THE HEART OF A SPY

The Hearts of Adventure Sweet Romance Series

THE HEARTS OF ADVENTURE SWEET ROMANCE SERIES

⚜

CHLOE FLOWERS

F&F
Flowers and Fullerton

Published By: Flowers & Fullerton LLC
www.flowersandfullerton.com
Cover Design by: Dar Albert, Wicked Smart Designs

ISBN: 978-1-63303-946-9

Disclaimer

Author's Note

*"Courage, endurance and luck. Forged by fire and will, a young nation
defied the odds and won."*

A special thanks to *Arcadian Books* in New Orleans, who sent me
home with two fantastic reference books on the Battle of New
Orleans:

Edited by Smith, Gene A. *A British Eyewitness to the Battle of
New Orleans, The Memoir of Royal Navy Admiral Robert Aitchison
1808-1827*. Gainesville: University Press of Florida, 1999. Print

Lacarrière Latour, Arsène, Edited by Smith, Gene Allen.
*Historical Memoir of The War in West Florida and Louisiana in 1814-15
with an Atlas*. New Orleans: The Historic New Orleans Collec-
tion, 2004. Print.

The battle of New Orleans is a fascinating study.
Close to 4,500 Americans faced off against nearly 15,000 battle-
hardened British troops (this number fluctuates, depending on
the source). The British lost 2,000 men. The United States casu-
alties were around 100. In all practicality, the Americans should
have lost this battle. If it wasn't for the multitude of calamities

that befell the British, the American forces probably would have been decimated. The characters in this novel are indeed fictitious, but have been placed in many scenes that actually occurred during the fight for control of the Mississippi. Some of those characters became instigators of a few of those calamities, for the readers' enjoyment and entertainment.

Additional factual information on the Battle of New Orleans can be found here:
http://www.history.com/news/6-myths-about-the-battle-of-new-orleans-3
http://www.history.com/topics/battle-of-new-orleans
http://battleofneworleans.org
http://www.knowla.org

Dedication

My grandmothers were amazing cooks.
So, of course both my parents became amazing cooks as well.
It's the kitchen, isn't it...where families gather, memories are
made and stories told?
It's with deep gratitude that I dedicate this book to my family.
To my grandmothers, Dollie Flowers and Madeline Holbert,
and my parents who taught me the importance of family time
spent together.
To Tess, Cole and Cade: remember our family gatherings.
Tuck them safely in your heart.
They'll become more even more precious over time.
I love you always
(And after that).
-CAF-

Be sure to check out the Creole Jambalaya recipe at the end of the book!

Foreword

Download the first Hearts of Adventure book FREE! Click here.

Dearest Reader,

As always, I have left a gift for you at the end of the book. The recipe for **New Orleans Creole Jambalaya** is one of my favorites. If you enjoy this book, please consider leaving a review and loaning it to your friends. It means a lot to writers when you do!

Thank you from the bottom of my heart for reading!

Fondly,

Chloe

"We will expel the invader from every spot on our soil, and teach him, if he hopes for conquest, how vain it is to seek it in the land of freedom."
-General Andrew Jackson

Chapter One

NIGHT VISIT

Saint Maria Abbey, Jamaica
November 1814

E va sprang from her cot before the abbey bell's metallic echo
faded. Living in the back alleys of New Orleans, sleeping in
doorways, listening to drunks retch in the street, avoiding toe-
nibbling rats and feral dogs, all forced her to learn how to jerk
awake at the slightest sound, the tiniest movement.

Things were different now. While she no longer crept in the
shadows, she was still hiding. The nuns at the Ursuline Convent
had lifted her from that horrid life nine years ago, taught Eva how
to be a healer, then sent her on a mission to the Jamaican abbey.

The bell's sharp ring sounded again. No time for shoes.
November weather made them less of a necessity here than in
New Orleans this time of year. The air was thick and hot, even at
night.

She dragged her hair away from her face, and her fingers
brushed the ragged scar on her cheek. She threw an open-sided
tunic over her robes, then drew up the hood, thankful for the way
it kept her marred face in shadow.

An urgent fist thudded on the entry door. Her heartbeat quickened. The back of her neck tingled, as it always did when danger approached. She shook it off. This was not unusual. As the abbey's healer, nighttime visitors asked for her most often. In most cases, it was a frantic family member assisting a woman in labor. Little babes rarely picked convenient times to make an entrance. She lit a lantern and ran, bare feet flying across the cool stone floor.

Eva gripped the handle and tugged open the thick wooden door, barely managing to step back fast enough to protect her toes before a massive figure swooped toward the threshold. A determined boy shadowed him, casting worried glances at the child in the man's arms.

"I need Sister Eva." His voice was low and taut, like twine tightly stretched between two posts. His bulk spanned the doorway. She tilted her head up and lifted the lantern. She'd not yet taken vows, but decided not to correct him.

Intense gray eyes glittered in the light. Short, black stubble covered his chin and jaws, along with several small scars, including one angling up from his eyebrow to his forehead.

Blade marks.

The scars indicated this man was a fighting man. The dark brooding aura suggested he was a brigand, pirate or privateer, which explained the tingle on the back of her neck earlier. Long ago she learned to listen to those signals. Still... something about him seemed almost familiar. Did she dream about this encounter?

Even scarred, he had a handsome face in a rugged, roughly cut way. Near-black curls poked free of the crumpled collar of his coat, which he'd apparently thrown on in haste. He had the aura of a man of power and order; making the turned collar incongruous. Her fingers itched to flip it back and straighten it.

Although her perusal took less than two seconds, he made an impatient sound, and she found her voice. "I am Eva." She directed her attention to the child. She was a young girl, maybe ten or eleven years of age. Flushed face, long nearly black hair stuck to her cheeks and neck. She was fevered, always a bad sign, no matter the climate.

He tilted his head, more to indicate himself than in deference to her position. "I'm Drago Viteri Gamponetti. I require your help. You are a healer, yes?"

She bristled at his tone. He required help, not needed it or asked for it. It was an order expecting compliance. Military? His accent suggested Spanish heritage, although it was likely Italian. It most certainly was not French. Dark eyes glowered at her. She gripped the door tighter and glanced at the limp body in his arms. Fevers were never easy to banish. Had he arrived in time for her to save the child? What would he do to her if she failed?

"Yes, I am a healer." Her voice almost didn't tremble. Sister Beatrice usually rose at the bell to assist. Even if the older nun was slow and arthritic, she was helpful. Too bad the woman had complained about an ache in her knees and asked for a sleeping draught this evening. Eva was on her own.

He shifted the girl, then shouldered his way past her into the foyer without waiting for her to invite him inside. He kicked the door shut behind him hard enough to rattle the leaded window frame, and she jumped like a skittish rabbit.

The man's impatient expression bordered on disgust. "This child needs immediate consideration. She's caught a fever, and it's lingering." His voice was clipped, dark eyebrows lowered. "There are red patches on her arms, as well. You are a healer, so get to work." His voice rumbled like an approaching storm. He lifted the girl higher, almost as if to dump her into Eva's arms. The muscles in his cheek jumped, and his glare told her that if his large hands hadn't been otherwise occupied, he would have used them to grip her shoulders and shake her into compliance.

Eva turned on her heel. "This way." She hurried to the first empty chamber and gestured to the pallet. "Put her here and let me examine her." She placed the lantern on a squat table near the bed. The man settled the lifeless child, careful to avoid any jerky movements. The scent of the sea, tobacco and leather surrounded her as he looked over her shoulder while she pulled away the blanket.

She glanced toward the corridor. It would have been helpful if one of the other sisters had awakened. She was the only healer in the abbey. Since Beatrice attended her most times, it gave the others a convenient reason to roll over and go back to sleep.

Breathe.

Releasing a quivering breath, she pressed her palm on the girl's cheek and resisted the urge to spin and run for Sister Beatrice. The gentleman's thick-lashed eyes flicked around the room, then back to her. She liked to believe she had a stronger constitution than most women, but something about him, beyond his brusque manner, raised the goose flesh on her arms, and she had an uneasy notion this man brought darkness with him.

You're not a superstitious ninny.

Her responsibility as a healer forced her attention back to the child, who let out a soft whimper.

"When I returned home, I was told she'd been out in the sun and bade her come inside, which she did, but perhaps she stayed out too long?" Gamponetti whispered in her ear, her heart stammering as his warm breath heated her neck. The hopeful tone that should have accompanied the words was missing, in its place one more commanding.

He stood too close. Waves of heat crashed into her back. She released a slow breath to calm her pulse and ran her hands over the girl's cheeks and arms. Both were on fire.

"Did she complain of pain elsewhere—her ears, stomach, or head? Was she bitten by a spider? A jellyfish? Did she brush up against a vine with fine, thin thorns?" Fever caused by a sting or a bite was easier to treat than one generated by a more serious sickness.

"She didn't complain about anything to me." The man

straightened and shot a thunderous look to the boy hovering nearby. "Julian, did she say anything to you?"

"No, captain, she didn't say she felt poorly or was bit." Peering at the girl, the boy grasped her limp hand.

Captain. Perhaps the man was indeed military. He certainly carried himself like a commander, shoulders back, chin up, legs braced. A ship's commander.

Focus!

Julian pushed up her sleeve to expose several angry patches. "When she returned from fishing with Manuel, she had big pink spots on her arms. She said they burned."

"They look like burns," she murmured. What caused red blotches besides heat? Too much sun, as the captain had suggested, but the heat and redness wouldn't move beyond the exposed area, confirming the girl had a fever.

She turned her attention to the youth. "What day did she go fishing?" Julian looked to be about eleven or twelve. He might be a powder boy for one of the British vessels gathering in Negril Bay.

He flipped his fingers, counting. "Four days ago."

Four days ago, following a storm that had blown through. Jamaica had an odd, highly toxic tree—the Manchineel tree. Stepping on the fruit had caused her problems in the past. Some of the juice had seeped through the hole in her shoe and burned her foot. After a rain, even water dripping off the fruit and leaves can burn the skin. That explained the burns, but not the fever.

"Has her appetite been normal? Has she kept her food down?"

"Yes," both answered.

Eva reached for a nearby pitcher, which forced the captain to step away. Thanks to the early morning rain, they'd been able to collect an acceptable amount of fresh rainwater. Otherwise, if they wanted drinkable water, they had to trek the three miles to the caves where an underground spring flowed into a small cavern pool in the side of the bluffs. The cave water was crisp and cold, a blessing in this tropical climate of smothering heat and humid air.

Hoping to rouse the child, Eva dampened a cloth and placed it on her forehead. Pale eyelids twitched, and she moaned softly. "What's her name?"

"Jacqueline. She's my twin sister." The small Adam's apple in Julian's throat bobbed up and down. He darted worried glances between Eva and Jacqueline.

Both males breathing down her neck made it impossible to focus. "Leave me a moment if you please, so I may examine her for any wounds or stings."

The man and boy departed, and Eva pushed up the girl's skirts and examined her legs, unfastened her dress and peeled it away from her heated body, checked her belly and back.

Nothing.

The child's long, dark hair clung to her forehead and neck in an untamed, knotted mass.

Eva's stomach twisted. If she couldn't determine the reason for the fever, she couldn't attempt to treat it. She learned that much as an apprentice of the Ursuline nuns' healer.

Probing Jacqueline's throat with her fingers revealed no lumps. She didn't labor to breathe. Eva pushed her belly, looking for anything hard or abnormal. The girl moaned. She caught her breath, shifted her hands to the girl's left side, pushed again and received the same response. Perhaps her stomach or bladder caused the illness. If her appetite had been normal, then it was probably her bladder or young womb. The knot in Eva's belly tightened further. Not easy things to heal.

She gave her shoulder a gentle shake. "Jacqueline? Can you wake up?"

The child's long black lashes twitched, and she mumbled something incoherent.

"*Mon enfant,* can you open your eyes a moment and talk to me?" The girl's eyelids fluttered. Hope blossomed in Eva's chest.

The young girl opened her eyes. "Are you an angel? Am I in heaven?" she whispered, her glassy, fevered eyes widening.

Hallucinations, no doubt. Eva smiled and shook her head. Since she dressed as a novice nun, her robes were white. "I'm a healer at the abbey in Port Royal. Tell me where you feel the most pain."

The girl moved her hand to the center of her abdomen. "I spotted blood—"

"Where? When?"

"When I... relieved myself... it was pink," Jacqueline's whisper wavered.

The bladder must be the origin of the fever. A tea would help the girl. Thankfully Miss Kalia, the old Obeah healer who lived in a hut in the jungle, had tutored Eva to use Jamaica's healing plants. She could treat this ailment.

Miss Kalia. *She* was the reason for the uneasy feeling when they arrived earlier.

The old woman had approached Eva while shopping at the market, the first week she arrived in Jamaica, nearly five years ago. Pointed out different local roots and herbs needed for healing. Eva often wondered how the woman knew she was a healer. None of the sisters dared look the Obeah woman in the eye.

Shortly after their awkward meeting, Kalia started with the premonitions.

People who weren't from the island called the old Obeah woman a white witch, and they were careful not to raise her ire in case she was a black witch, as well. A slight chill skittered across her shoulders. The woman's gifts sometimes made Eva uncomfortable.

Especially the visions.

Kalia's latest premonition had been even more unsettling, and Eva had driven it from her thoughts until now.

"A dark-hearted mon wit a sick girl-child 'bout to cross you path. Him be drawn to de light in you. You light—it might can save him, but be

warned. Him dark is strong. Him dark desire yearns to draw you into him doomed shadow."

Eva shook the black musings from her mind, and yet again returned her focus on Jacqueline. The next step was clear. They must cool her fevered body and should leave for the caves right away. She sent a prayer of thanks for the luminescent full moon, and ask God for His protection and healing touch. Just that brief moment of intent introspection and meditation soothed her.

Unfortunately, a trip to the caves meant a trek through the jungle at night with the "dark man" from Kalia's premonition. She reached for the door and hesitated. Sister Beatrice could join them.

Except... the cart wasn't very big, and the old mule could barely haul it empty. The path there with three adults and two children would be too taxing for the creature.

Eva drew in a lungful of air and released it, searching again for calm. If she were to help the child return to good health, she'd need ingredients for the tea.

Eva picked up the lantern and opened the door to find the captain pacing the hall like a panther in a cage. As he spun toward her, his coat lifted enough to reveal a dark red, silk lining, a brace of pistols and a long gleaming sword. In two strides, he was in front of her.

His eyes locked on to hers in the dim light.

Piercing.

Intelligent.

Cunning.

His shoulders relaxed slightly, which meant he read her expression. Sensed her confidence. He was very calculating, indeed.

Pirate. Definitely a pirate. So much for actively avoiding the more insidious tendrils of humanity. She'd met a few pirates in her youth. Some had been ruthless and thirsted for violence. Others less so. Still, all lived by the same code, the same rules, creating a loosely woven net of frayed order.

Chances were, her novitiate robes alone would do little to protect her among such men. Her value as a healer, however...

She raised her chin. "I believe I can heal the sickness with a special tea, but first we must take her to the caves to cool the fever." Her voice echoed in the chamber; she'd spoken a bit louder than she intended. She gestured toward the barn. "If you and Julian go to the stables and hitch the cart to the mule, we can leave right away."

Captain Gamponetti nodded, whirled and withdrew, taking his shadows with him, the boy once again bobbing at his heels like a juvenile duckling.

The tingling on the back of her neck returned.

Chapter Two
KALIA'S PREMONITION

The silent, brooding Captain Gamponetti with his storm cloud eyes and catlike grace settled Jacqueline and Julian in the back of the cart, then handed Eva up to the bench. She tried not to flinch at his touch. Instead, she propped her sack of herbs and salves between her feet while he sat in and gathered the reins, giving them a flick of his wrist to spur the old mule into motion.

She'd roused Sister Beatrice long enough to inform her of their planned trip to the caves. Eva shot a sideways glance at the man next to her, a mountain of muscle and bone. At least if she didn't return, the sisters would know where to search for her body. While she had no true outward cause to be so wary (other than his presence and Kalia's premonition) remaining cautious was more for self-preservation than anything. Truly, the fellow merely delivered words and sentences in a crisp, terse manner. Still...

Stop it.

Those ominous statements only added to this discomfiture. Allowing them to churn in her mind didn't help at all. Her duty was to treat and heal the girl. But even so, she'd be on her guard every moment.

Eva pulled the hood lower over her head. Keeping her scarred face in the shadows came instinctively for her. The hoods and veils were less to protect herself these days. She'd learned if she kept her scars hidden, it saved others from being affected by the sight. Their reactions no longer surprised or mortified her like they once did. Just a numbing punch to the gut.

Children cried.

Ladies spoke in hushed whispers as they stared from behind their fans. *"What a horrible thing to happen to a young girl. I wonder how she was maimed."*

"It's likely she's a prostitute. I've been told older women in a brothel will attack and scar the younger ones, so they don't steal their customers."

"Oh, how do you know she's a...a..."

"No chaperone, no protector, what else would she be?"

Five summers ago, the young man who'd promised love, marriage and a life outside the convent, had recoiled in horror when she finally found the nerve to remove the veil. He soon disappeared and left her with a shattered heart. The malicious, bloody shards still jabbed at her lungs when she allowed the memories to invade. Long ago she'd accepted the fact she was too damaged for any kind of romantic relationship. Hugo, in a drunken rage, had seen to that.

At least now she had value. Aside from God, her friendship with Sister Beatrice was as close as she would ever get to love.

"Are you expecting the waters to heal the girl?" The captain's dubious tone broke the quiet, startling her.

Another quick glance revealed a grim set to his jaw. The healer in her wanted to ease his worries and keep him calm by any means possible. The rest of her wanted to shake bells and shout warnings to the villagers.

Fighting the unease as best she could, she kept her voice soothing. "The cave waters are cool and will reduce her fever, which I suspect comes from her bladder. She must drink a medicinal tea and a *lot* of it over the next fortnight, to dispel the sickness."

He shifted on the hard wooden seat, shoulders tight and coiled. "Have you healed someone with this type of infirmity?"

"Of course—"

"Did the treatment work? Did they live?"

"*Capitaine* Gamponetti, I may be young for a healer, but I assure you—"

"She's such a little piece of fluff, but she's as stouthearted as any of my men." He jiggled the reins, giving the mule the opportunity to keep up his pace without getting a crack on the rump for lagging. "I haven't been around many small girls, but I believe she's stronger than most." His voice bore a hint of pride; daring her to argue.

"I know you're worried about her and I promise I'll do everything I can to help her."

"But what of the burns?" The steadiness of his words did nothing to disguise his concern, nor the stern resolve in the angle of his frown.

"Your daughter probably played beneath a manchineel tree after the storm."

He released a long breath, glanced at her, then dipped his head, trying to peer inside her hood. She couldn't stop herself from ducking. The observer's expression after that first glance was always the hardest to observe.

He scowled. "They're not my children, although I am responsible for them at the moment," he said.

His explanation gave her pause. Some tightness eased from her shoulders. He had a kind heart then, surely. Although he appeared composed, she sensed a hidden menace lurking beneath the surface, like an alligator submerged in the murky waters of the bayou. Waiting.

"Where are their parents?"

"Dead."

Eva nodded, understanding. Thankfully, the abbey had room, should the children need a home. The nuns never turn a child away; she was living proof. A question ripped at her stomach. *Dead by whose hand?*

"Are you related?" she asked, hoping with all her heart the answer would be "yes."

He shrugged. "No, but their family is very special to me. I'm an unofficial guardian of sorts. Their uncle, cousins and brothers run a hotel and gaming house in New Orleans, which was destroyed by a fire. I offered the twins a place to stay while it was being rebuilt." His mouth twitched. "To keep them out of the way."

"Are you with the British troops?"

He shook his head. "I have my own schooner."

"He's a privateer," Julian piped up from behind her.

Even as Eva sent up a brief prayer of thanks, a shiver ran down her spine. Privateers were nothing more than pirates with permission to plunder, some spurred by loyalty to their sovereign, others by greed. Worse, in times such as these, said permission wasn't regularly sought. Letters of Marque were not always obtained, nor were they often authentic. Privateers were thieves and marauders, the lot of them—a people and a lifestyle she avoided with determined vigor. And she'd done so quite well, up until tonight.

A wisp of hair tickled her chin, and she tucked it away. She should have grabbed her long veil. It draped diagonally across her face and over her shoulder, covering the puckered, maimed skin on her cheek.

She peered through her lashes at the man next to her. He had a restless aura about him, loose limbs ready to snap into action. Charcoal eyes carried a hint of leashed violence. Which type of privateer? A devious one might not concern himself with children, although it would take a veritable demon of a man to deny minor aid to a child, like taking her to a healer.

Well, the man couldn't be completely black-hearted. Miss

Kalia's strange insights might be helpful here. Her mind returned to his schooner. There was indeed a reason he knocked on her door tonight, beyond the girl's sickness. Perhaps beyond the prediction.

Providence.

She'd prayed and prayed for guidance. God had answered her prayers and sent someone to help her and the Ursuline nuns. They were in dire need of a protector to save their relics from being stolen. A responsibility that could cause an unambitious man to shirk away, but surely once properly presented, might not be so immense a quest for a privateer. Once she explained everything to the captain, he'd understand that, too. This quiet moment offered her the opportunity to voice a plea. How to start?

"I believe, *Capitaine* Gamponetti, the divine hand of God has sent you to me."

Silver-hued eyes held a hint of humor. "Pardon my lack of conviction, Sister, but I doubt God's hand would send a man like me to someone like you."

A man like him? Perhaps her observations had been correct, then. Not that it mattered, overmuch. The only thing concerning her now was whether she could trust him a reasonable amount.

A direct approach might be best. "Oh, but I honestly believe He has, *Capitaine*. You will deliver the children back home to New Orleans soon, no? I am part of the Ursuline order there and I have a desire to return to the convent. When it's time for you to depart Jamaica, I would happily act as the children's chaperone." Surely he'd relish the opportunity to divert more of his attention to his ship, rather than split it with keeping a watchful eye on the young twins.

He repressed a snort and cut her a quick dark glance. "Had you been acquainted with the two of them while both were in stout health, I doubt you'd make the same offer."

"Are you saying they're rascals?" His warning made her smile. Just the fact that he made an attempt at levity allowed her to relax somewhat (as much as a person could relax with a coiled panther seated four inches away).

The corner of his mouth tipped up. "They are rascals of the highest degree and much too smart for their own good. The two of them together... especially dangerous."

She laughed. "I shall endeavor to stay alert when they're nearby. How long will the twins be with you?"

He twisted and cast the twins a concerned stare.

Eva followed his gaze. Julian was sitting with his back against the box seat, his sister leaning against his chest. He tightened his arms around her as the cart rolled and jolted over the bumpy trail. Still, she remained asleep, her head lolling on his shoulder.

Gamponetti's lips flattened. "They were to stay with me until early spring. I had been preparing to journey south to Cartagena. I have a trade route to run and a timetable to keep."

Had been. Would they delay or leave earlier? "Have your plans changed?"

The captain shrugged once more. "I might return the children to their uncle in New Orleans before I go, depending on Jacqueline's health."

Eva caught her breath. Here was the opportunity she needed. "I should very much like to accompany them. As I have a need to return also, I would be happy to look after them during the journey." She'd repeated herself. She had already offered herself as an escort. Now, she must sound desperate. Which of course she was, but she didn't want to raise his suspicions.

He remained silent. Too late. She'd raised his suspicions.

Drat.

The hesitation sent a mixture of trepidation and relief to her chest. He might consider it, but was not yet convinced it was a good idea. She must think of a way to persuade him to take her with him. Perhaps appealing to his ego would help. "I have talked with every merchant ship's captain in Port Royal, begging for passage back to New Orleans, but all were too cowardly to assist me."

One had gawked at her like she had an octopus on her head. "I ain't sailing into them waters, Sister. Not with them British blighters—pardon my language—not with the British and their war with the States. Too dangerous. Only a fool or a madman would even try."

Gamponetti shifted, giving her a full view of both narrowed gray eyes. "Why are you so eager to return?"

Before she could answer, the captain's shoulders straightened and his attention whipped around to focus on the right side of the trail ahead. Broad leafy shadows crossed the moonlit path. Nothing moved, no sounds.

No noises at all.

No beetles buzzing, no night creatures rustling in the underbrush, no chirping tree frogs. Her lungs tightened. Jamaica wasn't without its dangerous beasts, both human and animal.

"What is it?" she whispered, gripping the edge of the cart seat, staring wildly into the dense flora.

"We're being watched." Easing a pistol from his belt with one hand, he pulled the reins with the other. The mule's ears twitched; he stopped abruptly, attention forward, listening. The captain spoke in a low voice. "Easy."

A lone figure stood on the trail a few yards ahead of them. "Why you be travelin' dis time o' night, Sistah Eva? You gots troubles?"

She slumped with relief. Next to her, the captain stilled, his hands gripping the reins as if they kept him from falling into a burning pit of lava. "I'm taking a sick child to the caves, Miss Kalia."

"Girl-child then. Who wit you?"

She swallowed. The premonition. "*Capitaine* Gamponetti."

Miss Kalia grinned then cackled a short laugh. "Ah, yes, yes.

Last time him saw I, him come from de red house. Long night wit de rum. Bad day next, eh Drago?"

The captain had turned to granite beside her, likely embarrassed (as well he should be) that Miss Kalia had seen him leaving a brothel. Eva chewed her lip. It was possible she misread the man. Allowed desperation to dictate her earlier impressions.

The old woman approached the wagon, swaying like seaweed with the tide, perhaps due to aching joints, but on a night like this, it was bewitching and unnerving, like an adder mesmerizing prey. The moonlight subdued her brightly patched skirt into shades of grayish-reds, greens, blues and yellows. Colorful feathers poked out in every direction from the silver hair piled high on her head. A streak of white paint trailed from one ear, ran along her jawline, across her chin, ending at her other ear like a gruesome grin. Eva fought the strong desire to squirm closer to the pirate for protection. Except that would give her as much reassurance as jumping from an alligator's jaws into a jaguar's mouth.

Kalia hummed as she peered over the side at Jacqueline. "T'ought so. Eva, see I in a vision just now. Surrounded by thunder and frost, perched next to a jaguar black as night. Woke I wide up." Before she could respond, the woman scampered up into the wagon bed, bringing with her a strong tang of wood smoke.

Julian didn't take his eyes from her, but still leaned away as she bent over his sister. She placed her palm against the girl's cheek, her brown hand contrasting sharply with the pale skin, even though it was still flushed with fever. She tilted Jacqueline's head back, pressed her chin down to open her mouth. Sniffed her breath.

Unsure what to say or do, Eva dragged her gaze from the old woman to the captain. How long had those two been acquainted? His storm-gray eyes followed the crone's every move.

Miss Kalia hopped down and slipped to Eva's side. The old healer grasped her hand and pressed a cluster of herbs against her clammy palm. "Her need dis. It make best tea for de girl." She nodded toward Captain Gamponetti and lowered her voice until it was barely there. "Him must drink *dis*." She caught her gaze and held it as she slid a small flask under the herbs. "Den dat what you want by him, you get."

Eva shoved them into her bag, afraid to refuse them and unsure of what else to do or say.

The old Jamaican woman stepped back and lifted both hands in farewell. Or some sort of blessing?

Maybe a curse?

A white witch. A "good" witch, if there was such a thing. Sister Beatrice would say there was not. But Eva had seen too much to denounce anything outright. There was no telling what spell Kalia incanted or bestowed upon them. The pirate jiggled the reins and clucked the mule forward.

As they passed, Kalia spoke again, but this time to him, her voice both smoky and chiseled, eyes black and white. "Change in de wind, Drago. A time come near for you to make a choice. Choose wrong and die. Before de tree flowers bloom, you betray an ally... aide a foe... break a vow. Light beckons you, but de dark always a seductress." Her wild stare locked with Eva's. "Which voice will him follow? Him heart or him head?"

Tension radiated from the captain in waves of heat. Kalia had slithered past his stoney, rugged aura to poke the tiniest gap between courage and unease. The muscles in his jaw tightened, but he did not look at the old woman as they passed.

"I...I don't know how to answer her question." Eva peered over her shoulder, but the witch had disappeared. An awkward silence followed. The jungle remained paralyzed for several minutes while they plodded along the path.

He could have taken Jacqueline to Kalia. She peered at him again, now understanding why. A rigidity thrummed through his broad shoulders; he had a flare in his nostrils, a fierce glint in his eyes.

Then it hit her; *Kalia terrified him.*

Her curiosity flared. "Have you known her long?"

The captain expelled a slow breath. "Everyone knows Kalia. And Kalia knows everyone." A wry smile seeped up to his eyes. The edges crinkled, and a dimple settled in his cheek, giving him a roguish, but more pleasing appearance. Much like an unapologetic child holding a stolen cake. "In truth, I found there's no way to avoid her even when it's your intense desire."

She'd learned much the same. A strange sense of balance lodged between them. The vulnerability the old woman raked out of the captain made him less threatening. "The people here have great respect for Miss Kalia. It would be foolish to dismiss her or her methods. To do so would also betray the islander's trust," she said.

The captain slapped the reins again and muttered, "Kalia's black medicine attracts too much attention, especially from the white man. They do not understand it. White men fear what they don't understand."

"It's not black medicine." She corrected him. "Obeah is a very ancient healing practice." She shifted the tea and the tonic to the bottom of her sack, trying to ignore the twinge of foreboding they sent through her chest.

"Call it what you will, the white settlers and plantation owners fear it," he muttered.

How should she approach the last premonition? He had to be familiar with the old woman's visions if indeed he knew who she was. How would he react? Surprise? Disbelief? There was one way to find out.

"Miss Kalia stopped me at the market two days ago and told me a man would come to the abbey with a sick girl-child," she blurted it out before she could stop herself. He would think her a ninny, talking about an old woman's premonitions as if they were gospel, which they were not.

Yet, a flicker of surprise shot across the captain's face. "She did?"

So he was familiar with Kalia's visions. "Yes, and here you are."

"Indeed." His brows dropped in thought, or perhaps concern.

She couldn't, *wouldn't* confide what Miss Kalia had said next. That was something she dared not repeat.

"Him not what him seem to be," the old woman had whispered. *"But den, so not are you."*

Chapter Three

MISSION FROM THE KING

D rago Viteri Gamponetti selected a spot in the shadows of the rear wall, near the secondary exit of the tavern. After returning from the caves, an older nun, by the name of Sister Beatrice, helped them settle Jacqueline in a bed before sending him to wait in the kitchen. Julian refused to leave Jacqueline's side. Tighter than a rusted bolt, those two. He snorted. And most times just as vexing.

Drago's thoughts drifted to the ethereal Sister Eva in her gauzy white robes with the concealing hood. Petite, like a woodland sprite, but highly competent. And strong. Although he frightened her, she did her duty with steady hands. Commendable. She didn't scoff at Kalia's ways, which surprised him. Few showed even the smallest amount of respect for other cultures and religions, especially those of the cloth. Yet, she used the herbs and brewed the Obeah healer's tea for Jacqueline, with the caveat that if she saw no improvement within two days, she would use her own remedy.

Since she didn't require his assistance, he'd slipped away to keep his appointment.

This establishment squatted in one of the more dank sections of Port Royal. The late hour provided necessary privacy. Away from those who might raise a brow at a pirate breaking bread with a pair of French aristocrats.

He needn't have worried.

The man and woman approaching his table blended quite well with the area's populace, clothed in common frocks and worn shoes. One would need to examine them closely to notice anything irregular—the lack of calluses on the man's slender hands, the absence of raw, red skin on the woman's. Gone was the erect stature and elegant movement of the upper class; replaced by the slope of inevitable despair in their shoulders and reticent scurry in their footfalls.

Brilliant.

Two of the French king's most talented and dangerous agents approached his table. Their eyes met, and Guiraud gave a slight nod as he held a chair for his wife before sliding into his own. The years had been kind to that firebrand. In a line of work that could shorten a man's life twice as fast, the bloke managed to look half his age.

Guiraud slid an envelope toward him. "As always, King Louis sends his regards."

"*Capitainé* Gampo, *un plaisir* to see you again," the woman said. One had to look past the dark ash-colored circles under her eyes and the shadowed cheeks. She was a beautiful woman curled under the disguise, moving like a cat in the night and noticing everything. Their tone contained a note that, while not friendly, was at least familiar.

Drago inclined his head and gestured for two more mugs. "So, we are once again to work together for his majesty."

Lady Guiraud retrieved an unfinished piece of needle lace from her reticule and set to stitching, giving an air of boredom which quelled any curiosity the patrons or barkeep might have had regarding the topic of their conversation. Still, she cocked an ear toward Drago.

"Where is Moreau?" Drago asked, shifting his gaze past the man's shoulder.

Lady Guiraud's lips pressed into a flat line, deferring the response to her husband.

Guiraud shot a furtive glance behind him. Several other people sat in the tavern, but they were engaged in their own activities and paid them no attention. Letting out a frustrated sigh, he returned his gaze to Drago. "He did not meet us as planned. We fear he may be dead. There was talk of a Frenchman being stabbed and robbed on Bright Street last night."

"We must complete our mission without Moreau's help." Lady Guiraud murmured while working the lace. She took a sip of wine. "I regret that I feel a certain amount of relief. He was a talented man—when he was in his right mind."

Drago shook his head in disgust. Moreau and his craving for opiates always made him a liability, but his uncanny talent for orchestrating a mission's finest details to perfection kept him useful to the king. They all knew it was only a matter of time before either his dealings or his appetite led to his demise. Bloody inconvenient timing, this. Moreau's loss was catastrophic, akin to trying to cross an ocean in a canoe instead of a galleon.

Guiraud tapped the wax-sealed envelope. "Your orders."

Drago sipped his ale, shifted his attention to the missive. He broke the seal with his thumbnail and read it. He was to transport the couple to New Orleans.

Easy enough, and convenient as long as Jacqueline's health improved.

Guiraud's eyes flicked across the parchment before he leaned forward. "We are to reclaim the sacred bones of St. Louis of La Roche-Guyon and return them to their rightful home in France." He expelled a breath with a huff. "I can only assume the king demanded them after the Americans purchased the Louisiana territory and was refused. The solution has now moved beyond the reach of diplomatic fingers."

"So, by *reclaim*, he means sneak into the St. Louis Cathedral and steal them." Drago met Guiraud's bright stare. Some people were born with an innate sense of stealth. This man was such a person, light on his feet and swift with his hands. The ability to shutter his conscience came in handy, too.

Lady Guiraud sucked in a breath. "A mission that stirs up less danger is a welcome change, but I am not happy to take from a cathedral."

There was something about pilfering from a church that should have settled rather uncomfortably in Drago's stomach as well, due to his mother's diligent Catholic upbringing. Years of pirating and privateering dulled that edge of his conscience. Although it appeared to be justified, such a task should unsettle any Catholic more than a little. Would God understand the reasoning behind the theft? Or in the King's mind, the *reclamation*? Not that it mattered to him, Drago's orders were simple: take the couple from Jamaica to New Orleans.

Lady Guiraud kept her head bent over her work, her voice low and tight. "Without Moreau, we are crippled. You must take his place, *Capitaine*."

So much for simple. Drago's gut clenched, and he cursed softly. This just became anything but. "My instructions are to provide transportation."

Guiraud's gaze hardened. "As leader of this mission, I am making adjustments necessary to complete it. I'm sure you are not intending to refuse additional responsibility. Doing so would be... *detrimental*... to your well-being."

Anger flared at the thinly veiled threat. "You are a thief and a courier, Guiraud, not an assassin."

The man eased a fraction. "I am what His Majesty requires of me, no more, no less. However, you should know Fontaine has been alerted to our mission and instructed to confirm its successful execution. If we fail, we die."

In other words, there'd be no shortcuts like lifting a few bones from a pauper's grave and passing them off as a saint's relics. He'd never suggest such a thing. At least not now.

Fontaine. The king's favorite assassin. He'd smile and shake your hand, then slit your throat before you said hello. Guiraud was absolutely right. With him watching their every step, failure meant death. A certain one.

How could a cluster of bones be that important? He gave the spy a curt nod.

Guiraud slid the missive to his wife. She scanned it before quietly slipping it into her reticule. "At least this time, our mission doesn't involve placing our lives in torrid danger." Guiraud tilted his head; the corners of his mouth lifted slightly. "It shouldn't be hard to gain lodging at the abbey for a night or two if we disguise ourselves as traveling missionaries." He stroked his narrow, clean-shaven chin. "I shall grow a beard."

His wife nodded her agreement, still working on her lace.

Drago drummed his fingers on the rough wooden table in irritation. *Bloody Fontaine.* "We'll set sail within a week. I have business in Negril Bay to attend to first."

"You will alert us in the normal manner when you are ready to depart?" she asked.

"Of course." He had no choice.

Stealing from a church. As if his soul wasn't doomed enough. He gave a short laugh. What more did he have to lose? He might as well enjoy this earthly life and attempt to postpone fanning the fires of Hades as long as possible.

Kalia's words echoed in his head. *Choose wrong and die.*

"It will be a pleasure working with you again, *Capitaine.*" Noticing Drago's empty tankard, Guiraud signaled with his hand to gain the attention of the barmaid. "Let's drink to a safe journey and successful outcome."

"More likely we should appeal for divine intercession," Drago muttered. It looked like he shall be taking Sister Eva with him to New Orleans after all. During the crossing, they could learn about the cathedral and its treasures from her. With any luck, this would be his last mission as an agent and a privateer in the service of King Louis.

If he survived it.

Drago tried to ignore the unease gripping his spine, but it was impossible.

Change in de wind, Drago. Before it done, you befriend a foe... aid an enemy... break a vow. Light calls to you, but de dark is a seductress... which voice will him follow? Him heart or him head?

Befriend a foe. Aid an enemy.

Ridiculous. Although it wouldn't be the first time.

But break a vow?

It should have been easy to dismiss those words. Laugh at them. Ignore them. A tiny Jamaican woman had no say over his fate.

None at all.

Yet, raised goose flesh covered his arms, even as sweat trickled down his back. The more important question was, which vow would he break? A vision of his head on a pike in the *Place de la Concorde* in France crept into his mind. He would not defy the French king.

He would *not*.

He gave his word.

As a captain and commander of men, a vow was one thing he did not take lightly. Therefore, his men trusted him. With trust came loyalty (and he valued loyalty above all else).

A man entered this life with very few things of intangible value to offer. One was his opinion, which many would argue had little importance, if any. Another was affection, which was a precarious thing to extend (as was any intangible that occupied a specific space in the heart). Thoughts or emotions could seep in and out; expand and contract, shift and melt. Yet nothing else truly fit where affection resided. It left a gaping hole when removed.

Once one opinion was given, another stepped in at the ready. Not so with affection. If a man gave that away, he was left wanting. It was like taking a breath. The exhalation emptied the lungs, which then craved to be filled. It was odd, really. Affection is the only thing that must be refilled to retain its value. If you gave it to another, and they, in turn, gave you theirs, you were sated.

Content.

The most priceless intangible, perhaps even more valuable than love, was a man's word... unless, of course, he broke it. A broken vow was as useful as a leaky bucket. No matter how often you filled it, it would never remain full. No amount of sentiment could return a man to honor if he depreciated the value of his word.

His vow.

Drago Viteri Gamponetti had done many sinister and ruthless things, but he never broke a promise.

Him dat will break a vow.

No. Him would not break a vow.

If he ever ran into that old woman again, it would be too soon.

Thankfully, after she'd disappeared, they'd made it to and from the caves without further incident. He and Sister Eva had taken turns holding Jacqueline's head above the crisp water of the deep, spring-fed, pool. The way the wet robes outlined the young woman's curves made his muscles freeze and his thoughts drift to more sensual places. Her profile made him forget to breathe. Yet, she hid her beauty behind the veiled hood. He understood her to wish to stay unobtrusive. Not everyone here showed reverence for women of the church.

After a couple hours, Jacqueline's fever diminished, and the sister announced they could return to the abbey.

Thank God.

Now, they only had to wait for the tea to work.

Chapter Four

TALE OF TEA LEAVES

※◈※

The tea's pungent aroma still wafted through the kitchen. Sister Eva moved like a white shadow, setting plates of food in front of them. A gossamer veil, different from the hood, kept the details of the right side of her face blurred; it forced him to read her eyes to guess her mood. Although by the firmness with which she placed his mug on the roughly hewn table, something troubled her. For some odd reason, he wanted to know why. Perhaps the witch's words unnerved her as much as they did him.

He shook his head. He didn't believe in the old island woman's magic, but everything was suddenly out of balance. Kalia had that kind of effect on people. He'd like to think she didn't affect him. But he'd seen and experienced too many strange and fascinating things during his travels to close his mind to it entirely.

Julian dropped into a chair with an exhausted thump, then yawned. "Will we still get to sail with you to Cartagena next week?" he asked, reaching for a plate of fish, "I'm looking forward to seeing my sister and Captain O'Brien."

Drago let out a beleaguered sigh. A finger of guilt poked his chest. "I intended to leave as soon as I sold the sugarcane. Trust me, I wish as badly as you to join the rest of the fleet for a trade run but Jacqueline is ill, and she can't afford to be exposed to tropical fevers in her weakened state." That was a good excuse, considering his new assignment.

Julian grunted his understanding and deposited a second piece of fish on his plate. Toyed with it, before resting his elbow on the table, then dropping his cheek into his palm. "When?"

Drago glanced at the nun. "I have urgent business to conduct in New Orleans, Sister Eva. I've decided to accept your offer to chaperone and bring you along."

The nun straightened, hope brightening her eyes.

Julian drooped. "Uncle Bernard and Tristan will want us to stay. Can't we just remain here until you return so we can go with you to Cartagena? Please, Captain Gampo, let us wait here until you get back."

Sister Eva shifted her startled gaze from the boy to him and back again. "Captain *Gampo*?" Her last word ended in a squeak.

Drago reclined back in his chair. Ah, she finally made the connection.

Gamponetti-Gampo.

Yes, he was a former pirate under the command of Captain Jean Lafitte of New Orleans, and still wanted for smuggling stolen cargo into the city. He hadn't been one of Lafitte's men in over ten years. Not since he deserted Barataria Bay for France.

Would the nun wilt like a little flower in the tropical sun now?

She hailed from the area, which could account for her recognition of his name. He narrowed his eyes. Although, in order to know his name, she'd have to be familiar with people associated with Jean Lafitte and his Baratarian pirates. How would a nun...

"He's not a pirate," Julian reminded her, focused on his food. "At least, not anymore."

Allowing the boy to answer for him, Drago shrugged. "I recently shifted my occupation from privateering to the merchant trade."

"I see." Her brow smoothed a bit at that, although her eyes still held a flicker of wary apprehension.

He studied her. There was something familiar about her and yet, something completely foreign. Like a frothy memory from early childhood. Real or imagined, he couldn't pin it down.

She finally moved and retrieved a cracked plate and a small bowl from the cupboard. "A French privateer. I suppose that's a less...dangerous vocation than pirate," she said. He didn't need to check her eyes this time. By her tone, her frown had deepened. She was unconvinced.

"Except if you're a woman," Julian said, oblivious to the sister's discomfiture. He washed his fish down with a gulp of diluted coconut milk. "Women bring bad luck aboard a ship."

The nun pressed her lips together and huffed, apparently aware. "I don't understand why mariners keep that old superstition alive."

Drago propped his elbows on the table and entwined his fingers. It wasn't that hard to reason. "Having a woman on board, even a woman of the church, is seen as a significant risk. My crew comes from varying countries and religious backgrounds, but they all firmly believe it brings doom."

The last skirt was Jacqueline, who'd been eight at the time, and she nearly cost him his ship *and* his life. A long scar from his shoulder to his lowest rib served as a reminder. Still tingled when he twisted to the left.

The actual truth he couldn't vocalize to a nun: ladies made trouble. They caused a man's primal urges to control his brain. He gave himself a moment to put his thoughts in order. Best to choose words carefully with God, nuns, abbey and all. "There's a more practical reason than mere superstition. Women are... distracting. Skilled sailors tend to become peacocks in the presence of the fairer sex. Men miss their watch, sails go unattended, things catch fire... all calamitous on a wooden ship in the middle of an ocean."

Julian looked up from his plate, a near miracle for the growing boy, who rarely spoke during meals because he was too busy shoving food into his mouth. Julian's appetite seemed endless these days. "If you gave Manuel the task of looking out for the sister, maybe the men would think less about it."

"Manuel?" Eva asked.

Drago released a long breath. "He's my cousin." How to explain Manuel? A loyal guard with a damaged mind? A child in a giant's body?

Julian cocked his head, pondering his words. "Manuel is strong and determined to do the right thing, but he's not able to understand complicated things. He is quite obedient. If Captain Gampo tells him to protect you, he'll do it with his life."

The sister laughed. How pleasing the sound was; it made him wish to see the smile the veil concealed. Novitiate nuns rarely wore veils, especially in the warmer climes. He couldn't help but wonder if she was that pious, or if there was another reason. Did she fear discovery?

She filled the bowl with broth. "I daresay, there'd be little need to protect me to such an extent."

Drago stiffened. "Do you not think yourself worthy of protection?" Where did that question come from? And why was it so vexing to hear she thought so little of herself?

"I..." She hesitated. "I'm undesirable in that respect, *Capitaine*." Her fingers fluttered at the fringes of her veil. It took her a moment before she steadied them. "Please understand that I value protection and safe haven of any kind." She gave Drago a smile which he identified only by the way the corners of her eyes creased with tiny lines. "You are fortunate to have a man so loyal to you."

His mind latched onto her first sentence. Undesirable? How could she mean that? Any man who breathed would desire her, with or without the dress and rosary of a novitiate Ursuline nun.

Last night, she wore a hooded tunic over her robes. While

she'd kept her face in the shadows, the water revealed what her clothing concealed. The cave spring helped Jacqueline, but it also made the thin white cloth cling to the curves of Sister Eva's body. And when the hood fell aside, she'd treated him to a stunning profile. Sleek raven hair, fine straight nose, full red lips. She was quick to cover her face again, but not before he had the pleasure of seeing her long slender neck, smooth skin and thick sooty lashes.

Now, *that* observation certainly didn't help redeem his pirate's soul. It would be better if he didn't think about her at all. Especially her curves, lips and neck. In fact, perhaps he should just direct his attention to Julian, and stop talking to her altogether.

Sister Eva made herself a mug of tea. He knew this because against his most recent advice to himself, he continued to study her. Undesirable? Who was the woman beneath the cloth?

More importantly, one who knew the name *Gampo*?

She approached with a fluid grace like the calm flow of water down a stream and placed the plate of bread and bowl of broth near him. Although she covered her hair with a veil obstructing his view of her cheeks and mouth, the white linen encasing her from head to toe made her dark brows and deep velvety blue eye more intense.

"How old are you, sister?"

She hesitated, then rubbed her eyebrow. Was she about to lie to him? *She's a nun, idiot. Not every beautiful woman lies.*

She sank into a chair across from him. "I'm twenty-two, *Capitaine*. And before you ask, no, I didn't grow up in the Ursuline convent orphanage. My mother died when I was eight. My benefactor—" She hesitated. "I took care of myself until Sister Beatrice saved me from an unfortunate accident." She lifted her hand up toward her face then caught herself. "She brought me into the abbey."

So... a former street rat. That explained why she had the eyes of an old soul. It also explained how she recognized his name. He picked up his mug, then eased back in his chair. He hated tea. Much preferred strong, black coffee if he was to drink something hot. But he wouldn't turn down the offered drink. It soothed his throat. The taste was sharp, but not bitter.

"What's in this tea?"

Her shoulders jerked as if startled. "Why do you ask?"

Her reaction made his skin tighten the way it did when playing cards in the company of a slick-handed gambler. "It has an unusual flavor." What was she hiding? He stared into his mug. The liquid was clear...

Why suddenly suspicious of a young nun? Should he be? What was wrong with him? He was in an abbey, for God's sake. He mentally crossed himself and sent up a quick apology for swearing in his head in a nunnery, in case it would do his rotten soul any good.

Although he really didn't know why he bothered with apologies.

Not true. He did know.

He bothered on the outside chance his black heart might not be lost completely.

A soft bed and a brimming cup of rum would help. Even a nap sounded very pleasant at the moment. Today's labors loading sugarcane combined with a sleep-deprived night stmust be taking its toll.

Time to go.

"Is the little ewe-white lamb out of danger?" He placed his empty mug down and shoved his chair back. "I have business to attend to, but I'll not depart until I'm assured." He paused. A fog seemed to descend inside his head. Thick and fuzzy, like cotton. What was happening? He blinked. The nun in front of him drifted into a ghostly white blur.

Her voice echoed from far away.

"... Fever has lessened... to drink more of the tea and confirm she dispels her fluids... manner before I can say... with... She... mending."

He reached up and rubbed his ears. Although she wasn't kin, Jacqueline was part of his family now. He wanted her well. He missed her crisp wit. If the little heathen didn't mean so much to him, he wouldn't give a rat's—. He looked up in time to see a startled look of surprise flicker across the nun's face.

Good Lord... had he said that *out loud?*

He had to quit cursing, even if it was in his own head. Pretty sure God could hear his thoughts. Fairly certain he was already cursed to walk in the flames of hell, but he did himself no favors with his impure observations and internal cursing. *And what was in this bloody tea?* Or was he just exhausted from lack of sleep?

He blinked. At least the nun came back in focus. "Sister Eva, if you wish to go to New Orleans, you are welcome to journey aboard the *Dragon*. Once I see to my business on the island, I'll return for you and the twins. If you don't mind, I'll leave both in your care in the meantime."

She brightened and gave him a wide smile. "Thank you, *Capitaine!* I shall enjoy their company." She rose and excused herself. "Finish your meal. I shan't be too long. It's time for Jacqueline to drink more of the medicinal tea." She filled a mug. "Julian, please bring along the rest." The boy picked up the bowl of broth and a chunk of bread, then followed at her heels.

Perhaps he should purchase some of that tea to keep in his stores, in case the child needed more later. Other than what rudimentary skills he learned from his ship's surgeon, healing, sickness and treatments remained an unpleasant mystery.

His new mission drove him to his feet. The world dipped briefly, then settled. Frowning at the strange sensation, he began to pace and think.

To plan the theft, he should learn more about St. Louis Cathedral. How could he engage the Sister Eva in conversation about the condition of the relics? Their specific location? Certainly, an opportunity would present itself during the voyage, no? She acted like a very agreeable woman. His chest constricted with that annoying and unfamiliar feeling of guilt again.

The sacred bones rightfully belonged in France.

They'd been entombed there and were removed from there. They should be returned there.

He would do his duty for his employer on this, his last mission in the service of the French king before becoming a merchant captain in his brother-in-law's trading company. It was time. Best to shift before age and fate caught up with him.

Sister Eva's innocent countenance and bright smile drifted back into his mind.

Blast it.

He sighed and sent up another apology, in case it helped at all. Departing the abbey sooner rather than later would be to his advantage before both his thoughts and his language spun his destiny's compass directly toward hell at a quicker pace.

Perhaps a gesture of goodwill would help. He brightened. He could offer a generous donation to the sisters, at least.

There, that placed everything in better balance.

The earlier dizziness had abated. Maybe the tea wasn't the cause. More likely lack of food and sleep. He glanced into his empty cup. And froze.

He didn't need Kalia to read the tea leaves to understand the meaning of the serpent shape coiled on the bottom of the mug.

Death and danger lie ahead.

Chapter Five
THE KISS

A pensive Gamponetti was staring into his mug when Eva stepped inside the kitchen. Jacqueline had begged her brother to stay to keep her company while she ate, and he complied. The faint fingers of dawn brushed against the window, chasing the dark from the room. She blew out the candles and filled a plate of food for herself. Bringing the man and boy into the kitchen was against the rules, but quite frankly, when *Capitainé* Gamponetti stopped and purchased fish and fruit from a peddler traveling toward the market square, then offered to help prepare it, she couldn't bring herself to banish them to the public room near Jacqueline's sick bed. Besides, he appeared to be a decent cook.

As she approached the table, he rose and pulled out her chair. The faint scent of spring water mixed with the musky smell of man and sea spray accompanied him as he pushed in her seat. He grunted at her nod of thanks and sat. She bowed her head to pray.

Dear God, thank you for this food and for sending Capitainé Gamponetti here to help me complete my task.

The chair creaked beneath his shifting weight. Her skin prickled from the piercing intensity of the captain's gaze. Perhaps he forgot to pray before he ate. Did he feel guilty he hadn't? Maybe he wasn't a very religious man. Few pirates were even former ones. She would pray for him too.

She prayed for God's intervention and guidance. To open the *capitaine's* heart. Open his mind. Open his eyes. Bestow upon him understanding, compassion, love, loyalty and commitment to their cause and to the church.

Finished, she reached for her spoon. He cleared his throat gruffly, and his chair squeaked again.

"Sister Eva," he began, then paused.

"Yes, *Capitaine*?" It sounded as if he was about to say something difficult, like telling her he changed his mind about the trip home. She shoved the negative thought aside.

Have faith.

"I have been thinking about the journey to New Orleans," he said. "I usually carry cargo in the extra cabins, but for your comfort, I shall keep one empty for you and Jacqueline. Her brother, I'm sure, will happily hang a hammock in the hold with the rest of the men."

She smiled her delight. "That is very kind of you. I'm grateful." The luxury of privacy was an unexpected surprise. That was much better than sleeping in a sail closet or some such out-of-the-way nook. Placing her napkin on her lap, she took a bite of fish as nonchalantly as she could.

"I'm happy you're pleased," the captain said, not sounding happy at all and likely dreading the glum reaction from his crew at her presence.

After listening to his opinions about women on ships, she didn't want to appear overly eager, lest he rethink his decision. It might be beyond her bounds to ask for more, but now seemed to be as good a time as any to approach her second request. After all, who better to defend against a thief than a pirate?

She fiddled with the loose threads of her frayed napkin. "Now that Jacqueline is improving, I'd like to explain to you why my need to return is so dire and to ask a favor."

"A favor?" He blinked, then narrowed his eyes as if he was having a hard time focusing. "What favor?"

"Capitaine Gamponetti—"

He scowled and flipped up his hand, silencing her.

He *silenced* her. How arrogant! The Ursuline abbey needed his help. The *church* needed his help.

And she was acting impatiently. Everyone was exhausted after staying up the entire night. It probably wasn't prudent to press her point now. She frowned. Disappointment muted her earlier joy at securing the passage home.

She'd placed too much faith in Miss Kalia. That stupid tonic, which was to help her "get what she wanted" from him, apparently was no longer working. If it had even worked at all. Perhaps he decided to grant her a berth prior to drinking it. Perhaps it was foolish of her to believe the old woman this time.

Sister Beatrice would have scoffed at her actions, but as a child, Eva witnessed too many strange things done by voodoo priestesses to dare scoff.

Besides, now he was rubbing his forehead (likely the after-effects of the laced tea). That realization brought a surge of remorse with it. His eyes had turned from a glazed bright gray to nearly black. He shoved his chair back, but remained seated, swaying like a ship on a turbulent sea.

"*Capitaine* Gamponetti? Are you well?" He just stared at her. *Oh dear*.

He blinked, then his left eye drooped. "What did you put in that —" He pitched forward and fell face first to the table, knocking over the nearly empty mug and cracking the plate with his forehead.

Eva shot from her chair, and her hands flew to her mouth. Her gaze halted on the overturned mug. What had she done?

What had the old woman used in that tonic?

Her heart lurched a sickening path to her stomach. Did it kill him? She darted around the table and shook him. "*Capitaine!* Wake up!"

Nothing.

She stared at his back, watching for the next breath to expand his ribs. Was he breathing? Unwilling to wait any longer, she placed her ear between his shoulder blades, hoping to catch something, anything, a heartbeat, an exhale. *Please*. She raised his head and peered at his slack-jawed face. There was no twitching of his eyelids or change in his expression. She put her hand under his nose.

There! A warm breath puffed against her palm. Thank God, he wasn't dead.

"Sister Eva?"

She started like a guilty thief and dropped the man's head back to the table with a dull thump, then winced at the likelihood of being responsible for a nasty bruise. She pressed a hand over her thundering heart.

Julian stood in the kitchen, holding an empty plate. "I'm sorry if I startled you, Sister Eva," he said. "Jacqueline fell asleep." He yawned, then noticed the slumped form on the table. His eyes widened. "What's wrong with Captain Gampo?"

She glanced from the boy to the mug to the unconscious man and tightened her hands into fists while her mind raced.

"I... I'm not entirely sure," she said. It wasn't like she told an outright lie. She suspected what might be amiss with him, but she couldn't be absolutely certain. "It's been a long night for the *Capitainé*. Perhaps he's exhausted?"

Julian's face blanked with shock. "He's not dead, is he?"

She laughed, and her voice warbled, "Of course not. He's just —sleeping." She glanced furtively around the kitchen, and her gaze lit on a nearby door. "There's a small bedroom next to the pantry used by our cook's helper, but she's with her family this week. Would you help me get him to her pallet? Perhaps he just needs to... sleep a while."

Julian eyed the bulk of the man slumped on the table and gave her a dubious nod. "I'll do my best. He's awfully big."

She shook the captain's shoulder again. "*Capitaine? Capitaine*, we shall assist you to a bed, but you must aid us. Can you stand?"

He mumbled a short string of garbled words. At least he responded, thank the Lord. Together, she and Julian looped his arms around their shoulders, then heaved him to his feet.

Miss Kalia and her wretched tonics and premonitions. How was this supposed to sway the captain's priorities and help her? The man couldn't even say his own name at the moment. How long until he recovered? Her heart lurched. *Would* he recover?

What if the tonic turned him into a blithering idiot?

She stared at the large, unconscious man. This was going to be trouble. Gamponetti was lean, yes, but also solid. Through the thin linen shirt, outlines of chiseled muscles crossed his chest and shoulders; hard ridges wrapped his ribs.

Although she nearly starved in the New Orleans streets before being taken in by the Ursuline nuns, her diligent work at the abbey had made her strong. Hopefully, it made her strong enough to support her portion of his bulk.

Even though it was a short walk, adjusting to the man's erratic gait proved difficult. He stepped on their toes. Halfway there, his right knee buckled, sending Julian to the floor. Eva staggered under the weight, causing the captain to teeter toward her before the boy could scramble up and regain control. When they reached the door to the small room she groaned in frustration.

"We can't all fit through at once," she said. "Julian, you must hold him long enough for me to slip inside."

"Yes, ma'am," he panted, face red with exertion.

"*Capitainé* Gamponetti, wait here," Eva ordered. She slipped in, intending to spin the man a quarter turn so the boy could follow quickly. Together they'd ease him down to the bed resting against the adjacent wall.

She realized too late that particular element of her plan was flawed. As she whirled to face him, he stumbled across the threshold and teetered, forcing her to shove against his very broad shoulders to halt him. Unfortunately, once he started to tilt, there was no stopping his momentum. He fell like a solid oak, squashing her between his body and the bed and pinning her arms against her chest.

She would have shrieked in surprise if the air in her lungs hadn't been forced out in a harsh whoosh. She squirmed, trying to free her hands and gain enough leverage to shift the massive hulk smothering her, but it was hopeless. Salt spray, leather and a musky scent tinted with something citrusy once again permeated her nose. Her belly did strange, annoying things.

"*Capitaine*," she gasped, struggling for a breath, "you're... crushing... me!"

His body jerked, and she glanced over his shoulder to find Julian tugging on his arm. The tall, lanky boy neared manhood. Still, he was no match for the captain's massive body.

"Captain Gampo! Wake up!" Julian's voice bore a slight note of panic. He braced his heels and leaned back, straining until the cords of his neck stood out against his throat.

"Find... Sister... Beatrice," she choked out. "The chapel... in the... north wing."

The jerking stopped, and the boy's feet smacked the floor in his panicked dash from the room, then echoed down the hall.

Wiggling her forearms between her body and the captain's, she tried to shift him enough to take a full lungful of air. Heat radiated from his chest to hers to swirl and dip beneath her ribs.

To her relief, he lifted his head, helping her cause a tiny bit. "Mmm... " Gamponetti's heavy lids flickered and opened part way. Liquid silver eyes traveled over her face. It was then she realized her veil had slipped. She couldn't reach it. "Waz this?" he mumbled.

At least he awoke. If only he'd get up. The effect his body had on her senses and emotions irritated and unnerved her. Breathing wasn't the only problem. Strange tingling sensations swirled low in her belly. "*Capitaine*, please shift your weight. I can't move."

He nuzzled her neck, sending a shiver rippling down her spine. "Move? Why'd I wan' you to move, *il mio caro*?"

A circle of heat splayed over her ribs, and a jolt of panic and awareness flashed through her. She tried to squirm out from under his hand but only succeeded in moving against him in a very intimate and not totally unpleasant way. "No, *Capitainé*! I'm Sister Eva! Not—"

"Theresa? Thaz a priddy name," he murmured, kissing her temple and sending a bolt of revulsion down the side of her neck. Definitely revulsion. Or fear. Probably both.

Her heart pounded wildly in her chest. "No, not Theresa...Sister Eva! *Sister*!" She'd shout directly into his ear if only she could take a deep enough breath. It didn't help that with every surge of her pulse, air escaped, and her body melted. Never again would she use one of Miss Kalia's remedies without first learning what was in it, and how it worked.

Blue-gray eyes, hooded by drowsy lids and inky lashes stared at her with a glassy mixture of dominance and languid heat. "You talk too much, Theresa."

Talk too much? Now she couldn't even remember what she'd been about to say and doubted her tongue could move if she did. Somehow, she managed a sharp gasping inhale.

His breath hitched, and he moved his lips across her throat, pausing at the vein pulsing with a chaotic rhythm. His body was granite hard. Panic welled in her chest.

"Cap—"

His mouth muffled her next objection, trapping hers in a kiss. Every nerve was diverted to focus on the sensation of his lips. All she could hear was her own jagged heartbeat. Every inch of skin tingled from the tops of her ears to the bottoms of her toes. His scent reminded her of fresh sea air and leather, both comforting and exhilarating. She yearned to be closer, breathe more of him in and at the same time shocked by the thought.

Although she had yet to take her final vows, she was practically married to the church, and what was happening now, what her woman's body apparently so eagerly desired to explore, was nothing less than adultery, which happened to be a huge sin.

That last thought was akin to tossing a bucket of cold water on a catfight. Her mind finally re-engaged, and she twisted her face away from the heady enchantment created by his kiss.

The minor victory was fleeting, as he set his lips to another delirious task, finding the tender skin of her neck, which wouldn't have been exposed had she taken time to dress in her coif and wimple last night.

Sister Beatrice's voice drifted into the room from the kitchen. "Eva? Where are... Oh!"

The interruption was enough to make the captain turn his unfocused gaze toward the door, providing sufficient room for her to swing one arm. Her palm connected with the captain's temple, slamming his skull against the wall with a solid thunk. He collapsed.

She gasped for air. The unmoving man still sprawled across her body, pinning her down.

Dear Lord, what had she done?

Chapter Six
TRUSSED UP PIRATE

"Now what?" Sister Beatrice wiped her brow on her sleeve.

The same question churned in Eva's mind. "Wait until he wakes, I suppose." It had taken a lot of pushing and pulling, but they finally freed her from beneath the captain's body, which was no small endeavor since unconscious, he was as heavy as an ox. Explaining the trip to the caves and Jacqueline's illness had done nothing to soften Sister Beatrice's demeanor.

"What's wrong with him?" Julian asked, eyes wide. "He acts like he's drunk."

Beatrice scowled. "Did he get into the sacramental wine storage?"

Eva sighed. How to explain? "No, that's not the reason for his current condition. I served him tea, which must have had contained some herbs that encouraged sleep. Perhaps paired with fatigue, it had a more elevated effect." That was the truth.

"What herbs?" Sister Beatrice frowned and glanced around the pantry at Eva's supplies organized in jars or drying overhead. She happily assisted Eva in her healing endeavors, but understood less about Jamaican plants. "What affected him poorly?"

Eva groaned inwardly. How could she respond in a manner

that wouldn't veer too far from the truth? Mentioning Miss Kalia's name would make things worse. Beatrice was terrified of the woman. If she knew it involved Kalia, she'd likely tell Father Andrew, who would demand an inquisition which would probably end with Eva's being ostracized from the order and possibly the church.

She'd have nowhere to go.

"I'm not sure what ingredient was the culprit." That was a good start since she'd no idea what the old woman put in the tonic. "I didn't mix it. None remains for me to examine."

Excellent. Not a single lie.

Sister Beatrice's expression relaxed, only to darken again. "I'm relieved the tea is gone, but why are you keeping a man in the kitchen storage room in the first place? If he's ill he should be in one of the sick rooms."

Julian's eyes widened. "We couldn't very well carry him anywhere. He's big as a horse."

Her stare hardened. "He shouldn't be in this area to begin with."

Eva winced. Breaking that tiny little rule didn't seem like such an egregious error earlier. "Sorry, Sister. It had been a long night, we were all hungry—"

"Yes, so you said." The sister waved away the excuse and harrumphed. "What if he awakes in the same temperament?"

Biting her thumbnail, Eva studied the man. Julian had explained his odd behavior to Beatrice when he fetched the old nun from the chapel. Indeed, what if the captain awoke in a mad frenzy? What if the potion lingered?

Would he remember *the kiss?*

Her stomach lurched. Would he remember she slapped his head against the wall? She swallowed. "Maybe it would be best if we restrain him until we're certain he's in his right mind." she thought aloud. Was that too drastic an action? Considering their specific situation, perhaps not. The great deal of uncertainty surrounding the tonic's ingredients and effects made it imperative, actually.

Sister Beatrice pressed her lips together and nodded. "That would be the safest thing to do. Father Andrew and I shall take the cart to the granary this morning, and the other sisters need not be aware he's here, they'll just make things more difficult. We don't want this to get back to—" Beatrice snapped her mouth shut.

It wasn't hard to guess her thoughts. The apostolic administrator in New Orleans first suggested Mother Marie Francis send the mission west into the wilds of Texas to teach the Word of God to the Caddo Indian savages. Mother Superior had swayed him in favor of tending to the neglected Jamaican abbey instead, which was less dangerous.

Beatrice propped her hands on her hips. "I'd feel better knowing the man's restrained. Let's collect some rope and straps from the stable." She shuffled toward the kitchen door. "Come on, boy. I could use your help."

Julian expelled a breath and rubbed his eyes with the heels of his hands before following. "If he ever finds out I helped truss him up like a boar on a spit, he'll whip the hide clean off my bones," he muttered.

"Well, he won't hear it from us." Sister Beatrice's voice carried behind her as she opened the door and stepped outside.

Since a chair wouldn't fit, Eva dragged a stool into the small room and sat, staring at the captain. She wanted to seek out Miss Kalia and demand to know what was in that wretched tonic, even though it would be senseless to do so.

The woman could only be found when she wanted to be.

There were many things that caused people go out of their minds temporarily or sometimes permanently: dozens of animal and insect bites, venom, flowers, roots, leaves of a hundred different plants. Trying to determine what combination the Obeah healer used was truly a hopeless endeavor. Even if she found out, there was no guarantee Eva would know how to counteract its effects, or if Kalia would bother to tell her.

They'd tied Captain Gamponetti's ankles to the corners of the bed and secured his wrists to the head.

"No one can know he's here," Sister Beatrice whispered.

"What? Why?" Julian asked.

Beatrice tossed a glare at her. "Because the other sisters would tell Father Andrew, and he would certainly write the Father Dubourg. Men are not permitted past the front foyer and sick rooms."

"He charged in carrying an unconscious girl, I couldn't very well forcefully toss him out," Eva hissed. In fact, she doubted she could force the man do anything.

"When he wakes, simply free one hand, and give him a knife to cut through the rest. Tell him he must leave. Open the kitchen door, then exit back into the abbey. Bar the entrance."

Eva gaped at the older nun. "You think he's just going to fly outside like a trapped sparrow?"

"Why not? What's the worst he can do? Ransack the pantry?" Beatrice shoved a filet knife into Eva's hand. "Explain to him why we bound him first. If he's in his right mind, he'll apologize and beg forgiveness. If he doesn't, cut one hand free and leave. By the time he frees himself, you can lock him out of the main part of the abbey." Beatrice pressed her palms toward the sky and looked up. "Pray to God he's up and out of here before we return!" She spun toward the door, her robes billowing behind her. "We should be back before dusk."

Eva studied the long, dark form. He was shockingly handsome in the light of day. Ebony curls had escaped from the leather tie at the base of his skull. Long lashes rested on cheeks covered with a neatly clipped beard. She touched her chin where it had rasped against the bristles, and a little shiver traced down her spine at the memory.

If he woke up angry he might refuse to take her home. That was unacceptable.

Eva straightened. He just needed a plausible reason as to why he was tied to the pallet frame. If she apologized and informed him she'd inadvertently provided him a sleep-inducing tea, which was basically true and explained why he passed out of consciousness, that might be enough of a reason. Before she slammed his head against the wall, anyway.

But it wouldn't explain why he was restrained.

She groaned in frustration. She'd have to reveal he'd become unmanageable. If he asked what she meant by "unmanageable" then she'd have to tell him about the kiss. What if he was so appalled and embarrassed he changed his mind about allowing her to accompany the twins?

That couldn't happen. She had an opportunity to prevent a wicked crime. Father Andrew had already given her a letter to personally deliver to Father Dubourg explaining his interpretations of a dying Frenchman's fevered ramblings. The priest had sent for Eva since her French was better than his. The mortally wounded man had begged absolution for a number of things, including agreeing to plot the theft of the sacred relics from St Louis Cathedral in New Orleans.

No. She couldn't mention *the kiss*. Of course, she wouldn't relate Kalia's part either. She'd tell him they feared he'd hurt himself, so they restrained him. That sounded practical, didn't it?

That settled it; she'd wait until he awakened then explain everything. Except Kalia's blasted potion. And the kiss. She'd also have the chance to plead her cause and beg for his assistance after they arrived at the Ursuline convent.

He mentioned earlier he was Catholic. How could he refuse a mission for the Church?

His jaw was slack, and he hadn't so much as twitched a finger. Surely Kalia didn't give her something that would permanently incapacitate the captain.

Would she?

There was one advantage having the stubborn man trussed like a boar on a spit, as Julian had said, and it made her smile rather wickedly. No doubt, her penance would be dozens of Hail Mary's and Our Fathers for stretching the truth and using nefarious methods to accomplish her goals, but at least she'd be able to help the Church.

"It looks like you'll be listening to what I need to tell you, after all, *Capitainé*, because I won't release you from these bonds until you do."

Chapter Seven

PENITENT PIRATE

This wasn't the first time Drago awoke tied to a bed. The last time, a lusty trollop made off with his entire purse as well as his boots and weapons. It had been inconvenient, but not surprising. He'd been drunk. Even worse, *that* was the morning he'd visited the Obeah witch's hut after he staggered, broke and barefoot out of the bordello, desperate for something to offset the effect of the rum and ease his misery.

SHE'D LIT her pipe and waved him inside. "Change in de wind, Drago. See you in I's dream. De demons hunger for you dark soul. Feed it them?" The scarlet paint on her forehead resembled a hideous red frown. Her raspy voice shot a chill down his spine. "A woman of light soon beckon you. Her a gilded place to trust you heart. Will her light your way, or will you extinguish her wit you shadow?

HE WAS CONFUSED. The last thing he remembered, he was dining with Sister Eva in the abbey kitchen. Now, he was bound spread-eagled on a small cot in an unfamiliar cupboard. His tongue felt thick in his mouth, and his head weighed ten stone, yet he hadn't taken a drop of rum. He closed his eyes and tried to swallow. They had drugged him. How?

Someone mumbled nearby. He raised his head. *Sister Eva?*

She was responsible?

He wasn't really a pirate anymore, but she knew of his reputation, which should have been enough to make her think twice about doing something like this. He shifted so blood flowed to his numb right hand.

Her head bent, the sister prayed in disjointed French and English. What on earth possessed a nun to drug and truss a pirate? It was insane to even consider it. He paused. Was she in her right mind? Did she fool him with her soft smile and meek countenance? Did her deep blue eyes and smooth, slender neck distract him from the madness within?

He almost apologized to God. Even the most pious would notice a beautiful pair of eyes on a woman, (sister of the Church or not). Surely the acknowledgment of her features wasn't a sin.

Was it?

Why linger on the question? He had no hope for redemption; why should he worry? Best to live a grand life while he had a life to live. God already knew he was neither a humble nor a decent man.

He stared at the ceiling and tried to think. Last night, she appeared to be in control of her wits. Even during Kalia's eerie intervention. In the cave pool, she cradled Jacqueline's head and spoke in low soothing tones, which had put the children—and even him—at ease. A mad woman couldn't possibly appear so sane for that long.

Could she?

He searched for the moment her demeanor changed, struggled to guess her motivation for drugging his tea.

Kalia.

Drago had plied the fickle waters of the sea a long time, witnessed and learned of too many strange and mysterious things for him to be arrogant enough to dismiss any of them as false.

The old woman possessed the gift of the sight, that was a certainty. Her own people both revered and feared her. She was a known witch, after all. Did she possess other powers? It wouldn't be a stretch to think she might be able to place a curse on him. What if the novitiate had fallen under her witchery?

He sucked in a breath. Were the two in league together? Was it a *black* witchery?

It couldn't be. Jacqueline improved after the treatments.

So, if it was a curse, it had been directed to him alone, but why?

Questions circled in his head like vultures. None more than why she restrained him and what Sister Eva planned to do with him.

His mouth was drier than sun-baked sand. His mind mocked him by creating visions of Kalia and Sister Eva carving out his heart and dancing under the full moon until a darker thought loomed. A strong aftershock of terror thundered straight through his bones.

Kalia had mentioned his departure from a brothel. Did Sister Eva mean to punish him for the infraction? There were worse sins, and he'd committed most of them, but the sister couldn't possibly know of it.

A commandment or two broken. Probably three. No penance could redeem him.

That horrible decision which led to his doom returned to torment him yet again. Along with that horrible day and the horrible act which secured his spot in the fire...

WHEN THEY HAD FIRST TRACKED the pirates to the coast of Portugal eight years ago, he'd been ecstatic. The markings on the hull and patches on the mainsail matched the one who took his sister. After gunning down their mizzen mast, his crew boarded the vessel, hoping to find Risa, but were disappointed. The only information they wrenched from the captain concerned a girl matching Risa's description, who had escaped from his ship with a member of his crew.

An Irishman by the name of Fynn Ahern.

Their father had placed Risa in Drago's care. He failed to escort her from Elba back home to San Vincenzo safely. Failed to protect her. Pirates kidnapped her to sell as a virgin bride at sixteen.

They had separated the captive women into two groups while aboard the pirate's ship. It was obvious the men had mistreated the older ones. The younger girls were in better condition—most likely virgins. Worth ten to twenty times the price of a regular slave on the block.

The Persians placed a high value on virgin slaves.

It had been difficult to convince the prisoners that his crew did not intend to mistreat them or sell them back into slavery. After being released from the hold, the Negro warriors tried to fling themselves, chains and all, overboard. Before his men could stop them, several succeeded, sinking into a cloud of bubbles.

After that, they secured them in a storage room, determined to keep them from harming themselves. Raul, a huge Cimaroon on his crew, had been able to settle them a bit and communicate somewhat. The man was as dark as night and wore nothing but a loincloth with a weapon's belt around his waist and one of Drago's old shirts, sans sleeves. The two of them had been through a lot together; he was one of the few men Drago trusted with his life.

At least he now had a name to use in his quest to find his sister: Ahern.

If Ahern sold Risa to those Persian curs, he'd travel to the end of the ocean searching her. Then he'd hunt Ahern down and kill him.

Slowly.

The wind had picked upand aided their efforts to be away quickly. Drago gazed dispassionately upon the pirates chained around his mizzen mast. Their captain had lost consciousness an hour ago. He wouldn't have to endure witnessing his brig and his livelihood, sink. The closest port could have them.

The most valuable cargo had been off-loaded and stowed away aboard the *Dragon*. All that remained was to scupper the other ship. He wasn't about to make it easy for the pirates to slither back into the slave trade.

It hadn't taken long to rig the pirate's vessel to blow. A few spilled kegs of powder in the hold, a trail of oil-soaked rags, and it was ready.

One of the rescued women became hysterical from her place at the stern. Not only had he not understood her language, he hadn't understood why she hadn't been relieved to be saved from the brigands. No matter, he'd been confident they'd find a way to explain things once they had executed the current task.

Time to go.

Raul had strung a rag-wrapped arrow dipped in oil in his bow. Tapping the tip to a lit torch set it aflame. After careful aim, he let it fly.

"Make sail!" Drago had shouted. "Lead along topsail sheets, and halyards lay out and loose!"

"Lay aft the braces, ye dogs! Starboard main and larboard head!"

Sails puffed out their bellies, then stiffened as the breeze filled them. The *Dragon* lurched into motion, and soon they were flying away.

Harvey handed Drago the spyglass. Thick, rolling gray and black clouds billowed from the deck.

A slight movement near the capstan drew his attention, and the small form of a young girl stumbled toward the rail, her white shift flapping around her, dark hair swirling across her face.

Drago's heart had stopped. Why was the child still on the boat? How had they missed her? Horror knifed through his gut just as an explosion sent a thunderous black plume billowing upward.

The woman screamed and fainted.

He'd wanted to drag the glass away from his eye, but he couldn't. Of course she was gone, but still, he found himself looking frantically for her as the wind blew the black smoke away. The ship itself had blown in half. Stem and stern both speared the sky for the briefest moment like twin peaks, then tilted and within minutes disappeared into the depths.

The ocean roared in his ears. The image of the waif in white, hair blowing, would haunt him the rest of his days.

Anger, shock and sickening dread flooded his chest. Drago fought to inhale. He'd never taken the life of an innocent soul before. A child, no less.

It was unforgivable.

☙❧

Drago forced the horrific memory and the weight of the guilt away. He opened his eyes and stared at the foot of the bed where his legs were spread wide, strapped to the posts.

He whipped his gaze to Sister Eva, his breath frozen in icy terror. Beside the kneeling woman, a long, slim filet knife rested on a stool. His stomach tightened. Maybe as punishment, she intended to castrate him!

Dear God.

A leather strap was wrapped several times around his right

hand, his left, restrained with a rope. He couldn't move his legs. He was completely at her mercy. His heart ricocheted off his ribs.

She prayed on her knees near his feet, likely praying for his precious soon-to-be-departed tender parts. Thankfully, she was yet unaware he awoke.

He tugged again at the straps securing his wrists, then examined the pallet. It was ancient. If he broke the frame, he could free himself. He'd have to be quick. The old wood would create a lot of noise when it splintered apart. He braced his arms, ready to heave his body to the side.

A grating creak echoed in the tiny room, and her eyelids flew open. She looked up, her velvet blue eyes widened and locked with his.

His mouth went dry. Although his soul was undoubtedly lost, he prayed.

Dear God in heaven, I sincerely, deeply and humbly apologize for admiring Sister Eva's eyes. And curves. And neck.

Amen.

Chapter Eight

PIRATE PERSUASION

*C*apitaine Gamponetti finally woke up!

Eva held her breath, waiting for him to react. Until he said or did something to indicate his current state of mind, she wouldn't be able to tell if he was coherent or still demented. If he remained under the influence of the tonic, the restraints should hold him.

Strangely enough, he stayed silent, which was not a comforting sign. He should be demanding his release and blustering with outrage. At the very least he should ask why she attached him to a bed, which she'd expected since he seemed the type of man accustomed to giving orders. And having them obeyed.

She stared, baffled. Why didn't he say anything? His eyes were open and alert, no longer unfocused. In fact, they were quite wide and decidedly focused. On her.

Was he frightened? Certainly not. More likely contemplating his next move or command. Maybe both.

Odd. Perhaps the tonic left lingering effects, after all. She'd been under the impression the man had a much more courageous constitution.

Maybe he was quiet because he'd already suspected the reason for the confinement and was preparing an argument or a threat. Did he remember exactly what happened?

Did he remember *the kiss*?

Lifting her chin, she gave him her most indignant look, which was challenging given the fact she trembled beneath her robes. "Do you know why I restrained you, *Capitainé*?" Her voice came out sounding harsher than she intended. Just the thought of that stupid kiss had her flustered, raising her ire as well as her voice.

His Adam's apple jerked up and down. Heavens, he was as pale as sun-bleached bones. His eyes shifted to the dagger on her stool, then widened into a glare.

Eva straightened her shoulders; she would not be intimidated by his glares or his dark reputation. She would have her say, and he would listen. Perhaps she should reiterate her question. "*Capitainé*? Do you know why we restrained you?"

He glowered, opened his mouth, shut it, coughed, then spoke with a chilly calm. "I believe I might suspect the reason."

Oh dear. So, he remembered, and from his tone didn't condone her actions. "Then you should understand why the restraints are necessary until I am certain you won't duplicate the offense." She awaited his apology. She certainly deserved one.

"Well... Sister," he carefully chose his words. "I think perhaps you might have slightly... overreacted."

How could he possibly believe that? "*Capitainé*, your actions were appalling!" He should be ashamed, begging her to forgive him, although at the moment she had a hard time even considering forgiveness. This inflamed the guilt because a woman in her position should pardon readily. Unfortunately, she had a harder time than most with that particular grace. She could now also add "lying" to the list of sins to confess.

Insufferable man.

Conceited brigand.

Irritable bully.

He was ridiculously thick-headed, if he believed she over-reacted.

He reddened. "I can understand why you would say that Sister, but surely you've known other men who've exhibited the same behavior."

"Not here, *Capitainé*, I assure you." The gall! What kind of man assumed she'd be familiar with other men who fondled women of the church?

His brows jumped up, and he looked around the room. "Well, not here. I didn't mean to insinuate the abbey would ever…"

Eva's cheeks were probably as red as his face. How naïve to think he might be somewhat honorable. She gritted her teeth. At least he had the decency to be embarrassed. There ought to be a stiff measure of guilt mixed in, which would satisfy her greatly, although it wouldn't exonerate him.

Not in the slightest.

Guilt was a powerful weapon. Sister Beatrice (an expert) wielded it with uncanny precision. Perhaps now was the time to utilize the same tactics. "You behaved in a most disrespectful manner, *Capitainé,* and I am more than a little offended."

He sighed, and the edges of his mouth tipped down. "For that, I beg you to accept my sincerest apologies, Sister Eva."

Oh, no.

It wouldn't be that easy for the scoundrel. She rose from her knees and picked up the knife, then perched on the stool. If he wanted her to free him, first he would hear her plea and if he had any bit of respectability, feel obligated to assist her as penance, or to assuage his guilty conscience for forcing a lustful kiss on a novice nun.

And it was indeed a lustful, *lustful* kiss.

Her lower belly rippled under the surface of her skin.

"I'm afraid, *Capitainé* Gamponetti, your feeble apology isn't what I want from you. Not entirely, anyway."

Chapter Nine
NUN IN CONTROL

✦

Great Calypso!
       Drago fought the urge to jerk at his bindings like a leashed animal. Where was Julian? If he shouted for the boy, would he hear and come to his aid? He dismissed the thought almost as soon as it burst into his head. She had a dagger on her lap. He couldn't risk him being injured or killed.

Drago would rely on his quick mind and smooth tongue to negotiate and talk her into reconsidering. Perhaps he could offer her something she'd appreciate more than his nether parts; something to which he wasn't so intimately attached.

"Sister, you must—"

"I beg your pardon, *Capitaine*, but I think we can both agree I'm the one in control at the moment, can we not?"

He mashed his lips together to keep from saying something he shouldn't.

Perhaps he wouldn't be able to talk her out of castrating him. There had to be another tack he could take. Think, think, *think*. In the meantime, he must delay her from taking any drastic actions, and do anything to placate her.

Anything.

He nodded slowly. Keep her calm and keep that knife as far away from his jewels as possible. "You are indeed in control," he ground out as calmly as he could. It didn't help he wanted to spank her with his numb right hand until the feeling came back into it, and reason came back into her.

A smile crinkled the corners of her eyes. "Excellent, I will talk, and you will listen."

He snapped his mouth shut. No woman had ever spoken to him like this. Or man, for that matter. He clenched his jaw hard enough to make it burn.

Look pleasant. Nod frequently.

Her expression sobered, and she leaned forward. "I need your cooperation and assistance with something very important." The candlelight glinted off the blade in her hand, dappling his crotch and the body parts in jeopardy. God was playing cruel, vindictive tricks on him.

His tongue nearly tripped over his teeth. "Of course, Sister. I'm happy to assist you in any way possible." At this point, he'd commit to anything, whether he vowed it or not.

Surprise flickered crossed her face before she brightened and smiled. "Thank you, *Capitaine*. I'm so relieved to hear it." She sat back continued, "I discovered a scheme to steal sacred relics from the St. Louis Cathedral in New Orleans. I know this because Father Andrew and I tended a dying man who was given this task by the French King."

Drago closed his eyes and gave a mental groan of frustration. Moreau. The missing agent. He'd confessed in the presence of a nun from the St. Louis Cathedral of New Orleans. *The idiot.*

Of all the horrible luck.

If Moreau revealed the names of the other agents, then she'd known all along he was connected to that mission. What did she hope to accomplish now? Talk him out of his obligation to the King of France? He'd lose more than his nether parts if he failed to fulfill his duty.

A sharp steel blade attached to a guillotine frame came to mind.

He swallowed. Surely she didn't plan to replace the stolen relics with his—? He had to learn how much she knew. "The Frenchman died, so the plot likely died with him," he said carefully. If Moreau gave her names, he'd find out now.

But she shook her head. "It did not die with him. He was given this the task along with three other agents. The problem is, he mentioned no names, so I don't know who they are, only that there are three of them."

Drago's relief was temporary, mainly because she continued to run her fingers over the knife handle as she spoke. While horribly distracting, the insinuation was quite clear.

In addition to being in command, the nun was definitely light in the head. Worse, the fate of his bollocks lie in his ability to charm the weapon from her.

"*Capitaine* Gamponetti, I have an important request."

"I want you to understand that I will do anything you ask of me, Sister Eva." *Just please don't turn me into a eunuch.*

She released a long sigh. Her sapphire eyes flashed, and she once again leaned forward. "*Capitaine*, will you give both God and me your word that you will help?"

"I give my word to God and to you that I will help," he said solemnly.

At this moment, he didn't care what she wanted, he would promise it. The sooner he escaped this abbey, the better off he would be.

Crazy nun notwithstanding.

Chapter Ten

DRAGO'S VOW

Eva was ecstatic the man was being so agreeable. "*Capitaine*, once we get back to New Orleans, I need your additional assistance with a very important matter for the church." She waited, barely able to contain her trepidation and fear of his refusal.

While she didn't approve of the way Miss Kalia's tonic worked, she was beyond pleased with the results. *Capitaine* Gamponetti had indeed bent to her will. God answered her prayers, and yet again Miss Kalia's uncanny ability to predict Eva's future was horrifyingly accurate. "We cannot wait."

He was already nodding. "I'll do my best to help you."

"Truly?" Eva chewed her lip.

The captain's gaze turned stoney. "My word is my vow."

"Good." This likely forced him to adjust his trade route and miss the opportunity to bring in a healthy amount of revenue. It was a lot to ask. She shoved her guilt aside. Her cause outweighed a hefty purse.

By far.

He shifted. "I also have some much needed supplies I must

purchase while in Negril Bay. The *Dragon* will sail as soon as possible."

A nagging agitation wiggled in Eva's belly. That could be a ploy to delay. He could be lying and had no intention of helping her. Would he go back on his word after giving it to a soon-to-be member of the Ursuline order?

Quite probably. He was a pirate, after all.

She glanced around the room and caught sight of a Bible resting on a low shelf.

Decision made, she gave him one more careful scrutiny. The affect of the tea seemed to be completely gone. She prayed he wasn't simply going along with her demands—*requests*—because he was confined. Her old self would have believed the more pessimistic view, but if she was to become Sister Eva, the newest Ursuline novitiate, she would work to believe the opposite.

Have faith.

She gripped the dagger, rose and approached the bed. The captain's throat convulsed as he stared at the nicked blade. She sawed through the rope securing his right hand to the bedpost. As soon as it was loose, he shook it then moved it lower to hover above his... his... belt. She swallowed, a bit chagrined at keeping him restrained for so long. He must need to relieve himself by now.

She would hurry.

The cord around his left ankle untied easily. The right ankle's knot proved to be more difficult, but she managed it after a few minutes. As soon as she freed his leg, he crossed it over the other.

Not wanting to hold him much longer, she offered the Bible. "Will you swear an oath upon the Word of God to complete this mission for God's church?" Even pirates had to have some sort of code about swearing on a Bible (at least she hoped so).

He hesitated, almost as if he were reluctant to move his hand. If he'd been lying to her, he'd likely not swear. If he did, she'd just have to trust him to keep his word. As long as he took her with him, the worst that could happen would be his refusal to help prevent the robbery. She could perhaps persuade some parishioners to guard the sacred bones, if she became desperate.

His eyes darted to the knife and then back to the Bible. What did he think she would do, stab him if he refused?

Well, if he tried to kiss her again, she might consider it.

The kiss.

Do not think back to the kiss. In fact, never think about the kiss again. As far as using the blade, even in her former life, she rarely needed a weapon.

Perhaps there might have been a time when she was younger, when she'd thought differently, when she trusted people less, when she had to fight wild dogs for scraps, a dirk came in handy. The Ursuline sisters had taught her about compassion and faith, that the Lord loved and protected her; even still, she had hoarded crusts of bread and slept under her cot in the abbey for many months after Sister Beatrice found her.

Eva focused again on the pirate. "*Capitaine*? Will you swear to help me complete my mission?"

He closed his eyes, heaved a great sigh, and placed his hand on the book. "Yes, Sister. As soon as I deliver my cargo to Negril Bay, I will return and take you to New Orleans."

"And help prevent the theft of the relics."

His nostrils flared. Flint-colored eyes locked with hers. He spoke as if he had a mouth full of rocks. "And help you prevent the theft of the relics."

"There." She smiled. "That wasn't so hard, was it?"

Chapter Eleven

THE BRITISH THREAT

Negril Bay, Jamaica

"Ships ho, Captain Gampo!" The cry came from up in the topmast yards.

Drago exited his cabin. "What do you see, Razin?"

"Looks to be an armada, sir!"

They'd rounded the windward side of Jamaica toward Negril Bay. The *Dragon* rode low, pregnant with sugarcane. If the vessels anchored in the harbor were hostile, she'd be easily taken.

"What colors do they fly?" he yelled back.

"The bloody Union Jack," came the reply.

Dozens of British warships had amassed in the bay. Why? There was no need to overly worry since an English purchaser commissioned his cargo. The question at hand was this: where were they heading and toward what cause? Since Spain and England were allies, he ordered a Spanish flag hoisted and continued toward the docks.

After checking in with the harbormaster, Drago sent a messenger to alert the buyer of his arrival so he may inspect the shipment. The harvest should net a healthy amount of coin.

The tavern where they were to conduct business was close to the wharf. He sat to wait. As he sipped his ale, he let his mind wander back to the abbey at Port Royal. He should toast to his good fortune that, although the nun knew about the plan to steal the holy relics, the identity of the agents remained hidden. They could still complete their assignment with relative ease. He chuckled into his mug. In asking for his help, the nun had inadvertently paved the road to their success.

This mission just became much easier. What better way to determine the best path to their target than discuss vulnerabilities with Sister Eva? He'd develop a plan for posting guards, suggest a hiding place, and supervise proper execution. A normal man would have been plagued with guilt. He would be too if he had a reason to worry further about his soul. He ordered another ale, keeping with his latest vow to enjoy this life.

The next one would be a lot hotter.

He'd sail for America within a week, given that Jacqueline recovered her health.

Sister Eva may be a bit unbalanced, but she was indeed a talented healer. Her treatments worked well; by the time he had departed the abbey yesterday, Jacqueline was up walking about.

He shook his head. Long ago, he'd quit trying to understand the gifts God bestowed upon the common man (or woman). He'd witnessed a man calculate the total weight of a wagonload of baled cotton within two pounds. He'd listened to a young boy play the violin better than a grown man who'd been playing for thirty years. He'd never know how Sister Eva determined the little lamb's ailment or its cure, but he was grateful she had. Well, he was grateful as far as Jacqueline's situation was concerned.

But Sister Eva's behavior would keep him wary and vigilant.

She'd drugged him with bloody tea! It was unlikely he'd ever drink tea again. With her knowledge of herbs and tonics, he was probably lucky he'd been out of sorts for only a short while. Granted, he was unconscious long enough for her to tie him to the bedposts, but at least he came away with his purse still full and no lingering aftereffects of his visit.

And no missing or inactive body parts.

Drago scowled. He'd rather gather up the twins and take them to Cartagena and meet the rest of the fleet. Let the French couple handle the king's latest folly. If he had the children with him now, he could simply shove off from here. If the little skirt wasn't ill, and if he wasn't so opposed to parting with his head for failing the mission, he might actually give the thought longer consideration.

But then he'd break a vow to a king and to a nun which was infinitely worse than breaking one *or* the other. Either way, he was cursed. The king of France would call for his head, followed swiftly by the king of the Underworld demanding his soul.

Sailors by nature were a superstitious lot, and after placing his hand on a Bible and giving an oath to the Almighty, only the claws of death would normally keep him from fulfilling it.

The fact that he was coerced against his will provided a little leeway, as the vow wasn't a binding promise. Drago released his breath in an annoyed gust. He kicked the table leg, missing the fly that had lit there. Blast it, if he hadn't also sworn upon a Bible to take her back home and help prevent the theft of the same church relics he was charged with obtaining. He gave a sarcastic snort. There was a conundrum. Betray a nun or have his throat cut in his sleep by Fontaine?

He swirled the remaining contents of his mug and stared at the liquid as it stilled. Why did he bother to contemplate further? He already knew his choice.

Sorry, Sister.

"Captain Gamponetti?" A nasally voice broke into his musings. It belonged to a small, round man with wide droopy eyes, a bulbous nose and a sedate cut to his mouth.

"Shall I presume you are Mr. Winesap?" Drago stood and shook the man's hand.

Winesap tilted his head and gave him a thin smile. "Indeed, I am." He gestured to Drago's near-empty mug. "May I join you?"

"By all means." He signaled for two more ales as he sank into his chair. "Did you find my product to be of an acceptable quality?" The man bloody well should have. He'd gone to annoying lengths to select the best grade of cane and still offer a price the man accepted.

Winesap nodded, removed his handkerchief and wiped the sweat from his upper lip before taking a seat. "I did. I did. Beyond expectations, even." He removed a hefty purse from his pocket and plopped it on the table as a young Jamaican boy placed two ales in front of them. Winesap reached for his tankard with both hands and took a healthy drink. "We've nearly finished transferring the cane to my hold."

Drago picked up the leather pouch. It had a satisfying heft. He poured a few coins into his palm to inspect, and glanced at the dog-faced man, wondering if he knew something about the boats gathered in the harbor. "I've never seen such a large flotilla of warships anchored here."

"A grand sight, isn't it?" Winesap settled in his chair. "We are amassing for a final assault. Vice Admiral Cochrane awaits Captain Lloyde's squadron to join us from the Azores. Then we depart."

A final assault on whom? Drago flicked his gaze over Winesap. The man wasn't dressed in a Navy uniform, although he was obviously British by his accent and style. "Your vessel is part of the navy?"

Winesap's jowls jiggled as he shook his head. Thick shaggy brows converged at the center of his forehead. "I've simply been commissioned to transport the sugarcane fascines needed for the army. I suppose I'm accompanying them, but my ship is not part of the fighting force."

Cane fascines?

Fascines?

His cargo would be used to make fascines? Not rum? Not sugar? He'd selected the finest cane just so they could tie it in bundles and spread them across mud and muck for foot soldiers to trample over? It was enough to make a man weep. A slow burn began in his stomach. It took effort, but Drago relaxed his jaw and swallowed a careful sip of ale. "Fascines for the army? To what battle do they march?"

Winesap puffed out his chest. "We're finally going to take New Orleans from those dirty-shirt Americans. When we capture the city, we'll control all access to the Mississippi River. From there it'll be easy to separate the entire western territory from the American Union." He swept a hand in the general direction of the harbor. "We shall bring a fighting force of over fifteen thousand battle-hardened troops fresh from France and Baltimore. We also have our Spanish allies. Once we negotiate with the French and Spanish settlers and the slaves from the sugar and cotton plantations, which we will free of course, they'll all be eager to aid us."

Drago's mouth went dry. He stared hard at the purse brimming with coins. "So the sugarcane fascines?"

Winesap smiled. His eyes remained patronizing. "If you've ever been to the Louisiana Territory, Captain Gamponetti, you'd know it has a vast area of swampland and mud. Fascines will be required for the soldiers to traverse across marshy areas. Cochrane will certainly procure additional cane from plantations nearby, but for the initial landing, I'll accommodate him. The admiral shall probably make landfall through Lake Pontchartrain, cut the straightest path to the heart of the city and take it quickly. Less than a week after we arrive, either New Orleans will be ours or it will burn."

Chapter Twelve

DRAGO'S OATH

D rago strode toward the abbey; the heavy purse in his pocket pulled at his coat and his conscience. This new information changed things considerably. The knowledge he'd just contributed to the fall of New Orleans left a bitter taste in his mouth. If he'd known the British plan for the sugarcane, he'd have found a different buyer.

It was too late now.

He spent the last two days getting the *Dragon* ready to sail. New canvas would be delivered soon. The sheets would be repaired en route. There was no time to do otherwise. Winesap had said Cochrane would wait for Lloyde's fleet to arrive before departing, which could be a week from now or it could be tomorrow.

Dusk was descending, and he was grateful for the cooler temperatures following sunset, although he might have a different opinion once he arrived in New Orleans to the early December chill.

A stout woman with a permanent pucker and an accusatory glare opened the door. By the wisp of gray hair poking out of the coif around her face, he'd guess she was in her late fifties.

"What can I do for you, Captain Gamponetti?"

"I—" Drago hesitated. He never met this woman. How did she know his name? "I'm here to speak with Sister Eva," he said carefully. "She's been tending my ward, Jacqueline Sauvage."

The nun narrowed her eyes and snorted.

Had he done something to offend? He almost reached up to straighten his collar before stopping himself. He cared nothing of her opinion of him. He was the captain of his own ship. He had a crew of men who either respected him or feared him. Regardless, it put him in control. When he was in control, things fell into place. When things fell into place, life was easier. Tasks were successfully completed. Outcomes were accurately predicted. Men were handsomely paid. He didn't care what they, or anyone else, thought of him, including this hag of a nun.

He mentally winced. What was it about this place that drove him to be at his worst?

She continued to scowl as if she'd read his mind. Finally, she swung the door wide. "Follow me. I'll take you to her. She and the children are in the garden."

At his arched brow, she shrugged. "It's cooler to work this time of day."

Still baffled by the cold reception, he followed her awkward gait. She rocked side to side before lurching forward. He quickened his pace before she disappeared around a cluster of tall, shiny ferns.

The garden rioted with vines, flowers and leafy greenery in the center of the courtyard, well-protected from hungry, four-legged herbivores. Which of those plants had been used to drug him?

"Eva," the nun called out. "The captain has returned."

Sister Eva looked up from her work. "Thank you, Sister Beatrice." She dropped her trowel in a small wheeled cart and stood, pausing to press her hands against the small of her back and stretch, reminding him of the curves revealed in the cave waters the other day.

Turning his attention to his young charges, he was much relieved to see Jacqueline working beside the nun. There was a splash of color in her cheeks and a smile on her face.

"How are you today, little skirt?" he teased.

"Much better this day, Captain Gampo. Did you offload your sugarcane with success?"

"That I did." He couldn't return her smile. The weight in his pocket prevented it. As he greeted Sister Eva, his stomach tightened. It wasn't safe for her to make the journey. Besides, he needed her to care for the children. She wouldn't take the news well.

Julian propped a pitchfork against the stable door and trotted over, all elbows and gangly legs. "Hoy, captain! Look at Jacqueline. She's all better. Sister Eva's tea cured her."

Drago touched his hat and gave the sister a sincere bow of thanks. "I'm grateful for your administrations. It's clear you have a divine healing touch." Normally, his deep baritone compliments made most women blush.

Not this one.

"You're welcome, *Capitaine*." She wiped her hands on an old rag. "I'm thankful for God's gifts." She cocked her head and peered at him past the edge of her veil. "Now you've returned, shall I prepare my things? When will we depart?"

Instead of an answer, Drago pressed the pouch of coins into her palm.

"What's this for?" She straightened, and her brows converged.

He gestured to the twins and the structure surrounding them. "It's for you and the children." The nun's shoulders stiffened and although he rarely explained his actions or decisions to anyone, he had to fight the impulse to do so now. He clasped his hands behind his back and clenched them. The air became still and quiet. Even suffocating.

Jacqueline dropped her eyebrows. She was a smart little chit, already reading words unspoken. "What children? Surely not us."

She met Julian's narrowed stare with an incredulous one of her own.

Drago directed his attention to Sister Eva. He would not converse with a twelve-year-old petticoat. Hard enough to have the discussion with this particular nun. "I must leave the children in your care for a few weeks. The coins should provide both for their welfare and the abbey for an extended time."

Julian clenched his jaw. "I want to come with you."

Drago shot him a piercing glare. "You are to look after your sister. She needs your protection."

"From what?" Jacqueline asked, sweeping her arms out wide and looking around. "Mosquitoes?"

"*Capitaine* Gamponetti." Sister Eva's voice, although flat and soft, cut through the air like a gunshot, her sapphire eyes turned stormy. "You gave your word."

Drago pressed his lips in a frustrated line. It wasn't like he was intentionally breaking his vow to her. He had new information which demanded plans be adjusted. He may have done a lot of heinous things in his past, but he wasn't about to deliver women and children directly into an area about to become a battlefield. Even *he* had a conscience. It might be run down and threadbare, but it was still there.

He had other problems gathering strength like an approaching hurricane. He'd be the devil's handmaid before he'd let the cane he sold to the Brits end up in fascines to be used for English foot soldiers, and he could give a mangy cur's tail about the rest of the people there, but the twin's family had become trusted friends over the past few years. He would retrieve them, then bring them to safety after obtaining the relics.

He caught the sister's heated glare and held it calmly. "The British have amassed an armada of over sixty ships in Negril Bay. They will soon set sail for New Orleans. Their plan is to take the city as well as control of the Mississippi River. I cannot, in good conscience, deliver you and the children to imminent danger."

Sister Beatrice made the sign of the cross. "Dear Lord, protect us!"

Jacqueline paled. "What about Uncle Bernard, Victor, Adrian and Tristan? We must warn them!"

Julian crossed his arms. "I want to go with you," he stated again, "I'm nearly thirteen and of age to be a powder boy."

Drago scowled. "I'm not the Royal Navy. I employ men, not boys."

Julian's eyes sparked with defiance. "My family is in danger. I can't stay and hide in the abbey with the women."

The boy was treading on dangerous ground. It was likely he was unaware his sister was reaching an age where men were starting to notice her developing figure. She was already beautiful in the face. Ebony hair, long, thick lashes, sparkling blue or thundercloud gray eyes, depending on her mood. This was the safest place for her. For both of them.

"You won't be hiding in an abbey, you'll be protecting your sister," he snarled.

Jacqueline's voice cut through the evening air. "I'm going with you, too. I want to be with my family."

"You're not listening," Drago snapped.

Sister Beatrice gasped. "Watch your temper, Captain!"

He'd forgotten she was still there. He clenched his hands and shoved them into his coat pockets, striving for calm. He spun toward the children and did his best to keep his voice low and even. "You all must understand the British intend to bring a bloody battle to New Orleans. They'll have four times the number of soldiers than the entire population of the city and surrounding farms." He paused a moment while they digested this information and knew the second realization struck when the little skirt's eyes filled.

Jacqueline twisted her fingers in her pinafore. Her voice dropped to a terrified whisper, "Uncle Bernard will defend our family and property. Our brother and cousins will stand with him."

Julian paled. His hands hung limply at his sides. "The British will take over the hotel and loot the gaming house, then they'll kill them, won't they?"

Drago shook his head. Although it was indeed likely. "I will get to them before the British arrive. And yes, the army will probably commandeer the hotel as well as Tristan's gaming house. It's probable, however, if your uncle grants permission for them to use his property, they'll relinquish it as soon as the battle is over. They'll be less likely to sack the city if the people cooperate."

Sister Eva was staring in disbelief at him. Her cobalt eyes sharpened beneath long, inky lashes. "Cooperate? We are a free nation, *Capitaine*. We will not stand idly by and allow foreign soldiers to take our home without a fight."

Drago did his best to soften his tone further as he settled his hand on the young boy's shoulder. "I'm leaving at first light. I shall warn the governor and the city, then get your family. Once I have them on my ship, I'll bring them back here where they'll be safe."

He didn't vocalize the next thought. *By then the relics will be on their way back to France. My service to the king ended.*

Sister Eva gasped and brought a hand to her mouth. "That will be how the French agents will get into the cathedral... with the British army." Her fingers gripped the coin pouch until they grew white. "The sacred relics must be moved. Hidden. The nuns will need protection, as well." She pressed her hands and his purse to her stomach. "The British have little sympathy or respect for the Catholic Church."

Drago straightened; he would develop his own plan of action. "Sister Eva, I gave you my word I would help. As soon as I speak with the governor and Bernard Sauvage, I will alert Father Dubourg about the planned theft."

"What if you're too late?" Sister Eva's crystalline gaze tripped his heart. If his life wasn't at risk, he might have considered abandoning the French king's mission. "You placed the church last on your list. What if you aren't in time to save the sacred bones of St. Louis?"

Drago sighed. "I have sixty men on my crew. I will send one of them to warn the Ursuline nuns."

"Only one?" The veil hid most of her face, but her tone contained a barely restrained thread of anger, which in turn ignited his. On *his* vessel, the men would never question his decisions. On *his* ship... he closed his eyes and clenched his teeth together. Of course, he wasn't on his ship at the moment. The nuns had a completely different view of authority and who really wielded it. He'd compromise.

"Fine then, I'll send ten. In fact, we'll go to the cathedral first." Naturally. His primary objective was to find and take the relics.

She placed her hands on her hips and studied him, the tension in her shoulders almost visible. "I should go with you."

Absolutely not.

Now that he had a grand excuse to leave her behind, he'd rather bring a hornet's nest aboard. She'd already complicated his mission for the king. At least if he posted several men at the abbey, he'd be seeing to his obligation to "protect" the relics. Besides, how would he sleep knowing she was near, knowing there was a distinct possibility he could awaken tied to his own bed?

Or worse?

A better course of action would be to play the part of an honorable gentleman concerned with the welfare of both his charges. It would place him in a natural position of strength, where little debate should arise.

Sister Eva stepped forward. "I could accompany your men and alert the abbey while you raise the alarm. The children can stay here, with Sister Beatrice."

"I will not allow it."

She opened her mouth to speak, but he slashed the air with

his hand. "No argument. This isn't a minor campaign. 60 British warships, filled with thousands of seasoned soldiers, cannot be defeated by a meager American army and undisciplined militias, who may or may not attempt to defend the city. The American militia has a tendency to run, so I hear." He tried to ignore the frightened expressions on the children's faces.

Sister Eva crossed her arms. "I'm a healer, *Capitaine* Gamponetti. Battlefields are where I'm needed most."

Logical reasoning.

He would argue no more; chances were if he didn't leave now, she'd find a way to extort another oath from him. He was still trying to determine how to sidestep the last one.

In addition, there were a number of things to do before he could set sail. This conversation was delaying him. The quicker she understood that his decision was firm, the better. He plied logic of his own. "You are not the only healer in this hemisphere, Sister. Your duty is here. I'm holding you personally responsible for the health and welfare of these two children until I return. I've left you a handsome sum to assist in that endeavor."

Her voice trembled with barely leashed fury. "You cannot buy your way out of a promise, especially one to God."

He whirled back to face her. "I gave you my *oath*." The words were out before he had time to think, and harsher than he intended. Her eyes widened, and she stepped back. He followed, intending to drive his point home. "God can bloody well strike me down if I break it," he grated out.

A sharp silence fell over the courtyard.

What had he just done?

Chapter Thirteen

STOWAWAYS

"Hurry, Beatrice."

The older woman grunted as she lengthened her stride. "Those two will learn the price for disregarding instructions once they feel the sting of a switch on their little backsides."

Eva silently agreed. Although she wasn't sure she had it in her to take a switch to a child, she'd be fine with Sister Beatrice doing so, as long as it wasn't too hard. Or for too long. Or with too big a switch.

The twins had probably sneaked aboard the captain's ship in the middle of the night. She could think of no other place they'd go. She'd paused to check on them before preparing for her early predawn prayers, and her had heart seized mid-beat at the sight of the empty cots.

Capitainé Gamponetti's vessel stood proud and unyielding close to the pier. High tide was still a few hours away and would mark the time of departure. A sturdy plank connecting the schooner to the dock groaned and creaked; wood rubbed wood as the ship shifted and rocked. It meant someone recently departed.

God willing, that someone was *Capitainé* Gamponetti.

Eva detected no movement yet on the main deck. She tried not to think about how many of the crew might be in the brothel on the hill. The notion brought the handsome silver-eyed commander to mind, which had her clenching her teeth again. Miss Kalia and her prophesies and tonics. *Humph.*

"Him not who him seem to be..."

Well, he certainly wasn't the type to keep a promise made on a Bible. That was the pirate in him, of course. Although, if he kept the last half where he pledged to prevent the theft of the relics, she'd be satisfied enough to forgive him. Perhaps.

The water lapped softly against the hull as they crept on to the vessel. It was likely the children were hiding somewhere below. They surely wouldn't hide in the captain's cabin. Eva paused and bit her lower lip, suddenly nervous. They should have thought this through better. Not only were they unfamiliar with the layout, they were without a light. It had to be as black as a moonless night down there. No telling what they might run into in the dark.

A hatch nearby suddenly flipped open with a loud crack. Sister Beatrice grabbed her arm with a gasp. A giant of a man squeezed his shoulders through the opening and scrambled to his feet. His back to them, he strolled over to the rail and proceeded to relieve himself.

Both women froze in fear and mortification. While she was fast enough to dart below through the open hatch, there was no way Sister Beatrice could possibly make it.

The man finished, stretched, spun around and stopped in his tracks, eyes wide. His massive jaw went slack, and her stomach took a dive. The man had to be at least a head taller than *Capitaine* Gamponetti, which meant he was nearly seven feet in height. His face showed signs of battles hard fought. It harbored a crooked, flattened nose, and a scar split his left eyebrow into two heavy slashes.

A shocked silence hung between them.

Just as Eva opened her mouth, the man made the sign of the cross and gave them an awkward bow. "Good morning," he said, voice thick, slow and rumbling like boulders rolling down a mountain. Either his brain worked slowly as well, or English wasn't his primary language.

"Good morning, sir." Eva was not sure what to say beyond that. They were caught.

"Are you here to bless our boat?" The man clasped his hands prayerfully in front of him.

"Yes, of course," Sister Beatrice finally piped up. "We should like to start below." It had become obvious the man was more brawn than brain.

"I am Manuel," he said. "I would like you to pray for me. And my cousin, Drago."

Ah, so this was the captain's loyal, protective cousin. Sister Beatrice shot a doubtful look at her. Taking a chance, Eva stepped forward. "We are also seeking two children. Have you seen them?"

Manuel's eyes widened, slid to the open hatch, then down to his feet. His chest rose and fell in short, rapid breaths.

Ah. Not only had he seen them, he knew where to find them. More confident now, she switched to a polite, but authoritative tone. "I should like to talk to them, please. They fled my care without a proper goodbye."

Manuel's head rose a notch. He appeared to ponder her request a moment before releasing a lungful of breath. "This way," he mumbled.

The descent was steep and as dark as she'd feared. The tang of rotted hemp and saltwater assailed their nostrils. Once they reached the next level down, Sister Beatrice clutched Eva's tunic for guidance. Manuel led them into a sail room and turned up a lantern until there was enough light to identify walls and objects. Canvas, both old and new, stretched across the floor, some in piles, others folded in layers.

He strode across the room and opened a small corner closet, then stepped aside. Sister Beatrice limped up beside Eva and crossed her arms over her chest while glaring at the two-forms huddled inside. "Out with you both, now."

The children rose glumly to their feet. Jacqueline stared at the enormous man, aghast. "Manuel," she whined. "We told you not to tell anyone you saw us!"

Julian laced his fingers on the top of his head and closed his eyes. "You *promised* you'd keep our secret."

Manuel's lips smashed into a straight line. He propped his fists on his hips. "I didn't tell them I saw you. They only asked to speak with you. I told no secrets."

"It's the same thing," Jacqueline huffed.

"You fled without a proper goodbye," Manuel mumbled. His shoulders dropped along with his chin. He began to rock forward and back. Eva so wanted to calm him.

"You did the right thing, know that." She smiled and lightly patted his arm.

He jerked and stepped away. "No touching!"

Confused, she glanced at the twins. Julian grimaced. Jacqueline's wide eyes took up much of her face.

"No touching," Manuel muttered.

Jacqueline peered up at him. "Manuel, Sister Eva didn't know you don't like to be touched."

He nodded but still didn't raise his head.

Uncertain what to do or say to him, Eva focused her regard on the children. "You deliberately defied *Capitaine* Gamponetti's orders to stay at the abbey." She addressed Julian. "He trusted you to protect your sister."

The boy removed his hands from his head only to spread them palms up toward Jacqueline. "That's what I'm trying to do! I couldn't let her go without me."

Eva frowned. "Go without you?" She stared at the young girl. "This is *your* doing?"

Jacqueline's lips puckered and twitched back and forth, looking almost remorseful. She lifted her chin. "I very well couldn't leave Captain Gampo to do everything. Which would he do first? Go to the governor? Save my family? Rescue the relics? What if he's delayed? Who would warn my brother about the British invasion? Quite honestly, I'm not sure he can complete everything properly."

The same concerns had been swirling in Eva's mind since the man stormed from the convent dressed in his expensive clothes and his cloud of arrogant superiority.

She flicked her scrutiny to the girl's face. The traces of sickness had dimmed, her eyes now a bright silver-gray and her mouth fixed in a determined line. Eva narrowed her gaze. Jacqueline knew exactly what she was doing. Stirring the doubts and unease was easy enough to accomplish under the circumstances, and the young girl did it in an expert fashion.

Jacqueline's smaller hand clasped Eva's fingers, and her hushed voice interrupted her thoughts. "Come with us, Sister Eva. Once we arrive, you'll be able to travel immediately to the cathedral with the captain's men. Julian and I will alert our family. Captain Gampo can meet with the governor. We can all finish our tasks at the same time."

A strident clanking interrupted their discussion, followed by a sudden lurch beneath their feet.

"The anchor!" Sister Beatrice squeaked, gripping Eva's arm hard enough to leave a mark. They looked at each other. A decision had to be made now. Either she and Sister Beatrice drag the children up where Captain Gamponetti would see just how well she cared for his charges after a mere twelve hours under her protection, or lurk in the closet and delay the inevitable confrontation as long as possible.

It wasn't a difficult decision.

Eva dropped her voice low enough that only the nun could hear. "Do you think you can confront the captain and inform him it is imperative you travel with him? Release him from any obligation to see to your safety other than an escort to the convent. Perhaps he'll agree and even give you a cabin. That would help our cause. The children and I could hide there. The worst that can happen, is he'll deny you and send you back to the abbey."

Beatrice pursed her lips and nodded, a conspiratorial glint in her eye. "I'll see to it."

Eva addressed Manuel, who fidgeted with the pocket flap of his coat on the other side of the room. "No need for you to distract your cousin with news of our presence here. I will personally speak with him concerning the children."

Just not right *now*.

Julian's shoulders eased as the big man nodded and threaded his hands together. "Yes, Sister, thank you. Can you bless us now?"

Sister Beatrice made the sign of the cross and folded her hands in prayer. "Heavenly Father, bless Manuel—"

"And Drago."

"Heavenly Father, bless Manuel and Drago and the people aboard this vessel. Keep them safe on their journey to New Orleans. In the name of the Father, the Son and the Holy Spirit, amen"

"Amen." Manuel made a satisfied sign of the cross, then threw them a gap-toothed grin. He shuffled down the passageway. Sister Beatrice followed, a bit slower and grumbling about her knees.

Eva gave the children a stern glare. "You terrified me by running off like that."

At least they had the decency to appear somewhat contrite. "We're sorry, Sister Eva," Jacqueline finally said. "But we were so worried about Uncle Bernard and Tristan and our cousins, we couldn't take the chance you'd stop us."

She would have.

The ship dipped slightly, then righted itself, and she gripped the closet door for support. Muffled male shouts and laughter came from the upper deck.

Jacqueline ushered Eva inside; Julian followed and closed the door. She swallowed and blinked in the humid, inky darkness, beginning to think this might not have been the right decision.

No going back now. Their course was set.

Chapter Fourteen

NUN TOO SOON

D rago strode across the *Dragon's* deck, toward the helm.
He'd almost paused at the abbey after Mass for a last
farewell to the children. The thought made him shudder. His visit
would have provided another opportunity for the twins to beg
and plead to accompany him, which would have been more than
unpleasant. The unpleasant stuff would've been the begging, not
the actual accompaniment, which in all honesty he might have
enjoyed under any other circumstances.

He braced his stance wide against the subtle shifting of the
Dragon. The wind had picked up from the Northeast, a good sign.
That and the current through the Yucatán Channel should speed
their journey.

"Oy, Captain Gampo, sir!"

Drago's attention shifted to the wrinkled, grizzled form of Mr.
Harvey, as the man limped in his direction. Although the curmudgeon regularly threatened to quit Drago and the sea, he usually
appeared when it was time to hoist the anchor.

"Good morning, Harvey." He shouldn't hire on the old sailor
again. The man had a nice little hut situated among a grove of
mango trees. For the life of him, he couldn't figure out what

brought the old salt back. Harvey claimed he gave up seafaring after being awarded a king's ransom for helping the Sauvage family find a treasure hidden by an ancient relative (a famous female pirate named Anne Bonny).

The old man wasn't content to stay off the water and live out his days in sated leisure. Drago had sought to persuade him to remain in Jamaica this time, but the stubborn mule wouldn't listen. Even likelihood of danger wouldn't sway him. He insisted he go along and make sure "...that squid-brained son of a one-eyed cur"—meaning the twins' Uncle Bernard—"kept his arse outta harm's way."

The friendship the two men had developed during a harrowing sail from South Carolina to Jamaica a few years ago, was one worth protecting, it seemed. Admirable, but what did he think he could do among a New Orleans population of fewer than 10,000 Americans?

Take out half the number to account for women, and they were down to 5,000.

Eliminate the children and the sick or elderly and the city had, at best, 2000 healthy men.

Against 15,000 combat-hardened soldiers.

It would be a bloodbath.

How many Americans understood basic warfare? His guess: very few. Some didn't even own or know how to fire a gun. If he was feeling generous, which he certainly was not, he might agree half of the two thousand men might know how to both fight a war *and* use a gun. However, how many of the rest knew how to persevere in an organized campaign? Or even a disorganized one?

He was sailing into disaster and quite probably his death, unless he could escape before the British arrived.

At least the children were secure. Drago clasped his hands behind his back and inhaled a lungful of the fresh ocean breeze. There was something about the dawn of setting sail that always lit his blood on fire. Men steadily and methodically checked rigging and belaying pins, adjusted spars, joked, laughed.

"Is the crew all accounted for?" Drago finally asked Harvey. "Did the Guirauds board yet?"

"Aye, sir, the Frenchies be in the first cabin." He tilted his head up, one eye squinted nearly closed against the dawning sun. "I expected to see those two heathens running about. Don't tell me the little skirt is still feelin' poorly."

He shot a pained scowl at Harvey. "Jacqueline's much better, but I've left the twins with the nuns."

Harvey snorted. "I'm sure they weren't happy about that."

He winced. "Not a bit."

Harvey scratched his stubbly chin. "Will we be takin' on any more cargo? I noticed the hold ain't quite full."

Freight would slow them down. "No time. We must arrive well ahead of the British and get in and out of New Orleans as fast as we can."

A flash of black and white caught his eye. He whirled. Was that...? No...it couldn't be.

Harvey followed Drago's gaze and snatched the worn cap from his noggin as Sister Beatrice bounced toward them with that tottering gait of hers. She stopped short of the stair leading up to the helm, clasped her hands in front of her and lifted her head up, stoic and determined.

Drago groaned. Perhaps he *should* have visited the abbey. He glanced past her, expecting the novitiate in white robes on her heel, but curiously there was no sign of her.

"Where is Sister Eva?" An uneasy sensation seeped into his stomach. He didn't want the woman on his vessel, that was certain, but there was something almost alarmingly wrong with her absence.

Sister Beatrice's determined expression stuttered to one of wary confusion. "She's... with the children, of course."

He narrowed his gaze, still not relieved. It wouldn't have

surprised him if Sister Eva and the twins hovered at the elder nun's elbow. In fact, he half expected they'd be here somewhere and had intended to sweep the decks for stowaways prior to departure. The elder sister's information saved him the trouble. "To what do I owe the pleasure of your presence on my vessel, Sister Beatrice?"

The nun inhaled deeply, giving the impression she carried a significant burden on her shoulders. "I am in most desperate need of your assistance, Captain Gamponetti. As you are aware, Sister Eva has discovered a plot to steal our relics from the St. Louis Cathedral."

He nodded. Of course, he was aware; the solemn oath he made was never too far from his mind. So was the inevitable betrayal. Between the sugarcane fascines and the relic mission, Judas seemed like an innocent babe.

Sister Beatrice inflated her rather expansive lungs once again. "Captain Gamponetti, I should like to sail with you to New Orleans. We, the other sisters and I, decided we must alert the order personally."

"I already offered to deliver the message," Drago said curtly. Evidently, his word to do so wasn't enough. He mentally shrugged. Nor should it be.

Harvey's expression soured. "We don't need that kinda bad luck," he muttered under his breath, drawing a severe glare; the nun was well within earshot, apparently. "Beggin' yer pardon, Sister." He gave her a slight bow, but still sent Drago a sideways glower of warning.

He didn't share Harvey's dark, superstitious sentiment in this particular situation. If the nun accompanied them, he'd be keeping his oath, because it would mean he made an attempt to prevent the theft. Would it not?

"I'm happy to accommodate you, Sister. There is a vacant cabin you can use." He swept his arm to indicate the activity. "However, as you can see, I'm in the process of preparing to depart, and I can't delay more than an hour or two since the high tide is already past. I'll send an escort along to carry your things, unless you have them with you?" Her empty arms suggested otherwise, but he felt obligated to ask.

Sister Beatrice shook her head. "I fear I didn't take the time."

"My cousin Manuel will help you retrieve your trunk."

"You are most kind."

Drago smiled. "Think nothing of it. My hope is that your prayers for a safe crossing will travel to God's ears much quicker than ours and be given much more consideration."

His last comment got Harvey's attention, and the tar straightened as much as his bony frame would allow. "Kindly give me the honor to offer me own services to ye." He scurried down, then halted at her shoulder before nodding to her to follow.

Sister Beatrice gave him a quick perusal, confusion evident in her stare. Before she could voice a response, Harvey cupped his mouth with his hands and bellowed, "Manuel, git yer arse to the mizzen, ye blighter!" He cringed and spun to face the nun again. "I apologize fer me language, Sister."

"Oh... of... well..."

So that was how to silence the woman. Apologize before she had a chance to chastise. Drago would store that little snippet of information for later.

Manuel lowered a bulging sack from his shoulder like a mountain might let loose a boulder, propped it against a cluster of barrels, and lumbered over. "Aye, Mr. Harvey?"

The grizzled sailor jerked his chin toward the ramp. "C'mon, we're heading fer the abbey to git the sister's things."

Manuel nodded and stepped with him to the gangway entrance, where they bumped shoulders as each tried to step off first. Harvey ricocheted off the wall of muscle and bone, much like a bullet off a rock.

He staggered against the rail, almost careening directly into the water. The big man flinched and grabbed Harvey's collar and settled him. Hat jolted askew and now covering one eye, Harvey snapped, "Git offa me ye thick, lumbering sod!" He swung an elbow which bounced off Manuel's hip. "*Unmph!*" He paused to rub the bone. "Curse yer arse," he grunted. "It's like hitting a granite horse."

"No touching," Manuel muttered, stepping back.

An intrusive cough halted their conversation. Sister Beatrice stood calmly behind them, her hands tucked under her open-sided tunic.

Manuel's eyes widened, and he hopped to the side, an impressive feat for one of his size. Harvey reddened and sidled next to Manuel in an invitation for her to pass first, which she promptly accepted.

Manuel fisted his hands and knocked them together. "Is she mad at us?"

"Ain't no tellin'." Harvey heaved the words from his gut as if they weighed ten stone. "Them nuns are always scowlin' 'bout somethin'." He righted his hat. "Best not ter agitate 'em."

Manuel gave the sister's departing back a wary perusal. "Maybe you should go next, Mr. Harvey."

"Ye yellow-bellied coward," Harvey groused. He shoved his thumbs into the waist of his britches, then fell in behind the nun, although his steps stuttered just a little.

Drago muffled a laugh. A more unlikely trio of characters had never walked the streets of Port Royal.

"I'm no coward," Manuel mumbled. "But women scare me."

Harvey's voice drifted up the ramp. "Then don't go stirrin' one up. Yer more likely to keep yer bollocks that way."

In all of Harvey's seventy-one years, he'd never spoken truer words.

Chapter Fifteen
A SIXTH SENSE

It was bound to happen, of course. The *Dragon* wasn't as big as a Spanish galleon or ship of the line, with dozens of nooks and spaces to hide. It was a schooner. Who knew what had prompted Captain Gamponetti to inspect the lower decks and walk past the cabin where Eva and the twins hid.

Perhaps it was a sixth sense.

To their credit, they managed to remain hidden for two-and-a-half days.

The morning of departure, Sister Beatrice had returned with a trunk containing extra clothes, as well as a stash of dried fruit and biscuits. She also gifted the captain with a cask of the abbey's finest rum to show her gratitude, hoping it would keep him too busy to notice the goings on below.

The twins' temper shortened, and although Eva did her best to diffuse any arguments, the children became bored and testy. It started with a disagreement, followed by a quick yank on a braid by Julian and ended with his sister's enraged shriek. Soon after, an unexpected knock rapped on the door.

Jacqueline's eyes widened, and she clamped her hand over her mouth, too little too late. Julian fisted his hands in the hair at the top of his head and squeezed his eyes shut. "Now you've done it, Jacquie."

"*Me?*" she hissed. "You started it!"

"Shh!" Eva glanced around frantically, hopelessly. There was no place for all three to hide in the small space. Sister Beatrice had left to get some air, so the three of them would have to face whoever knocked on their own.

She examined their options, evaluated their rationale and tried to put together a solid argument, but they had only one option. Their reasoning was weak and her thoughts kept colliding, leaving her with a jumbled mess of useless words, so no argument was forthcoming.

Time to accept the consequences.

She checked her veil, more from habit than anything, took a deep breath and unlatched the door. All·muscle, sinew and bone, Drago Gamponetti blocked the doorway with his bulk. A dim lantern hanging behind him in the passageway outlined his body in a flickering fire, but cast his face in shadow. With dark hair loose about his shoulders, Hades himself could be standing there.

His face went through a series of expressions, starting with surprise and ending with rage. Storm cloud eyes flashed; inky brows slanted down, his face all straight lines and fury. "What are you doing here?" He ground out the words as if he chewed stone.

There were so many things she could say, but only one answer to his question, and it had to do with Jacqueline. She wasn't about to deliver the girl front and center for a whipping. Eva knew little about captaining a boat, but she did know the consequences if a member of a crew defied their captain's orders. They'd get at least three lashes for it. Perhaps a more general approach toward answering the question was in order.

"Well?" He glared, crossing his arms. He wore black boots, breeches and a shirt, the ties open, revealing an interesting V-shaped section of his deeply tanned chest.

"I'm sailing to New Orleans," she said in a thin voice, eyes still on his exposed skin and the light sprinkling of hair. It could be soft. Or coarse. She kind of hoped it was soft.

"You are *not!*" He pushed the door wide and ducked inside, causing her to flinch and jump back. She caught the scent of sea spray, leather and something sharp and musky as well. Her reaction seemed to startle him, and he gave her a wary once-over before he turned his attention to the children.

Jacqueline and Julian huddled together in the corner, watching. Probably hoping the nun might be able to provide some sort of divine intervention on their behalf. Unfortunately for them, she didn't possess that kind of influence.

Eva inhaled and resolved to bear a stronger countenance to the man. He couldn't intimidate or scare her any more than he had already. In fact, he would learn she was more than a meek little woman in a nun's robe and tunic who couldn't prevent him from kissing her. She ground her teeth and mashed her lips together. Now he had her thinking about *the kiss* again after she'd worked so hard to block that stupid memory.

She had responsibilities of her own, to her order, and to the church, a chain whose last link inevitably ended at God's feet. She was here for a good reason. A *very* good reason. She forced a more stern tone. "*Capitainé* Gamponetti—"

"It's not her fault, captain." Julian walked forward. He swallowed as if a shoe was wedged in his throat. "It's... it's mine. I wanted to come with you, and she came after me. I wouldn't return to the abbey, and Jacqueline wouldn't leave me."

Eva felt her eyes widen. What was he thinking? She gripped a handful of her tunic. Had he assumed she was going to expose his sister? She groaned. All Julian had done was stir the captain's anger.

Captain Gamponetti's face darkened as he spun to face the boy. "I told you to protect your sister," he snarled. "I entrusted her safekeeping to you. I assumed you were ready to be a man and embrace your obligations, but obviously, you're a still a little milksop." His gray eyes turned thunderous. He reached out and grabbed the youth's collar, then hitched him up against the wall. Julian let out a choked squawk. His fingers automatically clutched Gampo's forearms.

An instinctive quake skimmed through Eva's frame, both dreadful and familiar, freezing her bones. Her breath stalled as her throat closed in panic. A man enraged beyond his ability to control his actions brought pain and destruction, and left broken things in his wake. Bleeding things. Marred things.

A brace of lean muscle and power, Gamponetti was ruthless and commanding. The straight planes of his face severe and firm as stone, eyes sharp and furious. Gone was the concerned man she met at the abbey. Here stood Captain Gampo, the pirate.

Some women, brave women of grace and strength, could calmly soften a man's temper with a word or a touch. But for her, such a furor whipped her heart to a racing beat and her voice to shreds. As if a fistful of twigs had been shoved down her throat, she couldn't swallow, couldn't talk.

The boy didn't deserve punishment for her failings. She'd faltered in her responsibility, not Julian. She shouldn't have let the twins out of her sight. She should have—

"Stop!" Jacqueline's voice pierced the air at a pitch that could have shattered glass.

The captain jerked his head around, eyes round and white-rimmed. When the girl placed her thin hand on his wrist, the dark charcoal rings around his irises softened, even though his jaw stayed hard.

Jacqueline would be one of those strong women of grace someday.

"Please, Captain Gampo, stop." Her eyes darted to her brother, who gave her a slight shake of his head, an unspoken plea to be quiet. But the mighty little Jacqueline wouldn't be hushed. "It's truly my fault. I decided to run away from the abbey and steal aboard." She hung her head. "Julian wouldn't let me go alone, and Sister Eva came looking for us. I wanted to go with you, so I could warn my family." Raising her chin to meet his thunderous glare, she added the affront, "I worried you wouldn't get to them in time."

His lips flattened, and he allowed the boy's feet to slide to the floor before facing the girl. She stood perfectly still, the tiniest tremble in her lower lip the only sign of emotion except for the slight widening of her eyes. He leaned down until his face was even with hers. Gray eyes flashed a steely promise before he spoke, and his voice lowered further to a livid, offended growl. "I don't know what's worse, you defying a direct order, or questioning my ability to see a sworn duty done."

Jacqueline's face paled, her mouth opened, then closed. Gampo's nostrils flared at her silence. "You put yourselves and my men in a greater danger, because now I have to turn around and take you back, which will vastly reduce the time and distance between us and the British." He poked his finger at the girl. "And the time to move your family to safety." His tone shifted from that fire-lined growl to something even more terrifying, although Eva couldn't describe it. A tone of impending doom resonated from the deep baritone in the captain's voice. He studied Eva through slashed brows. "And the time to warn Father Dubourg. This was incredibly foolish of you all."

Well, when he put it that way, it did sound stupid and irresponsible.

Julian swallowed. "Sir—"

Gampo's fist still gripped the collar of Julian's shirt and jacket. His free hand whipped up faster than Eva could wince; a single index finger sliced the boy's sentence into silence. He swiveled his head back to Julian. "While assuming liability for your sister's transgressions is admirable, your previous admission brands you a liar," he said, voice chillingly soft. "I have no regard for liars." He released the boy, moved to the doorway and gestured with his hand for the three of them to precede him.

"Out."

The twins wilted; they shuffled as if heading for the gallows. She could almost see the thick cloud of dread draped over their shoulders.

"Where are we going?" Eva asked before stepping after the children. She couldn't keep the fear from her voice. It trembled. "What are you going to do?"

Gampo closed his eyes briefly before he expelled a breath. "I'm not holding you responsible, Sister Eva. I know very well how these two heathens can get under your skin and worm their way into your mind. Still, you'd do well to remember I am the master of this ship. If I can't maintain discipline, the men won't respect my authority." He grasped her arm and ushered her from the room, fingers biting into her elbow.

She wanted to jerk from his grasp; his hand was way too warm. "You haven't answered my question, *Capitaine Gampo*," she said. At her address of his pirate's name, he stopped. His brows slammed down, and he pinned her with a heated stare. A muscle rippled in his cheek. She shot a pointed look at his hand. "You're hurting me."

He let go as if burned. "You'll soon see for yourself."

The twins' countenance disturbed her, sinking like a rock in her stomach. What was about to transpire next surely wouldn't be to her liking.

Chapter Sixteen

THE PRICE OF REBELLION

❦

K eeping her head bowed and a hand on the hem of her veil near her jaw to keep the wind from blowing it up and exposing her face, Eva trailed the twins.

Sailors paused in their tasks and gawked. She studied them in return. They were a crew of every size, shape and color, some dark and bearded, others light and hairless. Asian, African, Indian, Persian and European blood flowed through the veins of these seamen, and some wore no shirts. Averting her eyes would be expected of a nun and should have come quite naturally, but she couldn't stop herself from using the opportunity to study their scars and ponder their origin.

A giant African stood at the helm, hand on the wheel. He wore a sleeveless shirt and a loincloth. Two leather straps crossed his chest; one held a pistol, the other a wickedly curved sword. His dark eyes flicked from Gampo to her, then back to the captain, his expression unreadable.

Another sailor, with a long beard, darkly tanned skin, and dressed in Eastern clothing, leered at her, then licked his lips before spitting on the boards an inch from her toes. His message was clear. Neither her church nor her religion had any authority over him. *Capitainé* Gampo had told her about the different beliefs and cultures his men brought to the ship when he explained why they believed women were bad luck. She gave herself a mental note to keep well out of that man's way.

Sister Beatrice stood chatting with a middle-aged couple near the rail. At Eva's appearance, surprise flashed across the nun's face. She made a horrified sign of the cross before she shuffled to Eva's side. The captain ignored her.

He turned and bellowed. "All hands to the sheets! Prepare to come about." Sailors leaped into action, hauling lines and adjusting spars, according to his continued instructions. The African turned the wheel, and the schooner canted to make a slow turn.

Gampo paused by the center mast. "Mister Harvey, a word," he said, voice curt.

The wiry man perched on a barrel glanced up. The rope he'd been repairing slithered to the floor. He hopped off and limped over.

A rush of panic fluttered across Eva's chest. They were turning around! She pressed forward, past the children until she was closer. "We can't go back now!" She had to get home!

Gampo impaled her with a flinty glare, and she clamped her mouth shut and bit her lip, realizing her error too late. She just questioned the commander's orders.

"We *can* go back, and we will." He spun on his heel. "Mister Harvey!" Gampo's voice roared across the deck.

"Aye, sir!" The old man took in the gloomy expressions of the twins and the serious set of his captain's mouth, then hooked his fingers in his belt and waited.

Gampo's jaw tightened. "Bring one of the longboat paddles to the mizzen mast."

"Aye, sir," Harvey muttered to his toes, then left to do his captain's bidding.

"Manuel!" Gampo thundered once again.

"Aye, sir!" The big man looped a rope around a belaying pin and strode over.

"Strap the boy's hands." He jerked his chin toward Julian.

Manuel started to step forward, then hesitated to glance back, his brows pinched in confusion. "The boy? You mean Julian?"

Gampo lifted an eyebrow and nodded once.

This confirmed Eva's suspicions. She focused on the captain, willing him to look at her, imploring him with her eyes and her heart to change the course of his intent, but he stood proud and stoic and stared past them to the horizon. If it wasn't for the muscle balled in his jaw, he would have appeared to be oblivious to what went on around him.

A short time later, Julian faced a grating, wrists bound high enough to pull him up on his toes. Jacqueline stood next to Gampo; she trembled, but to the girl's credit she made no sound.

"Harvey, step up." Gampo crossed his arms and glared at the twins.

Harvey thumped the oar handle on the deck "Right here, sir."

Thick brows shuttered the captain's eyes, and his tone was deceptively soft. "What's worse, defying orders or lying to your captain?"

The old salt scratched his bristly neck. "Can't rightly say, sir. Both seem ter be equally... offensive." Harvey's last word almost lifted above the breeze.

Gampo nodded. "Agreed. Equal paddles for both, then. Three for each."

Three for each? Was he going to paddle Jacqueline with a ten-foot oar? One swing would snap her in half!

Harvey looked from Jacqueline to her brother, strapped to the breastwork. He paled slightly. "Sir?"

"The boy has taken responsibility for the petticoat's actions, so he'll also take her punishment." He flicked his hand toward Julian.

A small sob escaped from Jacqueline's pale lips.

Harvey coughed. "Aw, well captain, sir, me hands don't grip so well these days—"

Gampo arched a sardonic brow. "You'd have me select another?" He glanced at the African. "Perhaps Raul?"

The seaman shifted his gaze to the giant behemoth still standing near the helm.

Eva finally released a breath. He had a heart, after all.

Harvey quickly shook his head, apparently realizing his captain's intentions. "No, sir! I'll do it, sir." He hopped up to the grate. "Ain't no young buck gonna take me place," he stated loudly as he hefted the paddle and straightened. He tucked his head down and muttered something under his breath, but Eva couldn't make out the words; it could have been another complaint, but unquestionably something he didn't want to be overheard or he'd have said it louder.

The rest of the men had halted their duties and gathered around the mizzen mast. The lines groaned, and the wind sang in the sails, yet the quiet was more distinct.

Harvey hefted the long oar back and swung; contact with Julian's backside broke the silence with a loud crack. The boy threw his head back and gritted his teeth, swallowing a grunt of pain. Eva's stomach clenched. It was a mighty long paddle.

Gampo stepped forward, and for a moment she thought he was going to stop Harvey. Instead, he spoke to Julian. "Don't you dare cry."

The boy dropped his head, and Jacqueline stared, eyes wide. Eva moved closer to Gampo's shoulder and whispered just loud enough for him to hear, "You are a vicious monster."

He cocked his head toward her voice, then shrugged, unaffected by her slur. "A tightly run ship requires discipline and obedience from everyone on board."

"You have made your point," she hissed. It was easy to understand the hierarchal structure and the reasons behind establishing a stringent set of rules, as well as consequences for breaking them. It was the same when dealing with children; if they sensed a weak character or a softening countenance, they'd press their advantage until they became uncontrollable. Rules and routines were necessary and important; both with sailors and children alike.

Jacqueline sniffled and closed her eyes. Gampo glanced down at her, his voice cold and flat. "You're not a coward, little skirt. Open your eyes and accept your punishment."

"Do you want respect or fear, *Capitaine*?" Eva moved closer. He was near enough now she caught his musky scent, triggering the memory of the kiss in the kitchen pantry, something that would not help her to think about at this moment.

He narrowed an eye at her. "Are you saying my men obey me because they fear me?"

What was it that made men thirst for the approval of their peers? Was it this need for respect that ignited their desire to reign over others like kings, whether royal-born or not?

She shrugged. "I'm saying there's a difference between respect and fear and a difference as well between discipline and cruelty."

The breeze suddenly lifted Eva's veil, and she snatched at the edge to restrain it, then paused.

Maybe her scar would drive understanding a little deeper into his mind. Best to get it over with; she delayed it too long, anyway. In all honesty, it was terribly vain of her to hide behind a veil, but it had become as much a part of her as the scar. She released the gossamer fabric and allowed the twist of the wind to fling it away from her face, to trail behind her like a comet.

She ignored the astonished faces. At least she tried to.

Shocked expressions and impolite stares were nothing new; she endured them for almost ten years. Children pointing, women talking behind fans, eyes on her until she noticed, then dropping their gaze or turning their backs. What was it about the macabre that lured people in and made them hunger for another glimpse?

She kept her eyes on the captain, waiting for the moment her face would draw his attention, and his eyes would widen in horror and disgust.

She thought back to the boy who'd wanted to marry her. Even a year-long courtship hadn't been solid enough to keep the ugly scar from interfering.

Still, her heart clenched when Gampo finally gave her his full attention. She stood in front of him and waited while his perusal followed the long, wicked trail from her chin, across the corner of her mouth, up her cheek to the flat tip of her ear before locking on her eyes.

No one had ever been able to mask their reaction, not even when they were forewarned she'd been maimed. Yet he did. The slight tightening of the corners of his lips was his only response. His gaze swirled with interest, intelligence, and residual anger.

"Cruelty is not interchangeable with discipline, *Capitainé*." She could barely choke out the words. Why did his reaction matter to her? Why did she care what he thought about her deplorable face?

Why did she hope?

Eva had noted his nicks and scars when they first met. Many of the sailors had multiple scars. Some had lost fingers. The cook had only one leg. Maybe disfigurement was normal to him and not something from which to recoil.

Either that or he was very, very good at keeping his feelings cloaked behind an impenetrable emotional shield and those thick black lashes.

Still, there had been a flicker of something else in his eyes.

It wasn't pity. She'd seen that enough to recognize it at once. A gentle breeze caressed her cheek, and the waning sun's last rays heated her face as the glowing orange fireball made its inevitable descent toward the horizon. She let her eyelids close for the briefest moment to savor the sensation on her horrible, marred, abused face.

For some reason a lump knotted in her chest, something that

hadn't happened in this situation in years; she struggled to tamp it down before it brought the tears along with it. Finding her voice, she met his tornado-laced gaze with her own. "Wise leaders know showing mercy also earns admiration. It can strengthen loyalty as well. I did not take you for a tyrant, *Capitainé* Gamponetti."

Harvey hoisted the oar. The second swing elicited another painful grunt from Julian, and he panted in quick, pained gasps. Jacqueline clutched her dress by its collar, tears streamed to her jawbone and dripped on her whitened knuckles.

Without releasing Eva from his iron stare, he spoke. "Enough, Mr. Harvey. I think I've made my point."

Eva shut her eyes, more to escape his perusal than anything. When she finally had the courage to open them, she glanced up to find him still studying her. His gray eyes now glimmered with... what? Appreciation? Curiosity? There was energy emanating from him in powerful waves, leaving her both invigorated and sapped of strength. For a moment, she forgot to breathe.

He continued. "On behalf of Sister Eva's gentle request for mercy, I commute the sentence to the two strokes served." He strode toward the helm and barked at his cousin over his shoulder. "Manuel!"

"Aye!"

"Take them back to their cabin and lock the door."

"Aye, sir."

Jacqueline ran to her brother's side. Her hands shook as she untied Julian's wrists. Manuel fumbled with the straps. Jacqueline's eyes still welled with tears. Her brother turned his head and met his sister's gaze.

"Don't you cry neither, Jacquie," he whispered through thin, pale lips.

Eva secured her veil and moved to help. She tried to shift her body under the young boy's arm, but he jerked away. Manual grasped Jacqueline's wrist and headed for the hatch. Julian followed, his head down, shoulders slumped. Sister Beatrice waited with hands clasped, her face blank and stoic. Eva chanced one last grateful glance at the captain's back, before following.

Inside the cabin, Jacqueline slid down the wall and hugged her knees; great gasping sobs shuddered through her willowy frame. Julian crawled into a hammock and rolled to his side, facing away from them. He curled into himself and stilled. She would leave him to his misery. It wouldn't do for her to embarrass him further by making her presence known.

"Ju... Ju... Julian—" Jacqueline hiccuped.

"Stop apologizing, Jacquie." The anguish in his tone tugged Eva's heart. "You know the captain was right."

"I know... but still—"

Julian huffed a shallow breath. "I'm just glad he let me keep my britches on in front of the nuns."

Why weren't they angrier? She would have certainly been upset. It had taken all her reserve to refrain from sending her fist into Gampo's austere, slashing mouth earlier. Strange, it seemed so hard and unyielding now when it was so pliant and soft when...

No. She would not think about *that*.

Instead, she turned and secured the door, her mind in a jumble as she went back up on deck, unsure if she wanted another confrontation with Gampo. Any arguments would undoubtably fall on deaf ears.

Eva made her way to the fore part of the schooner, where she could remain out of the way of the crewmen, ropes and sails. This was only her second voyage on a ship of this size. The speed thrilled her heart, along with the crack of the canvas and the way the sun warmed her face and the wind kissed it.

A cry came from the tops. "Sails ho! Sails ho!"

The captain's clipped voice boomed from the steerage. "How many?"

"A great number, Capt'n!" A pause. "It's... the British armada!"

Eva caught her breath and scanned the horizon, but could see nothing.

Captain Gamponetti issued additional commands. "Ready about! Hard a-lee the helm! Luff around!"

The African's voice barked across the deck, "Helm's a-lee!"

"Man jib downhaul! Raise and tack sheets!"

The *Dragon* exploded into movement, every man at some task with frantic focus as the ship began a graceful turn. Her sails shivered as she crossed the wind.

"Ho, Sister Eva!" Canvas flapped, and she spun to see Harvey scampering toward her. "Stand here, sister, so ye don'ts gits swayed away."

She shifted to the spot he indicated while the sails swiveled with the vessel as she came about amid shouted orders and replies. When she directed her attention back to the horizon, she barely made out the tiny white specks scattered there. Her stomach tightened.

The captain ordered the men to unfurl all the sheets, and soon the *Dragon* flew over the water, and the specks disappeared. He descended the steps and made his way to where she gripped the rail. The air seemed to shift as he neared. It sharpened and nipped at her skin, sparking a heightened awareness of his proximity.

He followed her gaze and spoke without looking at her, his voice gravelly soft. "It appears your request to continue to New Orleans will be granted after all, Sister."

She fought a smile by pressing her lips together, but the corners still pushed up. "That's the way God works sometimes, *Capitainé* Gamponetti." It was impossible to keep that tiny bit of smug satisfaction from her voice. One peek at the hard glint in his eyes, and she wished she'd tried a little harder.

Slowly, the anger seeped from his expression, replaced with a resigned annoyance, acknowledging the irony with a light snort and a smirk, pulling a dimple into one cheek.

"So it would seem, Sister Eva. So it would seem."

Chapter Seventeen

LET IT GO

The captain ordered the topsails reefed as the day waned. The *Dragon* traveled light and according to Harvey, continued to draw ahead of the sluggish British fleet.

Orange tinted lambs' wool clouds crowded the setting sun and dimmed to pink as it touched the horizon. Dusk glittered over the ocean, and a billion stars anxiously awaited to blink awake in the evening sky. Eva moved to the forward most part of the deck. She tugged the veil away, and let it fly behind her, relishing the silky caress of the ocean's breath upon her face. After years of the thick, tropical Jamaican air, the cool, fresh temperature felt delicious.

For a moment, the fresh wind's subtle magic erased the scar and smoothed her skin. For a moment, she stood alone with the current and the breeze and the lure of the moon. For a moment, she was a child of the water and the sky and the earth.

She was whole.

"I've never seen Drago Gamponetti reduce a punishment." Lady Guiraud's breathy voice shattered the moment like a rock through a windowpane. "He is a rigid wielder of justice. Always rules his ship with an iron fist."

So, Lady Guiraud knew him well. Perhaps that's the reason he granted them passage while leaving her at the abbey. Eva drew the long delicate scarf up and around the front of her shoulders, then dropped the tail behind her back, shutting away the touch of the wind and the effervescent sparkle of the stars. She made sure to properly conceal the scar before she turned.

The thin, petite woman was kind enough to wait until Eva covered her face before moving forward to lean her forearms against the rail. A restrained beauty hovered about her. Flawless skin, intelligent eyes and aristocratic edges to her nose, mouth and cheekbones appeared incongruous with the garb and stature.

"Have you known the *capitainé* long?" Eva asked. *And in what manner? Family? Former lovers?*

Lady Guiraud lifted a slender shoulder. "We travel with him, because he is resourceful, a strategist. He does not enter a fight he cannot win." Her eyes took on a cunning glint.

Yet, he made it quite clear defeat was inevitable against the British. "He believed this journey was too dangerous for the children and me." Eva waved toward the general direction of the enemy fleet.

Lady Guiraud nodded her understanding. "He protects those he cares about." She leaned in and lowered her voice conspiratorially, "We have a special arrangement. We pay zee *capitainé* extremely well to *not* care about us."

A special arrangement could mean many things. Since the Guirauds were French and Gampo a French privateer, it seemed logical the connection might be political in nature. The woman's relaxed manner came across as odd, as if pending death and danger was too insignificant, or too familiar for it to be a concern. Meanwhile, a knot of terror had coiled around Eva's chest the moment the watch sighted the flotilla. "Are you not concerned about the British invading the city?"

Lady Guiraud's caramel eyes widened. "Oh, *oui*! Very much. We won't be there long. My husband and I intend to visit zee cathedral then journey to Cincinnati. We will stay with my sister there until late spring."

Still, it was a big risk to take.

When she voiced the thought, she received another elegant shoulder lift. "I am not overly worried. Zee *capitainé* is a clever man. It is why his men are so loyal."

"Did you travel to Jamaica specifically to seek him out?" He mentioned having the children with him for several months. There was something askew about the Guiraud's—like a dropped stitch, easy to overlook when close to the needle. Further along, the error marred the pattern until it was the only thing you noticed.

Lady Guiraud flicked her hand in somnolent nonchalance. "It is understood he resides on Lamb's Tail Island. *Capitainé* Gamponetti tells me you hail from zee Ursuline convent in New Orleans," she responded airily, changing the topic.

She was done providing information about the *capitainé*, then.

"I grew up there."

Although Lady Guiraud pressed her lips together, they turned up a tiny bit in the corners. "*Mon père* told me stories of St. Louis when I was *le enfant*. I am most grateful to have zee chance to worship in zee cathedral bearing his name and his sacred bones." She straightened her shoulders. "It is my hope being in zee presence of his holy relics will please *mon père* in heaven. It would be a shame to be so close and not pause to see them before traveling upriver." She released a wistful sigh. "Tell me about zee cathedral. Is it beautiful?"

Eva smiled, suddenly more homesick than ever. "Truly, it is. My description could never accurately convey its wonder."

The woman tucked a long, sleek wisp of hair behind her ear. "Do you think Father Dubourg will grant me zee honor of praying over zee relics? They are in zee sanctuary, beneath zee alter, no?"

This wasn't an unusual appeal. Many pilgrims desired the same. Some wanted to kiss the sacred artifacts, others wanted to press them to the skin of the diseased and afflicted; still others merely called to pray over them. But, since protecting the relics occupied the forefront of her mind, the question raised her suspicions to an alarming level.

The Guirauds hailed from France and could very well be involved. She exhaled and attempted to steady her worries. Or they could simply be two more immigrants. Not long ago, New Orleans was part of a French territory; visits and immigration by her citizens were common and frequent. A large segment of her populace had roots in France.

"It is up to Father Dubourg to grant permission," Eva replied.

"Of course," murmured Lady Guiraud, glancing up at the movement of a sailor reefing a topsail.

Eva sensed their conversation was over. "I hope you enjoy your visit to New Orleans. We have a considerable French population, you should feel much at home, although your English is quite good."

The woman flashed beautiful white teeth. "Thank you, Sister Eva. A pleasant evening to you." The lady wandered over to the far side of the ship and struck up a conversation with Sister Beatrice. Probably making the same plea to the elder nun. Perhaps trying to gauge if the sister had a better chance of gaining Father Dubourg's ear.

Eva pursed her lips, deciding to keep a watchful eye on the couple, just the same. She didn't survive this long without a healthy dose of suspicion when it came to assessing people and their motivations.

A strange tingling pricked Eva's spine, along with the uncomfortable sensation she was being watched. Turning, she scanned the deck looking for the *capitaine*, then lifted her gaze to the sailor reefing the sails. High above her, the man who'd spat as she passed earlier glowered down at her. Caught staring, he released an oily grin which slid across his face, revealing dark gaps between his teeth. Although he was smiling, there was not a single glint of affability. He was not a friend. Suppressing an apprehensive shudder, she returned her attention to the gentle ocean swells.

The warm timbre of Captain Gamponetti's voice eased through the mild sea breeze. In any other situation, his voice might have been even more soothing. After the events earlier today, she remained wary, unwilling to be on the cutting side of his anger. He sauntered toward her. Even with his hands clasped passively behind his back, there was no mistaking his dominant stature and prowling strength. Dense muscles bunched and coiled beneath his skin.

Power and shadow.

It was the first time he acknowledged her since Julian's punishment. "It's a beautiful evening, *capitaine*," she responded softly. He stopped next to her, his shoulder so close she felt the heat emanating from it. She sneaked a furtive peek at his fiercely handsome profile. Wild black hair flew loose. However, his shadowed jaw was less tight, hawkish nose and inky brows less ferocious, eyes less stormy. Evaluating the horizon, he stood silent and commanding. Perhaps the sight of her face repulsed him enough earlier he'd avoid looking directly at her. She didn't have the courage to turn and face him. Instead, she tilted her head up and gestured to the billowing sails still unfurled, bellies full of wind. "Do you usually travel through the night?"

He followed her line of sight. "When the sky is clear enough to navigate with star charts, yes."

She cast a worried glance behind them. "How far ahead of the British are we, do you think?"

He shrugged a shoulder. "We sail light, thus more nimbly. I'm hoping to increase the distance tonight. Normally, they reef the sheets or drop anchor at sunset. Even so, the gulf current will continue to push them northeast, unfortunately."

The captain's contemplative attention remained on the ocean. It was a small thing, the desire for him to look at her. But the pain was sharp, the insult deep. Especially since the veil was back in place.

The corners of his mouth relaxed. "We have an escort," he announced, pointing.

She followed the line of his finger. "Porpoises!" She clapped, a sudden lightness in her chest. She smiled as the graceful creatures arched over the waves near the stern. "I believe they wish to engage us in a race," she laughed.

If he stood farther from her, his deep chuckle would have been swallowed by the whoosh of the hull slicing through the swells. "Let's oblige them." Cupping his hands around his mouth, he shouted, "Release the tops, Mr. Razin!"

"Aye, sir!"

She couldn't help giving him a startled sideways glance at his suddenly jocular disposition. The sight made her gaze falter. His profile in the waning, golden light of the evening was elegant. The proportions so perfect, a Greek sculptor might cry with longing. Such a man would never need to visit a bordello for a woman's company, yet he did. Who was he, really? Who had he been before he became a pirate? Was he from a loving family, or like her, forced to grow up early and alone?

She angled her head to observe the turbaned man, Razin. Now the size of a sparrow, he and another sailor quickly loosed the topsails. The ship rushed ahead. She gripped the rail and leaned forward, unable to restrain the joyful laughter bubbling from her belly. She was a bird, flying swift and free over the water, breeze under her wings and sea spray on her face.

For a moment, everything was light and tender and sweet.

Frisky fingers of wind flipped the veil from her face. It flew behind her like a long tail, sweeping away the moment like a breaking wave erases a footprint. Instinctively she spun to capture it, intending to re-wrap the fabric into place when a warm hand grasped her wrist, staying her motion.

Puzzled, she looked up into the intense gray and blue-flecked eyes of the captain.

His perusal studied without judging, devoured without consuming. No pity, no disgust, no morbid fascination. Wind combed his ebony hair, revealing the tanned angles and shadows of his cheekbones, the strong jaw, gentle cleft in his chin.

La Belle et la Bête. A tale her mother had told her when she was little about how a beautiful girl fell in love with a hideous monster. As a child, she always pictured herself as the belle.

A harsh irony.

Liquid pools of silver locked her gaze.

"Let it go," he said.

If only he knew how those three words terrified her.

DRAGO HAD ABRUPTLY DEVELOPED a vehement dislike for that bloody veil.

Like a lonely bower, it imprisoned her; keeping the tiniest pleasures at a distance, shackling her to the wound. Earlier, when the sun kissed her cheeks, her expression, like that of a child biting into a sweet treat, fascinated him.

Her injury was certainly the result of a violent confrontation. The angle and line of the scar insinuated a fast, malicious slash of a blade. The swirled skin on her cheek indicated the steel had been hot enough to brand. Meant to punish, not kill. What egregious error had she committed to incite such anger? Such cruelty?

He couldn't nudge aside the sense the young woman had once moved well beyond the simple routine existence of the Ursuline nuns, facets of her past shaded and hidden from view. One day, he'd uncover her secrets.

Sister Eva's laughter and joy lifted his spirits, lightened the air around him like a sunbeam through a thundercloud. An unfamiliar warmth curled around his chest, lush and calming against the unyielding turbulence ordinarily residing there.

Not only did she have spirit, she'd acted decidedly sane since he discovered her below. Either he was wrong about assuming her unbalanced, or this was a very, very impressive performance. Interesting that he wished the former to be true.

The *Dragon* left the porpoises behind as dusk transitioned to twilight. The bell rang, signaling a change of the watch. She lingered, wrapping the covering into place. "Thank you, *Capitainé*. I enjoyed the amusement."

The smile in her voice stirred the sensation in his chest again, stilling the tempest, shifting stone. He gave her a slight bow. "The pleasure was truly mine, Sister Eva." It truly was.

She gazed at the stars beginning to wink in the sky. "It is easy to understand why a man falls in love with the sea, so beautiful and open. Here you are alive and free. "

Her beauty mesmerized him. Long, thick lashes framed sapphire irises rimmed with charcoal. Her lips were parted, languid and full. "Yes," he managed to rasp, unable to rip his gaze from her stunning profile. "Yes, she is beautiful indeed."

Chapter Eighteen
ZEALOT'S ATTACK

She could see nothing. Eva skimmed her hands along the walls to avoid snagging splinters as she groped her way to her cabin. There hadn't been a lantern to take, although when she descended the ladder, she could see a faint glow beneath the far door where Beatrice had left one lit inside for her.

The old nun's snores vibrated the planks, promising a solid night of restlessness. Their berth was one of several compartments normally used for stowage, however they all had hooks for hammocks. All but three still had remnants of sugarcane and timber.

The next time she walked this passage during the day, she'd count the steps between each door, to find her way better in the thick, inky darkness. This fumbling along would eventually send her sprawling. Already, she had at least two splinters in her palms.

Gamponetti's countenance had shifted earlier. The familiar, caustic mantle had slipped away, revealing an interesting combination of a blithe yet intense demeanor. She rather liked it.

She paused and listened outside the twins' door. Silent. No doubt the events of the day had driven the children into a deep, exhausted sleep. Hopefully, the dawn will bring better spirits, since they were nearing their destination.

An eerie tingling shot across the back of her neck and she hesitated, about to call out when a hard, thin hand clamped over her mouth and pulled her sharply into one of the vacant cabins.

Her assailant shouldered the door with just enough force to shut it with a feathery click. Fear clawed at her stomach. She wrenched her head to the side and attempted to scream, but he slammed his body into hers. What little breath remained left in a half-scream. Panic crashed into her at the unyielding impact of the bulwark against her back. She kicked out into the darkness and connected with a bony shin. A pained grunt rewarded her efforts. He wrapped something around her neck. The vague realization he was using her veil to strangle her flitted in and out of her mind. She scratched at the fabric, desperate for air.

His ragged nails scraped down her throat, then clenched the neckline of her tunic. A violent jerk ripped it to her waist. A cold, desolate terror bored a hole through her chest. Rosary beads clattered to the floor. No stranger to the nefarious side of men, her choices now were few, and none of them offered a complete escape from ruin or torment. A cool rush of air hit her bare skin. She twisted frantically, still digging at the fabric circling her neck. Sharp talons of fear gripped her heart and froze her limbs. A sheer bolt of panic flashed through her lungs as she fought harder to draw a clear breath. Instead of a scream, she could only choke out gravelly puffs of air. It wouldn't be long before she lost consciousness.

A low, raspy voice hissed in rapid pants, "You are an insult to God. Your church speaks with a tongue like an asp, giving with one hand while taking with another. Your death will be quiet and quick." Hatred dripped from each word like acid.

Unable to loosen the veil, she blindly attacked with her nails, gouging an eye and scraping skin from his forehead, drawing a hostile, pained yelp.

A blow to her cheek slammed her against the wall, rattling her bones and jarring her teeth. She lunged back at him. If Hugo taught her nothing else, it was how to take a hit and keep fighting.

The metallic taste of blood coated her tongue, but a retaliating strike with her other hand to the ear caused him to lose his grip on the fabric. She struggled to inhale past the sharp shards of pain in her throat, but at least now she could breathe. She drove her knee up into soft flesh, hoping it hurt like the devil.

The faraway crack of the cabin door against the wall barely registered. A sick, yellow light invaded the room, bringing into focus her attacker, his ferocious face twisted in fear and pain. The sailor who had spat on the deck doubled over, clutching his groin, his dark, glinting eyes saturated with hate.

Razin.

An enraged roar thundered in the small room. Razin had just enough time to turn his head before a blurred shadow crashed into him. Eva sank to her knees and sucked in another lungful of precious air as she grappled with the tourniquet around her neck.

The shadows lunging in the eerie light turned into a raging, snarling demon, huge, muscular and agile. He pummeled Razin until the man crumbled into a bloody heap.

Saved by a pirate, she thought numbly. Air grated her throat as she pulled in a shaky breath. The cabin reeked of Razin's fear and sweat. Her heart hammered an erratic rhythm, jolting her ribs with every beat. She blinked and tried to focus. Captain Gamponetti whirled and raked a feral gaze over her, eyes flashing like fiery blades.

The movement made her cringe. He stilled, coiled and vibrating, chest heaving, fists clenched at his sides, eyes crackling gray fire, the angled planes of his face contorted with fury.

A chill skimmed over her skin. She numbly glanced down. Good Lord, her ripped tunic hung off her shoulders in pieces! She fumbled with the torn material; her hands shook violently, and she fought to quiet them. Her rosary was scattered everywhere.

She clung to the fabric with one hand and began gathering the beads with the other.

Gamponetti's tortured voice permeated her mind. "Please, let me help you."

Why won't her hands stop shaking? The restriction was gone from her throat, yet she couldn't take a normal breath. This vexing tunic, something was wrong with it. That evil man must have torn part of it off completely. She patted the floor, searching for a scrap. It had to be here somewhere. Two warm hands, knuckles raw and bleeding, wrapped around hers, stilling them. The coppery scent of blood mingled with the taste in her mouth.

"Let me help," Gampo said, his voice hoarse with emotion. He crouched next to her, blocking out most of the light.

Help her with what? She looked down, and two fat drops plopped on their hands, then two more. A ragged sob escaped her raw throat.

She was *crying*?

Not just crying, but sobbing so hard she shuddered with each breath. His gaze seemed softer now, so she nodded her permission, oddly unafraid considering he looked like the son of Satan clad entirely in black, ebony hair loose and wild.

She didn't object when he gently slipped his arms under her knees and behind her shoulders. He lifted her against the heat of his chest; she buried her face in his neck and clung to him. Pressing her close, he concealed her naked skin against his body and carried her to the upper deck in sinuous, smooth strides.

A soft sea breeze wafted across her cheek, but when she inhaled, she smelled *him*, the same musky spice forever branded in her memory from the night of the kiss. A warbled laugh escaped her lips. What a crazy time for that particular thought to float to the surface.

Startled voices shouted questions. His chest rumbled as he called for Manuel. "Put Razin in irons. He's below, in the second cabin."

"Aye, Cap'n." The worry in Manuel's voice tugged her heart. "Why is she sad? Is Sister Eva hurt?"

Gamponetti's long strides didn't slow. The best she could do was turn her head and give the man a small, tremulous smile. The rest of their conversation faded.

She dimly registered entering a cabin. Odd. No sound of Beatrice snoring.

Ah. It was *Captain Gampo's* cabin.

This one was well-lit and much bigger. He sat down with her in his arms, then shifted. The trickle of liquid into a glass. His husky voice rumbled in her ear. "Drink this."

He pressed the rim to her lips, and she gulped a mouthful. Fire tore down her throat and she gasped, which made the burning worse, and she coughed. After the fit of coughing ended, he lifted the glass.

"Take another. Smaller this time. You've had a long, trying day. It will help settle your nerves."

She shook her head and struggled to whisper, but the words wouldn't come.

He put it down and offered a tankard instead. "This one is simple grog, it won't burn as much."

His gentle, smooth voice reminded her of sun-warmed honey. She focused on his face. Even in the golden radiance of the lantern, his eyes were like a tempest.

So striking. So lethal.

As treacherous and menacing as he looked, she didn't fear him. Although perhaps she should. He was large and demanding and had been a pirate in command of brigands and cutthroats, looting and killing for spoils.

Was he also a murderer?

A thief?

It was likely. She'd recognized Gampo's name when she'd first heard it. He was a notorious pirate and Jean Lafitte's second before he left New Orleans for France to become a privateer. She smiled grimly. So what had she decided to do? Slip him a tonic and bind him to a bed.

Those actions were no less dangerous than running clandestine messages for Hugo. She'd escaped from that world nine years ago. A wave of near-hysterical laughter and disbelief rippled through her chest. She always feared Hugo would find her and drag her back. But willingly enter that society again? *Never*.

He pressed the tankard to her mouth again, and she drank. It was indeed grog, but it wasn't as diluted as he'd insinuated. Her shoulders still trembled, and it was so difficult to swallow. A faint gushing swooshed in her head. It sounded like enormous gasps.

He was talking, and she had to concentrate to understand him.

That gasping sound...

Good Lord, it was *her*! She was still sobbing uncontrollably. Her eyes were hot and burning. Like a reverse breath, the air left her lungs faster than she could pull it back in. She struggled to slow her breathing, and it was several minutes before the sobs reduced to sniffles. Living in the abbey had made her complacent. It had dulled her edges, made her weak, vulnerable.

But she'd felt safe there.

Gamponetti dabbed at her cheeks and bleeding lip with a cloth. He had a small scar near the cleft in his chin. She reached up and rubbed it with her the pad of her thumb, fascinated at the combination of scratchy and smooth. He stilled. The sensation of slight stubble rimming the soft raised flesh was intriguing. He seemed invincible, too unyielding to be scarred. However, even that small expenditure of energy was draining, and she dropped her hand and folded into herself.

He was right. The day had indeed been exhausting.

Capitaine Gamponetti offered her another sip of grog. "You're safe now, Eva. I'll protect you."

Safe? "I—" Words were so challenging to articulate. Warm bands of steel caged her body, splitting her attention. "You're a pirate," she murmured, taking the tankard and burrowing into his hard chest.

His grip on her tightened. "*Was*. Regardless, I have always lived by a certain code of honor. I have never broken my word. When I say I'll protect you, I will."

Liar.

"You gave me your word back at the abbey. Then broke it," she muttered. The long silence had her regretting her remarks. Was he angry or penitent?

He finally spoke. The granite in his voice suggested barely leashed anger. "One was a small agreement to take you to New Orleans. Not as binding as a formal vow." He uttered the words with a chilly calm. "And the other, an oath given... under duress."

Duress. That was funny. A cat coercing a panther. She almost chuckled, but she didn't have the energy. She owed him her gratitude, at least. "Thank you," she finally mumbled. "For everything."

He gave her a tender squeeze in response, his anger either set aside or forgotten for now. She brought the tankard up for another sip, but it was empty. She put it next to a rum bottle and eased back into the safety of his thick, corded arms. He stroked her hair and murmured melodic words of comfort in a language she recognized, but didn't understand.

Italian.

Chapter Nineteen

UNREDEEMABLE

D rago ground his teeth against the violence still surging through his veins. A torrent of rage screamed for him to go below and drive a blade through Razin's malignant heart. Only his need to ease Eva's panic kept him from doing so. In addition, taking things into his own hands would unsettle his crew. Charges must be brought to light, judgment determined, punishment dealt. Harshly.

So, instead, he refilled the empty brandy glass with rum.

When he tried to deposit the nun on his bed earlier, she'd clung to his neck, forcing him to sit and hold her. This, in turn, forced him to focus back on his fury with Razin to keep his mind from the exquisite warmth on his lap smelling of sunshine and rain.

Stroking her head seemed to soothe her, so he continued to use one hand to comb her ebony hair from her crown to past her nape, through the long, shiny strands to the ends.

Repeat.

She finally expelled the hysteria. For a brief moment, he feared he'd been mistaken about her solid state of mind and the insanity he dismissed earlier.

The brandy would calm her nerves and bring sleep. He eased the veil from her neck and gently covered her, cursing at the raw, red mark around her long, graceful throat and the bruise already forming on her cheekbone.

Thank God he'd arrived when he did.

Eva had left without a lantern. Below deck was bloody dark at night, the steps narrow and steep. He retrieved one from his cabin and followed. When he heard Razin attacking her... He sucked in another angry breath.

She stirred against his chest. "I... I'm sorry I caused so much trouble."

"You have nothing for which to apologize." He meant it. She did nothing to provoke the mangy cur, and it irritated him that she might think so. "The fault lies with Razin."

"My very presence offends him." She lifted her head and looked at him with watery blue eyes. "He has a vigorous hatred of the Catholic religion or nuns... maybe both."

"I was unaware." He couldn't have possibly known, yet he was furious with himself just the same. "He is new to the crew. This is his first sail on the *Dragon*. And last."

"I'm used to being shunned." She dropped her head. "It's the reason I stayed at the abbey after my wounds healed. I'm fortunate and grateful for the sanctuary."

He straightened. "Sanctuary? I assumed you were already a novitiate." She'd lived with the nuns beyond the age of eighteen. It would make sense.

She reached for his glass, shocking his eyebrows straight up. "Careful, that's rum."

Eva took a shaky swallow and grimaced, then rubbed her throat. "I'm not a novitiate yet." Her voice was raw and reedy, kicking his rage awake. Again he wanted to bury his saber in Razin's chest. Maybe he would. Later.

She let out a quick sigh. "Mother Marie Francois said I wasn't ready, which is why she sent me to Jamaica, among other things."

"Why did you need a sanctuary?" And what or who was she running from? And what *other things*?

The hand holding the glass wobbled near her temple. "To keep me safe from the man who did this."

His gut clenched. "Another man attacked you like Razin?"

She tilted her chin up and stared at him. The blank shuttering of her expression made his heart contract with a sharp spasm. He'd seen that look before in the faces of Negro slaves. His stomach gave a sick lurch. She was extinguishing emotion, blocking the cloud of horror from her vision.

"My benefactor did it. He was drunk and furious with me. I ran away and hid on the convent grounds, knowing he wouldn't search for me there. Sister Beatrice found me the next morning."

Drago unclenched his jaw before his teeth snapped off. "You are of age to lead your own life, now. He has no legal control over you. Why do you remain with the nuns?" He already knew the answer.

Fear.

Her shoulder shrugged against his arm. "They have accepted me. They care for me. It is a safe refuge. I intended to request true novitiate status when my mission in Jamaica ended, so I can begin my two years of transition into the order."

A thread of doubt tinted her voice; he tugged on it, curious. "Intended? Have you changed your mind?" Now that would make for an interesting situation, one he would very much like to explore.

She hesitated. "No, but I'm unsure if I'm worthy of the honor."

He frowned. There was something satisfying about her statement, while at the same time maddening. She underestimated her worth, greatly. "How could you ever be unworthy?"

Did he really just ask that? He should have said something comforting, like: 'better to realize it now than later' or: 'not everyone's meant to live that kind of life'. Something corroborating her theory. It was a bit selfish, but advantageous to him. Especially since he no longer had to call her "Sister."

She let out a soft huff of breath. "You don't really know me, *Capitaine*. Or who I was."

Her cryptic comment stilled his thoughts. A lone tear escaped and paused at the corner of her eye. The desire to brush it away was too strong to resist, or he was too weak.

He brushed it away.

It seemed like two poles within her warred against each other. A dichotomy of kindhearted compassion and rigid dedication, a flimsy sense of self-worth, yet a powerful talent for healing. She was a flower willing to accept the pain of remaining curled in its bud rather than face the terror of discovering what her unfurling petals would reveal.

He stroked her hair. "Who are you, Eva?" he murmured, his voice raspy and low.

Silence. The sputtering of the lantern on his desk broke the stillness. He sighed. "You don't have to answer my impertinent questions."

She lifted a shoulder, and it rubbed his ribs like a caress. "They aren't impertinent." She took another sip, lowered her head and rested her temple against his breastbone; the intimacy in the way she snuggled closer had him fighting between the urge to dump her on his bed and get out of the cabin, or draw her closer still.

"I lost my mother when I was eight." Her voice was heavy and soft. "I had no other family. When the landlord and another man came to take her body, I overheard something that terrified me. They spoke about selling me to a rich man who used young girls until they died. I climbed from a window and ran. I didn't understand then, what kind of monster the rich man was, but I knew that I didn't want to die. The streets became my home. I was half-starved when Hugo Dupré took me in."

Emotion roiled in Drago's chest like a gathering storm. "I'm familiar with the name." She had fled one nightmare only to collide with another. Hugo Dupré was well-known among Lafitte and his Baratarian pirates. He negotiated terms between buyers and sellers for Lafitte's stolen bounty.

She took another sharp swallow of his rum. Apparently, he wasn't getting it back, so he took her empty mug and filled it for himself. He needed it.

Eva leaned her head back and closed her eyes. "He trained me to be one of his runners. We delivered notes and packages to his customers. He also taught us how to pick pockets, which became a frightening pastime for all of us."

And an easy way to lose a finger. Or a hand, depending on whom you thieved from. That layer of society had a unique system of justice.

He snorted in disgust. Dupré was scum. He took advantage of desperate and impoverished women and children. Their activities lined his pockets from a safe distance.

He was savvy. Children moved about unnoticed. Women were distracting in their own way. If caught, they'd be punished, but perhaps not as severely as a man, children even less so. No doubt, Dupré had all ten fingers intact.

Eva plucked at a tie on his shirt. This was one of the ways women could be bloody distracting. "We all had a hidden pocket inside our coats where we put our takes and Hugo's missives. One evening, he arranged a card game. I was to lift something important Hugo wanted, a map from a player. I did as instructed. On the way to his bolt-hole, I passed an open window. On the sill was a tray of teacakes. I grabbed one and shoved it in my mouth."

She released the cord, smoothed it, and his breath hitched as she unintentionally caressed his chest. He opened his lips to attempt a word that might still her hand, but his throat went completely dry. Before he could utter a sound, she continued.

"Hunger burned my belly, I hadn't eaten in two days. I acted without thinking. Without paying attention to my surroundings. A man grabbed my arm. He'd seen me steal and threatened to drag me into the house for the master to punish. I panicked. I twisted, kicked and fought until I slipped out of my coat. I left it and the folded map I'd taken, just dangling from that man's fist."

Drago's tried to swallow. Her fingers were stroking in a way that was making him crazy. Finally, with a tortured hiss, he grabbed her hand to still it. She stopped and jerked her sapphire gaze to his face, eyes wide.

He closed his eyes briefly and swallowed. "That tickles," he lied.

Her lips parted with a faint gasp. Sweet Calypso, how he wanted to kiss them... He should leave. However, leaving would likely distress her. She seemed content in his arms at the moment. He was a pirate—blast it all, a privateer—but not a monster. He just got her calmed, holding her so she felt safe, stroking her head to ease the panic. Leaving was something he was unwilling to do.

Not because he couldn't, he simply chose not to go.

The corner of her mouth twitched before she bit her bottom lip. If she only knew how insane she was making him now, *she'd* leave. She curled her hand into a fist inside his, but didn't pull it away. He could feel his heart slamming against his chest beneath his knuckles. She smelled like sunshine and rain and felt like paradise in his arms, and all he could think about was how extraordinarily happy it made him that her decision to enter the cloister wasn't firm.

"I'm sorry," she whispered. "I... I didn't realize what I was doing."

He released her fingers. She couldn't have, or else she'd flee from the room. Instead, she set her glass next to the bottle and to his shock, refilled it. He reached to still her hand as she raised the glass to her lips, but the prospect of touching her skin made him hesitate. He settled for a verbal warning. "You should slow down, Eva. That's straight rum."

She frowned and stared at the glass, then took a small sip anyway, before continuing. "Hugo came home drunk and penniless. He lost his entire purse playing cards. He said it didn't matter, the map I lifted would make us wealthier than royalty."

Her gaze landed on the lantern, and the flickering flame captured it. She treated him to a breath-taking profile, a mixture of graceful angles and pliant edges. The sleek arch of her brow and long, curved sweep of inky lashes bordered eyes that reflected a blue-green fire.

"When he found out I failed, he became insanely enraged. Grime was burning off a knife blade in the coals. Had he not been so drunk and unbalanced, he would have slit my throat." She covered her scar with her palm. "He did this instead. I ran away to the Ursuline nuns, and they hid me and helped me to heal. I was thirteen."

The same as age Jacqueline. Drago's gut clenched at the pain she must have endured, both emotional and physical. In his opinion, the series of events that drove her to the abbey doubtless saved her life in more ways than one. At thirteen, her beauty would have been on the cusp of blossoming. Hiding in the convent for the next few years prevented a more insidious fate.

She expelled a long sigh, closing her eyes. "I still owe you an apology."

"In God's name, what for?"

Her delicate eyebrows slammed down. "Your language is appalling, *Capitainé*."

He matched her glower. "This is *my* ship."

She flattened her mouth and shifted, thinking through his response. She puffed out a sharp, irritated harrumph. "I shall better keep that in mind."

He inhaled. Of course, he could perhaps behave with a somewhat higher degree of refinement. "And I'll better attempt to control my tongue," he groused, stopping short of telling her that if she didn't like it, she should leave.

That would punish him more than her.

He lifted the tankard for a gulp. The drink would keep his mouth busy. For a little while, anyway.

"I truly do need to apologize for one specific thing." She eyed him as she sipped.

He raised his brows. "One specific thing?" Trussing him up like a pig on a spit by chance?

She focused on her finger, now tracing around the rim of her glass. "I shouldn't have given you Miss Kalia's tonic without knowing what was in it."

Devils bollocks! He choked, the rum exploded up his nose, its fiery fingers blistering tender tissue. "You gave me one of that witch's tonics?"

Her mouth opened, and he glared, daring her to admonish him again for his language. She mashed her lips together, wisely.

Well, that explained why his memory was foggy from that night. And the next morning. He was lucky he woke up with his mind intact. He ran his hands through his hair, grateful he had a scalp under it.

Eva's voice was humble and small. "After Jacqueline was out of danger, all I cared about that morning was persuading you to take me with you to New Orleans. When Miss Kalia said the tonic would help me get what I needed from you, I should have asked what was in it." She hiccuped. Her lids drifted shut for a moment, then opened. "I was desperate. I needed assistance. God sent you to me for a reason." Her words slurred a little, and she let out a short laugh. "Although I'm sure the reason wasn't to kiss me."

What? *What?*

He *kissed* her? "I'm sorry, Eva. I don't understand." What the devil had happened between the time he finished his meal and awoke tied to the posts? "I'm afraid my memory of that day is faulty," he ground out.

She heaved another sigh. "That's prob'ly because you don't 'member falling on me." She hiccuped again, then let her forehead plop down on his shoulder, where she mumbled, "You kissed me quite... thoroughly."

Dear God!

He kissed her. He'd kissed a *nun*.

Granted, she wasn't a novitiate nor had she taken her vows, but at the time, he had assumed she was a sister of the church. If he'd not been under the spell of one of Kalia's potions, he'd never have considered the thought. Certainly.

The shock of his actions and the ensuing guilt should have had him feeling like an ogre, but it was entirely offset by the fact that she wasn't truly a nun.

The image of Eva in the cave pool floated to the surface, but that was the simple admiration of her beauty, not a plot to steal a kiss.

For the most part.

The devil already held the deed to his soul, he had nothing left to lose by denying Eva's irresistible allure. Or lying to himself about it, for that matter. He clenched his jaw. What pitched stones into his stomach was that his actions had been as deplorable as Razin's.

No wonder she'd tied him to the bedposts.

Realization slowly dawned. She'd restrained him from *kissing* her again, not to threaten him with castration. He groaned, then snorted. Laughter bubbled in his chest and he tortured himself by quietly laughing at his assumptions; it was a long moment before he could speak.

He was a bloody *idiot*.

Perhaps an apology was called for, although it was a pity to have to apologize for something he didn't remember enjoying. "I swear I don't recall—"

She shushed him by sliding an index finger across his mouth. What he wouldn't give to replace the finger with her lips. That image made his stomach tighten, along with other things. It didn't help that she wouldn't stay still. Every time she shifted, he had to bite the inside of his cheek as a distraction.

Unaware of his errant thoughts, she smiled up at him. "Don't 'pologize. You kiss much better than Henré. I... I liked it."

That grabbed his attention. "Who's Henré?" And who was he to her? Not that he cared.

Her hand fell from his mouth, leaving him feeling abruptly exposed. She sighed and swirled the glass she still held. "When I was seventeen, Henré sighted me at the market. By then, I found if I wore the veil, then I didn't scare the children. Still, he asked for Mother Superior's permission to court me." She sipped carefully. "He wanted to marry me as soon as he completed his apprenticeship." A sad smile drifted onto her face. "I loved him."

"Why didn't you wed?" Why did he care? And why did the thought of her marrying Henré irritate him more than the thought of sleeping on a blanket of burrs?

She struggled with the words. "I wasn't right for him." Another shrug. "He asked to kiss me. I let him remove my veil."

It was easy to predict the ending to this story.

He was supposed to be trying to calm her, not forcing her to relive such a heart-rending memory. He gave her a gentle squeeze to halt her words. "I shouldn't pry. You've had a terrible fright, as well as a harrowing day, it's probably best that you rest. Sleep."

Her eyes lost focus, and she continued as if he hadn't spoken. "I feared his reaction," she murmured. "but still allowed him to draw away the veil. After he gathered his composure, he gave me a quick peck, like you'd give a small child or an old woman."

Drago's chest filled with an ache that twisted his lungs. He wanted to hit something. Repeatedly.

Her voice dropped to a ragged whisper. "When I opened my eyes, I could see it. The disgust... the revulsion. He tried to be brave, but I could tell the sight unnerved him. I knew then, that while he may have loved me before, he could never continue to love me." She closed her eyes and let out a harsh laugh. "I whirled and ran, praying to God that he'd call out to me to stop, then beg me to come back, but he didn't. I never saw him again."

She'd thought that milksop tried to be brave? Drago snorted. The young man was a coward and a fool. "He didn't deserve you." The words were out before he could bite his tongue.

She rolled her head back and scrutinized him, her eyes the color of dark blue silk. "That's a very compassionate remark, for a pirate."

"I'm not a pirate." He brushed a sleek tendril from her face. "Privateer. There's a distinct difference."

"So you say." The corners of her mouth quirked up even as she narrowed her eyes and studied him. "I think you are a better man than you let others believe, *Capitainé* Drago Viteri Gamponetti."

Guilt raised its hideous fist and landed a crushing blow to his gut; his voice came out in a sandy whisper. "No, Eva. I'm unredeemable."

She pressed her palm to his face, scorching it. "No one is ever unredeemable, *Capitainé*."

The ridiculous ache in his chest shifted at the calm conviction in her voice. "Sister Eva..." He'd changed his mind about the sister rule. Right now it was important that he call her Sister Eva, as an indicator that she was forbidden.

Forbidden.

If he could commit only one act of chivalry the rest of his life, it was this one: Consider her untouchable. *And then don't touch her.*

Regardless of her upbringing, Eva had a golden heart cradled with wings of white. He had no right to cast her into his shadow. Otherwise, he might lift her closer and show her precisely how those beautiful lips should be kissed.

Reverently.

Passionately.

Deeply.

His mouth had turned into a desert. Drago reached for the bottle and took a healthy gulp, welcoming the vicious trail of fire.

"If you knew the things I've done, you'd know I'm unredeemable," he growled, then gave a disgusted snort. "And it appears I should add forcing a kiss upon a nun to my list of transgressions." She stilled, and he instantly regretted his gruff tone. He gentled his voice. "Please accept my sincerest apology. It was disrespectful of me to have pressed my advantage. I deeply regret my behavior."

He wanted to cut his own tongue out the second her expression shifted. Calypso's blood! The despair he understood. But the resignation in her eyes destroyed him—as if she expected and deserved nothing better—it sliced his heart open from stem to stern. He tripped over his words, trying to repair the damage. "I'm... I'm not saying I didn't... want to or... or that I didn't enjoy it—"

She huffed a sarcastic laugh. "You don't even remember it."

"But—"

Again, a finger on his lips hushed him. "Don't." Dark lashes shuttered the blue glimmer from her eyes; words sparked from her lips, fierce and soft. "I'm *glad*. I'm glad you don't remember it. I know I'm repulsive. I've seen the effect I have on people. Many times."

An argument tried to escape his mouth, but her fingers blocked it. "I'm happy you kissed me, so there is nothing to forgive." The honest weight of her words groaned in his chest.

The warm lantern light bathed her face in a creamy glow. Yes, the angry, scarred burn would always be with her, but she needed to understand that it was only a small external mark. It did not define who she was as a person. The rest of her was exquisite. Her compassion and ability to see into his soul and still treat him with confident kindness amazed him.

He saw beauty. Not scars. Sapphire eyes. Narrow, pert nose. Full, pink, kissable lips. Long, delicious curves that had his fingers aching to follow them.

She was wrong.

Unarguably irrevocably wrong.

How could she be so blind? "Eva—"

She shook her head, silencing him. "Perhaps I should be ashamed and shocked that I didn't mind the kiss. But I'm not. Not in the slightest. It was a gift." She raised her glass and sipped. "I'm happy my first real kiss came from you."

Something close to primal satisfaction roared to life in his chest at the words "first real kiss."

She reached up to trace the scars on his chin, cheek and forehead, and threads of fire skittered under his skin. "During that moment, I didn't feel hideous, or repulsive, although I am both those things."

"Eva—" Her name gripped his throat. Her touch was tender, almost reverent,, and it was doing terrible things to his concentration. "You are neither of those things. You're beautiful."

Her eyes, twin pools of deep blue, widened then narrowed with suspicion. "You must stop uttering lies, *Capitainé* Gampo."

Gampo.

With the exception of his crew and the twins, who'd been introduced to him as such during a rather unsavory situation where he'd been forced to kidnap them, Gampo was the name used by strangers who feared or despised him but didn't respect him. From whose lips it fell had never concerned him.

Until now.

"Call me Drago." Or anything else. Just not Gampo. He could tolerate Captain Gampo from any other person in the world, just not from her.

She shrugged. "There's no need to save my feelings. They have been dead a long time."

His gut tightened, and he wanted to shake his words into her head. "I'm not lying."

"I know what I am and it's not *beautiful*." She bit off that last word and tossed down the rest of her drink. "Please do not attempt to placate me this way, it's insulting, Drago."

Frustration boiled up in his chest. Why wouldn't she listen to him? No one had ever discounted his words in such a manner.

Ever.

When he spoke, his men shut up and listened. They executed his commands without question. His opinions, orders and stratagems saved their lives. It filled their pockets with coin. It kept their bellies full.

They never doubted him. Yet *she* did.

She hiccuped. "I'm hideous and—"

Enough!

Before she could say another word, he pulled her fingers from his mouth then returned them to his lips, shocking her into silence long enough for him to shift his gaze from hers, a deep, limpid blue, to the slim nose, then on to her sweet, berry-tinted mouth.

God help him.

Lowering his head, he kissed her. She tasted like moonbeams and fire. Like a man dying of thirst, he drank as if she were the last drop of water. Tension eased from her body like a quiet exhale. He lost himself in the softness of her lips. She threaded her fingers through the hair at his temples. He cradled her head in his palm, amazed at the potent intoxication of her kiss.

If he didn't extricate himself now, he'd continue to consume the nectar she offered.

And perhaps the nectar she did not.

He lifted his head; her hand slid to his cheek. She tucked her face into his neck and kissed it, and he bit back a hoarse growl at the shivers that spidered over his skin. He rasped a warning. "Eva —" If she didn't stop, he'd either go mad or take her to his bed.

She inhaled, then blew a wisp of hair from her eyes. "Maybe Mother Marie Francois was right about me," she murmured. Her sigh reversed direction and ended in a hiccup. Her eyelids fluttered shut; sooty lashes brushed her cheeks. "This mission was a test, I think. I'm fairly certain I just failed it irrefutably."

Those last mumbled words barely reached his ears. Perhaps he wasn't meant to hear them, but they gave him a healthy jolt of satisfaction just the same. "Things might be clearer in the morning." He wouldn't press his advantage here, especially since the rum seemed to have gone to her head. Drago shifted to free himself, but her arms tightened around his neck.

He appealed to the heavens. If this amount of restraint didn't entice God to grant him some level of absolution, then Eva was wrong; he was *absolutely* unredeemable.

Expelling a lungful of air, he returned to methodically combing his fingers through her dark, sleek strands of hair. After a while, her hand dropped limply to her chest. Her breathing settled into long, deep breaths of sleep, providing him the opportunity to stare without being rude. The widow's peak at the top of her forehead and high cheekbones accented her heart-shaped face. Her lips were flushed from kissing. He traced the jagged scar from her chin to her temple, then brushed a rebellious strand of hair back behind her partial ear.

"You do not belong in a convent, Eva."

Something ethereal emanated from her; it seeped through flesh and blood and bone sending a steady vibration strumming through his body. His pulse bound the rhythm in a delirious dance. The shadow shifted, and everything expanded like a great inhale. Even the thought of separating from her cracked open a hollow crevice in his chest and left a bottomless cavity chiseled into his heart.

He lifted her hand and entwined his fingers with hers, then placed a kiss on each and spoke to her although she slept. "You belong with me, Eva. I will claim you. On that, you have my ardent vow."

And heaven help him, his affection.

Kalia's smoky voice echoed in his head. *"De light beckons you but de dark always a seductress."*

As the thought seeped into his mind, he embraced it. He

would seduce her. He was a bloody pirate, after all—unforgivable, unredeemable and unremorseful.

If he had to drag her into the shadow in order to have her, he would.

The promise he made in the abbey poked his conscience, although lightly. How was he going to protect the very items he must steal?

There had to be another way to appease both the king and Eva.

He'd find it.

He had to.

Persuading her to stay with him was now as important as breathing. He didn't deserve her any more than Henré, but he wanted her, and it was crucial that she want him in return. He rarely took "no" for an answer, but this was a delicate play. His betrayal would likely earn him her loathing.

He sat for a long time, rolling ideas around in his head. Different scenarios, options.

Eva, the Guirauds all ended up dead each time.

The single scene they did not, Eva ended up hating him.

And he ended up without her.

He shook his head. It was folly to think a solution existed. Either he sent the relics to France, or he did not. If he did, she would despise him. If he did not, King Louis' assassins would kill him and the Guirauds. And even worse, once Fontaine connected him with her, he'd kill her as well.

He picked up a silky curl and let it wrap around his thumb, the color as dark as the shadow gripping his soul. He was loath to betray this woman.

For now, he'd revel in the sweet form in his arms, breathe in her essence and memorize the blissful sensation of her lips against his. Once he took possession the relics such delicious pleasure would likely never happen again.

Chapter Twenty

A CAPTAIN'S SENTENCE

❧❦❧

T he scream that awoke Eva made the skin grip her spine as if an icy stream of water surged down her back. She jolted upright in bed, lost and disoriented, convinced she was still dreaming. Sunshine streamed through the small windows.

Sunshine? Her cabin had no windows. The unusual sensation of air hitting her bare chest drew to her attention downward. She still wore only her torn shift, which now gaped open. She clutched the fabric in her fist. Her robe was draped at the foot of the bed; it had been roughly stitched together.

"Good morning, Sister Eva." Jacqueline perched on a chair near the bed, bent over her needlework, tongue sticking out from the corner of her mouth. The young girl had a threaded needle in her hand and Eva's open-sided tunic on her lap.

A loud crack ripped the air, followed by another high-pitched cry. Jacqueline twitched and darted a glance toward the closed door, then returned to her mending.

It hadn't been a dream. Eva donned her robe and rose from the bed. "What is happening?"

Jacqueline ignored her question, but asked one of her own. "How are you?"

Some fleshy areas were sore. Bony areas ached. She gently prodded her bruised cheek before touching her tender throat.

Her brain throbbed. Did the captain give her *rum*?

"I'm fine." Not really, especially since she had a recollection of snuggling against a warm, solid chest. She didn't dream that part. She straightened.

He'd *kissed* her!

The kiss was similar to the first one, but different. Longer. Gentler. More tender. Without the impairment from a tonic. He kissed her of his own volition! She brushed her fingertips along her lips, savoring the memory. The kiss had been so gentle. So precious.

Had Drago told Jacqueline about Razin's attack? An involuntary shudder quaked through her shoulders. Eva studied the young girl's features, which were decidedly blank, thereby answering her own question.

He had.

She searched for her shoes and found them next to the captain's desk, which stood fixed against the wall nearby. Maps were strewn over a long table placed prominently in the middle of the room, as if every other piece of furniture was secondary in importance.

"Finally." Jacqueline lifted the repaired garment and bit her lip. "I'm finished. Although, I'm afraid my needlework isn't very good. I've only ever mended sails, stockings and ripped trousers." She said the last as if she wasn't sure if she should add mending trousers to her list.

Eva smoothed her fingers over the stitches. "Considering the condition this tunic was in before you started, I think your stitches are more than adequate."

A small, pleased smile darted across Jacqueline's face; she nodded toward the desk, to a shallow bowl containing Eva's destroyed rosary. "I wanted to repair that, too, but the crucifix is missing, and it needs a new cord. Manuel said he'd help me restring it after—"

Another loud clap interrupted her. The girl's smile disappeared. This time, the scream was shorter. Her attention once again slid to the door.

Eva shrugged into her clothing; she'd mend her shift later. "Jacqueline, *mon cher,* you haven't answered my question."

The young girl grimaced. After another quick glance at the door, she said, "Unless they are offering aid or following a direct order from Captain Gampo, they're not allowed to touch us."

"Who?"

"The men."

An understanding dawned. Razin was being punished.

The image of Julian tied to the breastwork floated to the forefront of her mind. Mister Harvey had used an oar. The stroke of the whip signified a much more severe form of discipline.

Jacqueline hesitantly gathered the needle and thread and stashed them in the sewing box. "You shouldn't go out there. Manuel is standing guard. He won't let you pass. He'll follow his captain's orders no matter what."

Eva arched a brow. Most likely, that was experience speaking. Drago had warned her about the twins' antics, had he not? She eased open the door and peered out. Manuel's back was to her. Like everyone else aboard, he focused his attention on the activity near the center of the ship. Shackled to the breastwork grate, Razin was stripped to the waist and had several long thick gashes crossing his back. The African, Raul wielded the cat-o'-nine-tails. Drago stood near the stair leading to the helm, a foreboding figure of authority and judgment.

He stood with his feet braced wide, corded arms folded across his chest. As usual, he was dressed in black from head to boots. A fierce scowl darkened his face, stoney eyes flashed beneath lowered brows. The quartermaster drew back the whip, flicked it and looked at him.

Gampo gave the slightest nod, and the cat whistled through the air. It made contact with the man's skin and clawed around his ribs. His body jerked violently before he let out a ragged cry.

Once again, Raul looked for direction. He received another inclination, and the whip hissed. This time, Razin's voice was a crumbled warble. As if sensing her presence, Drago turned his head toward her. His expression teetered for a second, between potent interest and flat dismissal. His shout cut through the morning air. "Manuel!"

The hulk of a man started before twisting his chin over his shoulder. He pulled the hat from his head and worried it in his hands. "Mornin,' Sister Eva. I'm sorry, but you must stay in the cabin. Captain's orders."

Before she could respond, he stepped forward, blocking her view of the deck, grasped the door, and swung it shut with a commanding click.

Chapter Twenty-One
LIGHT BECKONS

❧❧❧

"Raise the lantern higher, Manuel." She transferred the basket of supplies to her other arm as she peered into the makeshift cell. They were down in the hold. A couple inches of dank sea brine sloshed to and fro with the swells, dampening her hem and soaking her feet. He complied, and she scrutinized the form sprawled facedown across a wooden pallet. Angry red slashes crossed his exposed back. Dried blood stained the waistband of his britches from yesterday's lashing.

Manuel unlocked the iron gate and stepped inside, leaving just enough room for her to squeeze in next to him. Razin opened his eyes and glared. When his gaze struck her, it faltered in surprise. He recovered swiftly and eyed her with a wary stare as he started to press himself up.

"Stay where you are please, Mr. Razin," she said. He stilled at her words, shot a look to Manuel, then back to her, before he eased down to his stomach. Dark eyes flashed with loathing and distrust.

She withdrew a small wooden bowl. "I created a salve that will help your wounds to heal. If you'll permit me to apply it, you'll discover it also relieves the pain somewhat."

His jaw rippled as he pressed his lips into a thin line. Finally, he gave her a curt nod. Manuel moved closer to his feet, giving Eva room to work.

She poured a tincture on the gashes, and he flinched at the sting. "In a moment, your discomfort will subside, but only temporarily. I'll be able to rub in the salve without causing you additional discomfort." She concluded her administrations efficiently, gathered her supplies and stepped toward the door.

"Why?" Razin's voice rasped, dripping with bitter hatred.

Why indeed? She'd have asked the same question had she been in his place. The answer was simple.

"To please God," she answered. His face remained hard, but his eyes seemed to flicker ever so slightly. She took just two steps before coming nose to nose with Captain Gamponetti. She stopped so fast, her basket swung forward and struck his hip. She braced a hand on his chest to avoid a collision. Rigid tension curled under her palm, and she snatched her hand back. She didn't think to request permission to treat Razin first, although it appeared she should have.

"What are you doing?" His voice was brittle, the question deliberately articulated.

She tilted her head, struggling to read his expression in the dim light, to determine if his features mirrored his tone. His eyes glittered with shards of flint.

It did.

"This man paid for his crime. I assumed you still require his services, so I sought to speed his recovery to the best of my abilities."

He folded his arms over his massive chest. The steel in his voice hardened his words. "Were I still a pirate captain, this bilge rat would have been given a dozen lashes, then tossed overboard as a pretty meal for the sharks, for his crimes. As per the articles."

The visual made her cringe. She placed her palm on his forearm, which was solid as a granite boulder. He slowly unclenched his fist, the muscle beneath her hand almost easing imperceptibly as he unfolded them. "We must forgive those who trespass against us." She nodded toward Razin. "That's what I have done." If only her anger at Hugo would subside as easily. Forgiving Dupré was toughest for her. It always had been.

He studied her. "You have a very complex nature. You're much more merciful than I." He offered his arm. "Watch your step."

She slid her hand into the crook of his elbow, perhaps a little too tightly.

Manuel followed them up to the main deck before speaking. "Sister Eva?"

She stopped and faced him. "Yes?"

He plunged his meaty hands into his pockets. "I—I tried to fix your prayer beads." He rocked forward and back.

"That was extremely kind of you, Manuel." His distress was palpable. She smiled, hoping to put him at ease.

"The pieces were scattered everywhere." He shifted his weight and withdrew a new rosary, beautifully restrung, with a hand-carved crucifix.

Eva sucked in her breath, reached out and ran her fingers over the cross. "This is exquisite. Did you carve it?"

He nodded. "From a piece of ivory. I've been working on the cross for a long time." He let the rosary pour into her open hands.

To think he went to so much trouble and worked so hard to make this for her was overwhelming. Aside from the nuns, the only person to show her such kindness had been her mother, and more recently, *Capitaine* Gamponetti. She smiled through watery eyes. "Thank you so much."

"You're crying!" The big man's face crumpled, both hands clenched his hat. "I know you're sad that your rosary was broken. I couldn't find it all." He swayed, distraught, and stared at the floorboards.

"These are not unhappy tears, Manuel. I am overjoyed." She patted his arm lightly before recalling his aversion to touching.

She jerked her hand back. How could she forget? He went still. His eyes drifted to his cousin, then back to her.

"Oh." He examined the spot where her hand had been. "Drago said I must let healers touch." He released a long breath and looked at the captain.

Drago nodded his confirmation, and Manuel relaxed a little.

She admired the gift. Meticulously knotted beads and shells strung on a strong, silky twine. The crucifix glowed a soft white. No one had ever made something especially for her.

"Manuel, this is the best gift I have ever received."

"Ever?"

"Ever." She draped the rosary around her neck. "I shall carry it always."

His face broke into a wide smile. "I'm glad."

"Oy, Manuel!" Harvey shouted. "We needs ye aft, ye blighter!"

He dipped his head. "Good day, Sister Eva." He pulled his cap back on and, still grinning, ambled away.

She met the curious perusal of the captain, grateful for his foresight with his cousin. He inclined his head, then walked away. If she wasn't mistaken, his lips had tilted up in a slight smile.

Chapter Twenty-Two
MANUEL MAKES A CHOICE

New Orleans
December 1814

Drago's gut churned as he watched a small contingent of his men accompany Sister Beatrice to the convent. He'd kept his word to provide protection for the relics, even if it was in a very unscrupulous manner. No sailor would dare attempt to stop his captain.

The twins asked to introduc Ev to their Uncl Bernard, so she accompanied them, as well as Drago and the Guirauds to *La Maison de la Fortune* hotel and Gaming House Harve and Manuel were both stepping lively in anticipation of a good meal.

Much progress had been made to rebuil,d and the area where they gathered was lush and inviting. Tall, round columns braced the two-story entranceway. Plush chairs and settees upholstered in deep, rich colors and patterns rested against the walls.

Bernar Sauvage descended the leagan,y curved staircase. "What brings you to these golden shore,s you ornery son of a one-eyed goat?" he barked.

Ev held her breath, preparing for nclepat confrontation, but the humorous glint i Harvey' eyes, along with his toothy smirk, had her observing curiously.

The old sailor stepped forward, arm extended. "I expect to haul yer sorr ars outta Satan's hearth again, ye lice-ridden, three-legged sea dog."

Bernar snorted. "Don't bother. My arse is perfectly roasted for Lucifer. He likes tough, trail-hardened meat."

Two young, broad-shouldered menascwnded behind Mr. Sauvage. By the resemblance alone, one could tell they were his sons. They were all dressed in rich jewel-toned jackets and waist-coats with fawn trousers. Bernard's chuckle rolled through his chest, and he shook Harvey's hand.

Laughing, Harvey pumped his arm. "How fare ye, me friend?" He clapped each of the young men on the back. "Adrian, Victor, how be ye, lads? Read fe a lesson in brawling?"

Adria chuckled. "Absolutely not. You cheat. Come in, sup with us, and give us the goings on." He smiled at the children. "Hello, little cousins!" He opened his arms to the twins, who filled them immediately, all giggles and grins. "We didn't expect you back so soon. Did you outstay your welcome again?" At their sudden quiet, his eyes widened. "You did!" Although he lowered his brows, his eyes brimmed with laughter. "What did you do this time?"

Jacqueline darted a furtive glance a Drag before speaking. "Nothing destructive Adrian, we promise."

Victor' gaze flicked to him Drag crossed his arms and leaned a shoulder against one of the huge round pillars. The little heathens wouldn't dare lie with him listening.

"We only sneaked aboard Captain Gampo's ship—"

"*Again*? Victor' face blanked in surprise. He shook his head and groaned. "You're lucky you didn't get thrashed."

Well—the truth will come out, eventually.

Drago introduced the Guirauds, who inquired about a room.

Bernard signaled for a servant to settle them in and orderedthe couple a supper trad.

A panel on the side wall shuddere, before hinging inward. A tall, sinuous man stepped out, then turned to pull the door shut with a soft click. Smart family, building secret passages in the walls of their new establishment. His dark coffee hair pulled back into a queu.,Hhe was slightly taller than Drago, although not as broad.

"Tristan!"

Drago couldn't tell which twin shrieked, but it didn't matter. Both launched themselves into the arms of their brother. Sometimes Drago wondered why he tortured himself by maintaining a friendship with this group. Equal parts of camaraderie and longing always warred with each other in his heart when he was around them. Maybe his chance at having a family would come when he completed thislnstl mission.

He and Manuel were pressed into service aboard a pirate ship at fourteen, not much of a warm family atmosphere there.Dragoe glanced at Eva, and his heart clenched at the longing in her expression as she quietly observed the reunion. He wasn't the only one who desired the same.

Trista squeezed the two until they squeale, before releasing them. "Jules! You're as big as a horse." He cuffed Julian's ear, then lightly tugged Jacqueline's braid. "Hello there, Biscuit. I guess we should thank you for bothering to leave us a note outlining your summer sojourn, otherwise we'd have given you up for dead," he growled. "It was weeks before Captain Gamponetti's letter of explanation arrived." He lowered his brows. "I hesitate to ask what calamities you've caused."

She placed her palms on both her brother's cheeks and squeezed just enough to pucker his lips. "Well, I try so hard to be good and avoid trouble when I can Tristan, you know I do."

"Do I?" His expression remained stoic.

Jacquelin arched a brow and tilted her head. "Of course, you do!"

Drag fought to keep his smile masked. If the gambler believed any of that, he was a fool a hundred times over. The imp was a cheat, a liar and a thief. The first came from growing up above a gaming house with brothers and cousins running the business. So, it's entirely possible cheating was a family trait. The last two characteristics were courtesy of Drago and his crew. Additionally, if he had more time with her, she'd also be a better shot. At least she could clean, load and fire a gun.

Protect herself.

The little skirt displayed a confidence and vitality he grudgingly admired. Should he have a daughter one day, he'd want her to exhibit the same spirited character. Although, perhaps a slightly less devious one.

"Then why are you here? Trista said, suspicion building in his voice.

Jacquelin crossed her arms and lifted her chin in Drago's direction. "Would you believe Captain Gampowtetrptned to leave us behind in Jamaica?"

Little minx, always leaving out the fine details.

"Apparently he didn't," Tristan observed dryly, glancing a Drago. "Since you are definitely here."

"Obviously, Jacquelin sai,d as if they had just decided the world was round.

Trista quirked a brow at his little sister.

It was the Ev stepped from the shadows in a movement both smoky and fluid. Beauty and grace emanated from those exotic, azure eyes, which were smiling. "I'm afraid we didn't give th *capitain* a choice." She tossed him an amused grin, and the impulse to smile back was impossible to restrain.

Jacquelin beamed at the youn novitiat nun.

No, wait—not *yet* novitiate.

"Tristan, I'd like you to meet Siste Eva." Jacqueline grasped

Eva's hand and pulled her to her brother. "She healed me when I was ill. Siste Beatric traveled with us, too, but she's gone ahead to the convent." She prattled on, describing the sickness and Eva's treatment.

Part of him wanted to correct the introduction, but he refrained, something possessive forcing him to keep the secret to himself. Besides, being known as Siste Ev kept her safer.

Trista smiled and bowed, all languid charm and glowing confidence. "Sister, you have my lifelong gratitude. Welcome to th *La Maison de la Fortune* Trista Sauvage at your service, now and always."

She waved his words away as if they were undeserved. "Thank you, Mr Sauvage." She was uncannily at ease here, while earlier Beatric had shifted from foot to foot until he asked some of his men to accompany her home. She practically flew out the door *La Maison de la Fortun* was, after all, a gaming house, and one could only imagine the other games that might transpire within the walls besides gambling.

Yet Ev exhibited no such trepidations, as if the place were a familiar one. He narrowed his eyes, contemplating. A few years ago she was one of Hugo Dupre's runners; it was likely she'd been in theildr establishment before. Perhaps many times.

Bernar Sauvag ushered everyone to a large table where they enjoyed a friendly meal of rice, corn cakes and stew, along with a crisp claret. The conversation revolved around the twin's latest adventures and the newly renovated hotel.

Finally, Drago pushed away his empty plate. As delightful as it would be to continue such pleasantries, it was time to discuss more dire matters. He leaned his elbows on the table and addresse Bernard. "Earlier you asked the goings on Sauvage. They're about to become more serious. We've barely arrived before the British. I've been told they intend to invade the city and take command of the river." He described the flotilla which had amassed in Negril Bay and was now heading for the Louisiana territory.

Bernar sobered, his shaggy gray eyebrows sagged. "We've been expecting an attack for some time. The Brits came around a few months ago and tried to seduce our own Jean Lafitte. They wanted his knowledge of the bayous but he went t Claiborn instead."

Harve placed his goblet on the table with a decided thump. "Claiborne? Who be he?

"Our governor, Bernar replied. "And you know the ways of those that govern. They talk in circles when they possess no ohlaentr plan. The merchants are in a frenzy at the possibility of their businesses being sacked and razed." He tossed his napkin on his plate with disgust. "So, they'd rather hand it all to the Redcoats than see it burned. But, the President sen Jackso and his troops to defend the gulf coast. He well knows if the enemy takes control of the trade up and down the vast river, they'll take back the country, and we'll once again bear the yoke of the British crown."

Harve harrumphed. "An' what is that soggy, milk-sopped field mouse of a Governor plannin te do about it?"

Bernar straightened. "Jackson's gathering men and militias. I formed one with the other tradesmen. We intend to fight to the last man."

Fools. Even Eva' lips thinned. This bit of news could thwart Drago's plan to whisk away the family to the safety of his Jamaican home. Hlmus o be more persuasive with the Sauvage men. Drago reached for his wine. "A battle might well happen sooner rather than later. That hefty battalion of British soldiers is barely a day or two behind us."

Bernard's mouth tightened, but an unrestrained zeal flashed in his eyes. "Our hopes and loyalties lie with the command of Genera Jackson. He only arrived two days ago and has begun to talk about imposing martial law on the city. He's set a strict curfew as well as a call to arms for every able-bodied man. Our numbers grow every day."

"How many men?" Drago asked, already aware of the answer. If he could ge Bernar to come to an honest conclusion, it might be possible to persuade him to put everyone on the *Dragon* and depart New Orleans with haste.

"Nearly 4,000," Bernard said proudly.

Four thousand.

Eva's shoulders dropped, and she bent her head then gathered herself, obviously devastated by the lack of numbers. Drago's earlier calculations were alarmingly correct. He'd hoped he'd been wrong. There was no way such a small fighting force could fight off 15,000. The city would be overrun, sacked, and burned.

"Please, Uncl Bernard," Jacqueline broke in, her gray eyes wide and pleading. "Captain Gampo offered to take us back to Jamaica until the British leave. All of us."

Julian took his eyes from his plate long enough to pipe in. "To keep our family safe," he added.

Ah. There was a tactic he'd not considered. The twins were littl hellion of the first order, but they were smart little hellions, preying on the tender and sturdy bonds of blood which Bernard and the other Sauvage men treasured above all else.

It was a commitment easy to understand and respect.

The men exchanged looks, then shifted in their seats. A tightening of their shoulders indicated a disappointing lack of consent.

Harve cleared his throat, an amazingly polite way (fo Harvey) of directing the conversation toward him. He nodded toward Drago. "Captain ain't once steered us wrong. W ain' never gon te a battle w ain' won, b'acsez w ain' aroun fe those we couldn't." He stared hard at Bernard. "Best ye follow his lead, my friend."

If possible, the family patriarch straightened even more in his chair, jaw set. "This country fought for her freedom and will always strive to maintain it. America is not for the taking. We are a free republic. We plan to stay that way."

The loyalty and spirit were commendable and brave, but useless in this kind of battle. "You'll be ridiculously outnumbered," Drago said flatly. "Fifteen thousand against four?"

Tristan clenched his knife. "We've already offered our services to Jackson." He cut a last bite of meat, then stabbed it with his fork, his mind made up.

Adrian's expression was somber, but like his father and cousin, determined. "We are to meet with the general tomorrow to go over maneuvers and battle training. You should atten, and give your report, Captain Gampo. It might spark the additional patriotic fervor we need to recruit more men."

"Tristan," Jacqueline said softly, suddenly looking small in her seat. She swallowed, and her lower lip quivered. "You've never been a fighter."

He lifted his chin. "I am now."

"But... Tristan—"

He silenced her with a stern glare, although the way she fidgeted, it was unlikely she'd stay silent long. "Quiet, Biscuit."

Bernar shifted his attention back to Drago. "I know you're not an American, Captain Gamponetti, and this is not your fight. However, you and your *Dragon* would be a great help on the lakes protecting the city with the rest of the gunboats on Lak Pontchartrain."

Because the river offered a more strategic escape route, Drago chose the more arduous path, tacking back and forth up the Mississippi rather than enter from the East through Lake Bourne and Lake Pontchartrain. The lakes, while connected by channels to the Gulf, were too shallow.

In addition, Bernard was correct; this was not his war. Drago had a responsibility to see the relics safely away before the battle began. They'd have tohqrrly. Today. Tomorrow at the latest. He leaned back. "I won't speak for my crew, but I'm afraid I have other obligations, Mr. Sauvage. As you said, this is not my country's war."

Eva locked gazes with him, imploring him with her eyes to stay. She had such hope. Such confidence.

He sighed and propped his elbows on the table. "However, I'll assist in any way I can before I'm required to depart."

Where had *that* come from?

One second, he was convinced he'd not get involved, the next he was offering to help. He was going daft. Engaging in a war with fifteen thousand British troops would both endanger his men and his ship. He wasn't quite sure in which order he should list his priorities, but his life and the lives of his crew had always been in the top spot.

Well *above* an American battle.

Julian, however, had paled and stared at him in disbelief. Drago leveled a cool gaze at the lad. "No need to look so crestfallen, boy. As you have clearly stated in the past, I am a privateer which means I have a duty to my employer, the King of France, a final obligation I must see through to the last unless I lose affection for my head."

But when Eva's face fell, his chest constricted in pain.

Manuel paused with a corn cake halfway to his mouth. "I will fight, Drago." He gestured to Eva and the twins. "I wish to drive the British away and protect their home."

Drago scowled. "I cannot force you to remain with m,e Manuel, nor can I condone your decision. It is, however, yours to make. You may present your argument tomorrow, and I will give mine, then we shall decide together."

Manuel nodded, temporarily satisfied.

Tristan sent a meaningful look to Drago. "Take the children with you. Keep them out of harm's way."

"No!" Julian jumped to his feet, tipping his chair in the process. He clenched both fists at his sides. Bright spots of pink stood out high on his cheekbones. "I won't leave! I won't run like a coward. I want to stay. I want to *fight*!"

"Julian—" Trista began, eyes narrowing.

"We want to help," Jacquelin interrupted firmly. She gave her older brother a fierce glare that could scare a roaring lion silent. "You know we will find a way."

Tristan tensed. "Jacquelin Louisa Sauvage…"

Now those sounded like words that should mute a twelve-year-old. Yet they didn't. Not that he was surprised.

Jacqueline wisely shifted her stare to her uncle, while Tristan glowered. "Sister Ev will need assistance tending the wounded. If she will permit it, I'll assist her."

Hard to argue with the girl's logic. Whatever that little schemer had in mind, at least she'd be with Eva. The best way to watch the little sprite was to be tied to her. Eva's eyes caught his, a slight twitch of her brow had him returning a nearly imperceptive nod. They would be safer at the convent.

"I'd be grateful for their help," Eva said. "And they would be better protected," she added, leaving the rest unsaid.

More than they would be on a black-hearted privateer's ship.

"It's settled," Bernard said, reaching for his glass as the servants cleared the table. "They may assist Sister Eva at the hospital." He tossed the wine down. "Should the battle claim us, the children will remain at there." Bernard shifted his gaze to Drago.

Drago nodded in silent understanding, even as frustration coiled in his gut. "I shall return for them should you leave instructions that they be released into my care."

He'd failed to persuade the family to travel with him to safety. Failure was something he was unused to addressing.

Or experiencing.

He gave an order. It was obeyed.

That was the way things worked. How was it he suddenly had almost no power? He frowned. Actually, it appeared he had no power here at all. The children would stay at the conven until he came for them. The Sauvage family would not be accompanying him to Jamaica Manue had expressed a desire to fight, which, of course, he would not be permitted to do without him, and he was not staying to risk losing his ship to the British.

Drago had always been Manuel's keepe,r an Manue always had Drago's back. They grew up together. Manuel wouldn't react well to someone else shouting out commands. He'd look fo Drag to confirm, as he always did, then panic when Drago wasn't there. An, Go sav the poor wretch who made the mistake of pawing at him.

No, Manue would be aboard the *Dragon* when they sailed downriver.

However...

There was the matter of the sugarcane. He'd be cursed heart and liver if the bloody Redcoats used it for fascines. While he sure wasn't going to march across a field toward fifteen thousand armed and battle-trained soldiers to his death, he could certainly cause a satisfying amount of aggravation to the British by finding a way to sabotage thos fascines. The odds of success would be better with a small group of men who were both trustworthy and cunning.

And perhaps a little insane.

Chapter Twenty-Three

BETRAY AN ALLY

"How much further to zee cathedral?" Mr. Guiraud flipped up the collar of his coat.

"Only a short way," Eva said. Even in such horrible weather, this was home, and she was happy to see it. The first thing she would do when she got into the abbey would be to retrieve her long woolen cloak. She curled her hands under her tunic for warmth and released a relieved sigh.

True to his word, the captain had provided guards. They'd accompanied Sister Beatrice earlier, lifting the tremendous weight of worry. At least, as far as the relics were concerned.

The shadow of war approached, and now there were worse things creating concern.

"I did not expect eet to be so cold here!" Lady Guiraud drew a thick gray shawl closer around her shoulders. It didn't help matters that their carriage was missing a door, allowing the chilly December wind into the coach.

Drago curled his fingers deeper into his pockets. He claimed to prefer the chill to sweltering heat. Usually. "Mr. Sauvage said this has been the coldest winter in the past twenty years," he said.

"Then I should have brought a heavier cloak." Mrs. Guiraud

shivered. "I should like to light a candle for my dear *pére*." The petite brunette rummaged around in her reticule. "Will zee church accept francs? I have not yet traded for American currency."

Eva smiled. "All forms of tithe are accepted. There is a bank nearby, however."

"Excellent, we shall go after we visit zee cathedral."

"When do you depart for Cincinnati?" Eva asked.

Mr. Guiraud shot a glance at his wife, who ignored him. "We board zee first steamship once we have prayed over the sacred bones of St. Louis," she replied, with a fleeting smile. "I am very happy to soon see my sister."

They dropped Eva at the convent gate, then continued to the church. The sight of the Ursuline convent brought a comforting warmth that tugged at her heart. It was indeed wonderful to be back, even under such dreadful circumstances.

She was greeted by the sturdy and stoic Mother Marie Francois. The older woman tilted her head, her snappy hazel eyes traveled over Eva's face and roughly mended robe and tunic. "I did not expect your return until spring. Are you well?" There was warmth in the crinkles of her eyes alongside the concern. She reached for Eva, and she stepped into the circle of comforting arms.

"The Port Royal Abbey is well-tended." Eva savored the warm hug from her mentor and friend and couldn't keep from smiling. She broke the embrace and gripped the older woman's forearms. "Did Sister Beatrice tell you about the danger?"

The Mother Superior folded her hands. "If you are here to warn us of the impending invasion of the British, we are well aware. General Jackson is assembling an army to defend the city." She swept her arm, indicating the convent. "We are in the process of converting much of our space into a hospital." She smiled and patted Eva's shoulder. "I'm happy God brought you back to us. Your healing skills shall be most welcome, child."

Had Beatrice said *nothing* about the relics? Perhaps the older nun hadn't expressed the dire necessity of action and the danger facing the sacred bones. "There is another threat!" Eva gripped her arms tighter. "Three French agents of the crown have been assigned the task of stealing the holy relics from St. Louis Cathedral and taking them back to France. It's possible they will arrive with the British and use the battle as a diversion."

"Hmmm."

Hmmm? Their most precious and sacred artifacts were in jeopardy, and she said *hmmm?*

The elder nun linked arms with Eva, and they began to walk toward the church. "God will protect us and the sacred bones in the manner he sees fit. The greater danger is to the residents of New Orleans. We must focus on preparing hospital space in the convent to treat those wounded in battle. We need beds, blankets and supplies." Her usually erect stature drooped a little, and the pleasant crinkle in her eyes faded. "I fear there will be much bloodshed."

Drago's prediction rang in Eva's ears. *"It will be a bloodbath."*

If every single resident marched to the battlefield, those fifteen thousand redcoats would not even be *slowed*.

Mother Superior's attention seemed so committed to the upcoming confrontation with the British, she didn't completely comprehend the seriousness of the French plot. They should, at the very least, protect the relics. "Can we move the relics to a safer place until the battle is over?"

"It would be difficult, but not impossible." Mother Superior squeezed Eva's arm. "Tell me about your time in Jamaica," she said, smiling.

Eva swallowed her frustration and related her observations and experiences with the Jamaican people, their culture, and their landscape. If she'd been able to plan her return voyage suitably, she would have brought back some breadfruit. She also talked about Kalia and the old woman's strange healing practices and stranger intuitions. She told Mother Marie Francois about the captain, the twins, and how she ended up stowing away in the sail closet.

Eva faltered at the tale of Razin's attack and the punishment Drago dealt. Too many conflicting emotions were tied to *that* night. She wanted to keep them to herself. The freedom of lifting her bare face to the setting sun, the thrill of the race with the dolphins, the steely warmth of Drago's arms...

"You've become quite the adventuress! Tell me more about this captain," the Mother Superior whispered, excitement lacing her tone.

A strange tingle fluttered in Eva's chest. His kiss was forever burned into her memory. Gray eyes smoldering with interest, lips moving against hers. A twinge of guilt tried to elbow its way into her conscience, but she shoved it aside. Plenty of time for that later...like during confession.

"*Capitainé* Gamponetti brought us here from Jamaica. He's also the guardian for the twins, one of whom I treated when she was ill. He's a hard man, but I believe he has a good heart. He's a strong leader, and his men are loyal to him. I asked him to assist me in protecting the relics, and he gave me his word he would."

No need to relay every single detail of that oath. She suffered through the inner cringe at the image of the massive man tied to the bedposts.

Eva gave the abbess a sideways glance, but her expression was rather blank. How could she tell her that Drago Gamponetti was the most handsome man she'd ever seen? True, he had battle scars, but his face was as chiseled as a sculpture. Silver eyes rimmed in with the thinnest ring of midnight blue sparkled when he was amused, became thundercloud gray when angered. The iron bands of his arms gave her the softest shelter of comfort when he held her and stroked her hair. Her heart clenched with longing.

"He's a good man then?" Mother Marie Francois gave her a

soft smile. Her voice broke into the turbulent thoughts and images twirling and bouncing in Eva's head like beads on a drum.

Good? She pondered for a moment. "He has a tender heart for children, but wields a harsh sword of discipline. I think, deep in his heart, he desires to be a good man. He was a pirate, then a privateer for many years, and it seems that type of life prodded him in a direction he has come to despise."

What had he said?

I'm unredeemable.

She disagreed.

"In times of duress, he steps behind a brigand façade— part dark-hearted pirate, part loyal privateer of the French crown. But I have seen him show tenderness and devotion, too. Even love." The words hung in the air like a flock of gulls.

Where did *that* come from?

She tried to peek surreptitiously around her veil at the older nun's face. The Mother Superior's mouth was pressed together in a firm line, yet the corners curved up. "Do you care for him?" Marie Francois asked.

Of course, she cared for him. But certainly *not* in the way, the Mother Superior was insinuating. She shook her head, baffled. "He is a complicated man."

"That was not my question, child." The nun tilted her head to look at Eva, who avoided her gaze, uncertain how she felt. Or why.

It would do no good to delay her answer. With a resigned sigh, Eva nodded her head. "Yes, I care for him." That was true, she really could not deny it. "He took orphans under his protection and asked nothing in return. There is a distinct line he draws between following orders and breaking rules. He protected me from a man who tried to attack me. He allowed us to journey with him without requiring payment of any kind, even though it would have been within his rights to do so."

The abbess wove her fingers together. "Do you consider him a truly honorable man? Attacking enemy ships and stealing their cargo to deliver to the French King does not sound honorable to me."

"It is his obligation to his employer," Eva objected. "The letter of Marque granted to him from King Louis states he is to capture English vessels and bring them to France. In exchange, he and his crew are paid a set share of the value of the ship and her cargo. To not do his duty is to betray his sovereign." It sounded suspiciously like she was trying to defend the man, which she was not. She was simply reciting the facts as she knew them. "While I do not like the role of privateer he plays, he takes his duties quite seriously. Before I pressed upon him my urgencies to return to New Orleans, he had plans to join a fleet of merchant ships and become part of a trading company."

A slight stab of guilt needled through Eva's chest. She looked at her hands, unable to meet her mentor's gaze. "He wants to lead a more honest and honorable life." Somewhere far away, like Cartageña.

"Does he care for you as much as you do for him?"

Even as she shook her head, a trickle of uncertainty invaded her mind. She the recalled the captain's affections, his kisses. That didn't mean he *cared* for her. It just meant he desired to kiss her. The fact her heart gave a desperate lurch at the memory didn't imply anything.

A realization hit like a cold drop of water on hot skin. "You think I have fallen in love with him," she whispered.

Marie Francois stayed silent. And stared straight ahead.

She didn't love him. It would be terribly foolish of her if she did. He hovered on the fringes of a life she had spent the last nine years avoiding. She couldn't go back there. She *wouldn't*. "I said I cared about him, not that I loved him. I do believe those to be two quite different things."

Fine, she cared about him, but she didn't love him.

She *didn't*.

Mother Marie Francois expelled a great sigh. "Eva, I love you like I would a daughter, and I pray every day for your happiness. While I am glad you are here among us at the convent, I question whether you should stay."

No! The tears pricked the back of her eyes, and her throat hardened until she couldn't swallow. This was the one place that should never reject her. The only place she was safe and accepted.

Mother Superior paused and studied Eva. "Are you here out of obligation or fear? Are you serving or hiding? Here, you can hide from everyone except yourself and God. Search your heart, child." She grasped Eva's hands, squeezing them tightly. "If it tells you that it would be happy never seeing your captain again, if it assures you that you would be content with us more than him, if you don't wonder what it would be like hold his child in your arms, if the notion of creating a loving family does not bring you joy, then by all means, stay with us. Take your vows, and bind your heart and soul to God and His church." She stared at Eva with eyes swirled with shades of green and caramel and wisdom and love. "Be true to yourself. To lie to yourself is to lie to God."

Mother Superior's words stirred up a storm of emotions. Love, longing, obligation, failure, guilt, sadness, fear.

Questions drenched her mind like sheets of rain in a gale. What manner of person would she be if she abandoned the church for a man? What manner of person would she be if she chose to hide in a convent? If she stayed, would it sadden her to watch the opportunity to experience heartfelt love for a family—*her* family pass her by?

Tears burned the back of her nose; her voice came out rough and reedy. "Why are you saying these things to me?" To have worked so hard to become valuable to the nuns, only to be driven away by the few who accepted her cut sharply. Deeply. Painfully.

True, the captain accepted her. There were no horrified stares, no glances dripping with pity, no murmured words of disgust by his crew. It didn't mean he loved her.

With the exception of Mr. Razin, the crew had been courteous, even kind.

A memory surfaced from several years ago, of the small child who'd awakened from a fever only to scream in terror when he saw her face. She had been fourteen. She had to leave the room before his mother finally calmed him. She began wearing the veil after that.

The nun hummed a moment before speaking. "I should tell you, the captain came to see me earlier. He felt the need to explain why you returned with a torn tunic."

She started. He departed the ship and came directly here before joining them at *La Maison de la Fortune*. She'd assumed it was to place a guard near the relics. He'd told her it was his first priority.

Mother Marie Francois enveloped Eva's hand with hers. "He also felt the need to tell me he cared deeply about you and asked me to send word to him if at any point you changed your mind about joining our order." The nun gave a half snort, half smirk. "Then he had the gall to tell me he would do what he could to dissuade you, then ask me to pray for his success in the endeavor."

Eva's heart jolted in her chest. He cared about her? Drago would come back for her if she changed her mind! But—

Mother Superior reached up and gave her a little shake. "He *loves* you, Eva." She squeezed her shoulders before releasing them. "I believe that."

He *loves* her? He loves her. Could it be true? Would he tell her if he did?

Suddenly she needed to know.

Eva drew the veil away from her face and wrapped it around her neck while her stomach gave a panicked flip. "Then I would hear it truthfully face to face."

His beautifully sculpted, handsome face to her horrid, scarred, exposed one.

Mother Marie Francois pursed her lips and released a soft huff of breath, then nodded her understanding. Henré had also proclaimed his love until she removed the shade.

They had arrived at the cathedral.

"Lend me your arm, child," the abbess panted. "These steps never get any easier for my old knees."

They entered the narthex, attracting the attention of a cluster of sailors gathered immediately inside the front doors.

"Where is he?" Eva asked, ignoring the smug smile from Mother Superior.

"He be in the nave with them Frenchies," one of the men answered.

She slipped into the center of the church and looked about. Her heart was both light and jittery. Did he *really* care about her? Did he really want her with him? Did he really... *love* her?

The area was empty. Eva stopped in her tracks. Confused, she hurried toward the sanctuary alter; a cool breeze caressed her cheek. The back door always blew open unless the latch was correctly set. The normally serene air of the sanctum bristled with disquiet.

An uneasy tingling swept up her spine.

"He be in the nave with them Frenchies..."

Mr. and Mrs. Guiraud!

She glanced at the altar as she passed. The lid to the relic coffer was neatly aligned with the box, but there were fingerprints and smudges in the dust covering it.

The sacred bones!

Without checking, she knew they were gone. The blunt force of sickening dread thumped her like a punch to the stomach. How could she have been so naïve?

How could she have been so *stupid*?

Three French agents were ordered to steal the relics. The Guirauds were two. And Drago Gamponetti worked for the French King.

He made three.

The blood drained from her face so fast her cheeks clenched as if pricked by a thousand needles. She'd led them directly to their target. She couldn't have made it any easier for them than if she simply handed them the bones.

Captain Gampo used her as a diversion. He used her to complete his mission.

He'd used her.

Her heart jerked just before it plummeted, crashing in a painful convulsion. Her lungs clenched tightly, and she couldn't swallow past the vise clamped around her throat. She staggered against a wall, unable to fend off the sting of betrayal skittering under her skin, forming an aching web that spread through the center of her body. It cracked through her very bones. The tears burned like acid, and no matter how hard she tried to ignore them, they tore from her eyes anyway, leaving hot tracks all the way to her jaws. She choked out a hacking sob.

This wasn't how this was supposed to be. She'd allowed herself to *hope*.

Had she wanted to trust so badly that a man like Drago Gamponetti could be honorable? Apparently, that deep-rooted desire had blinded her. She tried to gain control of her breathing, but her lungs could scarcely open, and her heart kept slamming itself against her ribcage like a panicked bird.

He had *told* her who he was. His allegiances had been clearly identified. He was a French privateer.

But he was much more than that, wasn't he? Bitterness coated her tongue. She coughed out a laugh and clutched her arms around her stomach, then slid down the wall. She wanted to curl into her own misery and stupidity.

She'd been foolish. Stupid.

All these years, she'd protected herself from this. She made herself valuable to the order as an important cog in the wheel, one that would jolt everything into a frantic panic, like frightened sheep, without her. She became their best healer for a reason.

Yet, for just one moment, she had dared to hope.

More foolish, she.

Her heart slammed a thick black door on the next thought. The one involving a promise. An oath. A Bible.

A man with molten metal eyes.

A vow.

Because if she considered it too long, those tiny pieces of glass forming that protective netting around her heart would splinter, flinging shards of misery everywhere.

A chill wafted over her, and she turned her face toward it. The thieves had gone out the back door! Anger boiled in her chest, and she scrambled to her feet, then ran toward the rear of the cathedral. The door was still ajar. The Guirauds were to catch a ferry up to Cincinnati, but was that just another lie?

Think.

If that was just a story, where would they have to go to find transportation? Where would they run?

The ship. The river?

She stumbled to a stop, awareness draped over her like a royal mantle. *Was* that why Drago wouldn't commit to helping Bernard fight... because he had to get the relics and the Guirauds out of New Orleans?

And he had to do it before the British arrived and cut off every escape route.

That horrible feeling, the one that twisted pain filled with longing, along with unfulfilled promises and seedy betrayals threatened to envelop her. Shoving it aside, she dashed through the door, her brain tapping into the city map she'd memorized as a child. They would head down Toulouse Street toward the river, then north along Levee until they reached the commerce section.

Larger piers.

The *Dragon* was docked there.

She wanted to scream and rail and shred something with her bare hands. Her fingers, out of habit, snatched her veil and twisted it over her face as her feet flew down the street, hugging the buildings and avoiding the thick mud.

She recognized the surge of energy bolting through her body. She'd experienced it many times before, long ago, before she was old enough to know the frigid grip of real fear. When she was young and almost invisible, quiet as a cat.

Who was she now? The meek marred nun swathing her horribly scarred face so children wouldn't cry, and women wouldn't stare? Or the street rat so effortlessly slinking into the corners?

A movement, a shadow.

Two low booms shook the ground, and her steps faltered.

Were those artillery blasts?

It was impossible to tell if it came from Lake Borgne or Fort Charles, but they could mean only one thing.

The British had arrived, and they were attacking the American gunships on the lakes.

Her pulse hammered a desperate rhythm in her ears. This was wrong. She was needed at the convent to prepare to treat the wounded. Yet her heart, still aching and fragile, dragged her toward the river and the relics and the man who had made a promise.

Already people of New Orleans were running, some toward Lake Pontchartrain, others toward the Mississippi. Merchants were closing up their stores. Militia patrols and Jackson's soldiers trotted toward the square for orders. Groups of men pushed wagons and dragged carriages and crates to block the streets.

The *Dragon* was anchored and tied off near the docks. Everything happened on the river. Drago would attempt to return to France.

She clenched her jaw. She may have made it easy for them to steal the holy bones, but she wouldn't make it easy to keep them. She secured the ties of her cloak against the chilling bite of the

December air. Clutching her skirts in her fists, she sprinted until she caught sight of the three.

Lady Guiraud clutched her reticule to her chest. The men each had a hand on her elbow, hauling her along at a pace that almost had the woman trotting.

Eva hopped over ice-crusted puddles and kept close to the buildings, both for shelter and smoother footing, cutting through alleys. By the time she reached the dock, her lungs were burning, and her face was warm. She paused long enough to scan the area.

There! Just turning the corner across the street, the three hurried along toward the *Dragon*. If she crossed quickly enough, she could cause a small collision. She didn't have time to construct a plan or decide what she would say. Instinct took over, and she plowed into Lady Guiraud hard enough to knock the breath from the woman.

"*Mon Dieu!*"

"Oh, my!"

In that flash of a second, Eva slipped one hand into the reticule while grasping the woman's other arm to steady her. Her fingers latched on to a silk pouch lumpy enough to be carrying the bones of St. Louis. She twisted and stooped, pretending to lose her balance as she hid it under her tunic and tucked it behind her belt.

"Sister Eva?" Mr. Guiraud's expression stuttered with alarm, then surprise.

For all the world she prayed she was wrong, prayed the Guirauds acted alone, even though she knew better.

"What in the world—" Mr. Guiraud sputtered, helping his wife regain her balance.

She hardly heard the Frenchman speak. The moment her gaze met Drago's, she knew. The world slowed around her as if she was in a dream. His thundercloud eyes transitioned from surprise to horror to a cold, flat storm.

He realized she'd discovered his deception.

Her heart splintered, snuffing the last fragile flicker of hope she'd stupidly allowed to remain in case she was wrong. Her chest seemed to implode upon itself, and every hope of a life of love with Drago died, leaving nothing but a frigid, stark wasteland. Even Henré's repulsion had done less damage.

Everyone stood like statues. The caustic fingers of heartbreak clawed at her throat, her words coming out raspy and raw. "I wanted to bid you a safe journey to Cincinnati." Eva barely choked out the lie to Lady Guiraud. To Drago, she added, "Goodbye, *Capitainé* Gampo."

Unable to look at him another moment, she spun away just as a large hand wrapped around her elbow. She jerked away and ran, hoping his surprise would temporarily paralyze him. She needed a head start. He'd chase her; she couldn't risk getting caught.

Tears blurred her vision as she raced across the street, narrowly dodging a moving coach. Ignoring the angry shout from the driver, she ducked down an alley and pressed against a recessed doorway. As she hoped, the wagon blocked her from view long enough for Drago to lose sight of her. It would be easy to disappear into the throng of people in Market Square; he'd go there to look for her.

Surely by now, they'd have checked Lady Guiraud's reticule and noted the missing relics. It would have been smarter if she'd planned far enough ahead to have a hiding place in mind. The sanctuary coffer wouldn't do, of course, nor would her room at the convent. She could hide them in an empty tin in the convent's kitchen pantry. Perhaps she should avoid any place associated with the church altogether. Jacqueline would help her find a secure place at the hotel. No doubt there were dozens. She crossed to the next block, darted into another alleyway, and headed toward *La Maison de la Fortune*.

Lost in her thoughts, Eva cried out when her shoulder was gripped from behind. How had Drago caught up with her?

She stumbled and ended up face to face with a short, thick man.

His lip curled up in a humorless sneer. "I thought I recognized you."

Eva's heart jumped in her chest as she cast a horrified stare at the face of the one man she had hoped *never* to see again.

Chapter Twenty-Four
HIM DARK IS STRONG

Hugo Duprè's murky brown eyes flashed with recognition. He grabbed her chin and tilted her face up. "It *is* you. There'll be no more hiding at the nunnery for you, Eva Trudeau."

"Let me go." She couldn't keep her voice from shaking. Fear made it nearly impossible to gasp out the words.

He barked a harsh laugh. "Not this time. You got away from me once, but it won't happen again." He scrutinized her from toes to nose. "I can still find a use for you, especially now with the British at our doorstep."

Blood pounded in her ears. After her mother died, Hugo was all she had. She had no one and no place else to go. He took her in, fed her, taught her how to survive.

She was eight.

"I no longer work for you." She jerked her shoulder away, then stumbled back.

He shook his head and followed, stalking her. "Eva, Eva. You were my best courier and my best picker. Small, quick with your fingers and..." He pointed to his balding head. "Quick with your mind. No lock or pocket was safe from you. Come back to me. I need your skills." He gave her a humorless, oily smile.

She barked a bewildered laugh. He was insane if he thought she'd ever return to thieve for him again. "Why would I ever do that? I live a different life now."

"Do you?" He crossed his arms and smirked.

Guilt pricked her conscience for a fleeting moment, and she fingered the silk bag of bones hidden beneath her tunic. This was not the same. She was helping the church, not picking a fat purse from a French trader, or running messages to Lafitte's pirates.

"You'll have everything you wish, Eva." His eyes gleamed. "I own a house in town now. You'll never want for food or shelter ever again. I'll buy you gowns and send you to parties with the city's elite."

Expecting her to steal jewelry? She bit back a cold snicker. "You'll send me to parties for what purpose, Hugo?" She pulled the veil down, revealing her disfigurement. "A gruesome, freakish curiosity?"

Hugo's eyes widened slightly before he shrugged. "That was a regrettable accident. You should have told me what you did with the map." He moved closer, reeking of onions and ale.

Accident? She glared her hatred, re-wrapping her veil and securing her cloak into place. "I told you—I lost it."

"That's a lie." He gripped her wrist and wrung it, sending a sharp pain up her arm. "You figured out its value, didn't you? You hid it." He pulled her to him, his voice viciously soft. "I want it back."

"Here now, what is this?"

Eva stared in alarm over Hugo's shoulder at a small group of men armed with muskets and pistols, one of the local militia.

Before she could speak, Hugo whirled and shook his fist. "Caught her lifting my purse, I did."

Her jaw dropped. "That's not true!" It took three tugs, but she finally pulled her wrist free.

"You caught her doing what?" One of the men said in an incredulous voice.

"She's not a nun," Hugo growled. "This is a disguise." She cried out as he yanked the hood back and clasped the hair at the nape of her neck, revealing her maimed face. "Look at her. Does she appear to be a pious and kind sister to you?" He shook her again. "She has fooled you! I recognize her, this is Eva Trudeau. She's a pickpocket. Throw her in a jail cell and rid the city of her trickery."

The militia shifted their weapons, clearly uncomfortable.

She finally found her voice. "I'm from the Ursuline abbey. Take me to the convent, and Mother Superior will confirm it." Mother Marie Francios would always provide Eva sanctuary.

Hugo sneered. "You are not a real sister of the church."

Little fingers of deceit scraped up her spine. She couldn't actually dispute his claim. At least not absolutely. He pounced on her lack of rebuttal. "They always travel together and are never out this late." With a dark glare, Hugo pierced the man who'd spoken first. "I want her charged with thieving."

"You have no proof!" Eva hissed. Almost immediately she regretted her words. A light sparked in Hugo's eyes as he shook her arm hard enough to clatter her teeth together. She wrenched it away, and something jingled in her sleeve, then plopped to the ground. They all looked down.

There, in the mud between her feet, was a leather pouch. The militia leader's face hardened.

"Good evening!" The unmistakable voice of Drago Gamponetti intervened.

Eva groaned, not sure which was worse, Hugo's mischief or the rigid undertone in Drago's overly cheerful voice.

The captain stood a head above the others. The aura of confidence and authority he carried with him had them all taking a step back. Everyone except Hugo, whom he approached with a straight back and a cold smile. "I believe you dropped something. I saw it fall from your coat." He stooped down, picked up the small muddy sack, then shook it. "Light as it is, you'd probably loathe losing what little remains, eh?" He tossed it to Hugo, who scowled and snatched it from the air.

Hugo glanced at the other men, who now eyed him with various expressions of disgust and annoyance, then returned the captain's icy smile, although it looked more like a grimace.

"Thank you, sir, but as I was explaining to these here militia-men, this imposter—"

But Drago's attention was no longer on the short, bald man. "Sister Eva? Mother Marie Francois sent me to find you," he said. "She was worried when you didn't return from your errand."

The militia leader scowled at Hugo. "This city is about to go to war, and you're wasting our time with this foolishness."

Drago quirked a brow and leveled a chilly glare at the men. "Is everything at rights? Did any of these men affront you, Sister Eva?" He swept his coat back to reveal a gleaming saber strapped to his hip and a brace of pistols tucked behind his belt.

Flinty eyes narrowed at Hugo, who had the good sense to back away a few steps.

The leader of the group cast another annoyed glance at Dupré before facing Drago. "No sir; seems we've had a simple misunder-standing."

"Ah, then. We'll take our leave." He touched her elbow. "Shall we be off? It's near dusk and it's not safe to be out after curfew." Drago tipped his hat. "I'm certain these brave soldiers need to be on their way to the town center where General Jackson is preparing to address his troops."

Eyes turned to the leader, who threw his shoulders back and jerked his jaw toward the square. "Let's go." They turned and trotted down the street.

Hugo narrowed his eyes at her before he whispered in her ear. "Consider my offer, *mon cher*."

She managed a short, sardonic laugh. Resume her activities as a novitiate, or as a thief... or worse? She'd already started the slide back to her old ways today by picking a lady's reticule. She wasn't far from transitioning completely in either direction, depending on her true nature.

"To lie to yourself is to lie to God."

Had she been lying to herself these past few years? Perhaps it was as Hugo said. She was nothing but a street rat and a pick-pocket. The years with the Ursuline order had done nothing much to change that.

Drago lifted her hood back over her head. "The chill creeps in with the setting of the sun. Best to stay covered to keep out the wind."

That single act of tenderness would normally have warmed her heart, but she wouldn't be fooled in by his charm and charismatic flair this time. The sting of his betrayal slashed her soul as sharply as the sword at his side. That brief flare of courage from exposing her face dissipated like a drop of ink in the ocean. He just made it perfectly clear it was time again to cover up.

She was such a fool.

She allowed the captain to lead her away from Hugo Dupré and indisputable trouble. Staying hidden from him had been easy with the nuns. Would he harass the convent, now he knew for sure she was there?

As soon as they rounded the next corner she spun and attempted to flee, but Drago would have none of it.

Her outrage roiled, churning with the torment in her chest. "Let go of me, you Judas!"

He only pressed her closer to his side. "Stop this. You don't want to attract any more attention."

She glanced back in time to see Hugo duck into an alley. "Then take me home," she snapped.

He gripped her elbow tighter. "I'll do no such thing until you listen to what I have to say."

Listening to his explanation and believing it were two different things. "You could say nothing I would be foolish enough to consider. Not this time." Never again would she believe his assurances. Now, however, the more important thing was to secure the relics. Even if she could escape his grasp, he'd only chase her down. Raising an alarm to her predicament would only draw the wrong type of attention. Hugo was watching. Waiting for another opportunity.

It was convenient when Drago escorted her into the foyer at *La Maison de la Fortune*.

Bernard Savage greeted them. "Captain Gamponetti, the blue salon is at your disposal, as you requested." His smile faltered when his attention turned to her. "Hello again, Sister Eva. Is—"

Drago gave him a clipped nod. "Thank you, Mr. Sauvage. We shan't be too long."

Thankfully, the twins were nowhere to be seen. The captain's duplicity was painful enough on her. The children would be crushed. There was nothing he could say that would sway him back into her favor. The Guirauds stole the relics with his help; she had the proof tucked into her belt.

He opened the door and gestured for her to precede him. Two steps past the threshold, she paused.

The Guirauds sat at the captain's table.

Liars.

Thieves. The lot of them.

It was almost laughable, the company she now kept.

Drago pulled out a chair for her. "Sit, Eva. There are things we need to discuss."

Mrs. Guiraud slumped in her seat, her reticule discarded next to her. "The relics are missing from my bag, *Capitainé*." Her voice trembled with each word. "I don't know what happened. I initially hid them under my cloak, but I had to put them in my reticule blindly. Perhaps I dropped them by mistake."

Mr. Guiraud rested his elbows on the table, his head in his hands. "We are all dead," he whispered.

Eva's stomach plummeted. "Dead?" *How could losing a few bones be deadly?* "I don't understand."

Gamponetti let out a long breath and scrubbed his face with his hand before dropping into his seat. "The penalty for failing a mission of our King is death by guillotine—or his assassins, whichever is most convenient."

Lady Guiraud stared at the tablecloth in shock. "It is likely the butcher is already here. When we don't contact the courier, he will find and kill us."

"It will be Fontaine," her husband said. "He left a message earlier. *He* is the courier."

Drago muttered a low curse. "And, no doubt, the assassin."

Cold fingers of fear gripped Eva's throat, and a rolling roar tumbled in her head. It had seemed an easy enough task to disrupt the theft. It hadn't occurred to her there might be such dire consequences.

Was it worth three lives?

Was it worth God's wrath to let go precious relics? Eva fingered the pouch at her waist as she studied the hard angles of Drago Viteri Gamponetti's face. He regarded her with a cool set to his jaw, eyes sharp and piercing. Although he reclined in his chair, beneath his skin, muscles coiled.

It really wasn't much of a dilemma.

Even though he'd betrayed her.

She was wrong about one thing when she described him to Mother Marie Francois. Trusting him was a mistake. Hot fury and chilling heartbreak warred violently as she made her decision. Still, indignation bubbled to the surface, and the words were out before she could think. "Those relics belong to the St. Louis Cathedral."

Mr. Guiraud slapped his palm on the table, eyes sparking with righteous fervor. "They are the bones of St. Louis of France, therefore they belong to France. We were entrusted to deliver them to their rightful home, our grand cathedral."

Guiraud's words made her pause. "*Your* cathedral?" This changed things considerably.

Mr. Guiraud was slow to respond, his mind most likely on Fontaine. He nodded absently. "*Oui*, in Paris."

Why would God care which church housed the saint's relics? As long as they were treated with the reverence they deserved, it couldn't possibly be a sin to prevent their transport from one to another. Father Dubourg would not be happy, but certainly, he could acquire others for the sanctuary. She wouldn't be responsible for the deaths of the Guirauds and Drago, no matter how badly she wanted to hate him right now.

Eva withdrew the silk bag.

Lady Guiraud's eyes widened before cupping her hands to accept Eva's gift. She pressed the returned bones to her chest.

Guiraud stood dumbstruck, his mouth open. He found his voice first, although he still could only manage to sputter like an overheated teapot. "What... h-how... did you...?"

But there was a bright gleam in Drago's eyes.

Guiraud sat with a thump. His arms dangled at his sides as he stared at her. "You picked it from her bag." Guiraud's tone was laced with a note of wonder. "On the street, when you collided with us."

Eva nodded but could no longer make eye contact with them. It certainly wasn't something of which she was proud. Stealing was a pretty big sin. In fact, it was one of those major, ten-commandment-breaking sins, regardless of the reason.

Still, the jagged throb in her chest from Drago's duplicity and deceptions made her want to find a dark corner and curl into a ball. Her eyes welled with unshed tears while anger set her ribs on fire. She was naïve when she should have known better.

She'd spent years in the abbey, trying to follow a righteous path, learning how to be meek and pious. Humble and forgiving. Worthy of God's love. Where had it taken her?

Nowhere.

It just circled her back to the same place.

A world of deceit and greed and darkness.

Him dark is strong. It pull you into de doomed shadow wit' him.

It would *not*. She straightened her shoulders and leveled a flat stare at the Guiraud's. "I wanted to prevent the theft and sale of the relics for personal gain at the expense of the church." She pointed to the pouch in Lady Guiraud's hands. "As long as they remain in God's house, where they can be cherished, does it matter in which room it resides?"

"*Merci,* Sister Eva." Lady Guiraud smiled and gently replaced the relics in her bag.

Drago's voice rolled like an approaching storm. "We need to talk."

"No." She slashed through his words with her hand. Tears pooled in her eyes. She let anger's hot, red hammer drop. "You're a traitorous wretch, *Capitaine.* Your soul apparently is cursed to the devil, and I'll be too, before I pray for your redemption." She ignored the couple's shocked expressions and whirled toward the exit.

A nun would never say such a thing, but she wasn't a nun. Not yet, and probably not ever. Mother Superior said as much.

She didn't really belong.

In a flash, Drago bolted from his chair to block her path. The movement triggered an instinctive response. One palm contacted with his cheek followed quickly by the other on the opposite, taking everyone, including herself, by surprise.

For a beat of silence, everyone stilled.

Air, she needed *air*.

Eva surged toward the door, but Drago wrapped an iron arm around her waist and pulled her against him, grasping both her hands in his other before she could strike again. She shrieked her wrath into his hard, muscular chest. Tears streamed down her face, and she squeezed her eyes shut in a vain attempt to restrain the flow.

Blast this man!

She'd placed her faith in the wrong person. Looking back at

recent events, it was foolish of her to have done so in the first place.

She should have *known*.

The moment she was introduced to the French couple, she should have known. The only person upon whom she could truly place blame for her gullibility and stupidity was herself.

Mr. Guiraud coughed. "We shall gather our things and meet Fontaine," he muttered. A chair scraped the floor. The rustle of his wife's skirts followed.

Capitaine Gampo spoke over her head, his chest vibrating against hers. "You'll have to follow the contingency plan. The British amassed their armada on the far side of the Chancery Islands and are preparing to cross from Lake Borgne into Lake Pontchartrain to take the city."

Lady Guiraud gasped, and her husband muttered a curse.

Eva froze at the news, her tears forgotten. She had to get back! War was upon them, and the nuns would need her. Maybe she could yet persuade them to take her back into the fold.

As a true novitiate this time.

The door closed behind the couple with a soft click, as if the gentle treatment of the door latch would diffuse the tension between the captain and herself.

He finally released her; she jerked away from him and headed for the door.

He stepped in her path.

"Allow me to pass, *Capitaine* Gampo," she snapped, intentionally using his pirate name. It suited him best, anyway. "I must get to the convent." She shoved with all her might, but it was like pushing against a house.

Hs brows slammed down; his stormy eyes glared. "Not until you permit me to explain my position."

His gloomy countenance would not intimidate her this time.

"I already know your position, pirate!" She tried to dart past him, but he captured her around the waist again.

"Eva..." His voice held a barely restrained hint of warning.

She ground her teeth hard enough to make them ache. "Let. Me. Go."

In answer, Drago picked her up as if she was a sack of sugar. He exited a small door in the back of the room and ascended a short staircase. Too stunned to utter a word, let alone draw a breath with his solid muscular shoulder wedged into her belly, she thumped his back ribs with her fists. Her rage intensified along with the bruising ache in her knuckles from vainly beating against rigid rows of bone. They stepped into a room, and before she could scream, he dropped her on a bed, blanketed her body with his, then yanked her wrists above her head.

She squirmed and spat like a wet cat. Whatever this black-guard had in mind to do to her, it wouldn't be easy for him; she'd fight with every ounce of strength she possessed. Another benefit of fighting dogs for scraps when she was eight.

He released her, then moved to sit on the edge of the bed. Wary, she tried to move but found her gown twisted around her legs and her hands immobile.

He *didn't*.

She tugged against the restraints.

Dear Lord, he had.

A growing flow of panic seeped into her chest to churn with her rage.

Drago just smiled, the small dimple in his slap-reddened cheek offset by the dangerous silver glint in his eyes. "There's a saying referring to turnabouts as being fair play, but I rather like the concept of simple irony." He laughed softly. "Now then, shall we agree I am the one in control here?"

Unwilling to give him the satisfaction of attaining her reticence, she merely pressed her lips into a hard, thin line. Uttering the words "go to the devil" came to mind. It took a great deal of self-control to keep them in her mouth.

To say the irony vexed her was like saying the Mississippi

River was a tender little stream. Drago eased back, muscles shifting under his shirt. A hungry fire in his eyes flared as he raked his gaze down the length of her form, pausing at the sight of an exposed calf.

Anger and trepidation mixed with an uneasy sensation that resembled anticipation. She couldn't draw a breath. If only he wasn't so wicked. If only she could trust him.

He reached toward her, and she closed her eyes, both fearing and hoping he would touch her. The fabric of her gown brushed against her leg as he drew it down over her exposed calf. She turned her face to the wall, swallowing her disappointment.

Perhaps Mother Marie Francois misunderstood the captain's feelings toward her. He didn't act as if he desired her. In fact, since the encounter with Hugo, all he'd done was attempt to cover her.

And hide her distorted face and undesirable body from the world.

Drago's low, anguished whisper echoed through the room. "Eva, please let me explain."

His words were a beautiful poison. Although she took in a deep breath to put more force into her voice, it still came out hot and raspy like a dry wind over a sun-baked desert. "There's nothing you could possibly say with that sugar-coated, forked tongue of yours that will change my opinion of you... you black-hearted scoundrel." *Ugh*. That was weak. She drilled her attention to the lamp, determined to avoid looking at him.

He sighed. He only had to stroke her skin with a finger, and her entire spine tingled. There was a smoky resignation in his tone. "There are things you don't know. This was to be my last mission. I'm eternally grateful it ended on my terms, instead of at the hand of an assassin. Rather than risk your life or anyone else's."

Her life? She clenched her fists. "I've been so gullible! I want to scream." She transferred her focus back to him. She looked into those beautiful, gray eyes of Satan's son, the betrayer, the manipulator. "You have what you wanted. Now let me go and leave me alone."

The humiliation of being so easily deceived crept up her neck in a slow, spreading burn. Unable to move, unable to divert her eyes away from the mesmerizing quicksilver stare, she could only suffer helplessly on the bed.

"I hate you," she whispered. And she did. She hated everything about him.

She hated the way he made her stomach flip when he entered the room.

She hated that the intoxicating, sultry timbre of his voice that made her want to close her eyes and just listen like she would a song.

She hated his mouth for betraying her and leaving her with the memories of fiery kisses to torment her.

She hated—

Drago leaned forward and grazed his finger over the edge of the scar at her temple, and the world stilled. She was too stunned to even flinch.

No one had ever attempted to *touch* it.

He traced the terrible thing, a searing trail of shame and revulsion. Heat spread over her cheeks and chest until her skin caught fire. When his finger reached her mouth, he brushed his thumb over her lips before cradling her chin in his palm.

"Please," he rasped in a pained whisper. "Don't hate me, Eva." He touched her lip once more, causing a shiver to shoot down the back of her neck. "You must know by now that I care for you very much."

She shuddered as a powerful jolt rippled through her body. For a moment, she couldn't speak. It was as if a spell had stopped time, freezing the entire world, stilling her breath, her thoughts, and the wild throb of her pulse.

"What... did you just say?" How could he treat her so ruthlessly, then say something so cruel? Did he really think those words would lessen the raw scrape of his deception? Repair her tattered heart? Even in its mangled state, it skipped, and her mind continued to howl, *"Liar! Liar!"*

He said that to weaken her defenses. The sad thing was that she was desperate to believe it. She longed to dismiss what he'd done to her in exchange for something richer, deeper.

How pathetic.

How weak.

How utterly and absolutely stupid of her.

His eyes locked with hers. Twin orbs of steel and black. He had to be lying. He *had* to be. She stared at him. Were the eyes not the windows to the soul? The lie couldn't hide there; it would flake away and float to the surface. But there was nothing but an open contemplation. No shifting sands of a falsehood. No amusement, no jest, no murky swirl of deception.

Or was she only seeing what she desired to see?

He did not say he loved her, only that he cared for her.

Don't do it. Don't fall.

Be strong. Be brave.

Protect yourself.

A moment passed before she found her tongue. "I don't believe that for a single second." Great. She sounded like a little girl. Even *she* heard the hope in her voice. He caressed her cheek, and she felt it all the way to the arches of her feet.

"Eva." He braced his arms on either side of her shoulders and captured her gaze with his. Heavens, she couldn't look away now if the world's survival depended on it. She thought back to his kisses, and part of her wanted the satin pressure of his lips again. He was trying to seduce her with his worthless words and amber, honey-coated voice. She knew this. She knew this. She...

He kissed her, and she lost her next thought. His lips feathered against hers so lightly it sent every nerve sparking. His hands cupped her cheeks, thumb caressing the trail of her scar, and for once she didn't want to shy away. He was gentle, almost reverent.

A deep sadness settled in her chest. It would never be enough. She loved him. Yes. And she despised herself for it almost as much as she despised her horribly maimed face and his malicious pirate's heart.

A stony, pessimistic voice in the back of her mind still raised the question. What if there was something else he wanted, and he was simply manipulating her to assist him? He'd fooled her thoroughly before.

Her soul yearned to believe him.

The voice prodded for her to be wary.

Pride awoke and demanded she not let him fool her again.

He lifted his head and searched her face. For what? Confirmation she cared for him? That he bent her to his will again? He had her under his spell, there was no denying that.

But she couldn't stand the *pain*. Just being this close...

"Please," she struggled to whisper. "Don't ever touch me again."

The sharp flicker of hurt sliced across his eyes, wrenching her heart still more.

An urgent pounding on the door shattered the still air of the room.

"Captain! Come quick! There's trouble."

Chapter Twenty-Five

A VOW

"**D**evil take me," Drago hissed through his teeth. "You need to hear what I have to tell you."

It didn't matter what he wanted to say. Best for her heart to wall itself off from his effect on it.

From love.

From emotion.

From pain.

Eva writhed against her bonds. "There is nothing you could say that I would possibly believe. I. Don't. Trust. You."

He called himself a captain, but a captain is a *leader*. He's nothing more than a tyrant. A blackheart. A pirate. A thief. Betrayer. Judas. Repeat. Repeat. Repeat.

He cupped her jaw. "If I release you now, you must promise you'll listen to what I have to tell you when we have the opportunity again to converse privately."

The pessimistic voice interrupted her thoughts.

Don't fall for his tricks and lies.

"I don't have to promise anything." She dropped her brows and pursed her lips.

His eyes flashed like an approaching storm. "As you wish!" he snapped, launching his large body from the bed with the sinuous grace of a cat. A low rumble reverberated through the room. More rain. The streets would be impassable soon. If she was to make it back, she had to leave now. And *run*.

Was he leaving her here like this? "Wait!" It pricked what remained of her pride to agree to his terms, but she had no choice at the moment.

Arching an ebony brow, he glanced at her over his shoulder. She pressed her mouth into a hard, slim line before expelling a short, irate breath. "I'll do as you requested. Now, set me free."

His eyes narrowed. "How do I know you're not just saying that to get me to release you?"

She gave him a sardonic smirk. "My word is my vow," she said, mimicking his statement to her from weeks ago in the Jamaican abbey. "The same as yours." Why should she keep hers when he cared so little about keeping his promise? *Gah*! The tenacious grip she had on her new life just slipped further, thanks to him. Now, she was contemplating deception. First stealing. Now lying. She dared not ask what came next.

Drago paused as he reached for her bindings. He straightened, eyeing her warily. Dark brows slashed an inky line across his face.

She felt her eyes widen. "What are you doing?" she cried. "Untie me!" He wouldn't dare leave her like this, would he? "Drago, release me at once!"

Instead, he whirled and strode to a desk and rummaged around in the drawers until he found what he sought. She glanced at the object in his hands and wanted to thump him over the head with it. Repeatedly.

He smirked, a single dimple swirled on his right cheek. Was her face so easy to read? She groaned. There was definitely no other man on this earth more vexatious, more annoying, more exasperating or infuriating than Captain Drago Viteri Gamponetti, pirate, spy, blackguard... and whatever other derogatory terms existed that described him. *Thank you, pessimistic voice.*

He sat and placed a warm finger under her chin, tapped her mouth closed, then pressed a Bible against her right palm. His eyes glittered, sharp and bright with victory. "Will you swear an oath upon the Holy Bible that you will grant me an audience to speak with you when I request it?"

What choice was there? Another roll of thunder echoed through the streets.

That pessimistic voice piped up again. *You'll regret it.* "You are a rake to the core." And he knew it. It was apparent in the satisfied twist of his mouth. His very sensual mouth.

Stop. Not sure which voice that was, but it needed to be quiet.

He tilted his head a bit. "Your word, *mio cara*? I await your vow."

Part of her wanted to bite her tongue and refuse. *Thank you, pride.* But what would that accomplish? She'd stay locked in this room until he returned. Freed, she could head to the convent and help with the preparations. "You have my word," she muttered.

He flashed that devilish grin then kissed her forehead before reaching over and yanking on the knot securing the cord. The binding slithered to the floor. He was gone before she could even sit up.

Chapter Twenty-Six
A NEW PLAN

❧❦❧

E va ran down to the hotel foyer, where a group of militia stood gathered around a messenger. Harvey and Bernard were with them. Drago leaned against a wall, arms and ankles crossed, listening with keen interest. The set of his jaw and tension in his shoulders told her the news was not good.

"The British have attacked our gunships protecting the Rigolets and Chef Menteur Passes between the lakes," the man was saying.

Eva glanced out the front window. Large, fluffy grayish white clouds drifted in the sky. There was no storm outside; the thunder she detected earlier were guns.

Harvey spat. "The lakes be too shallow for them British warships to pass."

The messenger acknowledged Harvey's speculation with a nod before he continued. "They're using longboats with a gun, maybe a Demi-gun, and rowing right up to the hulls and putting holes into 'em. Ain't no gunboat can blow fifty rowboats outta the water fast enough. Some rowed close enough to fire. Then the wind dropped, so now our gunboats are like sleeping geese in a frozen pond." He exhaled, shaking his head. "It's only a matter of time before they take 'em."

As if to accentuate his words, a distant rumble of gunfire echoed again in the distance.

A sick wave of dread shot through Eva's chest.

Drago's face was grim. "The longboats can hold twenty to twenty-five men. That's nearly a thousand British soldiers against two hundred Americans spread out in five gunboats."

"Ain't got a chance," Harvey muttered.

The booms in the distance—from the guns of the American boats or the British, she couldn't tell—made her chest shudder. The people would fight. Many would die.

The upper two floors of the convent had already been converted into a hospital. She was a healer. She needed to get back.

Her gaze was once again drawn to Drago. What would he do now? His mission was complete, but rather than set sail toward a new life in Cartageña, he found himself trapped in New Orleans. How would he protect his precious ship?

A shrill whistle sliced through the crisp December air.

The men paused.

Bernard Sauvage waved the sound away. "It's a steamboat. She must be arriving from upriver."

Eva headed for the door. Before she could escape, Drago slipped up behind her and gripped her elbow, then clipped a command to Harvey, Manuel and a few of his men to fall in and accompany him. "Let's go."

She tried to snatch her arm away. "What are you doing? Where are we going?" Eva struggled to keep up with his long strides. "I *must* go back to the convent. I'll be needed there."

The muscles in the captain's jaw rippled, and his mouth was set in a firm line. "Perhaps eventually you will, but for now, I need you with me."

Why? To torment her with his presence? Use her again?

"Don't be ridiculous, What good am I to you now? You've completed your precious mission."

With a low growl, he stopped and gave her the full force of his attention; his granite gaze bore into hers.

Searching.

Searching for what? More gullibility? Stupidity? She straightened and stepped back, and a flash of hurt flared and disappeared from his gaze.

He sighed. "Eva, the Americans are outnumbered and outmatched. Without more men and ammunition, this city will fall within a day, if not sooner."

She rolled her eyes. "Why do you care?" She wouldn't be fooled by the concern in his voice and expression.

Nefarious pirate.

Spy.

Thief.

He had no conscience. He had no soul.

At that thought, hers ached even more. Why did she let herself fall in love with this man? She was so *stupid*. She grew up quick-minded. The past few years with the nuns had softened her head.

And apparently, her heart. Where was that voice of pride when she needed it?

She ran from the old life, confident that she could be a better person. A good woman. Trusting, patient, pious. But trust made her vulnerable. Patience made her too late.

And because she was pious and damaged, Razin attacked her. She glared at the broad chest of the chiseled man in front of her. *Glared* not stared. "You don't worry about anyone but yourself, why would the fall of the city concern you?"

He looked toward *La Maison de la Fortune* and tensed.

Manuel spoke from behind them. "The American people will always protect their freedom, Sister Eva. The Brits have no right to take it away. Right, Drago? Isn't that what you said? Uncle Bernard will fight. We will help them."

Did Drago say that? When? To whom? She didn't understand what was going on. He wouldn't flee without the twins, so what was he planning?

The *capitainé* tugged his hat lower on his brow and buttoned his coat against the chill.

"Drago?" Manuel's thick finger tapped his shoulder. "That's what you said."

Drago gave his cousin a clipped nod. "Yes, Manuel. That's what I said. The Americans will battle, but they can't win without additional men and supplies." He exchanged looks with Harvey.

He had a plan.

The old sailor snatched off his cap and scratched his head. "I know what ye be thinkin' Capt'n, but we dinna leave the man on the best of terms. Ye, sure ye want to poke a sleeping gator?"

Drago shrugged and flattened his mouth. "He's the only man who can supply this city the arms she needs to defend herself. Besides, I heard his brother is in jail."

Harvey jammed his hat back on his salty pate. "Well, that don't do no good fer us."

Drago's eyes sparked with secrets, and a small smile tugged the edges of his mouth. "On the contrary, it gives us a very lucrative advantage."

She almost asked whom they were talking about, but wasn't quite sure she wanted to know. Chances were, he referred to the Baratarian pirates who smuggled goods and stolen cargo up and down the Mississippi. If it was the Baratarian pirates, then he'd have to negotiate first with Jean Lafitte, their leader. She'd run across some of his men when delivering missives for Hugo. Not people she wanted to be around. *Ever again.*

That was all the information she needed. "I'm leaving," she said, turning toward the convent. "We stand on the precipice of a battle! The hospital needs me."

Drago pulled her closer, his voice low and urgent. "Eva, please, *I* need you now. I can't fully explain at the moment, but unless you help me, British forces will destroy this city. Jackson himself said if the people of New Orleans don't come together and fight, he'll turn his own cannons on her, rather than give her up."

She glared. "How can I possibly be that important to your cause?" It didn't make a bit of sense.

His men shuffled and milled around them, both uncomfortable to be privy to their conversation and wanting to listen at the same time. He completely trusted only two of them—Manuel and Harvey. She'd not get specifics from him here.

He closed his eyes for a brief second, then gave her the full focus of his thunderous gaze. "There is only one man capable of tipping the scales in the tiniest amount, and he's unlikely to support us unless he has a good reason. I plan to offer to deliver his brother to him in exchange for his cooperation."

Deliver his brother. Will she soon add kidnapping to her list of vices? "Again, what has that to do with me?"

The corner of his mouth curled slightly. "I need you to assist me in breaking Pierre Lafitte out of jail."

What?

Drago raked his gaze up and down her ragged tunic. "We must stop at the convent to pick up a few things, including Sister Beatrice and a Bible, but first we must go into the bayou."

Chapter Twenty-Seven
INTO THE BAYOU

They stood shoulder to shoulder with a mass of people fleeing the city. After Drago bribed the steamboat captain for passage, they boarded the *Enterprise*. It docked briefly to off-load supplies to General Jackson on her way down to Fort St. Philip.

Eva leaned against the rail. She rode on a steamship once, when she departed New Orleans for Jamaica. The murky water hastened toward the sea. Large flocks of various water birds lazed on the long masses of mud running along the banks, broken on occasion by enormous bulrushes. Islands of floating debris flowed beside the boat. Passengers, eerily quiet, spoke only in hushed tones, pausing with each low boom of a cannon.

It made no sense to go south, not with the British amassing off the coast.

Two merchants exchanged murmured words as they leaned against the railing.

"It would be better for the city if we just let them take it."

"Jackson is determined to defend it."

"If we fight, they'll storm the town and burn it to the ground!

I say it's best to suffer them to come in and occupy it. After a while, things will go back to normal."

"There'll be no *occupying*, Smitty. Looting, that's what they'll do. Loot and burn. There'll be no more normal, no more freedom. We'll be servants to the crown. Again."

Hopefully, Drago's plan to persuade Lafitte to aid the Americans would work. She still wasn't convinced Drago truly needed her with him.

Her mind replayed his words. *I care about you very much.*

Her breath hitched; *that* was the catch.

The trick.

The deception.

That pessimistic voice saved her again. *To what depth did his affection actually go? Perhaps it was as shallow as his word.*

She adjusted her hood and stole a glance at his profile, taking an inventory of his weapons: inky long-lashes, straight nose, a lightly stubbled strong jaw, thick curly waves of ebony hair secured with a leather tie then covered with a tricorn hat, absurdly handsome, tall, hard-ridged, smooth-tongued, sharp-witted, in command and in control at all times, commanding men who followed blindly and faithfully. They trusted him.

Easy enough to do until betrayed.

She cared about him, too, probably more than he did for her. To him, she was a mark, a tool he needed now. She had little value beyond that, right? It all made more sense now. He valued her, yes.

But he didn't love her.

Oddly enough, the pain of that realization was slightly offset by the solace of his presence nearby, which was both agonizing and reassuring.

They departed the steamboat at the mouth of the Baratarian River. A shanty squatted on the bank, its roof a patchwork of palmetto leaves and cypress branches. A rowboat tied to a piling bobbed over the wake from the steamboat's passing. After a few minutes of negotiating with the two free black men living there, they all climbed into the craft and, racing nightfall, began the cloudy journey toward Barataria Bay.

⊗⊰⊗

"HOW MUCH LONGER?" Manuel asked.

"Not much."

"Hungry," the big man said. He took a turn with the oar, which kept him from fidgeting. "Will Captain Lafitte have supper?"

Harvey snorted. "If we live long enough to sit at the table, mayhap."

Again, the mention of the possibility of animosity between Drago and Lafitte. "Why are you worried about *Capitainé* Lafitte?" Eva studied Harvey.

The old pirate pressed his lips together, and for a moment she thought he'd decided to ignore the question. "Ain't only two things what can turn two brothers of the sea against each other," he muttered. "Greed and women."

Such a curmudgeon. Eva almost smiled. She was becoming accustomed to the old tar's caustic air. "Which of the two was it then?" Not sure she wanted to know about another woman.

He snorted. "A greedy woman."

She glanced from Harvey to Drago, who scowled at the old pirate.

Harvey clamped his mouth shut and pulled his pipe from his coat pocket, grumbling beneath his breath.

The trip was mostly quiet, except when the boatmen chanted their songs to regulate and beguile their strokes on the river. Their sweet, rich and harmonious voices lulled the rest of them into silence. The men kept busy by watching for hazards. Keen eyes swept the bayou for sunken stumps or sudden shallows. Occasionally, an alligator luxuriated in the slime or hung in the water submerged except for the eyes and nostrils... waiting. Cypress trees dripped their veils of Spanish moss into the water, flanked by palmettos and Paw Paws.

Occasional huts and small houses popped up along the bayou. Some appeared abandoned, but others appeared quite occupied with smoke rising from the chimney or a freshly skinned alligator carcass hanging from a thick cypress limb.

As peaceful as it was, something made the skin on the back of her neck tingle, as if more than just the alligators followed their movements.

"I gots witchy eyes on me neck," Harvey groused, peering up into the dense canopy of trees. "They be watchin'."

Chapter Twenty-Eight

A LAFITTE ALLIANCE

Barataria Bayou

A loud splash shattered the peace of the bayou. Eva clutched the side of the boat, and the *capitainé* gave her a sideways glance. "It's probably just an alligator."

Harvey was studying the cypress grove. "That weren't no hungry gator. It were a signal."

They rounded a crook in the waterway, and she gasped. In the trees, on flat rafts and dead stumps, clustered dozens of men. Probably close to a hundred. And all armed.

By habit, she draped the veil across her face and around her shoulders. Harvey's pointed Adam's apple bobbed up and down in jerky movements under the gray stubbled skin of his neck. The two black men had ceased their song and retired to squat on the floor of the boat, allowing Manuel and Drago's men to work the oars.

"You tol' us you could pass through safe," one of them said. "If you has any magic words, now's the time to spit 'em out."

Drago's posture projected nonchalant composure, always the leader. He scanned the group of men with an almost bored countenance. "We're here to speak with Monsieur Lafitte," he stated. Although he didn't raise his voice, it carried as if he shouted from a treetop.

The reply came in French. *"He'll ask who desires to grace him with their presence."*

Drago responded in English. "Tell him Gampo requests a word."

A derisive snort followed. *"Gampo does not have the bollocks to return to Barataria."*

The captain tipped his hat back a little and shot an amused glance at Eva. She frowned her bewilderment back. He responded in perfect French. *"Gampo does since both bollocks are still securely attached."*

"This way, then."

The house seemed to float on the water. Harvey informed her it wasn't as magnificent as the one on Grande Terre. Parts of it were still under construction. The main dwelling was completed; a single story with a tall lookout on top. The wings were still bare bones. A narrow wooden walkway circled the structure.

The boatmen tied up the vessel, and everyone piled out. Eva ducked behind the wall of muscle that was Manuel and Drago and did her best to become invisible. A voice finally broke the silence.

"It's not much yet, I know. After watching Grande Terre burn to zee ground, my heart hasn't been in zee design of this one like it should have been." The rich French baritone of Jean Lafitte made the hair shoot up on Eva's forearms. He was eloquent, intelligent and brutal. If one held that in the forefront of their mind, one tended to live longer.

Ah. The pessimistic voice was awake.

Lafitte was shrugging into a dark navy coat as he emerged from the house. Tan breeches and black boots gave him the countenance of a military man. Commanding. Hard.

His coloring was like Drago's, but that was where similarities ended. Where Drago was broad and packed with muscle, Lafitte was lithe and smaller in stature, yet the same powerful aura surrounded him.

"So, Drago, did you come to make good on your threat to gut me, and feed me to zee alligators?" Lafitte sauntered closer. The men surrounding them adjusted their weapons, eyes following every move.

Drago's cheek rippled as he clenched his teeth. To keep from saying something he'd regret, most likely. Finally, he offered his hand to greet their host. "Jean Lafitte. It's been an age."

"Long enough to heal old wounds?" Lafitte shook the captain's hand, brow raised.

Lafitte's expression was languid, but his eyes were sharp and wary. Drago straightened, muscles coiled and taut. "That is not why I am here, *Capitaine* Lafitte." His dialect shifted smoothly into French Creole.

Lafitte spoke conspiratorially. "I'd say I got the worse end of zee deal, my friend. I had no idea such beauty disguised so much... petulance."

Drago's only response was a slight widening of his nostrils. "I do not wish to enter into a discussion about her, Jean. There are matters of greater concern that darken our future."

Lafitte's edges relaxed ever so slightly. "Then let's leave zee chill and retire indoors." He clapped the old pirate on the shoulder. "Harvey! You're still alive! Devil's been preoccupied of late, I see."

Harvey managed a gap-toothed grin, although it looked more like a snarl. "Me place is well-reserved in the fires, Capt'n Lafitte. I ain't in no hurry just yet ter fuel 'em."

Lafitte chuckled and stopped before Eva. "Who's this willowy thing?"

Before Drago could introduce her, Lafitte reached over and moved her veil aside with a finger. Drago flattened his lips, a hard flinty sheen flared in his eyes. Lafitte's eyes widened. "Eva? *Le Petite Renard?*" A ripple of surprise flickered across his features.

Nearly ten years spent in the service of the nuns with an intense desire to leave the old life behind mattered not. Granted, she already teetered on the precipice between light and dark after lifting the relics, contemplating various other sins, but *Capitainé* Lafitte tipped her in with one phrase... *Le Petite Renard, the Little Fox*.

Harvey's shaggy gray brows slammed down. "Le Petite what?"

Lafitte laughed abruptly. "Eva Trudeau, is zat you... disguised as a *nun*?" He grinned. "It is!"

Drago's face blanked in shock for a half second before his gaze tuned suspicious. "You know her?"

Jean waved his hand and smiled. *"Oui."* He peered closer at her scar. "Hugo's idiotic outburst healed well. Stupid man. He drinks in excess too often. His greed will bring about his end." His eyes hardened. "I no longer engage his services. Unreliable. No loyalty." His voice was lethally calm, and the chill had Eva suppressing a shiver. Lafitte released the veil and patted her shoulder. "Zee Ursuline nuns are talented healers. I heard you'd disappeared after zat incident." He paused. The only tell of his thoughts was the tiniest flare in his eyes. "Are you here on business for Hugo, or—"

"No," She responded quickly. "I no longer work for Hugo. I only recently returned from Jamaica. The Ursuline nuns sent me to help with the abbey there. *Capitainé* Gamponetti gave me a return berth on his ship."

Lafitte's keen gaze moved from her toes to her head. "You wear zee robes of a novitiate, so you did not yet take your vows," he observed, his tone both casual and penetrating.

She focused on the thick, gray bayou water. He called her the little fox, but it was he who was cunning and intuitive beyond measure. Lafitte and Kalia could take over the world. "That's correct." She would say no more. Both questions and answers would be too painful.

Will you take your vows soon?

No, I am no longer a novitiate.

Why is that, mon cher?

Because Mother Marie Francois discovered I fell in love with Drago Gamponetti, and she released me.

Are congratulations in order, then?

No. I'm nothing more than a pawn he sacrificed to get his prize.

A gullible little lamb, were you?

Yes. Gullible and foolish.

Pirates never change, after all.

I should have kept that fact in mind.

Lafitte's quizzical regard lingered a moment before moving on to Manuel, either losing interest or acknowledging her stubborn silence would just continue. "Good to see you again, Manuel." He started to clap the big man on the shoulder, then stopped himself. "You're still bigger than a brigantine. Hungry?"

At Manuel's enthusiastic nod, Lafitte headed toward the house. "Come, join me for *un repas*."

Once inside, he gestured for them to precede him into a large dining room. "Drago, we've missed your wily strategies upon zee water."

Lafitte moved to the head of the table; Drago sat at the pirate's left. A big, broad-shouldered tar with an explosion of curly red hair dropped into a chair on Lafitte's right, before withdrawing a pistol from his belt and putting it beside his plate, his meaning quite clear.

Lafitte sat. "Dare I hope you've come back to join us?"

Manuel prodded Eva into a chair then sat next to her, his cousin to his right. Harvey shuffled over to a seat on the other side of the table from his captain and slowly sank into it, his right hand at his waist, near his pistol.

Drago shook his head and pinned Lafitte with a flinty stare. "An infestation moves toward New Orleans. I came to discuss strategy."

Lafitte unfolded his napkin and put it on his lap. "You talk of zee British swine about to attack zee city."

At Drago's curt nod, Lafitte exhaled a beleaguered sigh. "They've already requested my services."

They were too late.

But Drago nodded in understanding. "They wanted a guide. A strategist."

Harvey grabbed his fork and gripped it in anticipation of putting it to good use.

"*Oui*." Lafitte reached for a decanter. "I was offered zee rank of Post Captain in zee Navy, as well as zee command of a frigate, plus thirty-thousand dollars and a pardon for all past offenses." He poured a liberal splash of rum into his glass.

Harvey had dropped his fork at the mention of thirty-thousand dollars.

"Most men would find it difficult to refuse such a fortune," Drago mused.

Lafitte snorted. "Payable in Pensacola or New Orleans. But I ask, how? When?" He sat forward. "Am I like most men? No. Why would I serve his Britannic Majesty? Did they forget who taught Napoleon's commanders how to use a sword?" He gained momentum and like a round stone rolling down a steep hill, and continued. "I will never trust them." He filled another glass before passing it to Drago. "I'm a pirate, yes, but I possess high principles, my friend."

Drago smirked and took a sip. "Of course you do. You're a Baratarian, not a barbarian."

Lafitte threw back his head and laughed heartily. "*Oui, Capitainé* Gamponetti, *oui!*"

He nudged the decanter toward Harvey, who needed no further urging. Lafitte continued. "Napoleon's war is at its end, so I am now supposed to be a friend of Britain? I think not."

"Did you learn their plans?" Drago asked.

Lafitte shrugged, then rested his elbows on the table, steepling his fingers. "Apparently, I was of zee greatest worth in carrying on operations they had planned against Lower Louisiana. As soon as they claimed possession of the state, the army would penetrate the upper country and merge with forces in Canada, where, I was told, they were prepared to carry on war against zee American government most efficiently."

Lafitte tossed down his drink and refilled his glass. "Instead of agreeing to their terms, I dispatched a letter to Mr. Blanque of zee Louisiana House of Representatives and Governor Claiborne, recapitulating zee offers of the enemy, so those two gentlemen could have zee opportunity to conclude, on their own, zee importance of the hold I occupy, as well as my desire for my men to enlist in zee American cause." Lafitte tilted his glass so the glow of the candles illuminated the amber color of the rum. He studied it, observing the character of the liquid. "In exchange for full pardons, of course."

A slight bit of tension seemed to lift from Drago's frame. "Did they accept your proposal?"

Lafitte sighed and refilled Drago's glass. "I fought zee British. I've been attacked by zee United States, who caused a conflagration upon my island home then stole a dozen of my ships. Both attempted to either destroy me or turn me. Despite all this, *mon ami*, I tell you now, I will depart this country for zee other side of zee world before I side with zee redcoats." He snarled, raising his glass. "*Vive l'Amérique!*"

"*Vive l'Amérique!*" his men and Manuel repeated, raising their glasses and draining them.

Lafitte settled in his chair and smiled smugly. "I am a patriot, a *combattant*."

"You are a hater of the British," Drago replied dryly.

"*Oui*, that too." Lafitte smirked. "Nothing fuels zee flames of discontent more than zee ignorance of zee entitled, no?"

Before Drago could answer, the door on the opposite end of the room opened and several servants entered bearing trays of food, pitchers of ale, corn fritters and fried fish, and a large bowl of steamed shellfish which they perched prominently in the center of the table.

The *Dragon's* men dug in with gusto. Manuel put his face near Eva's ear and whispered, "Drago and Jean were partners once. Friends, too. Until Jean took Camille." He filled his mouth with a piece of fish.

"Camille? Who's Camille?" she whispered back. A woman? A ship? Why did she care?

Manuel swallowed and reached for his ale. "She was Drago's betrothed." He washed the fish down and wiped his mouth with the back of his big hand. "It made Drago really angry, so we set sail for France."

A woman. His love. Something lurking in her chest that felt a lot like jealousy kicked and churned. Eva processed the information while Manuel piled corn fritters on his plate before plopping some on hers. No wonder Harvey had been nervous to come here. Greed and women.

Capitainé Gampo conversed easily enough with Lafitte, but there was still rigidity in the captain's spine and jaw, a shady wave of unrest. His face was stoic, the lines hard.

And although Jean Lafitte laughed and joked, the humor never quite reached his eyes.

Former friends.

Now, reluctant allies.

It was obvious—Drago didn't want to be here, but he was here just the same. Why? Had he been backed into a corner? His ship was shackled by the mighty river on one side and the Royal Navy on the other. How would his smooth tongue talk its way home from here?

"So, Drago. Tell me why you are truly here." Lafitte sipped his wine. The air crackled with tension.

Lafitte's second picked up his pistol and examined it nonchalantly. Eva's mouth went dry, and it was hard to hear with the sound of her heart slamming against her ribs. Drago reclined in his chair but remained tightly strung, like a panther in a crouch. He barked a curt command. "Put the gun down, McLeod. You know bloody well, if your *capitaine* believed us a threat, he would have disarmed us before letting us depart the skiffs."

The air in the room shifted.

Lafitte's mouth twitched, and he gestured for McLeod to put away his weapon. Drago planted both forearms on the table and brought his fingertips together. "We can't wait for a response to your demands, *Capitaine* Lafitte. Jackson needs men and ammunition now if he's going to have any chance of engaging the enemy in any capacity. The city is in a panic."

Lafitte snorted. "You speak as if zee redcoats already won. Did not 'Old Hickory' bring his army?"

Drago shrugged. "He did, but they are outnumbered. The British brought over fifteen thousand men."

A lungful of air whooshed from Lafitte's mouth. For a moment, he stared at his glass, then at Drago. "I'd say it was hopeless if zee battle were any place other than here."

Drago lifted his brows.

Lafitte placed his palms on the table. "Think, Drago! We have bayous and cypress swamps. They need boats that are shallow on the draft and a good number of them at that, to ferry troops close enough to deliver an attack. Jackson only has to block zee passes on Lake Pontchartrain and zee canals leading into the city to force the redcoats to trudge thirty or forty miles through zee swamp." Lafitte's eyes brightened. "Zee Choctaw and Attakapas Indians, traders and trappers are expert marksmen. Sharpshooters who could easily take out zee regiment commanders." He pounded his fist on the table. "Cut off zee snake's head, and zee body can only writhe onto itself!"

"A sound plan with the right tools." Drago stared at Lafitte intently.

Lafitte pulled a blade from his belt and used it to trim a nail. "I might be willing to provide necessary items in exchange for immunity from American persecution for me and my men." He looked up. "Including my brother."

Ah. So that's why Drago wanted her to help him. He anticipated Lafitte's terms. Very smart.

Drago leaned back in his chair and crossed his arms. "Jackson can't order the release of Pierre. He's sentenced to hang."

Lafitte's eyes turned stony. "Still, those are my stipulations."

Drago took a casual sip from his tankard. "If you commit your men to the cause and bring guns and ammunition, I'll have Pierre out of jail before sunset tomorrow."

Jean's eyes sharpened, and he studied the brooding privateer in silence for several ticks of the clock before nodding. "By zee tip of my saber, I hold you to your word. Fail and you shall not see zee next sunset."

Drago inclined his head in agreement He caught her gaze over the rim and winked.

Winked.

He acted as if removing Pierre Lafitte from his cell was no more difficult than taking a stroll through the city square.

What was he thinking?

Eva's jaw unhinged. The jail was well-fortified and manned, its cells made of the heaviest iron cages.

The captain had just promised the impossible.

Chapter Twenty-Nine

THE LIGHT BREAKS

The woman Drago once thought he loved enough to marry sat a few feet away. He'd lost her the moment he introduced her to Lafitte. Her beauty was breathtaking, to be sure. Camille, a black swan, graceful and elegant, but brutally selfish and greedy. Jean Lafitte's charisma, charm and immense fortune had made him a valuable catch.

Usually, that memory generated a hot, familiar twinge of jealousy, regret, and betrayal.

Strangely, this time it did not.

Eva drew his rapt attention. Head bent, she tore off a tiny bite of fritter and raised it beneath the veil to her mouth. Scarred on the inside as much as the outside, she was strong but kind, trusting but intuitive, brave and selfless. His admiration for the woman had grown over the days and weeks since he brought the little skirt to the abbey. He fought to quell the uncomfortable churning in his gut.

He'd taken advantage of her.

Used her.

It was regrettable but necessary. He longed for the chance to explain, apologize and kiss her until they were both breathless.

Would she give him the opportunity? Could she forgive him? Would she ever trust him again?

She had an uncanny intuition, or perhaps it was a connection between them that he felt. As if she sensed his perusal, she tilted her head and returned his stare. For a brief second, her deep blue eyes welled with sadness and defeat, causing a slash of pain to rip through his heart. As quickly as it swept across her face, it dissipated. In its place was a mask of insouciance. Subconsciously, she adjusted her veil to drape over most of her face again.

If they were anywhere else, he would have ripped the cursed thing off and tossed it into the bayou. He'd tell her she didn't need to hide. He'd protect her and cherish her without it. He'd tell her she was beautiful. He'd tell her... Drago's heart constricted with an imploding spasm, pushing air from his lungs.

God save him, he'd fallen in love with her.

Chapter Thirty

DARK ALWAYS A SEDUCTRESS

New Orleans

Drago was too tall for the priest's robes, which was perhaps a good thing while traveling the muddy streets of the city. Eva, though, had both fists filled with fabric as she struggled to prevent her hem from dragging through the slime.

This was a ridiculous plan.

They paused at the door to the jail; Drago quirked an inky eyebrow at her, gray eyes focused and alert, although they softened slightly as she tucked a stray wisp of hair into her wimple. "Ready?"

She expelled a breath and nodded, dropping her chin piously. It was time to fulfill their end of the bargain. Drago hunched his shoulders, somehow managing to appear twenty years older, and proceeded through the doorway.

A spindly, young man slowly rose to his feet and spat a long stream of tobacco juice on the floor as they stopped at his station. Another lounged in the corner, half asleep.

"May I help you, Father?" the guard asked.

"*Sí.*" Drago nodded vigorously before turning to her.

"He is still learning English," she said softly. "I am his translator. Father Giuseppe has arrived to hear confessions from the wretched, so that when their days are done, they may enter the gates of heaven with a clean conscience." She shifted her satchel to the opposite shoulder. "It is especially important for them to repent now, since the British have brought war to the city, and Jackson will call all able men to fight."

The young man withdrew a key ring from his coat pocket. "This way," he mumbled.

Eva made to follow, but trod upon her dragging hem and stumbled forward with a small cry. The deputy whirled and caught her by the waist and righted her.

Drago snapped his brows down in a dark scowl, and the man removed his hands as if they'd been scalded.

"Oh!" She exclaimed breathlessly, still gripping the man's arms for support. "Thank you. I thought surely I was about to fall." She gathered her skirt and tunic in her hands and raised them to where they barely brushed the tops of her boots. "I shall have to shorten this."

The man gave her one more uncertain glance, before leading them to an iron door. He unlocked it and followed them into a room containing several holding cells.

Drago grabbed the man's sleeve and spoke in rapid Italian. The young man looked at Eva in confusion.

"Father wishes to sit during confession. The pallets are fine. He would like to start at the end."

"He wants to go *inside*?" The deputy glanced around the room. "I'm afraid I ain't allowed to do that, Sister. It wouldn't be safe."

She looked around the room. "Surely these men honor God enough to restrain themselves from doing us harm. How many violent murderers are in here?"

"Well, uh..." He paused in thought. "I don't rightly know."

She moved to the first one, occupied by three young men who looked to be brothers. "Sirs, what are your crimes?"

One stood and ducked his head. "Thievin', sister."

"And you?" She asked the men in the next cell. "Out beyond curfew," came the reply.

She reached Pierre Lafitte at the far end. He looked remarkably like his brother, except shorter and the several days of growth covering his unshaven jaws and cheeks. By this time, most of the prisoners had risen to their feet in interest, including Pierre.

Eva studied him. "You, sir. For what offense have you been imprisoned?"

He gave her a grand bow. "I've been detained for the act of self-preservation, Sister. I was challenged to a duel with rapiers, and in the process of defending my person, I mortally wounded my foe." He rose and met her gaze. A brief flicker of recognition passed over his features, followed by a pleasant smile, despite the dry, cracked lips. "I am quite remorseful and should very much like to offer my confession."

Eva approached the deputy and dipped her head. "We shall accommodate you, sir, and remain outside this man's cell. However, since the others are less nefarious, Father Giuseppe insists he sit inside with the rest."

He shrugged. "I suppose I can allow that."

Drago belched loudly and grasped his stomach in apparent pain. Eva put her hand on his shoulder. "*Stai bene, Padre?*" Drago had taught her to say this one sentence in Italian. Hopefully, she got it right, although it probably didn't matter.

He answered her in Italian and waved her away. She shrugged and addressed the guard. "Apparently Father Giuseppe ate something disagreeable, but he feels well enough to proceed." She gestured to Pierre. "Father shall stay outside the cell of this violent criminal. As his crime is most heinous, we'll start with him."

She opened her satchel, and Drago reached in and pulled out a stole and a bible. He placed the garment around his neck, then made the sign of the cross.

Eva began her "translation" in English. She spoke fluent French and Spanish and could read Latin and Russian, but unfortunately never learned Italian. Since the deputy didn't know Italian either, Drago's actual words weren't important, since she could recite the rites in her sleep.

"In the name of the Father, the Son and the Holy Spirit, I grant blessings to you," she said.

Pierre interrupted. "Pardon, sister, but do you speak my native tongue, French?" he asked.

"Of course."

Pierre's eyes lit up. He spoke to the guard in French, but the man waved his palms. "I can't talk Frenchie." He looked at her, irritated. "What did he say?"

"He simply asked if you spoke either Italian or French," she answered.

He shook his head. "Just use whatever will help move this along."

She nodded, turned back to Pierre and spoke rapidly in French. *"Follow our instructions exactly. We are going to get you out of here today."*

He responded in French as well. *"Eva Trudeau? Is that really you? My, but you have grown up!"*

Drago snorted and addressed Pierre again in Italian so she could "translate." But before she could respond, Pierre chuckled.

"What is so funny?"

"He said my brother is a horse's ass, and he's only doing this to restore his own honor and self-respect."

Eva looked at Pierre in surprise and continued in French. *"Do you speak Italian?"*

He nodded, leaned over and whispered in Drago's ear.

Drago raised his chin and glared at Pierre, again responding in Italian. He shifted to stand in front of her.

Eva shifted her gaze between the two men. *"What did the capitainé say to you?"*

He grinned. *"I said you have blossomed into a beautiful flower. He responded by telling me if I laid a hand on you, he'd cut it off. Are you two in love, Eva?"*

She rolled her eyes. *"He's a liar and a thief."*

"Then he is perfect for you, little fox."

Drago huffed, made the sign of the cross, and mumbled in Italian.

Pierre's grin widened. "He understands French, as well. Our fun is ended, *mon cher*."

"How much longer is this gonna take?" The guard sighed and shifted his weight.

Eva spun to respond and once again stepped on her hem, this time falling right into the guard's arms. Both struggled for balance; he attempted to set her upright while she clutched at his arm with one hand, reaching for her rebellious skirts with the other. After a moment of fumbling, she was back on her feet.

She adjusted her clothing, and her stomach gave a horrified lurch when she realized her veil had slipped off her shoulder. Although the deputy quickly lowered his gaze, she didn't miss the brief widening of his eyes when they fell upon the scar. She put the garment back in place and cleared her throat in embarrassment. "Thank you, sir."

"Yes, ma'am." His eyes darted from the floor to her and back to the floor again.

The hardest part over, she clasped her hands under her tunic, careful to clutch the keys to keep them from clinking together. Once a street rat, always a street rat, apparently. Hugo would have been proud.

"In reply to your earlier question, this will be quite a while longer." She frowned at Pierre. "This man neglected attending mass for a long time. He has much to confess."

The guard expelled an annoyed breath.

Eva brightened. "I have an idea. If you leave the door ajar, I can come let you know when we wish to move to the next poor soul, and you can come back in to let Father Giuseppe into the cell for the next confession."

The deputy gave her a relieved nod, spun on his heel and withdrew before she could change her mind.

Drago quickly doffed his robes while Eva moved to the door with the keys she'd lifted from the guard's pocket. Pierre took off his coat and gave it to Drago, who handed him a bag of coins before stepping inside, collapsing on the pallet and covering himself with the coat.

Pierre slipped into the priest's robes, drawing the hood up over his head. He grinned at the men in the other cells and put his finger to his lips. He proceeded to distribute the money among the smiling prisoners, with words of thanks and encouragement.

She moved to Pierre's side. He looped his arm across her shoulders and pretended to lean on her heavily. They shuffled to the iron door; Eva shouldered it open, appearing to struggle to hold the priest upright.

The guard was once again on his feet. "Did something happen?"

She gave him an apologetic smile. "It seems Father Giuseppe is not well after all. He asked me to take him back to his quarters."

The deputy held open the door. Pierre, nearly doubled over, released a pained moan as he passed, along with a loud belch.

The deputy snickered, and she shrugged. "Bad beans."

His eyes smirked in sympathy, and he stepped aside. The chink of metal hitting stone made them all pause. She glanced down. "Sir, you dropped your keys."

He patted his pocket, and his eyes widened. "So I did, thank you, Sister." His face reddened, and he retrieved them before retreating inside.

Chapter Thirty-One

SISTER BEATRICE TO THE RESCUE

Ashort time later, Drago heard Sister Beatrice's shrill voice echoing through the jail. "I beg your assistance. Father Giuseppe must have lost track of the time. He was to return quite some time ago to prepare for evening mass."

There was a panicked pause. "The father ain't here no more. They departed over an hour ago."

"Did they happen to say to where?"

The guard's tone suggested confusion. "Back to his quarters."

"With whom did they converse?"

"The prisoners."

Sister Beatrice harrumphed. "Perhaps they overheard something that can help me find them."

The metallic jingle of keys accompanied the deputy's uneasy voice. "They said they was going back to the church."

Her eyebrows lowered. "Well, they did not arrive."

The latch released, and the door squealed open. Both men rushed in, heading straight for Lafitte's cell. One of them banged on the bars. "Lafitte! Wake up!"

Drago didn't move.

The guard fumbled and dropped his keys twice before finally

opening the door. When he reached out and shook Drago's shoulder, he was rewarded with a low moan. Drago rolled over, and the guard cursed.

His partner rubbed his forehead. "The sheriff is gonna kill us."

"Oh, Dear Lord!" exclaimed Sister Beatrice, clasping her hands together. "What happened to Father Giuseppe? Is he hurt?"

The guard swore again and helped Drago to a sitting position. For good measure, Drago held his head and groaned again in pain.

The nun wrung her hands. "Please, sirs, if you would help him to his feet, I'll attempt to guide him to the cathedral."

Both guards half-dragged, half-carried him outside, apologizing as they went. Sister Beatrice huffed. "Impersonating a member of the clergy! How horrible!" She shook her finger at them. "You must catch those two imposters."

Now the deputies were sweating, even though the day was frigid. "Yes, Sister," the first guard mumbled miserably.

Pierre Lafitte had long ago boarded a small boat along with several of his brother's men and was probably celebrating in Barataria Bay, drinking rum and reveling in his freedom. Drago was confident Jean Lafitte would keep his promise and bring firearms and ammunition to Jackson's army. He had no reason to doubt it. Lafitte may be a pirate and a criminal, but he was also a man of his word. An odd combination, but still a favored son of the city.

Drago and the nun shuffled down the street and around the next corner before he straightened and gave her a satisfied grin. "Sister Beatrice, if you ever decide to leave the church, you could always find a career on the stage."

She blushed and swatted his arm. "Oh, hush, you." She still smiled, though. "I rather enjoyed myself."

Chapter Thirty-Two

TRUST IN LOVE

Lightning flashed in Drago's stormy eyes. "Sit. You promised to listen. Let me explain." Dressed in his usual black from his head to his boots, he removed his pistols and placed them on the desk. A saber leaned against the wall behind him. The *Dragon* tugged gently on her tethers as the Mississippi hurried by. All that disturbed the silence was the shifting creaks of the vessel as she breathed.

He crossed his arms and rested a hip against his desk. Eva glowered in a chair facing him and crossed her arms over her chest in response.

Drago growled, then pushed from the desk and prowled over to her.

"I'm listening," she snapped, pinning an icy glare at the wide expanse of his very impressive chest.

"You're like a beautiful tempest when you are angry." He cupped her chin. "At least look at me, *il mio amore*."

A collision with those churning silver eyes would do nothing to preserve her anger or her self-control. "Nothing you say can repair the damage you've done to my trust and my... life" She faltered. Had she any pride remaining, she'd say no more to him.

He wouldn't care that he broke her heart. Her return to street rat from a near novitiate was practically complete, thanks to him.

"I am marked. The deputy saw my face. The scar—I can no longer hide in the abbey or behind the veil." Tears burned in the back of her eyes, but she pushed them away. "I'll be recognized immediately either way." Perhaps she might persuade Mother Superior to send her back to Jamaica for asylum. She dare not remain here.

Nine years in the nunnery hadn't changed a thing, except now she had an innate sense of guilt for the deception at the jail and stealing of the relics from Lady Guiraud, though at the time she felt in the right. Letting them go also felt strangely right. The sacred bones would continue to be cherished by people who'd treat them with the deep, solemn respect they deserved.

She let out a frustrated sigh and raised her gaze. It was harder to focus when she looked at him. Harder to avoid appreciating the sharp angles of his jaw and the sensual line of his lips. Harder to keep her fingers from reaching out to trace the thin scar from his eyebrow to his hairline, before tucking the ebony curl back behind his ear. His hair was loose, giving him an almost maniacal mien. And his eyes were nearly as wild and predatory.

She hungered for him in a way that obscured the edges. Made it almost impossible to concentrate. His aura shouted an authority and dominance unaffected by her intentions or words.

She swallowed past the knot forming against her throat. "I considered you an ally in a common cause. You betrayed me."

Yet, he personally tended to her after Razin's attack and had defended her against Hugo. Why? Out of guilt? To gain her confidence again because he intended to use her and lie to her and betray her? Either way, it worked. She'd done his bidding, and he had accomplished his goals.

Just as she'd feared, the darkness in Drago Gamponetti had crept from the shadows; he'd lured her back into the dank swill she'd fought for years to leave behind. The Ursuline nuns had shielded her from people like Hugo, who'd exploit her talents for their own gain and people who couldn't hide their revulsion and disgust. Now, even the option to join the abbey was gone. Mother Marie Francois might offer her sanctuary, but would not accept her into the order. At least, not as long as she suspected that Drago was in love with Eva.

How was she going to recover from this? She couldn't tell her heart how to behave. It didn't matter if she wanted to care for him or not. She did.

There was a good man inside. She'd seen him. Sensed him. Listened to him. Drago may believe he was cursed, doomed to the devil and already lost, but she would not.

Could not. Contrary to the earlier words she'd spat in anger.

She'd witnessed his compassion and his righteous sense of patriotism, which he disguised as practical mercantile decision-making. All those were little elements of light that did not normally come from black-hearted pirates, sons of Satan.

Drago's eyes never strayed from hers. The color shifted with his emotions. Sometimes they were a thunderous gray, sometimes silver flecked with icy blue or even molten mercury. Today they were the intense hue of a turbulent sea, roiling with determined impetus and anger. They caressed even as they raked her skin. Such a fierce study would usually have her looking for a reason to excuse herself from the room. But, unlike the stares from others, his perusal didn't shred her self-esteem. The energy emanating from his silver-rimmed irises stilled her. He was so devilishly handsome. Even when leaning casually against a piece of furniture, power and danger swirled around him like restless twin sharks.

A slight thrill skittered up her spine. What would it be like if he loved her as much as she loved him?

He rubbed his thumb along her jaw. "Eva, from the depths of my heart, I am sorry. I was wrong to lie to you." He brushed a strand of hair from the side of her face, caressed her cheek, then dropped his hand. "I'm truly sorry, Eva."

Words. Those she might be able to fend off. But the raw energy that encompassed him was impossible to ignore. He was so close, the heat of his body penetrated her skin, his musky scent mixed with spring air and damp wool. Her heartbeat quickened whether she willed it or not, and her breath was barred from her lungs. He rose and placed both hands on the arms of her chair, his hair caging them. Her heart shifted its beat; she let her gaze fall to his mouth and battled the yearning and knew he had no idea...

The muscle in his jaw bunched and rolled. "I realize there's nothing I'll be able to do to redeem myself. This life was all I had to lose, so I chose to protect it at the expense of my soul, which, if it wasn't before, is unquestionably cursed now. I've been a pirate and a marauder for a long time, Eva. It seems to be the only thing I can accomplish well." His voice, like smoked honey, seeped into her bones.

The apology should have lightened her spirit a little, but instead it made it heavier. Loving a man like Drago Gamponetti would only lead to misery. It would take her back to a cage in the underworld. A return to that life would shatter her like a clay pot against a wall.

He finally met her gaze. Something glinted in his eyes. Satisfaction? Confidence? "St. Louis' bones still rest in the cathedral here," he whispered.

What?

"How—I don't understand." She narrowed her eyes. More trickery? She wanted to believe him. Believe *in* him. "I held them in my hand, Drago. Lady Guiraud took them and left." He made no sense.

He kissed her forehead, then slowly pulled off her veil. "Bones of the saints are scattered all over France and Europe, Eva." He grinned, and both dimples poked his cheeks. "King Louis couldn't

possibly know how many were *here*. I removed less than half."
Inky brows slid up his forehead. "Can you forgive my duplicity?"

She could only stare at him in shock. If what he admitted was
true, then he did *not* break his pledge in the slightest. As
promised, he sent men to guard the relics. They would be
protected within the walls of a French cathedral in Paris, and here
as well. The murky sludge of hurt and betrayal slid away, leaving
her breathy and buoyant. She almost laughed. Forgiveness had
never been so easy.

The ragged edges of his voice tore through the quiet cabin.
"Can you, Eva?"

"Yes, I forgive you," she whispered, unable to restrain the
longing or the tears. Drago was brilliantly cunning. No wonder
Jean Lafitte wanted him back in Barataria.

His eyes flooded with relief. He reached for her hand, and she
let him take it. "*Il mio amore*, I have something to ask of you."

She stiffened. There it was. Would she always play the naïve
fool for him? She tugged her hand, but he wouldn't release it. He
wanted to use her again for another task. Hurt sliced at her heart,
but she wouldn't let it show. He might try to bend her to his
whim, but this time he'd be disappointed.

If he sensed the shift in her demeanor, he didn't show it. He
dragged a stool in front of her and sat. "Do you think..." He
stroked her palm with his thumb, the sensation amplified by the
fact he was *touching* her.

Finally, he raised his head. His eyes were rimmed in deep navy,
and she stared, transfixed and amazed at the way he paralyzed her
limbs with just a look. She had no choice except to wait for him
to continue. It wasn't like she was able to jump up and leave.

"Do you think you could ever love a man like me?"

His words rammed her like a punch to the chest. *Heavens, if he
only knew!*

Could you, Eva?" His voice was raw emotion, scraping through
the surrounding stillness. Proud captain, leader of men. His pres-

ence filled the cabin beyond his bulk. Yet, it was that tentative tone which made her pause, rather than respond with a vexed shake of her head.

She touched her hand to his cheek. He closed his eyes and sucked in a sharp breath. Her heart melted. "Oh, Drago, loving you has always been the easy part." Tears seared the edges of her eyes. The words came out so effortlessly. Yet left a painful emptiness behind.

His expression opened with a bright hopefulness, eyes light. "Then why do you cry?" He smoothed a tear away with the back of a finger, before pulling the veil from her head and cupping her jaw in his palm.

The knot tightened. Would her words pain him to hear as much as they hurt her to say? "Because *trusting* you is the *hard* part."

Chapter Thirty-Three

IL MIO AMORÉ

Instead of hurt, a glint of understanding surfaced in Drago's expression. "Ah now, *non petite renard*, but St. Louis's bones still rest in the St. Louis Cathedral. If you ponder it all for a moment, you'll see I *kept* my promise. You can indeed trust me."

She gave him an exasperated laugh. "*You* are the fox, Drago Gamponetti."

His devilish smile faded quickly. "Fontaine would have killed us had we not acquired the relics." He sucked in a ragged breath. "Even worse, he would have killed *you*. This was the only way to keep you safe and give him what he expected, *mio amore*. I vowed to protect you, Eva, and I always will." Hope, sincerity and something like longing shone in his mercurial gaze. "You can trust me for at least that much, no?"

Dear God, she wanted to.

She needed to.

She was *terrified* to.

Still, she found herself nodding.

He smiled, and that wicked dimple dove into his cheek once more. She rubbed it with her finger. "I'll simply have to get better at learning the way you think and scheme," she said. "Deciphering your mind will keep me alert and *you* out of too much trouble."

He pulled her to her feet and took her hands, and they disappeared in his. His words were gravelly with emotion. "I am lost without you, Eva. You are my light in the dark, my sun in the day, my brilliant star at night."

She'd never been anyone's star. The knot around her throat unraveled, the tension gradually easing. Hope blossomed in her chest.

"I love you, Eva Trudeau," he rasped.

Her heart flipped so fast it kicked the air from her lungs. She could only stare. He'd just said he *loved* her.

Her. The unlovable one.

His hands skimmed up her arms; threads of lightning flickered under her skin. Heat pooled low in her belly, and a deep longing thrummed through her veins. Warm hands squeezed her shoulders. "Eva? Did you hear me?" He tilted her head up and searched her face like he was memorizing every tiny detail. "Eva?" The touch of his thumb on her lower lip jolted her from her stupor.

How could he actually love her, of all people? She was scarred, maimed, hideous. Her voice was a reedy whisper. "Yes?"

Brows shifted up, and he cocked his head to the side. "I was hoping, well—for a bit of reciprocity of some sort."

The man was *serious*. She was still in shock. "Reciprocity?"

Drago's eyes flooded with crushing panic. Fear, hurt, sorrow shadowed his features. "I love you, Eva."

Dear God, he meant it.

He loved her.

Drago's throat convulsed. The hard lines of his face melted. "I want the type of reciprocity where you grant me absolute and unadulterated adoration, to be bluntly honest." There was a strained note of teasing in his tone, and he looked like he needed to take a breath, but couldn't quite manage it.

She had to know. He'd said it himself—so many years of

pirating and marauding— "But can you be *honest*? I cannot commit absolute and total adoration to a lying, thieving pirate." She bit back a smile, but that statement was shockingly true.

Two short vertical lines creased between his eyebrows. "Unconditionally." His eyes heated; he drew her hand to his mouth and kissed it, prickling the hair on her wrist. White teeth gleamed with his quick grin. "In addition, I resigned that profession. When the Guirauds deliver the bones to the king, they will also give him my resignation."

That changed things considerably. Wings fluttered in her stomach and stretched up through her chest, sending a delirious current of joy through her body. "Truly?"

He finally exhaled. Silver eyes softened, and he gave her a tender smile. "Yes, *il mio amore.*"

"You are my love, too." She captured his face in her hands; the short scruff from a day's growth tickled her palms. The shadows shifted. A feathery lightness filled her heart. "And I shall bestow upon you complete and honest reciprocity."

The corner of his mouth jumped up. "Completely and honestly?"

She circled her arms around his neck, joy tripping her heartbeat. "Yes, I completely and honestly love you, Drago Viteri Gamponetti. I have for a long time."

He bent and kissed her. His lips moved with a surprising gentleness, both insistent and seductive. She dug her fingers into the hard corded muscle of his shoulders and kissed him back, letting the passion he stirred orchestrate every movement.

He combed his fingers through her hair, then traced the scar from her ear across her cheek until he cradled her jaw in his hand. He pulled away, his eyes flaming with both heat and exhilaration. "If I give you my vow to love you until the end of my days, will you trust me with your heart, Eva? Will you marry me? Will you become my wife?"

Her heart clenched so hard with emotion it hurt. A warm tear slipped over her cheekbone. Joyful laughter bubbled from her chest. She cradled his face, darkly tanned and angular in her herb-stained hands, the pale white of her skin almost glowing against his. Their eyes met, and in his she saw rolling thunderclouds clashing with a stormy ocean, raging for *her* and suddenly felt the intensity of his emotions crash through her like violent waves against a sheer rock face, each one pounding the shell around her heart, drenching her, washing away the fear and the scars and the dark memories before striking again. "Yes, I will marry you, Drago Gamponetti, you wonderful, honorable, brave, sly, protective pirate."

His face split into a grin; he lifted her up and twirled her in a circle, laughing at her squeal of delight as she clung to his neck. The world kept spinning even after he stopped and lowered his head and kissed her again. She answered the kiss with all the love in her heart, eliciting a sound of raw emotion from him. The warmth of his palms seeped through the fabric of her robes, creating streaks of fire as his hands moved along her ribs and around her waist.

He attracted her to him with an invisible magnetism, and before she could register what she was doing, her fingers wove around his neck. He answered her kiss with such savage tenderness, the center of her throat coiled tightly with emotion.

"I can't believe I finally have you," he rasped, sending heated words over her skin. "You are everything to me, Eva. The sun, the wind, the earth and the sea." He smelled like sun-warmed sand and leather. "Eva." He whispered her name like it tortured his lips. "You are so beautiful."

She forgot to breathe.

His words were so raw and honest, his gaze so thoroughly enraptured, Eva almost lost her ability to stand. Things warmed and glowed inside her. Beautiful. He called her *beautiful* and even more amazing...he meant it.

He touched his forehead to hers. "I love you." His whisper

rolled over the skin of her cheek, tickling her ear, sending shivers down the side of her neck.

She reached up and stroked his face, the rough rasp of his short beard abrading her palm. "This kind of love is new to me, Drago. It's terrifying to be so exposed after hiding my face and my life behind the abbey walls for years. You're the only one who wants me for who I am inside. I'll always trust you with my heart, Drago."

He swallowed and continued to search her face as if he needed to see her to breathe. "You are beautiful, Eva, outside and in. I love you because of who you are *here*." He kissed her heart. "And here." He kissed her temple and then rested his forehead against hers. Warm breath caressed her lips.

She combed her hand through the dark curls caging her face. "I love you too, Drago."

His words caressed the skin behind her ear. "You have stolen my heart, *il mio amore*."

She smiled knowingly and rested her hand on top of his. "And you have healed mine."

Chapter Thirty-Four

A CHOICE

T he clock chimed on his desk, and Drago groaned, planting a kiss on the tender skin of Eva's neck, as they shared one last embrace. "I have managed an invitation to attend a special meeting called by General Jackson. Come, I'll escort you into the back door of the convent first." He kissed her brow. "I want you safe, in case the redcoats manage to elude Jackson's lookouts. We'll leave at first light if it's not too late."

Her forehead wrinkled. "Leave? To go where?"

He gave her a baffled look. "Downriver, toward Barataria Bay. I want you and the twins out of New Orleans. The British will probably not detain us, and if they do, they'll find nothing in my hold. We'll hit Lamb's Tail Island in about three weeks if the weather holds. From there, we'll fill the *Dragon* with cane and casks of rum and begin the run to Cartageña..." His words trailed off, and he slowly released her as she stepped out of his embrace.

She couldn't believe what she was hearing. "You're *leaving*?" Hadn't Manuel said they decided to stay and fight? "What about General Jackson? Your friends, the Sauvages? Even now, they're preparing to defend our home. How can you leave when we need you?"

Drago straightened. "I will persuade them to join us." He sighed and rubbed his brow. "I can't keep you *safe* here. It will take the enemy less than a day to decimate the regulars and the volunteers alike. They are a force the people of this city cannot defend against. Eva, you must see that it's hopeless."

Run when her people needed her? "It is not hopeless. We have *hope*, Drago."

He stepped away and paced the room like a caged cat. His eyes were as wild as his hair. "If we wait, then the Royal Navy will attack and commandeer my ship! The best decision I can make for you, my men and my ship, is one that involves taking the *Dragon* out of the gulf entirely. It's the only way to save our lives. If the river wasn't so treacherous at night, we'd already be underway."

Her fingers curled against her chest, where her heart jerked with every painful beat. She treasured the calm security of his protection, but she wouldn't cower behind it. "I'm not going anywhere."

"What?" He spun to face her, eyes wide in shock.

She tried to take a calming breath. It didn't work. How could this be happening? "I'm needed here. There will be a battle, which means there will also be many wounded—"

He spread his hands. "You are not the only healer in this city, Eva."

"This is my home." Words caught in her throat. "These are my people. This is my nation. I will not abandon them in their time of need." She choked, tears streaming freely now.

She met his astonished gaze painfully. He didn't understand. "This country was built on the foundation of freedom. We cherish that foundation. We defend that foundation. We won't stand idly by while it is threatened. I won't flee to save my own skin." She clenched her fists beneath her tunic in frustration. "If I have to pick up arms and fight, I will."

He released a long breath. "Eva—"

She backed toward the door. "I'm staying, Drago. I love you, but I'll stay here, in New Orleans. Until the end. I'll pray for your safety every day. Godspeed."

He lunged at her, eyes wild and panicked. "Wait!"

She jumped back, whirled and ran from the cabin, choking back a sob that escaped as she hastened down the ramp to the docks. People paused and stared at the crying woman running down the street to the convent. Without her veil, her anguish was as exposed as her horrid face.

For once, she didn't care.

Chapter Thirty-Five

WE FIGHT

T he city was in a panic. The townsfolk were boarding up windows and doors. Wagons and debris now blocked almost every street and passageway.

Drago hadn't bothered to chase Eva down. If he'd caught her, then what? She'd made her decision. And now he'd made his.

Drago entered the house serving as Jackson's headquarters with Bernard and Manuel. Bernard was there because he lead the city's militia. Manuel was there in case Jackson attempted to arrest Drago, which was a strong possibility. He hadn't left New Orleans, or it's governing body on the best of terms several years ago.

When Andrew Jackson strode into a room, it suddenly became smaller. Drago respectfully rose along with the others. The general was pale and drawn. Drago had heard the general was suffering from dysentery. Yet here he stood, a commanding presence with keen eyes and a confident jaw.

Drago attended the meeting to propose an alliance. The Americans needed men. Lafitte employed nearly a thousand Baratarian pirates.

Lafitte needed a pardon. Jackson had the ears of the White House.

It was all a matter of pride. Jackson refused to negotiate with a pirate.

Lafitte refused to beg.

The gray mood in Jackson's temporary residence on Royal Street clouded the atmosphere. Five American gunships had been overrun by the British flotilla on Lake Borgne less than ten days ago.

The loss was catastrophic. Survivors were now prisoners aboard the enemy ships. The Americans possessed no other vessels to defend access to New Orleans through Lake Pontchartrain. The only thing that saved them had been the shallow depths. England's warships were too deep in the draft.

The British now had to transport foot soldiers via another route, which thankfully involved a long thirty to forty mile march through marshes filled with razor-edged reeds, murky cypress swamps, using the bayous and their muddy banks.

Now the Americans had an idea where the British might make landfall, but no way of protecting the city from the water if the enemy brought in vessels with a shallower draft. So far, none had been spotted.

Drago's stomach twitched. His window for a safe departure downriver would close fast. He admired Eva for her courage. She was loyal to her country. People with her spirit had toiled for freedom once before.

And succeeded.

Americans were fierce, and the raw necessity to triumph shoved away the fear of blood and death. The fire of righteousness burning in their hearts sharpened the blades of victory and justice.

It was quite possible the British would underestimate them as completely as he had.

The pirate in Drago wanted to sneak into the convent, snatch

Eva from her cot, and stash her safely aboard the *Dragon*. He'd have already done it if he wasn't loathe to stir her hatred. He might yet do it still and ask for forgiveness later.

Jackson's gritty scrutiny raked over the men at the table. Leaders from every militia, regiment, tribe, and nationality were represented. All had gathered to go to war for their country. The general cleared his throat, and the room went quiet. Flinty eyes pierced each man one by one. "A threat prepares to blast open the door to the West and cripple our great nation. By my count, we've amassed nearly 3500 men, including the Kentucky rifleman and the Dragoons of Mississippi." He nodded toward a thick-shouldered man dressed in buckskin from head to toe. "Mr. Logan, your report?"

Logan unfolded his arms. "Generals Coffee and Hinds mustered nearly a thousand riflemen and cavalry. They are all excellent marksman and are capable of navigating the wilderness with speed and precision. Unfortunately, there's a great shortage of guns, flints, and ammunition."

Jackson pressed his thin lips into a slashing line. "That seems to be the common issue. We are in urgent need of all three."

Drago shifted in his chair. He hated what he was about to do because he hated the Baratarian pirate almost as much, but he had no alternative. New Orleans was a growing city, teaming with people of every color, class, and culture. As proud and enthusiastic as they were, without resources and a capable leader, they had no chance in fending off fifteen thousand British soldiers.

Only one man in Louisiana had the men, the means and the power to offset those odds a bit. Small as it was.

"I have a suggestion, sir," he said.

Jackson raised his bushy eyebrows. "Captain Drago Gamponetti, correct?"

At Drago's nod, the general said, "I'll hear it."

Drago clasped his hands together on the table. "Understand sir, that under any other circumstance I would not consider this."

No bloody way did he want to be in the same room as Lafitte again if he could avoid it. If the need wasn't so dire, in all honesty, he wouldn't be introducing him.

Now, it was beyond dire. It was hopeless. The Americans would need to secure a pact with the devil to give them any possibility of putting up a decent contest.

And he was about to introduce Jackson to Lucifer's right-hand man.

"I know a man with a great many resources, a thousand men at his command and large stores of ammunition and weapons." He studied Jackson.

The general's eyebrows jumped.

"However," Drago chose his words carefully. It was prudent to apprise him of all the potential pitfalls and traps that may come with forming such an alliance while distancing himself as much as possible from his former colleague, lest Jackson place him in the same category, and put him in jail, which was still entirely plausible considering his more recent activities *and* his past ventures in Barataria Bay. "This man is known for his dealings with pirates and slave traders, as well as playing loose with the law."

General Jackson's slash of a mouth quirked. "We are not in a situation that allows for us to be picky, Captain Gamponetti. I will turn away no man, whether he be pirate or pastor, free or slave, black, white or savage, as long as he is prepared to do his patriotic duty to his country."

The general's willingness to recruit even the wild Indians betrayed his desperation. Although he'd allied with the Cherokee, his recent decimation of the Creek Red Sticks had been ruthless and bloody. Rumor had it that all Indians were savages in his mind, regardless of alliance.

Jackson pierced Drago with a calculating stare. "In fact, I'll be more than agreeable to write letters to the president requesting pardons for past crimes in exchange for such allegiances."

It was Drago's turn to bite back a grim smile. Of course, a pardon topped the pirate's list of demands.

"Who is this man to which you refer?" Governor Claiborne demanded. "I know of only one in this area like you describe, and I hesitate to be seen in the same room with him. He's crafty and belligerent, with absolutely no regard for the government or its rules."

Drago gave the governor a tilt of his head. "You very accurately described Captain Jean Lafitte."

"The Baratarian pirate?" Jackson asked, eyebrows jutting upward.

"You have heard of him, then?" Drago asked. A rhetorical question. Jackson likely had his own intelligence.

The general leaned back in his chair. "Indeed. A most unsavory fellow, I've been told." He tapped his finger on the table in thought. "However, in this instance, I would be a fool to refuse to speak with him." He stared at the Claiborne until the man dropped his gaze to the table.

It was time to see whether the gamble was worth the risk. "I hope I haven't overstepped my bounds by retrieving the man in case this topic arose. It's my understanding that there is little time to spare or waste. Captain Lafitte is waiting outside." Drago gestured to Manuel to open the door while Claiborne sputtered like a boiling soup pot lid.

Jean Lafitte swooped into the room like an Emperor. The air went still. Drago almost contained a derisive snort at the effect he had on the room, gaining a raised eyebrow from Jackson.

"Gentlemen," the pirate said, chin raised, voice firm. "Jean Lafitte, at your service." He gave them a lavish bow.

General Jackson rose to his feet. The other men did not seem inclined to stand or show the pirate any respect at all. Jean snapped to attention and gave Jackson a smart salute before extending his hand in greeting.

"*Generale*, I am honored." He snapped his fingers, and two

slaves entered the room carrying platters of cheese and fruit, freshly baked bread and bottles of port. A third set a large basket on the table, then began unwrapping crystal glasses from scraps of wool. Mouths dropped open, mute and dumbfounded.

Jackson sat and observed with narrowed eyes and a sagacious slant to his mouth. Clever man.

Jean Lafitte plucked a grape from a platter and waited until servants put a filled glass next to each man before he spoke. "My reconnaissance teams informed me there's a vast number of his Majesty's best foot soldiers weaving through the bayous." He flicked his gaze to Drago, then back to the general. "According to *Capitainé* Gamponetti, there is a great host of ships anchored on Lake Borgne. I also know there are more ready to sail up zee river past Fort St. Philip."

"Please sit, Captain Lafitte." General Jackson pointed to an empty chair across from Drago. "Captain Gamponetti informed me you may be able to assist us in acquiring arms. If we are going to defeat Pakenham, we are going to need men with stout hearts and sharp eyes in addition to guns and munitions."

Lafitte sipped his port. "My stores are at your disposal, *Generale*. I ask in return for two simple things. Zee first being zee release of my brother Pierre from confinement. A second being full pardons for his indiscretions, as well as my own and those of my men."

While the pirate spoke, Claiborne's skin flushed to a furious red. Unable to remain composed any longer, he slammed his fist on the table. "That's impossible! You, sir, are nothing more than a criminal. Pierre Lafitte is little better than a thief. I shall *not* sign my name to any document that releases you or your brother from the consequences of your actions."

Jean regarded Claiborne with cool disdain. "Regardless, those are my terms."

The governor jabbed a finger at him. "Your brother already escaped from his cell."

Lafitte feigned astonishment. "Truly? When did this event occur?"

Claiborne lowered his brows and growled, "I'd bet my last nickel that you know bloody well—"

"Gentlemen." Jackson, fingers steepled in front of his chest. "The Committee of Defense has already accepted Lafitte's proposition, Claiborne. All that remains is your proclamation inviting the Baratarians to join the standard of the United States."

Drago stifled a smirk. This was interesting. The general, it seemed, was savvier than he expected. The game of politics was indeed fascinating.

Claiborne had no choice but to do as ordered. He scowled. "Such a proclamation is only valid if you act as patriots and help us win the upcoming battle."

Lafitte tilted his head and smiled. "Agreed."

Jackson picked up his port. "The governor will draft it, I shall enforce the conditions, and add my own. I need every able-bodied man, Captain Lafitte. Without weaponry, we are crippled. Without able bodies to use them, we are lost."

Lafitte swept his hand in the direction of the river. "This minute, a force of eight hundred highly skilled Baratarians await your orders, *Generale*. My gunners are the best you'll find anywhere. They will run your armaments with order and precision." His cool stare shifted to the Kentucky sharpshooter. Lafitte shot Logan a bland smile, suggesting there wasn't much in the way of friendship there either.

Drago sought to even out the temperature of the pool of pride they all seemed to be soaking in. "Mr. Logan, the Choctaw are expert marksman and trackers." At Logan's raised brow, he continued. "They are excellent scouts and can find secure niches for your sharpshooters and marksmen. I suggest you instruct your snipers to shoot first at the men on horseback. They will be the highest officers of rank in the field. Redcoat foot soldiers tend to behave like startled goats when deprived of command."

Suddenly, muted shouts of alarm interrupted the conversation. A sharp rap on the door followed. "Enter!" Jackson barked.

The door flung open, and a young man, perhaps in his late teens or early twenties, stumbled into the room, muddy and out of breath. "The British have landed, and they've captured Villeré plantation!"

"How do you know this?" Jackson demanded, rising to his feet.

Lafitte leaned toward the general. "This is Gabriel Villeré, son of the owner."

The young man grabbed the hat from his head, then stared at the table of food and licked his lips. "I jumped from an upper bedroom window without being seen. I came straight here to warn you."

An aide stepped forward and laid a map in front of the general. "Show me where they are," Jackson said.

"Here." The man pointed to a spot. "Villeré is here, eight miles southeast of the city."

"That would mean that they traveled up the waterways, *which*," Jackson ground his teeth and glared at the young man, overshadowing him with both fortitude and height. "I had ordered blocked."

Villeré paled and clenched his hat until his knuckles whitened. "Yes sir, General, but we couldn't finish in time."

Scowling, Bernard Sauvage finally spoke. "Didn't finish? It could have been done in two days. You've had over a week, Mr. Villeré."

Jackson's nostrils flared. "Sergeant, take this man into custody until we can determine his intentions."

Claiborne stood, face red with anger. "If we find that Villeré received bribes from the enemy to leave the bayou open, you'll be charged with treason."

"I...I..." the man stuttered, his eyes wide. "My father is still a captive!" He lifted his shoulders; his cheeks took on an indignant flush. "Father told them your army boasts over twelve thousand, so the commander decided to wait for reinforcements before marching on the city." He straightened in indignation. "If my family supported the intentions of the British, then the redcoats would have pounded on your door this day, rather than me."

An uneasy quiet descended upon the room. Perhaps it just now sunk in. The enemy was about to pounce like a mighty lion and the town little more than a mouse cowering between its claws.

General Jackson expelled a lungful of air and braced his hands on the table. "Mr. Lafitte, I accept your provisos. Both Claiborne and I will use our influence in the Council of State to make sure your personal wishes be acceded to. I trust the next time we meet, you will be in the ranks of the American army."

"With pride, *Generale,*" Lafitte gave him a respectful nod, placing his hand over his heart.

Jackson pounded the table. He looked each man in the eye, his eyes bright with zeal and determination. "By the eternal, the British will not sleep on our soil tonight!" He addressed the aid. "Send word to Wagner to muster the men. Alert the *USS Carolina* to make ready. She's going to attack their camp from the Mississippi, while we engage using Indian warfare tactics under the shelter of darkness, thereby taking them by surprise. Their troops are tired from the forty-mile journey through the bayous." A thin smile sharpened his features. "Our soldiers are fresh and ready. We strike *tonight.*"

Drago looked on the scene with both excitement and trepidation. The plan was either brilliant or insane. Here was his opportunity to break free. He'd follow the *USS Carolina*, using her for cover.

Eva's velvety-blue eyes, rich with passion and patriotic fervor, permeated his mind. He grumbled a curse.

The truth was that he'd rather die for Eva than live without her.

Drago stood. "General Jackson?"

The officer paused at the doorway and turned his attention to Drago.

"I offer the services of my ship and crew. I can take enough men to load and fire the guns. We can trail the *Carolina* and assist. The rest can help with the armaments. They are highly skilled with weapons of every sort."

Manuel's chest expanded.

Drago ignored the satisfied gleam in his cousin's eyes and continued, "I'm also aware that the British require sugarcane fascines to traverse the soggy terrain. I would like to take a handful of men to find and destroy them. That should help to hamper their progression toward the city, if only a little."

He was going to regret this. But he'd be dragged through fire and brimstone before he turned tail while Eva and the Sauvage family fought for their lives and homeland.

Manuel growled his approval. "We fight!"

The general gave them a satisfied nod and something that resembled a stoic smile before he departed.

By this time tomorrow, they'd either be setting those fascines aflame, or they'd be dead.

In either case, there was fire in his future.

Chapter Thirty-Six

DRAGO'S CHOICE

Drago stood at the helm of the *Dragon*, while the current carried them south, downriver toward the Villeré plantation and war.

The low glow of campfires dotting the riverbank made it easy to spot the British troops in the distance. The night air was crisp, and the tip of Drago's nose was already numb. Thankfully, Eva stayed behind the lines and away from danger with the hospital wagon, along with the twins, who insisted on aiding her.

He'd sought her out to tell her of his plans to assist Jackson, earning him both smiles and tears. Her concern for his safety warmed his heart, but the despair in her eyes struck his heart like a sharp dagger.

If he thought he could persuade her to join him, he would. He couldn't protect her if she stayed in the city, and he did not. And he was uncertain if she'd be safer with him or the convent. Uncertainty never sat well in his gut.

What if the British broke through and bombarded New Orleans with rockets before he could get back to her?

He wasn't prepared for the stab of fear that seized his lungs at the possibility of Eva in danger, nor the metallic ache in his chest when he left her.

Again, he briefly engaged in the thought of simply kidnapping her, but cast it aside. Thoughts and actions like that would never earn her trust. Her disappointment and anger would shred him.

The *Dragon* drifted like a ghost in the mist, her sheets furled and yards bare except for a few of the crew who climbed up to keep watch for ever-present cypress trees, uprooted by the rain sweeping along with the rest of the debris toward the mouth of the Mississippi.

In front of them, shrouded in the swirling mist hovering over the river, the *USS Carolina* slid with the current. Several regiments of American soldiers crept through the trees lining the water, waiting for the gunboat to unload on the unsuspecting British camps. Her attack would be their signal to advance and fire at will.

Flanked by the swamp and the Mississippi, the only maneuver the redcoats had now was to march straight ahead to the city. Unless the Americans could drastically reduce the troops tonight, or at least ruffle them enough to cause a delay, the redcoats would hit the American line of defense hard, and by sheer force of numbers, break through it. Gabriel Villeré's lie, which nearly tripled the size of Jackson's army, bought them precious time while the British awaited reinforcements.

Lafitte's men and the Choctaw scouts returned earlier with information on enemy movements. "Zee Brits only used barges and small crafts to move the soldiers from Lake Borgne to land," Jean Lafitte had said. "Their march was a quagmire, there were not enough boats. Zee men are cold and tired and morale is drooping faster than a *debutant* in July."

With that knowledge, Jackson had given a rousing speech, filling the Americans' hearts with fire, hope, and breathless courage.

The *Dragon* slipped quietly downriver in the *Carolina's* wake, the water drowning out the creaks and groans of the hemp ropes and timbers.

"The Redcoats will have no rest tonight," Manuel murmured, shifting his rifle. He had a predatory glint in his eye and a stubborn set to his thick jaw. Drago didn't have the heart to tell him he wouldn't be fighting with the Americans on the riverbank. There'd be no stopping him if they did. The big man would charge into battle, raging like a fevered bear. He'd get himself killed. Manuel would have ample opportunities to fire off a shot or two from the ship. Hopefully, that would satisfy him.

Everything else involved stealth over might, something Manuel greatly lacked.

"Stay close to my starboard side, Manuel. We fight together, you and I. Eh?"

Manuel nodded and clapped Drago on the back, nearly knocking him off-balance. "We're brothers of the sword, right cousin?"

"That, we are, Manuel."

The big man's voice dropped. "I miss Harvey."

Somewhere in the trees and swamp were fifteen hundred American soldiers, militiamen, sailors and pirates. Among them marched the twins' uncle, Bernard Sauvage, their brother, Tristan, and a militia of New Orleans businessmen.

Harvey had abandoned the *Dragon* in favor of solid ground for once. "Someone's got ter have this boneheaded flounder's larboard flank. He's as good with a rifle as a blind puppy, and can't swing a blade any better than a crawfish," he said, jerking a thumb at Bernard.

"Don't slow us down, you old, creaky, sea dog," came the grunted reply.

Drago exhaled. "Harvey made his choice."

Manuel rocked on his feet. His fingers twitched at his sides. "We should be beside Harvey. We fight together. Always. We should be fighting with Harvey. For freedom. For Jacqueline and

Julian." He stared out over the misty river, flowing murky and silent. "Who will protect Harvey?"

"Bernard has Harvey's larboard side, he'll defend him."

"But who has Bernard's?"

Drago sighed. If he said Tristan, then Manuel would ask who would have Tristan's. Sometimes silence was the best response.

Harvey and Bernard were creeping through the thick night with the Lafitte brothers, and a group of about a hundred Baratarian pirates headed toward Villeré. On one side crept the Mississippi Dragoons, circling ahead near the river and on the other, General Jackson moving directly opposite along the cypress bog. The American forces formed a crescent, intending to strike first with a frontal assault, accompanied by a surprise from the flanks.

It had better work.

The *USS Carolina* had orders to fire on the encampments closest to the river, then continue on to Fort St. Philip to deliver a portion of Jackson's troops and some of Lafitte's men to defend the mouth of the Mississippi. The *Dragon* would rake them as well, but then follow her downriver. With any luck, the confusion would allow the sleek schooner to glide through the night past Villeré. The final task was to locate a quiet bend where they could ground and secure his vessel, conceivably getting her out of harm's way during the battle.

If only the same could be said for Eva and the twins.

Navigating in the dark presented a different problem. It'd been many years since he pirated with Lafitte. Hopefully, his memory of the great river's flowing currents and turns was sound enough to keep them from getting scuppered by a shallow section.

Although Drago had tried, the Sauvage men wouldn't be moved from their mission to help Jackson protect the city. He clenched his teeth until his jaw burned. How he wanted to deliver them from this abysmal place! Away from the greasy mud and the damp cold. Away from the bloody British.

And death.

Americans go about their daily tasks, "making do," as they called it. None led a leisurely life, not even the women and children. They all worked to live, and they did it content with the knowledge they were free to do so.

Their governor wasn't appointed, he was elected by the Louisiana constituents, and they were proud of it.

Stubborn and proud.

And doomed.

And his sugarcane had likely been used for fascines aiding the enemy march. Even worse, it made him, although indirectly, a British resource. If it wasn't for the Sauvage family and Eva (*especially* Eva) he wouldn't have cared.

He glanced at the longboats and canoes secured on the main deck. The more he thought about that smug fop, Winesap bragging about the imminent attack and their use of his cane as fascines, the hotter his blood ran. At least this was one small thing he could do for the American cause.

The redcoats would not use *his* sugarcane to assist their efforts to destroy freedom, and snuff out the pride of these stubborn, stupidly courageous Americans.

Chapter Thirty-Seven

A MISSTEP

Eva stood at the rear of the small barge (which was truly not much more than a glorified raft with short sides that kept the water from breaking across the deck). It belonged to Hugo. He didn't know she took it, of course. He might not even suspect. There was some satisfaction in that.

Borrowed. She'd *borrowed* it.

He still kept the boat nestled in a tangled patch of willows and swamp grass just below the city. It would have been better for Hugo if he rotated his hiding places; lucky for them he hadn't.

"Sound carries far and fast over de water," Raul said, his big hand on the tiller. "Stay quiet."

The huge Cimarron was a reassuring presence, and Eva was grateful Drago assigned the quartermaster to her and the twins for protection. He'd traded his loincloth for buckskin trousers and a long wool coat. Finding boots his size had been impossible, so he settled on Indian moccasins and seemed satisfied.

The wagons brought an ample supply of bandages, ointments and other items needed to treat the wounded. After they became mired in the slick mud a fourth time, the decision was made to take to the river. The plan was to drift as far as Chalmette plantation, then set up a mobile hospital camp just upriver from Jackson's planned assault.

If they had to evacuate, they'd use the rafts and barges to cross the river and trek up to the ferry.

Much to Eva's surprise, Sister Beatrice insisted on accompanying them. Her exploit at the jailhouse apparently inflated her bravado, along with her sense of adventure. She and the children clutched long poles and knelt at the side of the barge, poking away the branches and logs floating with the current.

They fell behind when their raft snagged on a submerged trunk. It took several minutes to work it free.

"Keep a keen eye open for the Chalmette landing," Eva whispered. If they missed the landing area, it would be difficult to find a safe place to tie up behind the battle line.

A large boom echoed over the water, startling them. Ahead, bright flashes lit up the evening sky as the *USS Carolina* opened fire on the British encampment. Gunshots followed, but were drowned out by more artillery charges from the river. Campfires flickered out as the panicked redcoats doused them, explosions from rifle muzzles, and the mouths of canons illuminated the night; the reflection doubling the brilliance.

"Sound does carry far and fast over water," Julian said, wide-eyed. "It's so loud, it's as if we are right next to them."

"Don't worry, child," Sister Beatrice said soothingly.

"Chalmette landing is way north of the Villeré plantation where the British are encamped," Eva added.

"All eyes stay sharp," Raul added.

The bombardment continued and was now joined by shouts of alarm, war cries and screams of pain. The fires along the bank loomed nearer, the rifle shots grew louder. Nervous fingers of fear gripped Eva's chest just as something smacked the water in front of them and sent a splash across the raft.

This was trouble. *Big* trouble.

Realization hit like a kick to the stomach, and caterpillars of panic skittered down Eva's spine. "Get down!" She whispered as loudly as she dared. "Everyone, stow your poles, lie flat."

Jacqueline paused, lifting her pole. "But how will we find the landing?"

Eva pulled the girl down next to her and gripped the rough wooden side. "I'm afraid we've passed it." Her heart pounded hard enough to jar the barge. "Stay quiet and don't move. Hopefully, we can just float past without being noticed."

"Oh, dear, Lord, preserve us." The rattle of Sister Beatrice's rosary beads followed her exclamation, along with a breathy whispered prayer. "Hail Mary, full of grace—"

The twins' tiny voices joined in, but were soon muffled by the chaotic conflict ashore. Thundering explosions surrounded them. Sharp tongues of fire from muzzles and guns slashed the darkness, creating flashes of twilight shrouded in fog.

Illuminated by a large explosion, two hulking shapes in front of them became clearer—the *USS Carolina* and a schooner. Eva's heart beat a frantic staccato in her chest. It was the *Dragon,* and she was taking heavy fire. Her guns spouted lethal grapeshot with a fiery roar, the temporary illumination making her an easy target for British bombardment. Her yards empty of sails, like the *Carolina*, she allowed the sluggish river to carry her along.

Eva gripped the raft tighter and pulled Jacqueline closer. Her past as one of Hugo's runners taught her many things. One was that rarely did the first runner get caught, but nearly always the second one did. The *Carolina* inflicted substantial damage and turmoil on the camp, then drifted away before the enemy had time to respond. Unfortunately, Drago and his ship had no choice but to drift into their sights, taking the greatest barrage.

Eva had been both frightened and elated when Drago came to her with the news he and his crew decided to aid Jackson. He stayed for her and his friends, and her heart swelled with pride and love. Not the unredeemable blackguard he professed to be, was he? But his choice, although valiant, put him in more danger.

A loud whistle ripped through the air, accompanied by an explosion in front of the *Dragon's* helm. Shouts, screams and the snap of cracking timber avalanched Eva's heart into her stomach.

Drago!

Thick, acrid smoke stung her eyes, blinding her. Jacqueline trembled at her side, either with stark fear or racking sobs. It was hard to tell.

A gunshot, a scream.

Stray bullets impacted the surrounding water. Raul grunted, then sucked in a sharp breath. Eva sliced her gaze back in time to see him sink to his knees. Before she could crawl to him, he tipped and fell into the water.

No!

"Raul!" Julian hissed a hoarse whisper, grabbed a pole and scurried to the edge of the raft, ready to pull the big man back. They frantically scanned the fog-blanketed river for movement. But he was gone.

They were floating blind now, either from the gunfire's thick choking haze or the fog. Perhaps both. The harsh stench assaulted her nostrils, along with the metallic scent of blood.

Screams and shouts pierced the darkness. Eva sank back next to Jacqueline and held her tightly.

"Fall back! Fall back to Chalmette! General Jackson's orders!"

"Help me! I'm shot! I'm shot!"

"Fall back!"

Eva wanted to scream in frustration. She was helpless, trapped on this stupid raft. She couldn't even try to save them. And they were dying less than forty feet away.

Muffled cries in French, Spanish and English drifted behind them while the ever-continuous current carried them on.

It was the fog that saved them.

It swirled, masking them in a misty cloud. They floated so near the bank they could hear the splash of soldiers running through the marsh grass and the wet slimy suction as it gripped their boots, belching as they broke free. Had she been on her own, she might have tried to ground the raft and slip from the river to help. With Beatrice and the twins aboard, she couldn't risk their lives. Priorities had shifted from aiding the injured to keeping the children safe.

Without the bright flashes of battle, she could no longer identify the boats in front of them. When the sounds finally diminished enough to chance a look around, Eva peered through the mist.

"Where are we?" Jacqueline asked.

The cold damp air crept down Eva's cloak as she stood. "I'm not sure, exactly."

"We have to search for Raul!" Jacqueline choked, her voice thick with tears.

Eva tried to swallow the knot of dread gripping her throat. The river rarely gave up its victims.

Chapter Thirty-Eight

MEET THE ENEMY

They came across the first dead body about three miles from where they exited the river, just as the sun's glow seeped up from the horizon. It was a British soldier, his face twisted in death, fingers loosely wrapped around his rifle. The twins paled, Jacqueline reached for her brother's hand, but he put his arm around her and pulled her close enough she could bury her face against his shoulder as they passed.

"I should like his coat." Julian shivered as they stepped around another fallen soldier. The boy's thin shoulders were covered with a fine frost.

Jacqueline had finally swallowed her fear and squeamish tendencies, determined to be as calm and stoic as Eva. "It's soaked in blood and muck, Julian," his sister said in a hushed tone. "You'd regret it. Besides, taking it wouldn't be right."

Beatrice made the sign of the cross over the man. "The British will soon be back for their dead."

Eva rose from another futile effort to check for signs of life. "We must keep going," she added, shifting her satchel to the other shoulder. They each had one filled with medical supplies. She cast a sideways glance at Sister Beatrice, worried about her ability to walk such a long distance. Had they reached the Chalmette landing, they'd have been placed on a hospital wagon straight away. No one had anticipated a sloppy trek through the frigid mud.

They trudged in silence. Almost silence. The sound of teeth chattering interrupted the surreal tranquility. Eva's feet were no longer cold since they were now numb. Jacqueline was slogging in a mud-covered stocking because her foot had come out of her boot when the muck wouldn't release it. Julian wrenched it free, but not until after his sister tripped forward. Their lips were blue and shivering.

Being the one responsible for their misery leaked guilt into Eva's stomach. She prayed to God for protection, for Raul's soul, and their safe return. For Drago and his men too, uncertain if they were alive or dead. Her heart twisted and sank, leaving a raw gaping hole in her chest. She wanted to scream her grief and anger into the cruel new light of dawn.

Like a specter in the mist, a gray horse limped a few yards to the right, heading in the opposite direction. Julian tried to capture the creature, but it spooked and ran. The harsh winter wind cut across their faces with brutal nonchalance.

They stayed as close to the water as they dared, thinking the British might avoid the river, worried there were more gunboats drifting along.

Julian picked up an abandoned pouch of musket shot and tossed it into his satchel. Jacqueline followed behind, warily scanning the trees. "It's too quiet."

"That's because every living thing's been driven away by the battle." He surveyed the surrounding devastation. "Or destroyed. Look at this tree."

A young oak with a circumference of a barrel was sprawled across the ground, Its trunk had been shredded by a cannon shot, great splinters flared in a fan of jagged spikes; its top hidden in a tangle of brush.

A low moan perforated the stillness.

Jacqueline's eyes widened, and she stopped. "Did you hear that?"

Julian tapped his finger to his lips. Together, they listened.

His sister pointed to a cluster of willow bushes. "It's coming from in there." Her voice trembled.

Eva shifted her supply bag to the other shoulder. "It's probably someone who's wounded."

Beatrice grabbed her arm. "Or it could be a bear or an alligator."

She gave the elderly nun an exasperated glance and whispered, "It sounded quite human, Sister Beatrice."

Julian picked up a short branch and threw it into the bushes. "If it's a critter, it'll run."

No bear ran off, no alligator thrashed its tail.

Another moan, louder this time.

Eva started toward the noise. The boy bravely stepped up to join her, pushing branches out of her path. She came upon a soldier, his blue coat and orange facings indicating he belonged to the British Light Dragoons, a mounted regiment. The lower half of his body was hidden within the leafy top of the downed tree. He looked to be near twenty, by the sparse covering of blonde whiskers on his cheeks.

Jacqueline knelt beside Eva and used the corner of her cloak to wipe away the blood streaking his face. "He has a wound on his forehead."

Sister Beatrice leaned in. "How bad are his injuries?"

"It's hard to tell, half of him is hidden," Eva said.

The man's eyelids flickered and then opened.

"You have very blue eyes," Jacqueline stated calmly, sitting back on her heels. "What is your name?"

The young man blinked and stared at her a moment before he answered. "Blackwood, miss. Major Ethan Blackwood." He tried to raise his head and winced. "At your service."

She flattened her mouth. "That's unlikely. You've got a gash on your forehead." She pointed. "Just there. It doesn't seem to be terribly deep. I'm Jacqueline Louisa Sauvage, at *your* service, since apparently, you're the one in need."

His baffled gaze hopped from one face to the next. "What happened?"

Jacqueline gestured at the surrounding foliage. "It appears you have been felled by a tree."

Eva attempted to pull away a branch for a better view. "Don't move just yet, try to find your bearings first." She scanned him, looking for wounds. If his lower body was unscathed, with no injuries or breaks, they may be able to help him merely by freeing him from the tree.

With a grimace, he raised to his elbows and looked down at his body. "Can't move my legs."

Eva's heart sank. *Not* good news.

"In fact," he said wincing, "there is a sharp pain in my left thigh." He took in the splintered trunks nearby, and his face paled. "Do you suppose it's been blown off?"

Eva gave him a small smile, hoping it was reassuring. "Not likely," she said.

Jacqueline piped up. "If it had, you'd have bled to death by now."

The man dropped his head back to earth. "Well, that's a comfort."

Julian crawled into the thick brush. "It doesn't appear you're under the trunk, but there is a rather large branch across your legs."

Beatrice straightened and flexed her gnarled fingers. "Well, we should attempt to move it, should we not? Come. If we all heave up, we should be able to lift it enough to free him."

The four broke branches and cleared brush away until they could grasp it. On Julian's count, they heaved. It was no willowy thing, but instead the size of a man's torso. Had his legs been pinned closer to the trunk, it would have been impossible to clear without an ax.

As it was, Eva strained until her muscles began to shake. She wasn't sure how long her grip would last. The shredded limb dug into her palms until they burned.

Julian grunted, his face red with exertion. "Can you move?"

The soldier squirmed, then grimaced in pain. "No."

"Jacqueline, crawl in so you can see what's wrong!" Beatrice gasped. "Quickly and with a will! I won't be able to keep my hold much longer."

The energetic girl dropped to her hands and knees and scurried in. "Oh, my. It looks like a smaller branch has punctured his leg. You must lift it higher before he can move away."

Eva groaned and rolled the load of the tree from her palms to her forearms. They braced their feet and shifted their weight for one final effort.

"We almost have it," Jacqueline shouted. "I'm going to wedge my shoulder under it from down here." The branch jerked upward. "Move, Mr. Blackwood! *Now!*"

The soldier dug his right heel into the ground and scooted himself back.

"My hands are slipping!" Sister Beatrice grunted, her face scrunched with the effort. Once the limb slid from her grasp, neither Julian nor Eva could support the weight. It drove both of them to the earth, and a short scream burst from the foliage.

Eva cried out in panic. "Jacqueline!" Her heart rammed against her ribs, sending blood pounding through her ears. The terrifying image of the young girl crushed by the tree had her frantically clawing for a better handhold. The muscles in her arms and back screamed in pain.

Beatrice struggled to gain a new grip on the limb, her hands were bleeding, and a small branch whipped across her face, leaving a bright red welt.

Ethan Blackwood, ignoring the oozing wound in his left thigh, rolled to his stomach and squirmed into the foliage of the tree until only his boots showed. A second later, he wiggled back out with Jacqueline clinging to his arm.

With a collective groan, they all collapsed. She started to crawl forward, to seek for signs of injury or blood, but her palms protested. The splintered wood had punctured the skin in several places, and it looked as if some of it was still there. She heaved her shrieking body up and staggered over to the brave girl and Blackwood, then sank back to the ground.

Jacqueline was gasping for breath, sprawled across Black- wood's chest, hair a tangled mass of twigs and leaves. She opened her eyes, and Eva marked the exact moment she realized her physical location. With a horrified gasp, she tried to push herself off the man but ended up floundering like a minnow out of the water. He pulled her off and to his right, where she landed on her backside with a very unladylike *oof*.

Relief had Eva sending up a short prayer of thanks.

Blackwood gasped for air with the rest of them. "It's a good thing... Miss Jacqueline... you are... not portly in the slightest," the young officer panted. A light sheen of sweat coated his face, giving it a grayish cast.

For once, the sprite had no retort.

Ignoring her own bloodied hands, Eva opened her satchel and drew out a small bottle and several bandages. "Let's have a look at that leg, major." She removed the cork. "This will sting, but it is necessary." She splashed a small amount of whiskey over the wound before wiping away the blood. To his credit, he only let out a soft hiss, although his face was drawn and pained. She prodded around and removed several splinters of wood before coating it with salve, bandaging it tightly.

"Thank you, sister," he whispered.

"You must care for this wound diligently, Major Blackwood," Eva instructed. "Otherwise you may yet lose your leg."

Julian crossed his arms over his chest. "I suppose he's our prisoner then."

Jacqueline rolled her eyes and gave him an exasperated stare. "What in the world would we possibly do with a prisoner?" She gestured at the soldier's long frame. "It's not like any of us are strong enough to carry him."

Sister Beatrice slammed her eyebrows down. "There'll be no taking of prisoners, young man."

They were here as healers, not soldiers. Jacqueline brought up a tricky dilemma, however. Eva took in the surrounding landscape, trying to get a better sense of how far south of Villeré they were. The fog made it impossible, though.

Jacqueline was running her fingers through her hair, pulling out debris. "We can't very well just leave him here, can we?" She said in that practical tone of hers. "The gators will get him for sure, lame as he is."

Blackwood swiftly shoved himself into a more upright sitting position. "Alligators? Here? This far from the swamp?"

Jacqueline shrugged, her eyes crossing as she focused on unknotting a tiny twig from a tangled lock of hair.

The soldier let out a piercing whistle, startling them. At their looks of surprise, he apologized. "I didn't mean to scare you, I'm calling Ferret, my horse, in case he survived and is near enough to hear."

Jacqueline wrinkled her nose. "You named your horse Ferret?"

Ethan Blackwood just gave her a small smile. "I didn't name him. However, he is quite intelligent. Much like a wily ferret."

The sound of a horse's hooves on the soft ground drew their attention. A gray gelding trotted into view, the same one they noticed earlier limping through the fog. But this time he had a rider. Or apparently, someone who was *attempting* to ride him. The man mostly bounced erratically on the beast's back.

The redcoat rider cursed. "What the devil, you blighter of a horse!" In one hand he gripped the reins, in his other a rifle fixed with a bayonet. His uniform was filthy and torn. Several coats, some red, some darker shades of brown and blue and one made of buckskin, were tied behind the saddle, along with a pair of boots and a half dozen rifles.

The animal stopped before them, its flanks heaving. The man looked up and narrowed his eyes at the small group in front of him. "What 'ave we 'ere?"

Jacqueline gestured to the horse. "Is this Ferret?"

Blackwood gave her a slight nod. His expression had darkened; cool, flinty eyes never left the soldier on the horse.

Julian brushed his hands on his britches. "Well, this works out then. You can ride together back to your camp."

Blackwood's mouth was pressed into a rigid line. He shifted and addressed the redcoat. "Your mount shows signs of abuse. He is injured and should not be hard ridden."

The man dismounted. "Is 'at so?" Small, hazel eyes darted back and forth, examining the scene in front of him. He glanced at the bandaged leg of the major, then switched his attention to the women and children. He ignored Sister Beatrice, then gave a glance of mild interest to Eva before perusing Jacqueline. A sickening chill spidered down Eva's spine at his lingering stare.

He turned back to Blackwood, and she took that opportunity to shove the girl behind her.

"Why did you do that?" Jacqueline whispered.

Eva reached back and gripped one of her wrists. "Just stay behind me," she hissed. "I want you to run and hide the first chance you get, understand?"

"An' who be you what knows about horses enough to say?" The redcoat sneered.

The officer answered in a voice icy and flat, his eyes flashing. "I am Major Ethan Blackwood of the Duchess of York's 14th regiment, and that is my horse."

It was obvious that Blackwood outranked the soldier, but by the redcoat's demeanor, that seemed to carry little weight. He'd been traveling along the river also, toward New Orleans. If he was heading back to Villeré, he'd be further from the Mississippi. That could mean only one thing.

Deserter.

The soldier barked a harsh laugh. "This ain't yer horse no more. And it don't look like you're in any position to right a challenge fer it." The deserter spread his arms wide and spun in a slow circle. "This be the land of the free, an' I be stayin' as a free man. We 'ave fifteen thousand men, no one will miss me." He jerked his chin at Ethan. "Or you."

That was a not-so-veiled threat.

He whirled and pointed his gun at Jacqueline. Eva's stomach lurched. How did she get all the way over by Blackwood? Why didn't she listen and hide?

"Get on the horse, missy," the man raised the rifle to his shoulder.

The girl sucked in an angry breath and scowled. "I will not."

Run, Jacqueline.

He waved the gun at Julian. "Put her on the saddle, or I'll shoot her, then you."

Julian glared at the soldier, his jaw clenching as well as his fists. Fear skittered through his sister's eyes, and she locked them on the rifle. The boy shuffled up to his sister and muttered something as he helped her up. The blood drained from Jacqueline's face so fast that even her lips turned white.

Julian quickly spun and charged the soldier who brought the butt of his rifle down then up in a wicked arc, catching him under the chin. Jacqueline screamed as her brother fell to the ground, motionless.

Eva was too far away, or she'd smack the horse hard enough to cause it to bolt. Instead, she grabbed a foot-long shard of the splintered tree trunk and threw it, hitting the horse's shoulder.

Ferret was a warhorse. A little piece of wood didn't even make him flinch.

The deserter swiveled the rifle to point it at Jacqueline, catching her just as she attempted to dismount. "Stay where you are, lovey."

She glowered a death glare at him and slowly settled back in her seat.

Sister Beatrice shook both fists at the soldier. "You wicked man, you have only the courage to attack children?" She took a limping step toward him, but Eva grabbed her tunic.

He'd kill the old woman without thinking twice.

The elder nun whispered over her shoulder. "He can only shoot one of us. You have scissors in your satchel. Follow me, and when I fall, you must strike."

Eva's heart hammered in her chest, even as the hopelessness of their situation weighed down her shoulders. There had to be a better plan. There just had to be, but none came to mind in this moment of dire need.

Beatrice gave her no time to argue; she spun and jolted toward the soldier as fast as she could hobble. "I shall not permit you to take that child!"

He raised his rifle and aimed down the barrel toward the nun. "I'll shoot. I won't hesitate."

"Neither will I."

The report of the gunshot cracked through the air. Eva screamed and started to run at the redcoat, but stumbled to a stop. Beatrice remained upright, dumbfounded.

The deserter was face down in the mud.

Jacqueline dropped the rifle that had been strapped on the saddle. She slid off the horse and ran to her brother, who was sitting up rubbing his jaw.

Major Ethan Blackwood reclined against the trunk, the pistol in his hand still smoking.

Chapter Thirty-Nine

CHOOSE WRONG AND DIE

The plan seemed like a decent idea at the time.

First, using a skeleton crew, follow the *Carolina* downriver, then bombard the British camp. Second, tie up the *Dragon* on the west side of the Mississippi, take canoes up the Le Courbé canal to Bayou Bienvenu and through the swamp far to the east of the battleground, find the cane fascines, destroy them, then continue on to New Orleans.

Except for the duration of the attack, the blast to the ship's stern and the unanticipated speed of the current, the strategy might have succeeded.

In the end, the overall engagement was catastrophic for the *Dragon*.

One shot hit the rudder, another pierced the bulwark above it. A third exploded against the mizzen mast, snapping it in half. The river took complete control of the ship. In the darkness, they missed the canal and rammed the riverbank only God knows where downstream, grounding her.

The good news was that they were too far away from the British headquarters to be easily captured. The bad news was that the *Dragon* was taking on water. They had a muddy trek carrying canoes from the waterway to the swamp and then a long row through the marsh back to the bloody fascines.

The oil lanterns coupled with a small bumpkin of gunpowder should be enough to set the cane afire if they ever made it there.

The sun was rising, or at least it appeared to be. It was impossible to see the yellow orb through the fog. The explosions and gunfire had long ceased.

Although he outlined the risks (in fact, his exact words were "We'll probably fail,") Manuel and four other members of his crew had volunteered to help execute his plan. Except for Raul, the rest had followed the Baratarian pirates, and either joined Jackson's army or traveled with Lafitte's men down to Fort St. Philip on the *USS Carolina* to defend the mouth of the river.

Manuel pulled his oar through the thick water. "Drago, do you think the twins and Sister Eva are safe?" His dubious tone gave away his distress.

Drago's thoughts swirled in the same pool of concern. "Raul is with them. They are behind the battle lines and won't be within the range of danger." The worry still burned a hole in his gut.

Jackson had ordered holes and ditches dug throughout the Chalmette fields. What if their wagon became mired in the mud, and the front line shifted, placing them in jeopardy? He wanted to know how well Jackson's troops fared in the nighttime assault. The British could be marching on the city now for all he knew.

He could only pray. He acknowledged the irony with a sarcastic snort, doubting his prayers made it halfway to God's ears. Although, it would undoubtedly please Eva that he considered making the effort.

A tiny consolation.

So many potential calamities ran through his head he could barely think, which was probably why the British were able to sneak up on him.

The crack of a gunshot echoed over the water. He shifted his gaze up to the trees where a dozen British marksmen crouched.

At least twenty boats emerged from the mist. If he had to guess, he'd say that they just paddled into a regiment heading for the British stronghold at Villeré plantation.

"We fight!" Manuel shouted, picking up his rifle.

"No!" Drago grabbed his arm. "There are too many. Look around."

He shook off Drago's hand. "We have to fight for freedom," he argued. "For Jacqueline and Julian. For their home, Drago. We *promised*."

Manuel and his promises. The man was slow in the head, but had an innate sense of right and wrong. What he lacked in smarts, he more than made up for in heart, compassion and loyalty. There wasn't a better man of honor on God's earth.

Therefore, he was constantly poking Drago's conscience in a most annoying fashion.

Cursing, Drago pushed the barrel of Manuel's gun down. "Yes, Manuel, we promised. But let's wait until the odds are more in our favor." Their best chance of staying alive was to surrender now.

He'd figure out a way to escape later.

The huge man lowered his weapon, his shoulders drooping. Drago gave his men hurried instructions on what information to divulge and what should be twisted, in case they were interrogated.

They rested their paddles on their knees as several longboats approached. The redcoats in them were the lucky ones. Others stood shin-deep in the water, lips blue with cold. And, Drago noted, carrying bundles of sugarcane fascines strapped to their packs.

His sugarcane, no doubt.

The commander sent men to take Drago's canoes, and it wasn't long before they were wading through the quagmire with the soldiers, hands tied in front of them.

By the time they emerged at Villeré, the sun had burned away the mist. His stomach plummeted, and for a brief moment, he thought he'd be sick. Manuel's high-pitched hum of despair pretty much summed up his own feelings.

Ramón one of his crewmen, crossed himself. "*Madre de Dios,*" his terrified whisper likely echoed all their thoughts. "We are doomed."

Spread across acres of fields hundreds of men worked, erecting straight rows of tents, cavalry regiments in blue coats, foot soldiers in red coats, some in kilts, some in trousers. Dozens of campfires sent thin fingers of smoke into the air, various slaughtered farm animals roasting on spits.

The raid disrupted only a narrow strip of the camp closest to the river. Splintered trunks, some still smoking, and ruptured earth marked the battle zone. Several freshly dug graves spotted an area further from the trees.

And this wouldn't be all the soldiers. Surely more waited aboard warships, planning an attack on Fort St. Philip at the mouth of the Mississippi, others in gunboats on Lake Borgne sailing through the passage to Lake Pontchartrain to strike Fort Charles, then the city herself.

Drago had only ever skirted the edges of combat, creeping in and out, doing reconnaissance, delivering orders, stealing, disrupting, sabotaging. Privateering.

This was indeed an army of thousands.

Sneaking in to destroy the fascines had been a fool's errand. Dread coated his stomach like thick, oozing tar when he thought of Eva and the children. He was helpless now to protect them. At some point in the near future, they'd be in the midst of a deadly battle. He'd rather bloody well die defending them in New Orleans than here, with his hands bound as a prisoner of war.

Drago and the others, shivering and coated with muck, were thrown into a small outbuilding. They huddled together for warmth, and he distracted them by calmly giving instructions to observe and mentally catalog as much as they could, to help plan their escape.

They *would* escape.

It was some time before the door opened, and a soldier sneered at them. "Whose duty is it to lead these dirty shirts?"

Drago stumbled to his feet and his cousin rose with him. "Sit down, Manuel," he hissed, trying to knock the hulk of a man off balance. It was no use.

Manuel's mouth flattened into a stubborn line, his eyes flared. "I go where you go, Drago. Always, I go where you go. We are brothers of the sword."

Shaking his head and glaring at his cousin, he stumbled out of the building, water still sloshing around in his boots. He couldn't feel his toes. Bloody British maggots.

Manuel's shoulder, a granite wall of muscle, brushed his. That small familiar sign of support gave him strength despite his concern that his cousin would lose both his control and his temper at any moment.

A wiry officer with a pinched face and small eyes coolly assessed them, before addressing Drago. "What is your name and rank?"

Rank? The idiot thought he was an American soldier. "Drago Gamponetti. And you are?"

The man sniffed and wrinkled his nose in disgust. One of the redcoats raised the butt of his rifle and drove it into Drago's abdomen, causing him to double over in agony. "You are in the presence of Lieutenant Colonel Brighton, and you'll do well to remember your manners," the soldier snapped.

Manuel lowered his brows and scowled, then moved to shield him. The man's eyes widened, and he stumbled back and pointed his weapon at him. "Step aside."

Manuel didn't budge. If Drago didn't do something quickly, his cousin would get himself shot. "Stand down, sailor."

Manuel stepped behind him. "Aye, captain."

Brighton lifted a brow. "Captain? So you are an American officer? This is your regiment?" He snorted in laughter, followed by his men.

"No," Drago said, voice steady now that he had his breath back. "I'm a simple merchant captain."

The lieutenant colonel narrowed his eyes. "Where is your ship?"

There was no reason to lie, but he didn't want the British taking the *Dragon* then using her against the Americans. "Downriver," he finally said. "We ran aground yesterday, and she was damaged too badly to continue." Hopefully, if they thought she was breached, they wouldn't bother looking for her.

Brighton curled his lip, eyes hard and intelligent. "Yet you were captured heading in the direction of the encampment." He clasped his hands behind his back. "Forgive me if I don't believe you. I shall provide you an opportunity to place yourself in a position of better grace. Let's start with the number of regiments, men in each regiment and their locations. Where are the American batteries located? How are they manned? Is the ground stable for the cavalry?"

Drago sighed and inclined his head. "While I thank you for the opportunity, I shall reiterate that I am a ship's captain, not part of the regulars, although I do recall overhearing a comment in a tavern that General Jackson amassed nearly twenty-thousand men and is expecting another ten from Illinois, Kentucky and Ohio by the Sabbath." Not a word of that was true, but he'd die before he told them that American troops scarcely reached four thousand.

The redcoat shifted his weapon and cast a nervous glance at his commander. "What about the batteries?" he asked.

He shrugged. "I don't know."

The officer's voice was brittle, laced with an undercurrent of impatient fury. "Where are the regiments stationed?"

"I. Don't. Know." He knew it was coming, but it still hurt like the devil. The butt of the soldier's rifle once again struck, this time in his ribs, leaving him wheezing. A stabbing burn greeted every inhale.

Brighton bent over him and growled. "What about the terrain? We need to know how to dispatch the cavalry."

This time, he tensed before the strike. "I'm a merchant captain—"

Another hit to his stomach.

The redcoat snarled. "Answer the question, you filthy maggot!" This time, the butt grazed his temple. A blinding white bolt exploded behind his eyes, and he staggered before his knees crashed to the cold, slick ground, jarring his bruised ribs enough to expel a pained grunt.

A growl reverberated from Manuel, and he charged the redcoat who'd struck Drago.

"Manuel! No!" He barely drew enough breath to speak. Shards of pain sliced through his ribcage. He struggled to rise, but a wave of dizziness shoved him off-balance. He fought to stay conscious enough to push up on one knee. Warm trails of blood streamed down his face.

Manuel roared, his eyes flashed lightning; thunder rumbled in his throat. "We fight! We fight for freedom!" He flung his bound hands into the side of the soldier's head, snapping his neck. Two others surged forward and grasped his arms.

Manuel's eyes went wide, white, and crazed. "No! No touching! No touching!" He shook off their grip as if they were drops of rain.

Drago's heart slammed into his pained ribs, and he tried again to find his footing. "Manuel, stop!" His voice was hoarse and the ground uneven.

Brighton shrank back several paces along with the two soldiers flanking him. Two other unsuspecting men ran past with sabers drawn. Manuel plowed both down before they could strike. Another raised his gun and squeezed the trigger. Manuel jerked back, and blood seeped through his shirt, but he continued to charge toward Brighton. Brighton's guards finally gained the courage to engage. Manuel took another bullet to the chest.

Drago's vision blurred, whether from the blow to the head or the blood flowing into his eyes he couldn't tell. He tried again to get through to Manuel, tell him to stop.

More soldiers swarmed toward them, rifles drawn. Two more shots brought Manuel to his knees, gasping for breath. His gaze, flooded with passion and agony, locked with Drago's. His hair was plastered to his face and neck, stubborn stone jaw quivering with animal rage.

"Fight for freedom... for Jacqueline and Julian...for Sister Eva...for our friends, Drago. We promised!"

Brighton raised his pistol, then shot Manuel in the head.

"No!" Drago screamed. Manuel! The world tipped and spun. He collapsed to the ground, tears mixing with the rivulets of warm blood streaming down his face.

Manuel, strong of heart and brawn. Courageous and loyal beyond measure. The two of them had watched each other's backs since they were boys. His cousin had saved him countless times. Today, when Manuel needed *him* most, he'd failed to reciprocate. By the sheer force of will, Drago lurched to his feet, vengeance burning in his heart. Hot pain sliced through his skull just before he blacked out.

Chapter Forty
ROAD TO VILLERÉ

E va's heart slammed against her ribcage. She knelt by the fallen deserter and rolled him over. The bullet went straight through his forehead. "He's dead." She looked at the major. "I hesitate to ask the penalty for killing a fellow warrior of the crown."

Blackwood holstered his pistol, his mouth set in a grim line. "He was a deserter, although 'tis best if we don't speak of it."

Jacqueline helped her brother to his feet. He held his jaw, eyes smarting with pain, face clouded with anger. He shook off Jacqueline and turned away.

"Let me see it," Eva said. He was trying to act tough, but she worried about a broken jawbone.

He let her pull his hand away, revealing a gash on his chin. She wiped away the blood. A couple stitches and it would heal well enough. "The scar will provide an exciting war story," she teased.

Julian actually brightened at that, probably already weaving a grand tale.

Sister Beatrice was still shaking, both hands pressed against her chest. "You saved our lives, sir." She dropped to a seat on the downed tree with a very unladylike grunt.

"And you saved mine," he responded. Blackwood gave Eva his full attention. "I only ask you to help me mount my horse, so I may return to my regiment."

Eva hesitated. How could she in good conscience release him? He'd be ordered back to combat American soldiers. Yet, after saving Jacqueline, how could she deny him his request?

Tilting his head, Blackwood perused her and the others, who were probably thinking the same thing. He gave them a wry smile. "My injuries will likely remove me from command. I shall not be fighting anytime soon. I'll barely be able to stay astride a horse as it is." He shrugged and rolled to his knees, wincing. "I have little choice but to try."

Jacqueline retrieved the horse's reins. "Well, there's only one way we'll know for sure. Julian, you and Eva are the strongest. Perhaps you should help him to his feet?"

Eva hooked her elbow under the soldier's upper arm, and Julian imitated her. "Sister Beatrice, will you support the injured leg?" She addressed the officer. "Are you ready?"

He nodded, lips flat with pain. Once upright, Blackwood grimaced and swayed.

Eva tightened her grip. "Keep your hold strong, Julian."

"Yes, ma'am."

The nun gently lowered the wounded limb. "How will he mount?"

"Like this," he grunted. Placing his arm on the pommel, he shifted his weight to the injured leg just long enough to allow him to thrust his other boot into the stirrup. He mounted smoothly from there.

Beatrice pressed her hands together, pleased. "Well! That was much easier than I expected."

No sooner had she said that than the man started to wilt.

"Grab him!" Jacqueline cried.

Eva clutched his jacket then tugged him upright while from the other side of the horse, Julian braced his hands on his hip and shoved. She glanced at Beatrice, wondering how to best phrase her thoughts. "Sister, I think you should ride behind him to keep the major steady."

They would also move at a quicker pace. The elder nun could only walk so fast. Obviously, they'd have to escort the soldier back to his camp. He wouldn't make it, otherwise.

Sister Beatrice's eyes widened. "Me? Ride *astride* a horse? I could never...it would be...I could *not*."

Eva wrapped her hands around the old nun's. "Sister, you must. You're strong enough to hold him in place. I know your knees pain you. Give them some ease, at least for a while." It was her legs Beatrice was likely worried about. A religious dress and tunic were not made to accommodate much in width. They would ride up.

The old nun pondered Eva's logic. Uncertainty and trepidation flickered across her face.

"Look, Sister Beatrice." Jacqueline pointed to the coats tied to the back of the saddle. "We can blanket your legs with these."

Smart girl.

Jacqueline's idea bolstered Beatrice's decision. "Fine, then. I shall do it. Julian, turn your head."

He was directed to the opposite side, assigned the task of keeping the steed still; both so the sister could mount as well as to keep the major seated. Finding a stump to make it easier, Eva and Jacqueline wrestled and pulled until Sister Beatrice was finally in position behind him. They draped two coats securely over her legs.

"Well!" Sister Beatrice's face was flushed from either embarrassment or exertion, it was hard to tell. With Eva shouldering her rump and Jacqueline guiding her exposed leg, it was probably both. "I admit, I'm a trifle nervous," she said.

Blackwood gathered the reins. "I'll do my best to avoid becoming a nuisance. Ferret is very-well trained and unlikely to bolt. Even so, we'll continue slowly for our safety as well as his."

At Eva's urging, Beatrice reached her hands around the major's waist. The nun paused a moment to get herself settled. "This isn't as horrible as I expected. In fact, it's quite a bit warmer." She blushed profusely.

Blackwood's face reddened, and he gave a choked cough.

"Let's proceed." Jacqueline took charge. "Julian and I will hold the major's boots to keep him balanced and astride."

Julian shrugged into the remaining coat the deserter had pilfered, a soft buckskin with a fur-lined collar, which he flipped up to cover his ears. He huffed out a nervous breath. "I guess we're off to Villeré." He looked to the northeast, where campfire smoke drifted with the wind. "I wonder how we'll be received."

There was no guessing. Eva could at least hide behind her veil. A knot of worry hardened in her stomach when her gaze rested on Jacqueline, who was obviously vulnerable and exposed.

At thirteen, she was even more at risk for abuse, especially from men like that deserter. With her dark, coffee-colored hair, silver eyes and full, easy smile, she was already transitioning from lovely to beautiful. In a few years, she'd be stunning.

Eva's gaze shifted to Julian, so ready to be a man. He could very well be forced into the army by the British, as was their wont. It was one of the foremost reasons the United States declared war against England. Too many American merchant vessels were ransacked, their crews pressed into service with the Royal Navy.

Anxiety and fear churned and clawed a hot path up her throat. If she'd insisted the children stay at the convent, they'd have sneaked out and followed her. It had become exceedingly obvious the only way to prevent them from getting into trouble, was to keep them with her, even though it didn't guarantee good behavior in the slightest.

The ground was uneven and pitted with ditches and holes, the American army's pitiful attempt to slow enemy troops. The major struggled to stay upright; each jolt drew a slight wince. He glanced down at Julian. "From your conversations, I've learned your given name is Julian, and your little sister's name is Jacqueline."

"Two minutes," Jacqueline said from the other side of the horse.

Blackwood gave her a puzzled look. "I beg your pardon?"

"He is only two minutes older than me, and I'll have you know I'm thirteen."

Julian puffed out his chest and grinned, enjoying the opportunity to nettle her a bit. "It still makes me older, *little* sister."

"Pfft."

Julian shifted the conversation before Jacqueline's temper got the best of her. "Have you always wanted to be a Dragoon?"

The man didn't immediately answer but stared at his hands holding the reins.

"Major Blackwood? Did you?"

He expelled a lungful of air. "No, but I'm content with my choice."

"Was your father a Dragoon? Is that why you joined?"

The officer let out a short, sardonic laugh. "No, definitely not. Truth be told, I did it to get away from him because I didn't want to follow in his footsteps."

This got Jacqueline's attention and by default, her imagination. "Why ever not? Was he a criminal? Not all criminals are bad through and through. We are friends with a pirate, although he isn't a pirate anymore. He actually saved Julian's life nearly at the expense of his own."

Eva's eyebrows jumped. Now there was a story she'd love to hear.

The major's thoughts ran along the same path. Either that or he wanted to nudge the conversation in another direction. "Saved by a pirate?" He gave Jacqueline a dubious expression. "That sounds rather unlikely."

Julian's eyes danced with excitement. "Captain Gampo truly did! I was nine—"

"Eight," Jacqueline corrected. "It was summer. We only just turned thirteen last month."

Julian rolled his eyes. "Fine. I was hiding under the captain's bed and found a stiletto. I heard the clash of swords and decided to help. He was fighting off Captain Brendan with a long sword, a saber. I attacked, surprising Captain Brendan. Instinct made him adjust his swing toward me, and Gampo flung his body between me and the blade."

Blackwood smirked. "That doesn't sound like a pirate."

No, it didn't. A small flicker sparked in Eva's chest, and she smiled to herself. Not at all.

Drago. Please be alive.

Julian's voice turned more somber. "If he hadn't, the sword would have taken off my head."

The major looked impressed. "That was quite brave for an eight-year-old."

Jacqueline snorted. "It was quite *stupid*."

Julian didn't argue. His own chagrinned expression drew the corners of his mouth down.

"Are you married?" Jacqueline asked.

Blackwood jumped at the sudden change in conversation. "No." He pressed his lips together as if annoyed the answer was startled out of him.

The girl focused her attention on skirting a large hole, but the corners of her mouth were tipped up.

He frowned, although his eyes twinkled with amusement. "You are quite talkative for such a young girl. In England, children are taught to be seen, but not heard."

"I'd like to visit London, someday. Although I cannot promise to remain silent the entire time," Jacqueline replied. The expression on her face led Eva to the conclusion that the girl likely wouldn't even try. The nice thing about the veil was that it did a wonderful job hiding smiles.

This time, the Major chuckled. "It would be a terrible shame if you did." The saddle creaked as he shifted in his seat. He winced. "Should any of you ever find yourself in London, it would be my honor to have you as guests."

Julian frowned. "You'd invite your enemies into your home?"

Blackwood stiffened. "You're not my enemy." He gestured to his wounded thigh. "I owe you a deep debt of gratitude for saving my life. If ever I can be of assistance, I hope you grant me the opportunity."

That opportunity might come earlier rather than later, depending on their reception at the British headquarters.

Sister Beatrice piped up, echoing Eva's concerns. "Your aid in keeping these children out of harm's way would be payment enough."

"Is your house big enough for us if we do come visit?" Julian asked.

"Quite."

"How would we ever find you?" Jacqueline asked.

"It shouldn't be too hard," he said dryly.

"I think I should like to marry an English aristocrat," Jacqueline mused. She brightened. "Perhaps when I'm eighteen, I can marry you."

The major barked out a preposterous laugh. "That is highly unlikely." He glanced at the young girl and abruptly bit his tongue.

Eva caught the shadow that flickered across the girl's face at his response, and her heart sank. Jacqueline's cheeks colored, and she moved away from the horse to hop a puddle, taking her time to return.

Blackwood shot her a sideways glance before clearing his throat and continuing. "However, I'm sure every gentleman in town will be begging for your hand."

Jacqueline's shoulders hitched the slightest amount before they straightened again. She didn't say another word.

In the distance, Villeré's house eased from the mist, a charcoal outline against a dreary gray backdrop. Eva's pulse quickened as several soldiers stepped from the fog and stopped. They were too far away to see their faces clearly, but close enough to notice their raised weapons.

"Halt!" The voice paralyzed everyone. A lieutenant came forward and raked his gaze over Blackwood's epithets. "Name and regiment, Major, sir?" he asked.

"I am Major Ethan Blackwood, Her Grace's Light Dragoons, 14th." He waved to Eva and the children. "These are civilian members of a medical detachment."

The lieutenant studied their group.

"We are from the Ursuline convent," Sister Beatrice offered.

By now, the rest of the watch had surrounded them. "You'll be accompanied to the Lieutenant Corporal of your regiment for formal identification," the soldier said crisply to Blackwood. Four of them flanked the horse.

Eva released her hold on the bridle and moved next to Jacqueline, who stood wide-eyed and quiet for once. Julian's expression wavered between fear and gritty bravado, but he stayed on the other side of the Major's mount. Beatrice remained strangely silent, perhaps waiting until her words fell on more influential ears.

She just hoped the major would find a way to protect Julian.

Blackwood nodded, then, "The women and children?"

The captain gestured for them to move along the lane with Ferret. "General Hampton will determine what's to be done with them."

Jacqueline cast a worried glance at her brother. Eva bit her lip. What would the British do with the boy? Would they treat him as a hostile prisoner and confine him or press him into the service of one of their officers? Her fears somewhat eased with Blackwood's next statement.

"I should like the boy to first care for my mount. I have a leg wound." The Major lifted the coat covering his blood-soaked thigh. Eva let out a sigh of relief.

The captain shrugged and gestured with his rifle for Julian to fall in next to Ferret. Hopefully, the Major would be able to see after him and keep him safe. They continued down the lane toward the main house. Near and far, dark specks dotted the landscape in a regular pattern of squares, looking very much like haystacks until they got closer. A sickening blanket of dread descended upon Eva's shoulders as she looked out at the hundreds and hundreds of tents spread out across acres of Villeré fields.

Until now, she hadn't been able to comprehend the terrifying magnitude of their numbers. Drago had understood the overwhelming odds against them when he'd seen the armada amassing in Negril Bay. Still, he came to New Orleans to warn his friends. Then he'd stayed and thrown his lot in with them. A bleaker thought made her stomach harden. The chance of his survival was tiny. They were a fledgling country fighting the strongest military force of their age.

This was not his war. This was not his land.

There was no patriotic fever burning in his chest for freedom and victory. He was, as Jean Lafitte had so elegantly pointed out, a pirate, after all.

Chapter Forty-One

AIDE A FOE

The skirmishes between the two sides continued for the next few days. Musket fire, the boom of Lafitte's big canons and British rockets testing their range and resolve interrupted the stillness of nearly every dawn. Eva's thoughts were of Drago every night before she closed her eyes and the first thing in the morning when she opened them. The thought he might be dead chilled the very center of her bones. She was thankful the British kept her busy.

Eva and Sister Beatrice worked in the hospital tent, tending the wounded and sick. Jacqueline stayed at her side, assisting, asking countless questions of both Eva and the patients they nursed.

"How does laudanum work? Why did that soldier still feel pain in his arm, when it was no longer attached to his shoulder? Will the surgeon insist upon removing Major Blackwood's leg? I checked it yesterday, and there was no horrible odor. He should heal quite well, don't you think? Why won't the doctor allow you to use your Jamaican herbs for this man? It seems very narrow-minded. Why do the British Negroes die from this cold weather more often than the British white men? Do you suppose it is due to their blood being unaccustomed to the chill? Does it flow too slowly here? Do you think Tristan and Uncle Bernard and Captain Gampo and Harvey are unharmed? I can't bear to think the worst, it makes me weep through my prayers."

When the young girl paused to breathe, Eva would slip in a few words, "The only thing we can do for your family is to pray, and hope Jackson can lead his troops to victory." Even as she spoke, her stomach dropped. Chances were nearly nothing that they would survive. How she prayed that Drago would come back to her so they could marry and be happy together! Her eyes burned with tears when she thought of a life without him.

General Pakenham had arrived several days ago and since then, the British made infrequent sorties to various parts of the American lines, testing for weaknesses.

There had to be plenty.

A young soldier came in the tent, scanned the area and when his gaze found her, headed her way. She recognized the boy, Edward Smythe, perhaps a year or two older than Julian. He shuffled toward her in boots too large; his jacket sleeves nearly brushed his fingertips. So boyish and lanky. How was he to fight in a battle when his weapon and pack likely weighed as much as he did?

He came to sit with another soldier soon after she arrived at Villeré. From the resemblance, they were related. Brothers, she later discovered. The elder brother had been gut shot during the December 23rd skirmish. Over the next couple of days, the cadet sat at his brother's bedside for hours and stopped in between his duties. Exhaustion blanketed his features, dark circles sank beneath his eyes. One morning she arrived to the sound of quiet weeping. His brother had died during the night. She hugged the young man a long time while he sobbed his horrible loss on her shoulder. A valiant boy with a kind heart, he was so much like Julian, yet they were forced to be enemies. Under different circumstances, things probably would have been different.

She, Jacqueline and Sister Beatrice had attended the burial, offering what little solace they could. They all soon became fast friends. Edward returned daily to help or sit beside dying soldiers. "William had me with him when he died. These men have no one," he said when Jacqueline finally asked how he could stand to return to the place where he watched his brother die.

Eva straightened and awaited young Edward's message. It wouldn't be the first time she was called away to attend an officer or his horse if that was what the cadet was about.

"Your presence is required at the main headquarters, Sister Eva. Bring any supplies needed to stitch a cut, if you would."

He waited while they gathered their things, but frowned at the girl. "You must stay, Miss Jacqueline. Only Sister Eva has been requested, I'm sorry."

Eva placed her bag on an empty cot. "As I am the girl's guardian, we shall go together, or not at all. She's too young and inexperienced to remain here alone." They'd both been the subject of more than a few indecent perusals from several soldiers already. After the harrowing experience with the deserter, she wasn't about to let the girl out of her sight.

He frowned. "Can she not stay with the other nun?"

Eva flattened her mouth and shook her head. Beatrice's knees had swollen, making it difficult for the woman to even walk. She carried a three-legged stool with her, to sit while changing dressings and cleaning wounds.

The medical bag remained on the ground, Eva's message clear.

Edward hesitated and opened his mouth, thought better of it and simply gave both a curt nod. "Follow me, please."

He led them toward the main plantation house. The day before it had rained and had become bitterly cold during the night; depressions in the earth captured standing water, now covered with a thin layer of ice. Eva tucked her chilled hands into her tunic.

Jacqueline skipped ahead and spoke to the private, her breath puffing a white mist in the brisk morning air. "Will you return to your family after the war is over? Do you have any sisters?"

His step faltered, although his expression remained stoic. "My brother was all that was left of my family." He paused to clear his throat.

Jacqueline's face dropped. "Do you not have anyone?"

The cadet raised his chin. Then he exhaled, abandoning the bravado. "That is why I followed him here."

Eva's heart broke. Another orphan. To her, he was a child. No child should be alone in the world. She of all people knew that much.

"Come with us!" Jacqueline blurted the words on the tip of Eva's tongue. "My brothers and I live with our uncle. We have a hotel and gaming house in town. I'm sure he would take you in and find a purpose for you."

The boy slowed his steps and shot a wary glance at her. "Would they accept a *redcoat* in their midst? They might have a different opinion after the war ends."

Jacqueline flipped his words away. "Posh. This country welcomes all nations. Why, if you just look around the streets of New Orleans," she swept her hand in the direction of the city, "you'd see Frenchmen, Spaniards, Indian savages from multiple tribes, islanders, British and even pirates." The last she added in a hushed tone, then smiled. "We have our own pirate in the family, Captain Gampo. Although he's not really a pirate anymore."

Drago was an American regular now. Where was he at this very moment? Was he safe?

Jacqueline gave Edward a close-lipped smile that looked like her mouth was full of pebbles. That child's spunk was going to get her into trouble. Eva tossed her a warning frown.

Little good it did. Jacqueline continued anyway. "Before that, he was one of Jean Lafitte's Baratarian pirates." She hopped over another ice-crusted puddle. "He's not blood, but we still consider him family." She looped her arm through Edward's elbow. "Julian and I would enjoy having someone nearer to us in age. Stevie is seven years older, but she's married and is with her husband on his merchant ship. Tristan is the next eldest, by ten years."

Hope flared in his eyes. "I've been told a man could travel into the western wilderness from here. Be his own man." The hope dimmed. "My commander would never release me until my commission is complete."

Eva touched his arm. "As an American, your freedom would be greater," she said. "But if the country falls back under the rule of the English crown—"

They fell into silence, pondering Eva's words.

After a moment, he answered, his voice gruff. "I'll consider it if I survive the battle. There is nothing for me back home."

"Survive the battle..." Jacqueline repeated in a horrified tone. "Cadet Smythe—"

"Call me Edward, if you please," he said.

Jacqueline grabbed his sleeve. "Edward, you must come with us to New Orleans." She nodded toward Eva. "We'll return as soon as it's feasible."

He gave her a shocked look. "But you're our *prisoners*."

Jacqueline rolled her eyes. "We're no threat to the British. Who'd stop three children and two nuns who decided to continue their journey?"

He shot her an irritated look, and she quickly made the correction. "Three *orphans* and two nuns."

Edward just shook his head and led them through the kitchen garden with its frost-coated plants.

A tiny mewling made Jacqueline pause. "Did you hear that?"

They stopped. "Hear what?" he asked.

But the girl was already on her knees, peering beneath a rose-mary bush. "Oh, dear, it's a soggy little gray and white kitten!" She reached in then dragged the animal out by the scruff of the neck where it dangled scraggly and forlorn. "Poor little thing. Where's your mama?" She lifted her apron hem and deposited the kitty in the makeshift sling.

"What do you plan to do with it?" Smythe shook his head. "There's barely enough food for the troops. How will you care for a kitten?"

Despite his words, Jacqueline smiled brightly. "I'll dry it off, and nurse it to health, of course. Have you noticed how the vermin on this plantation are out of hand? Not enough good mousers. Why, just the other day while fetching a bowl of rice, I had take a broom to a rat perched on the corner of an occupied cot!"

Eva suppressed a smile. She almost felt sorry for the rat.

Almost.

Edward just shrugged in defeat. "Come along, then." He opened the kitchen door and Eva, Jacqueline and her little mouser-to-be went inside. At the table sat an officer with a rag wrapped around his hand. Edward saluted. "Sister Eva, the General requires a cut to be stitched."

The man glanced up, and his eyes widened in surprise. "A *nun*? Dear sister, how have you come to be at this camp?"

Eva managed a small smile. "Apparently God needed me here, sir. I had been traveling back to the Ursuline convent in New Orleans with Sister Beatrice and two orphans when we came upon one of your wounded soldiers. We treated him and delivered him to his regiment. We have not been granted permission to return home." *God, please forgive my duplicity.*

Well, it wasn't a complete lie.

Jacqueline had dried off her kitten and had found a scrap of bread on the floor, which the little thing attacked with gusto.

The general frowned. "Thank you for answering the summons, nonetheless."

"Allow me to see the wound." Eva placed her bag on the table. The man removed the rag. He had a deep cut between his thumb and forefinger.

"It keeps breaking open," he stated. "The blood seeps out and prevents me from properly handling a weapon."

Eva nodded. "I shall stitch and coat it with a healing salve. If you keep it covered and dry, it will heal faster." Just as she flipped up the flap to her satchel, another soldier entered the room.

"General Gibbs, General Pakenham requests your presence immediately, sir."

The officer stood and glanced at Eva. "Come along. You can stitch it while I converse."

Leaving Edward in the kitchen warming his hands by the stove, Jacqueline scooped up the kitten, and they followed the soldier into the dining room, which had been transformed into a command center. The man she assumed to be General Pakenham, based on the manner of deference given, was seated at one end of a table littered with maps, while a young man to his left scribbled madly on a parchment.

Eva scanned the rest of the room, and her heart stopped. She could feel the blood wash from her face in a frigid wave.

There, in the far corner, stood a tall man with dark hair. His clothes were soiled and torn, but his posture was stilted and defiant. He stared out a window. Although she could not see his face, she could identify him by stature alone.

Drago!

How had he been captured? The cut on his temple, surrounded by a multitude of colors from the accompanying bruise, looked like it was a few days old. His lip was split and swollen. He carried himself as if his stomach or ribs pained him. All in all, he looked—

"Goodness, you look *horrible*," Jacqueline blurted, stopping in her tracks. Her eyes widened, her lips paled.

He whirled. Her words startled not only Drago, who appeared stricken at the sight of her but also the other men in the room. His gaze then locked with Eva's, and emotions crisscrossed his face, shock, relief, *despair*, before he swallowed and looked at

Jacqueline. He pressed his lips into a hard line, and he gave the girl a stern glare. Fingers on his left hand twitched.

Well, for once it wasn't the twin's fault they were in a sticky situation, but he couldn't know that.

Gibbs exchanged a look with Pakenham, then pulled out a chair for her. "Please sit, Sister." He settled next to her and presented his hand.

Her mind raced as she picked the things she needed from her bag. Drago's storm cloud gaze bored into her back.

He was *alive*!

Gratitude and glee washed over her clean and clear, and she thanked God for answering her prayers for his safety even as her stomach tightened with worry. He was obviously a prisoner of war. An abused one at that.

There was a rap on the door, then a sour-faced officer with small eyes and a pointed chin strode into the room and saluted. "Lieutenant Colonel Brighton, at your service, sir."

Pakenham pointed to an empty seat before turning his attention back to Jacqueline. "You are acquainted with the prisoner?" He studied her as the guard prodded Drago to stand at the general's shoulder. Both Drago's jaw and his stoney eyes hardened as he passed Brighton, tension rolling off him like heat from a bonfire.

Jacqueline blinked at the general, then at Drago. Another surreptitious look crossed between them, going unnoticed by Pakenham, as his concentration was focused solely on the girl. Jacqueline cocked her head as if to study Drago more closely.

"Not in the social sense," she answered slowly. "He's a merchant ship captain my uncle uses to transport wares to Mobil."

Eva shifted her attention between the two as she worked. Drago's expression cooled to a stony indifference.

They were up to something.

Brighton's nasally voice cracked the air. "He's not one of Lafitte's pirates? Is he American? Or French?"

A narrowing of the left eye from Drago had Jacqueline shaking her head. "Heaven's no. He's Italian. His name is Captain Gamponetti."

Pakenham gave a grunt of satisfaction, then shifted his attention to the officer next to her. "Lieutenant Colonel Brighton, I'd like to discuss the best place for your regiments to make the river crossing."

Eva sucked in a breath. Apparently, the officers didn't consider them enough of a threat to postpone discussing their plans. A good thing. They could at least provide Jackson solid information. If she had to send Julian on alone, she would. The boy grew up on the bayou; he could easily slip back to the city, especially if he didn't have the rest of them slowing him down.

Pakenham jerked his chin toward Drago. "It seems you were telling the truth, Captain Gamponetti, when you said you had no stake in this war."

The air thickened, and Eva's breath caught in her chest. A soul-crushing jolt of betrayal reverberated through her entire body. Either he'd lied to her before he left, or he was lying now. If it was the former, her heart would shatter. If it was the latter, he was risking his life.

Pakenham gestured to the map in front of them. "I assume you know the idiosyncrasies of the currents."

Drago nodded.

She bent her head and focused on her task, willing the tears burning in her eyes to go away. She'd stitch the wound as slowly as she could.

Pakenham shoved the chart toward Drago. "Where is the best spot to put in? It needs to be calm since we'll have to ferry several regiments across. The boats have to return without being swept too far downriver."

He tilted his head and studied the general. "Would you be willing to release me and my men from your camp in exchange for such intelligence? If my ship is able, I should like to sail home to Jamaica."

A guard lifted the butt of his rifle, then froze when Pakenham raised his hand. "I believe that is a fair arrangement."

Drago perused the chart, then tapped his finger on a point south of Villeré. "This is the closest place. It becomes too shallow further down."

Eva casually glanced at the spot he had picked, and her lungs finally allowed a breath to enter. From her days as a runner, she'd had to navigate the Mississippi many times with Hugo. The place the captain had selected south of Villeré was in no way as calm as he presented it. The depth of the water hid the steep slope of the land and the strength of the current.

Brighton caught her looking. "What say you, Sister?" His narrowed scrutiny raked at her nerves, and she forced herself to quell the prickly unease caterpillaring up her spine enough to shrug.

"I have only traveled the river a couple times since arriving at the convent. I'm afraid I can't be much help." Guilt almost nudged her conscience at the way the lie slid off her tongue like a fat raindrop off a leaf.

Pakenham seemed to accept her explanation. He directed his next command to the scribe at his elbow. "Send orders to all the commanders to ready troops for a dawn attack. We shall advance under the fortuitous cover of this fog." He shifted a cool stare to Brighton. "Lieutenant Colonel, you will cross to the west bank then march upriver to seize control of the American battery opposite Jackson's line. At my signal, turn the cannons on the enemy troops. We'll pinch Jackson in a deadly crossfire, and this battle will be won."

Dawn! Eva swallowed, a dark cloud of foreboding pushed down on her shoulders. Even if they were able to escape, they'd be hard-pressed to traverse the eight miles to the city in time to warn Jackson. Kept here, she and the children might be safer, but she'd have no opportunity to help her wounded countrymen.

Brighton stared at the map and frowned. "We'll cross in the predawn hours."

Pakenham ignored him and continued directing the young man scribbling notes. "Send an order to Mullins to have his regiment haul fascines and ladders to the front lines. They are to creep in before sunrise, and place fascines so we can cross that blasted water-filled canal. We'll need to scale both the ramparts and parapets."

"Yes, sir."

She could only move so slowly, tending the general's wound. She finished the stitches and reached for the salve and bandages.

"General Gibbs, you shall follow Mullins and attack from the right flank."

Gibbs nodded and lifted his hand to peruse the stitched wound. Eva held up the salve and raised her eyebrows in question. He stuck out his hand so she could finish tending it.

Brighton cleared his throat. "Begging your pardon, my lord, but would it not be prudent to await reinforcements?" His beady-eyed frown skipped from Pakenham to Drago and back. "We have been told by several New Orleans residents, slaves, and prisoners of war that General Jackson has upwards of twenty-thousand men."

Pakenham leveled a cool gaze on Brighton. "That scruffy army of backwoods miscreants would be no match for my troops if they had *thirty*-thousand men." He leaned forward and rested his elbows on the table, then laced his fingers. "They have little formal training, poor weaponry, and a severe dearth of courage. They shall wilt before the vigor of a British formation like a cut posy on a hot summer day." Pakenham sat back. "I will await my plans no longer. Tomorrow, as the dawn breaks, we will approach while this lingering fog can be used to our advantage, and attack them, full on."

Eva's pulse careened through her veins. Even if Drago's misinformation slowed the assault on the opposite bank, unless they constructed a way to upset the plans further or delay the army's predawn march, they were doomed. The general flicked his hand at Drago. "Return him to the stockade."

The muscle in Drago's cheek rippled even through the short stubble of his beard. His voice was cold, *livid*. "You said you'd let us go."

"Indeed." Pakenham reached for a biscuit. "I am a man of my word, Captain Gamponetti. After the crossing is successfully made, and the Americans defeated tomorrow, we shall release you with the rest of the prisoners of war. Following proper negotiations, of course."

Chapter Forty-Two
A DEATH SENTENCE

D rago could almost hear Eva's heart pounding while she tied the bandage around Gibb's hand. A small vein in her temple throbbed madly. By the firm set of her beautiful pink mouth, Pakenham's orders vexed her as much as they did him.

Still, she'd not acknowledged him since she first noticed his presence, and it took all his inner fortitude to refrain from swooping her into his arms and clutching her to his chest in relief. God, to breathe her in now would likely destroy him. But with her so close and so untouchable, tiny fissures in his heart splintered off with every tick of the clock.

How did they get behind the battle line? Where was Julian and Raul?

Something happened. His gut clenched at the thought of Eva and Jacqueline unprotected and at the mercy of the British army. Raul would not have left them willingly. One thing was certain, it would be much harder to execute an escape now. The risks he would have taken with the men would be too dangerous for her and the twins, if Julian was even still alive. And he wasn't leaving without them.

"Cadet Smythe, please enter." The opening of the door immediately followed Pakenham's order.

A young soldier burst in and saluted smartly. "Yes, my lord."

"Dispatch the ladies to the hospital and the captain to the stockade," he instructed.

Edward saluted and stood by the open door while they left the room. Drago's arms ached to grab both girls into his embrace. Instead, he whispered a short message in Jacqueline's ear concerning the feline. They walked as far as the kitchen garden before Jacqueline stopped abruptly.

"Oh! My kitten!" She spun, then paused to address the cadet. "May I go back for her? Please?"

He gave her a long blink and sighed. "Be quick about it, miss. We'll not wait long for you."

Eva calmly folded her hands in front of her. "Regardless of the length of her absence, I will await her here, if you don't mind."

The soft tone of Eva's voice contained both iron and silk, and Drago found himself once again admiring her strength and resilience. The robes and veil did more than mask her scar. It was easy to forget she spent most of her childhood as a street urchin.

The cadet frowned. "My orders are to escort you back to the hospital and him back to—"

"Digging latrines," Drago finished with false brightness. "A lovely task, that." He lifted a brow, determined to distract the soldier long enough for Jacqueline to complete her assignment. "What regiment are you in, cadet?"

He leveled a cool stare at Drago. "The 15th foot soldiers, led by General Mullins."

Eva took in a sharp breath. Slight as the sound was, he detected it and gave her a curious glance.

Her eyes widened. "That's the one just ordered to the front line!"

"Sorry to hear that," Drago said, playing along. They were

definitely going to need help with their escape. If they could turn this cadet, things might not be as bleak as he originally thought.

"Wh-what?" the cadet asked, eyeing both of them warily.

Eva swallowed. "Your regiment has orders to carry the fascines and ladders to Line Jackson so that the troops who follow can climb the levee and attack."

The young soldier paled, then swallowed. "How do you know this?" He whitened further when he saw the horrified expression on Eva's face.

The outlook truly was dreadful.

"We overheard General Pakenham give the orders," Eva whispered.

The young man would receive the full brunt of the musket fire from the Kentucky sharpshooters. It will not be just the sugar-cane fascines the other soldiers step on to traverse the water-filled moat.

The young cadet stepped back. He pulled up his coat collar, his hand trembling. "We...we must all do our duty to our king," he said hoarsely.

"Your courage at this moment is impressive. But futile," Drago observed. The recruit was a dead man walking. Or dead boy walking, sadly.

"Edward," Eva whispered. "Come with us."

Drago's eyebrows jumped off his forehead at Eva's words. Her compassion didn't surprise him, but what did she mean come with *us*? How did she know his given name? Had they already devised a plan to escape? That thought terrified him and elated him at the same time.

The cadet stiffened and ground his jaw. "I'm not a coward. I'll not be a filthy deserter."

Drago didn't miss the familiarity between them. "Young man, it's obvious that you're not a coward. If you wish to forfeit your life, that is your choice. If you help us get away from the camp, I'll see that you have a place aboard my ship for as long as you desire it."

"If you'd rather stay in America, you have a home here," Eva added. "You've become dear to me, Edward. It would break my heart if you met your end tomorrow."

Edward swallowed convulsively and looked away. "I cannot."

Chapter Forty-Three
THE PICK POCKET

"I found her!" Jacqueline's breathless pronouncement, gleeful as it was, did little to lift the mood in the kitchen garden. Smythe rolled his eyes and trudged back to close the door the girl left open.

She tiptoed gingerly up to Eva and Drago. "A rather cross man named Boyle, who, by the way," her voice dropped, "is to deliver tomorrow's orders and will exit the front door very soon, didn't believe my kitten was in the room." She burrowed her nose into the soft fur of the kitten's neck. "But he was wrong, wasn't he?"

Jacqueline gave Drago a pointed stare, barely restraining a grin.

His eyes glowed with humor and pride. "Well done, little skirt."

Eva lowered her voice. "Jacqueline, if you are thinking what I *think* you're thinking, we'll all hang before sunset." That should have scared the girl, at least a little.

"Only if they catch us," Jacqueline whispered, eyes bright. "Which, they won't."

It *should* have scared her, but it didn't. Eva shook her head in wonder. The young girl had spunk.

"What if we affect the outcome?" Jacqueline glanced at Edward, currently picking his way across the icy walk toward them, concern in her gaze. "What if we prevent the death of innocent lives?"

Drago's jaw flexed. "He's still the enemy," he reminded her in a flat voice.

Jacqueline pressed her lips together and scowled. "Not if he doesn't want to be." Her voice almost vibrated with anger and passion.

When Edward motioned for them to continue down the garden path, Drago used the opportunity to offer Eva his arm, and she gripped the corded muscle with all the love and desperation in her heart.

The bricks were slick with ice. Twice she slipped, and had he not grabbed her around the waist, she'd have fallen. To be honest, it was the warmth of his fingers on the tender skin of her inner arm that had distracted her from watching her step in the first place.

Drago leaned down to murmur in her ear. "If we hurry, we can intercept the Second Lieutenant. Eva, if you can relieve him of even one of his missives, it will help our cause."

"*Our* cause?" Eva's heart jumped.

His gaze locked with hers, a smoldering flash filled with both fervor and fury. "I've cast my lot in with the Americans. I plan to fight with everything I have to prevent these British dogs from taking New Orleans." He straightened. "On that, I vow."

Eva could barely breathe. It took all her constraint to keep herself from jumping into his arms and crying both her joy and terror at his words. But now, his life was in danger, and the fear of losing him in battle chilled her to the bone. They would fight together to help the American cause. To protect the freedom of her country and her people.

Jacqueline looped her hand through Drago's other arm. "How did you get here? Where are the rest of the crew?"

His mouth thinned, and his jaw rippled. "Four of us were captured. The other two were digging latrines with me until I was called away."

Eva frowned. "Other two? I thought you said there were four—"

The pain in Drago's gaze stopped her breath.

Muscles under the skin of his cheek rippled. "Manuel is dead. Shot by Brighton."

Jacqueline let out a small cry, and her hand flew to her mouth in shock. "Oh, no!" Her eyes flooded with tears.

Eva's chest constricted. Manuel, the mountain of a man with a tender heart. She gripped the hand-hewn cross on her rosary. Tears burned the rims of her eyes. She drew Jacqueline into her arms. The sweet girl shook with sobs; Eva stroked her head and murmured what words of comfort she could. Edward paused and watched in sympathy, giving them space to grieve.

Jacqueline composed herself and wiped her eyes with her sleeve, then stepped on ahead of them. Her thin shoulders still trembled with restrained emotion. The girl was strong, both outside and inside.

They'd almost made it to the edge of the garden where the bricks ended and the mud began when a surprised shout halted them. It was followed by a thud and a pained moan.

Jacqueline glanced over her shoulder. "Oh, dear!" She carefully tiptoed back to Edward, now sprawled on the ground, his forearm at an odd angle.

"Stay in the grass, little lamb," Drago instructed. "Else there will be a larger pile on the icy bricks."

Edward slowly sat up, cradling his arm. Drago reached down and easily pulled him to his feet. The young man winced, his lips and face pale with pain. "It's broken."

"Indeed, it is," Eva grinned, ecstatic. God was everywhere.

Edward grimaced, then frowned. "May I ask why you are smiling?"

The corners of Drago's mouth twitched. "She's thinking about how difficult it will be to load and fire your weapon tomorrow with a broken arm."

Edward's face blanked, then he released a long breath.

The sound of the front door slamming shifted their attention from the cadet. Drago glanced at Eva, his eyes conveying a silent message. If they were to steal any of the missives, now was their chance. She drew strength in Jacqueline's steadfast confidence and nodded. She'd do it.

Now was not the time to dwell on her actions or decisions, whether or not she was breaking a commandment by taking something that wasn't hers. She'd shed her sense of propriety, right, and wrong as surely as she'd shed her aspiration to become a nun.

But it all slithered around in her mind anyway, like a nest of Racer snakes.

The cadet provided an excellent diversion, but they had to hurry. They rounded the corner just as Boyle crossed the porch, and a skinny dog rose at the bottom of the steps, ears perked and curious. Boyle descended the steps, focused on shoving several missives in his shoulder bag. The cur bounced in Boyle's wake, probably hoping something edible would fall out. They closed in quickly. The collision with Drago and Edward took Boyle entirely by surprise.

"Oof!" he grunted and stumbled into Jacqueline, who lost her grip on her kitten, which vaulted to the ground with an angry hiss. This attracted the attention of the dog who lunged with an excited yelp, neatly clipping the back of the Boyle's legs, sending him on his backside with a bark of surprise then a grunt of pain.

They couldn't have planned it better.

Jacqueline shrieked as the kitten darted beneath the front porch. "Leave her be, you mangy, muddy cur!" She dove for the dog, barely preventing it from squirming under in pursuit.

All this commotion gave Eva the perfect opportunity to reach into the Second Lieutenant's bag and remove a couple envelopes before he'd even hit the mud. Her pulse raced so fast she could hardly take a breath, as she swiftly tucked them into the belt under her scapular.

Boyle smacked the ground with his fist. "You ignorant girl!" He slipped twice before he finally scrambled to his feet. "Look what you've done!" Sticky Louisiana mud clung to the back of his breeches, coattails and both hands.

"I'm terribly sorry," Jacqueline said, sounding contrite. "But, truly, 'twas you who stepped in our path."

Eva put her arm around the girl in an attempt to still her mouth before it got her into severe trouble. She gave the Second Lieutenant a remorseful and humble dip of her head. "We did not see you, our apologies."

Boyle narrowed his eyes, face pinched in suspicion. "What are you doing still here?"

Drago gestured to Edward, cradling his wrist. "This soldier fell on the ice and broke his arm. We were on our way to the surgeon."

Boyle jerked his muddied jacket back into place. "Then be about your business! I'm on an important mission for the general. Step aside!"

"Of course." Drago caught her gaze, and she gave him a slight nod. Silver eyes flickered with pride, and she almost grinned.

Boyle let out an annoyed huff and stepped stiffly down the path, clumps of mud plopping off his coat to the ground behind him.

Drago offered his arm once again to Eva. "Come then, Cadet Smythe. Let's get you attended to." He steered them toward the field hospital. Jacqueline was still on her hands and knees trying to coax the kitten from its hiding place. "Forget the cat, little lamb. I'm sure she can watch after herself. She's managed on her own, thus far."

"But..." Jacqueline peered into the dark shadow under the

porch, still grasping the scruff of the wiggling dog's neck. "Oh, bother." She gave the scamp a stern stare. "You leave that kitten be." The pup just blinked both forlorn brown eyes at her and gave a languid wave of its tail. Sighing, she released it and seemed pleasantly surprised when it made no effort to dive after the kitten. "Good dog," she praised.

This time it gave her a tongue-lolling grin and nudged her hand with its nose.

Eva shot a quick look at the front door, uneasy with the commotion they'd caused. "We should be on our way."

With one last longing look toward the porch, Jacqueline followed, with the scruffy canine panting happily at her heels.

"What is it about you and wretched animals?" Edward frowned, glancing at the muddy, burr-matted dog and cradling his arm closer to his stomach. "Do they always follow you wherever you go?"

"It appears so." Jacqueline flipped a wayward curl from her cheek as she passed them. "After all, *you're* still here."

Eva rolled her eyes. One day, that child's mouth would get her into more trouble than she could handle. Or talk her way out of.

"Halt!"

Eva's stomach plunged to her toes. Drago's arm stiffened beneath her palm. At the approach of an armed foot soldier, Jacqueline's face blanked and paled. Eva tucked her hands into her sleeveless scapular and pushed the missives further behind her belt, then bent them sharply so they hooked over it, before turning.

He addressed Eva. "General Pakenham requested I give you this." He handed her a small slip of paper.

She let out a small, relieved breath. "What is it?" she asked, unfolding the parchment.

"It's permission for safe passage back to New Orleans. He wishes for you and your young charges to leave at once, and return to the convent."

This time her smile was genuine. "Please pass our deepest gratitude to the General for seeing to our safety."

The soldier nodded and gave a crisp bow before spinning on his heel and marching back to the house.

"Finally!" Jacqueline breathed. "A turn of good fortune."

Chapter Forty-Four

FAMILIAR PEDDLER

"Thankfully, the skin wasn't broken. There is little chance of a complicated healing process," the surgeon said in a clipped voice. "However, I am required to assess you unfit for service until it heals, which will take two weeks or more." He scribbled a note on a torn piece of parchment. "Take this to your commanding officer. I've requested that he transfer you here. At the very least, you can take on minor tasks requiring the use of only one arm."

Eva tried to hide her joy at the news. Edward wouldn't be going to the front lines after all. Maybe now he'd reconsider, and they could persuade him to help Drago escape the encampment.

Private Smythe stood and saluted. "Yes, sir." He accepted the note, a relieved expression on his face, then addressed Drago. "I must return you to your assigned task."

Drago dipped his head. "Of course. Lead the way."

Eva smiled to herself. She'd passed the missives to him just as they entered the tent. She could think of no better home than the bottom of a latrine, newly dug by Drago Viteri Gamponetti.

A few minutes after Drago and Smythe departed, a soldier

stepped inside and addressed the surgeon. "Sir, there's a peddler just arrived with a variety of dry goods and supplies."

The surgeon paused and his eyebrows jumped, a hopeful gleam in his eyes. "Tobacco?"

"Yes, sir."

Both men exited the hospital tent. Curious, Eva and Jacqueline followed, the scrawny dog trotting at their heels. Jacqueline had wiped off a good portion of the caked mud, but nothing short of a long soak was going to get the creature's coat clean. No sooner had they rounded the canopy than Jacqueline squealed, "Tristan!"

The young girl's brother stood on the running board of a covered wagon. His head snapped around at the sound of Jacqueline's voice. "Jacquie!" His eyes lit with relief and joy as he hopped down and opened his arms. She ran into them, and he wrapped her in a hug, lifting her feet off the ground. "I've been worried about you, Biscuit. Is Jules with you?"

Jacqueline nodded, smiling. "He's tending horses. Are you going home? Can we come with you?"

Tristan cast a wary glance at the contingent of soldiers surrounding his wagon. "If it's permitted, yes." He lowered his voice. "I'm posing as a peddler to gather intelligence for Jackson."

Eva caught her breath and whispered, "We have information. Jacqueline can pass it along, but you must get the children out of here today."

"Here now, what's this?" The soldiers snapped to attention as General Brighton approached.

"It's a peddler, sir. Says he's newly arrived from the Carolina Territory. We retained him after learning that he was on his way to New Orleans," one of the soldiers said.

Brighton's sharp gaze landed on Tristan. "What business have you there?"

Tristan shrugged. "I am returning home to see my family." He flicked his hand toward the tents spread across the plantation fields. "I was unaware your troops were blockading the city. I meant no harm."

Brighton's eyes narrowed, and he addressed the soldier lingering at his elbow. "Sergeant, have you inspected the contents?"

The man gave him a stiff nod. "Yes, sir. It contains several barrels of tobacco, one of ale, four bumpkins of whiskey and twenty bags of rice weighing about two stone each."

"Commandeer the entire supply."

"Yes, sir!"

Immediately the soldiers swarmed the wagon, shoving the sputtering Tristan aside. "But...but..."

"Consider it a toll for an unmolested passage back to your family," Brighton said with a sardonic smirk. He pulled a pipe from his inner breast pocket, reached into an opened barrel of tobacco, and removed enough to pack into the bowl.

Tristan scowled. Jacqueline took his hand, a hopeful gleam in her eyes. "Does this mean you'll be permitted to take us home?"

Brighton looked at them in surprise.

Noting the officer's attention, Tristan straightened. "This is my sister. With your permission, I'd like to take her and her twin brother back home." He shot a glance at Eva. "Along with the Ursuline nuns, if possible." His countenance transitioned to one that appeared reticent and respectful. "You carry the countenance of a nobleman, sir. I'm sure you'd be the first to say that this is no place for women and children."

Tristan Sauvage. The smooth-tongued gambler had the charm of a gypsy fortune teller. Eva could only stand back and admire his performance.

Brighton slowly straightened like a swan stretching out its neck. "Certainly, but you must leave immediately to avoid being caught in any crossfire."

Tristan raised his brows. "Crossfire? You have not already taken the city?"

Brighton peered down his nose and snorted. "I assure you, it will be ours before midday tomorrow."

"Then I must deliver the children to the convent to keep them safe," Tristan replied, a worried expression etched on his face.

Eva pulled out the missive. "We already have our orders from General Pakenham to leave at once."

Brighton snatched the paper from her hand, read it then shoved it back at her. "Indeed." He glanced up as Beatrice hobbled up beside her.

"God Bless you for your kindness, sir," the elder nun said, smiling.

Brighton preened. "Sergeant, find the girl's brother, and bring him here immediately. I want the five of them out of here within the hour."

"Yes sir!"

Chapter Forty-Five

RESCUING DRAGO

D arkness descended quickly, and so did the chill. Being confined here meant Drago and his men couldn't sit near a fire; so they huddled close for warmth. The soldiers guarding the tent where he, Ramón and Chen hunkered chained together had stopped chatting, meaning that either they ran out of things to say, one of them was called away, or they took a short walk to the nearby latrine. The general hum of activity outside the tent increased.

Drago had spent a painful day helping the British dig a canal, leaving him wet, cold, and muddy. The troops planned to bring their shallow longboats from the bayou to the river, to ferry foot soldiers across the broad expanse of the Mississippi. It was easy enough to accomplish since the *Carolina* and the *Dragon* no longer antagonized the camp from the Mississippi.

Drago groaned. His abused ribs and stomach provided a constant ache, promising another sleepless night ahead.

Smythe had permitted him to stop at the latrine before bringing him to the detention area. Once inside, he ripped open the missive Eva lifted from the sergeant's bag to find it addressed to General Mullins. His orders were to take his regiments to the front lines with fascines to provide a path over the mud and ladders to prepare the way for Gibbs' men to scale the ramparts. He allowed himself a triumphant smile. His sugarcane wasn't going *anywhere*.

He dropped the missive into the latrine and urinated on it. With the ladders and fascines left behind, the British would have a difficult time scaling the anything.

"Drago?" A reedy whisper interrupted his musings.

His heart stopped. *No*. What was she doing here? "Eva?" He breathed her name in shock and dismay. No, no, *no*! She needed to go back. If they caught her, they'd kill her. Probably just execute her without asking a single question. At the very least, sneaking around the camp alone put her at horrible risk if she ran into anyone with less than honorable intentions.

The back of the tent rippled as she crawled inside. Chains clinked softly as the men straightened. He whispered as loudly as he dared. "Little fool! Get out of here." He wanted to crush her to his chest and at the same time shove her back out.

"Shh...I came to free you." She moved on her hands and knees until she reached him. He got a brief whiff of wood smoke, ash and crushed herbs. He strained to make out her shape. Was she wearing white trousers and the red coat of a *British cadet*? What did she do with her robe and tunic? They were the only things protecting her!

With a hushed cry of relief, she threw her arms around his neck, and for a moment he allowed himself the luxury of breathing her in. She cradled his face in her palms and pressed her sweet, warm lips against his chilled ones. "We must move quickly once I relieve you of these wretched chains."

Filled with warring emotions of joy and dread, he could only panic silently as she moved. She trailed her hands down his arms. Finding no bindings around his wrists, she groped for his feet.

Seconds later, the lock gave a soft click, and he grinned in the dark. He shouldn't have been surprised. How he loved her and wanted to shake and chastise and shout and scream at her for putting herself in danger. At the same time, he wanted the world to know how brilliant and brave she was. And her heart belonged to him.

One by one, the four of them crawled out into the darkness. Eva picked up a rifle she'd left on the ground near the tent, and they casually strolled the short distance to the edge of the cypress swamp.

The most important task was to warn both sides of the river about the planned British attack. They'd have to split up, and he wasn't letting Eva out of his sight, so the calculations were easy.

He wasted no time issuing orders for the others to head northeast to Line Jackson and help man the cannons beside Lafitte's crew. "Make haste, boys. There are no better gunners than you. Jackson's going to need every able-bodied man he can get. You proved your mettle a thousand times over behind the *Dragon's* guns. Take your skills and cast chaos and destruction on those bloody redcoats."

They straightened. "Aye, Capt'n. That we will." Ramón flicked his thumb over his shoulder. "We'll see if we can't slow those long-boats to the river, as well."

Drago grinned, his men were savvy. "An excellent plan. There has to be a weakness along the canal you can exploit. A small collapse would be catastrophic."

"We'll see it done, sir."

"For Manuel," Chen murmured.

Ramón's eyes gleamed. "Aye, for Manuel."

Eva squeezed his fingers. Drago gripped hers back, then released them, fearing he'd crushed her knuckles. He swallowed the painful knot in his throat and stepped forward to shake each man's hand. Drago couldn't allow his grief-ridden thoughts to invade his mind now. It was important to stay keen-witted. Focused. He'd mourn his cousin later. And he'd mourn him well.

The two men whispered their thanks to Eva, then disappeared

into the night toward the Chalmette plantation. He warred with the decision to send her with them, along with orders to escort her to the convent. The truth was that he wanted her with him. He needed her with him. It was the only way he could protect her.

There'd be no sleep for the British army tonight. The camp squirmed with activity. Twenty men still toiled dredging the canal from the swamp to the Mississippi. Regiments gathered, inspecting weapons and securing supplies. Thankfully, no one bothered to question why a cadet was escorting a civilian through the encampment. They had their own tasks and worries. A nervous unease rippled through Villeré plantation. Word had spread that Jackson commanded nearly twenty-five thousand men. Drago's exaggeration blossomed into a healthy rumor, which happily grew, as rumors tend to do.

When they were finally alone, Drago gripped her shoulders and pulled her close. Fear and fury welled up in his chest, and he gave her an angry scowl. "What you just did was dangerous. Do you realize you could have been killed?"

Eva calmly lifted her chin, her face a serene mask of courage. "You should have a little more faith in my abilities."

How many more did she possess? "The other disguise was safer," he growled.

She casually shrugged a shoulder. "Edward needed it in order for Beatrice and the Sauvages to smuggle him from here to the city." She looked down at her breeches. "I rubbed ashes into the coat and britches to blend into the dark a bit better. They fit fairly well, except for the boots. I put rags in the toes."

Drago hissed in a sharp breath. "Devil take me if I don't want to shake some sense into you!" She talked as if she did this every day. "You've lived in a convent for the past nine years, you know nothing of war and the dark intentions of men."

Eva hefted her rifle and locked her gaze with his. He could barely catch the glitter of her stare. "I understand more about the dark intentions of men than most women of twenty and two. These are precarious hours, Drago. Precarious hours call for indomitable decisions and desperate actions. I did what I had to do, and so did you."

He ground his teeth. She was right, of course, but that didn't make it easier. "I'd rather you were safely back in the convent."

"Well, I'm here." She straightened. "And I'm staying with you."

She was as stubborn as she was brave. "Then stay near me, because God help us, Eva, this is no place for a woman."

A tiny smile tugged at her mouth. "Is that a prayer, *Capitaine* Gamponetti?"

Prayers were for those who lacked the courage to cut their own path. Still, he managed a stiff nod. "It's as close to one as I'll utter."

She tilted her head. "God will help us." She pressed her palm to his cheek, melting him. "We'll look after each other," she whispered, then taking a deep breath, continued. "I am no stranger to the dark, Drago. Among other things, when I was a child, Hugo taught me how to become invisible in the night."

While he hated Dupré for the way that snake had treated her, he hoped those skills would keep her alive through this nightmare, because it was about to become more dangerous. He pulled her into his arms and held her, sinking into the soft warmth of her body, drawing strength from her calm and confident heart and hoping her faith in his protection wasn't unfounded. "We need to warn General Morgan about the dawn attack on the west bank. We can't let the British take that battery."

He felt Eva nod against his chest. "The information you gave them will slow their efforts." His heart nearly exploded at the pride in her voice. He kissed the top of her head. "Let's hope it gives us enough time."

They trudged downriver toward the raft Eva and the twins had hidden among the bulrushes. During the trek, she recounted the loss of Raul, the discovery of Blackwood, and the trip to

Villeré. Raul's death came as a surprise. The giant of a man had always seemed indestructible. Even after taking a knife to the chest, Drago had seen the Cimarron fight on as if it wasn't there. Turned out that his muscles were too thick and the blade too short to do much damage. He would miss the man. Loyal. Intelligent. Good in a fight.

They set off across the devilish river, heading to where the *Dragon* huddled on the bank. They needed weapons. He wouldn't charge into a battle unarmed. Crossing was a treacherous risk at night, partially submerged stumps and rotten logs clawed the bottom of the raft and bindings. A plunge into the icy water was deadly this time of year. Even if they swam to shore, the cold temperatures would seep into their bones, and they'd catch their death.

Drago's heart jolted against his ribs as horrific images of everything that could go wrong invaded his thoughts. It was one thing to look out for himself, yet another to protect the woman he loved. The rest of his life would become as dark as this night without her.

A few muted twinkles hinted stars above them. Night cloaked the land in a blanket of gloom. Drago barely breathed as Eva felt her way with a long pole. He knelt behind her, using a paddle as a rudder and stroking along the downriver side to keep them from progressing laterally across. No sounds but the current lapping against the raft. Even the night creatures seemed to sense the danger, wisely choosing silence.

The hulking form of the *Dragon* slowly revealed herself through the mist.

"Oh no," Eva breathed, stilling.

Drago cursed under his breath before biting his tongue. Why was his language always at its worst when she was near?

At least she was near.

He grasped her hand and gave it a squeeze. It was when they were apart that worry shredded his heart.

None of that changed the gut-wrenching fact that the schooner had been brutally violated. His prized vessel listed starboard due to the gaping hole in her flank. Blown apart from the inside out; her gun had been directed away from its port and pointed instead through her tender ribs. It would be a long time before they saw Lamb's Tail Island again.

Heart heavy, he climbed aboard the tilted vessel as noiselessly as he could; Eva waited below for his signal to follow. Aside from the occasional pained groan of her fibers, the *Dragon* was quiet and dark in death.

He didn't bother to check his cabin. It would have been the first place the marauders pillaged.

"Drago?" Eva's whisper cut through the silence.

He leaned over the rail. "It's abandoned. Can you manage the way up?"

She grinned and grabbed the thick hemp rope, soon scampering to his side. He slipped his hand into hers and led her toward the hatch. Together they made their way to the galley.

Drago rummaged around until he found the tinderbox and a rusty lantern. Within a few minutes, they had enough light to illuminate their surroundings. The stores had been picked through and cleaned out, save for what Cookie had hidden in the stove. Strange how no one seemed to think to check there. They shoved what they could into Eva's rucksack. Rice pebbled the floor. Thankfully, Drago found a few pieces of dried meat on the bottom of a tipped barrel, which eased their hunger and provided a needed boost of energy.

"I'm sorry about your ship," Eva said. Her eyes shone with sympathy. "I know the *Dragon* was precious to you." She touched his cheek. "You have lost so much."

He shook his head. Such tangibles no longer mattered. "*You* are precious to me, *il mio amore*." He enveloped her in his arms and held her. "I am thankful it was the *ship* and not you." He thought of his cousin and drew a ragged breath. "I sought to protect the people I love by removing them from danger. But Manuel understood that eliminating the danger was the only way to keep everyone safe. He fought to save your way of life. Your freedom. Manuel, in his slow, befuddled mind, understood that long before I did. He died fighting for a cause that lived in his heart."

We fight for freedom, Drago. For Jacqueline and Julian and for Sister Eva...for our friends. We promised. We fight for them.

But suddenly he needed more. "You must think me a coward for wanting to flee the city rather than fight. I'm not sure I deserve your respect. I have lied to you. And worse, I have deceived and betrayed you." A harsh band tightened around his chest, and he could barely breathe. What reason had he given her to trust him? He spent so many years taking what he wanted and needed, that he forgot how to earn it. Forgot the *importance* of earning it.

"I'll understand if you've changed your mind. I wouldn't blame you if you did." He didn't deserve her as his wife.

Then he felt it.

It was feather light at first. Her fingers fluttered over his side ribs, then froze. He bent his head and kissed her temple, unable to resist touching her skin with his lips. The sensation of her hands sliding over his side and around his waist almost had him shouting for joy. When she hugged him back, he grinned like a bloody fool.

"Eva..." He could only manage her name. He had so much to tell her. Guilt, truth, humility all pressed on his shoulders with a weight that threatened to drive him to his knees.

He choked the thick, hard words from his throat. "I've been an arrogant idiot. So many years spent looking out for myself had blinded me to courage. My pride blinded me to honor and valor."

How could the words, 'I'm sorry' mean anything coming from him? Telling her that he loved her was like dropping teardrops into the sea.

Meaningless.

He was cold and hard. She was warm and vibrant. He sauntered in darkness and subterfuge. She hid in the light.

What made him think he could win her? She had no reason to desire a life with someone like him. He had no right to ask. "I'm so sorry."

Her chest expanded with each breath, and he reveled in the pressure of it against him. He could almost feel the vibration of her heartbeat. He had to say something more. At least apologize again. Attempt to win her forgiveness, try to —

"Drago." Emotion thickened her whisper. "The past is in the past. Let's look to the future."

The world *stopped*.

Just like that, the darkness slipped away. His heart expanded to the size of a twenty-four pounder. He hadn't realized his eyes were closed until he opened them to look at her. To confirm the words just spoken.

Her gaze was bright and hopeful and honest. And she looked at him with love and devotion and yes... forgiveness.

"I love you, Eva. I know — " He allowed the last remnants of his pride to splinter and drop at his feet. "I know that I don't deserve you, but I'll spend the rest of my life endeavoring to earn your respect if you'll give me the chance."

She stilled, and he held his breath, daring to hope.

The warmth of Eva's hand scorched his stubbled cheek. He was in no way presentable to the lady, yet another dark mark against his character, but devil take him, he was desperate.

Drago cradled her face in his hands.

"I love you, Eva. When this is all over, will you still have me?"

Chapter Forty-Six
A COMMON CAUSE

Eva placed her hands over his, and together they cradled her marred face. Scarred, yes, but it no longer seemed as hideous or horrible. Drago made her whole. His molten silver gaze held hers with a strength and power that heated her from the inside.

Were they not both horribly flawed?

Perhaps that's why they suited so well.

Of course Eva would still have him. Emotion thickened her throat, and her words came out on the wings of a whisper. "I've loved you a long time, Drago. If you will have me as I am, then I am yours."

He pulled away, eyes wide with surprise, his mouth slightly open. "As you are? What other way could you possibly be?"

At that, she couldn't meet his eyes. "Well..." She gestured to her maimed face, unable to find the words to explain.

"Eva." Warm lips trailed kisses along her forehead, her nose, her chin, her eyes, then on her temple and along every twist and ripple of her scar. The sensation caused a panic to flare in her chest. She recoiled. His hands stilled her.

"No, *il mio amore*, you will not shy from my kisses, no matter where they land. I love all of you," he murmured against her cheek. "Every." He kissed the jagged part of the scar that jerked from her cheekbone toward her jaw. "Single." Lips, soft and soothing caressed the corner of her mouth. "Inch."

The touch of Drago's lips sent a jolt through Eva's entire body. The stubble rasped against tender skin, but it felt delicious.

This was not the same scowling pirate who rang the abbey bell in the middle of a Jamaican November night. She glimpsed this man several times over the past couple of months, however fleeting.

Until Villeré.

She sensed a change in him there. Here now, was the man she always knew could shift away from the dark shadow of the pirate. He just had to take one step into the light.

Her love for Drago expanded beyond her heart's capacity to hold it. She felt both bright and buoyant. He loved her. And she loved him.

They were together now, and that was all that mattered.

⚓ ⚓ ⚓

DRAGO EXPELLED HIS BREATH, buried his face in her hair and tightened his arms around her.

Eva's wisp of a sigh escaping almost made him forget where he was. She was his to cherish and cherish her he would. And as soon as this battle with the redcoats ended, if he was still alive, he was going to marry her; nothing would stand in his way.

There was no stronger motivation to keep her safe.

He slowly released her and kissed her forehead. "Come, we have a mission to complete." His heart jumped at her quick smile, and her cobalt eyes gleamed with excitement and determination.

Chapter Forty-Seven

A DEAD DRAGON

The door to the storage room off the galley hung askew by one hinge. Drago entered and reached beneath the lowest shelf. He felt around until he found a strap and tugged. Several sabers and three rifles dropped to the floor. Cookie didn't take any chances of getting caught by surprise. They emptied two other caches of weapons in other parts of the hold. He spent several minutes checking, cleaning and preparing them for battle.

Eva sliced pieces of old muslin into squares and measured shot and powder, preparing for the inevitable. She was oddly calm, given what they were about to do, and she attributed it to Drago's presence. She was stronger, more courageous when he was with her. She paused a moment to observe him. He'd tied back his hair with a short strip of the muslin, his long fingers moved swiftly and efficiently over the rifles. Outwardly relaxed, his body still had the tension of a crouching panther, waiting to pounce.

Before they departed the ship, Drago slipped into his cabin. Eva kept watch, even though she could barely see the outline of the railing, let alone an approaching threat. In the dark, she couldn't see the fog as well as she could feel it cling to her skin.

Everything was coated with chilled moisture. The thick night air seemed to muffle all but the most strident noises.

Drago emerged. When he was near enough, she could see a resigned expression on his chiseled face, small lines around his mouth and a stormy shadow in his eyes. The cabin likely had been ransacked; what hadn't been stolen was probably destroyed. Her heart went out to him. He'd lost everything in a matter of days— his cousin, his ship and by direct association, his crew and livelihood, as well as all his possessions, save what he had on him.

Drago hesitated, then rested his hand against the Dragon's wounded hull in farewell.

"I'm sorry you've lost her," Eva said softly. She hadn't missed the look of anguish when he first caught sight of his ship's carcass, half-submerged, bulrushes and tree stumps clinging to her jagged edges like remora.

He managed a grim smile. "She was a stalwart vessel. Saved our skins more than once over the years." He gave her a quick, silent nod, grasped Eva's hand, and together they slogged up the levee, away from the water and the destroyed ship.

They'd sneaked from the encampment while the troops prepared, but she wondered how much time they had until the attack. "Once they begin the crossing, how far down river do you think the current will take them?" The place Drago had suggested they put in was a deceptively still bend, hiding a sharp drop as it curved.

Drago grasped her hand. "Hopefully, it'll carry them at least a mile before they can paddle to the opposite bank."

That meant the British would either have to haul the ships back upriver or have the regiments trudge down to meet the boats, then once on the other side, march an additional mile or so back upriver to reconnoiter with their regiments. Every delay helped.

Eva tugged her boot from the greasy mud. Everything was just so wet and *cold*.

Drago's voice carried a tone of tension like a wire strung too tightly. "They have a great number of troops to ferry. It's likely they'll be delayed only a short while before they amass enough regiments to execute an effective march. They know we are not well-fortified on this bank. When I departed Jackson's headquarters, our generals and engineers were having a difficult time agreeing on the location of the line." His strides lengthened, and she slipped and slid along beside him. If it wasn't for his hand grasping hers like a vise, she'd have fallen several times.

He slowed, but she waved him along. They couldn't afford to waste any time. If she thought he'd do it, she would have already insisted he press ahead without her.

The darkness deepened during the time they were below deck. They shuttered the lantern, allowing for the smallest glow to illuminate the ground before them. Swirling mist seeped through the small cocoon of light.

An hour into their trek, Eva shivered and clenched her collar tighter around her neck. Her feet and her fingers were numb with cold. Drago had a layer of frost on his shoulders, and she had no doubt frost coated hers as well.

Her thoughts turned to the twins, Beatrice, Edward and Tristan. She silently prayed for their safety. She tried not to think of all the things that could have gone wrong, delaying or even preventing them from reaching Jackson's line in time.

"The sun's beginning to rise." Drago glanced at the faint glimmer in the east.

Eva inhaled a sharp breath. The enemy would attack at daybreak. And the Americans still needed to prepare.

He met Eva's worried stare with a concerned one of his own. "We won't get to them in time."

Her legs burned as much as her chest. "How much farther?"

He frowned. "It's at least two more miles."

"Well, then," Eva straightened her weary shoulders and

adjusted the rifles crisscrossing her back. "We're still ahead of them. You can move faster without me."

Drago's brows slammed down. "I'm not leaving you."

She scowled back. "I'll be right behind you."

"Halt!" The voice shot through the muffled stillness of the misty predawn. "Who goes?"

Eva's stomach gave a sick lurch. She shifted a rifle to her shoulder. They couldn't be captured. Not now.

Drago stopped mid-step and cocked his head. "Harvey?" He turned up the lantern.

"Zat you, Capt'n?" Harvey's grizzled frame drifted into the dim light. "Hoy! A sight fer my old eyes, ye be."

Eva exhaled a shaky breath, ready to collapse with relief only to gasp in surprise. Raul, dressed in buckskins, shrugged through the brush, his left arm in a sling.

Drago's brows jumped up his forehead. "You're alive!" A wide smile brightened his face. "Eva said you took a hit and fell into the river."

Raul responded with a sheepish grin. "Choctaw warrior pulled me out. We traded clothes. Dry is better." He reached forward and took a saber from Drago, clearly unable to reload a rifle. He hefted it, examined the grip, then sliced the air in a swift figure eight before nodding his satisfaction.

Drago clapped him on the back. "Glad to see you." He turned to Harvey. "Aren't you a long way from Morgan's line?"

Harvey snorted. "Morgan insisted we move downriver from Line Jackson. We be too few armed to defend the breadth of the new line, but the man won't listen to reason from no one." He hissed over his shoulder into the darkness. "Bernard! Bring yer sorry carcass over here. Tis the capt'n an' Sister Eva."

Bulrushes rustled, and soon Bernard and his bushy salt and pepper eyebrows poked out. "Capt'n Gampo? Is it really you?" Bernard elbowed his way through the weeds. "I'll be—Oh!

Mornin', Sister Eva." He tipped his cap. "I didn't expect you to be accompanying the capt'n. Last I heard you and the twins— " His eyes widened. "Where are the young ones?"

Before Eva could open her mouth to respond, Drago clamped his great hand on Bernard's shoulder. "They are on their way to New Orleans with Tristan. Both are in good health."

Bernard's shoulders relaxed for a moment. "Glad to see you, Captain. When we saw the *Dragon* scuppered, we thought the worst."

Drago released a dark breath before raising his chin and looking at Harvey. "Most of my men are marching to Line Jackson to help run the batteries. Some went down to Fort St. Phillip."

Harvey looked past Eva's shoulder. "And where is that big ox, Manuel?" His eyebrows jutted upward.

Drago's throat convulsed a second before he could speak again. His flint-colored eyes turned cold and steely. "A British dog by the name of Brighton killed him."

Bernard let out a low curse. Harvey's face paled, his watery blue eyes clouded, and his mouth flattened into a thin line. Suddenly he looked old, haggard, and beaten.

Drago's gaze raked over his men. "We'll have the good fortune of engaging the water-hearted cur within a couple hours, since he's one of the commanding officers of a regiment assigned to take the battery here." Harvey's eyes brightened at the news. Drago shrugged two rifles from his shoulder and handed them to him.

Bernard relieved Eva of two more. "There's little time to warn Morgan and Lafitte. We must make haste."

Drago nodded, his face grim. "We'll follow you. I'll tell you what I know while we're moving."

The soupy fog lingered, monstrous trees hunched along the levee, and dripped ringlets of Spanish moss from gnarled branches. Drago described Manuel's execution, the pleasure he had destroying the orders Eva had lifted ordering Mullins' regiment to haul fascines and ladders to Line Jackson for a dawn attack, Pakenham's plan for a simultaneous attack on both sides of the river and the rocket that would signal it.

Eva was glad she didn't have to talk. It was hard enough to keep up with their pace in silence. Drago slowed and reached again for her hand, and she drew strength from the confident line of his mouth and the steady purpose in his silver eyes.

She would not falter now. Sheer determination and a violent will to stay side by side with Drago kept her moving.

They burst into a clearing, and she staggered. A group of slaves frantically hacked away at a trench that barely crossed a third of the field. Her heart sank. They would never finish before the enemy arrived. Not only did they not have enough men and shovels, the area stretched for another half mile beyond.

A somber Bernard jerked his chin toward several groups of forlorn and dejected militiamen huddled around sparsely flickering fires. "They just arrived. Been marching for two days and nights straight. No rest. No food. And worse...they brought no weapons." Bernard made a face that was a cross between disgust and despair.

Anxiety clamped a hard band around Eva's stomach. They weren't even close to being prepared for battle. A separate cluster of militia hovered near the trench, dispassionately watching the slaves labor with the muddy earth. The sight of Hugo standing among them sent a chill down her spine like melting ice. When he looked up their eyes locked, and a tangle of fear and dread knotted in her chest. Hugo beamed with recognition, and a slow sickening grin split his face. She narrowed her eyes in what hopefully came across as an angry scowl, rather than the terror and unease twisting that knot even tighter. She held his predatory stare until a fellow soldier called him away.

A familiar form separated from a cluster of men. Jean Lafitte strode over to them, a long saber strapped to his waist, a pistol jammed in his belt and a rifle in his hand. "Drago, my friend, good to see you." His eyes glittered with humor, and he tipped his hat to Eva. "Miss Trudeau. You found a new disguise, I see." His amused grin flashed before he returned his attention to Drago. "General Jackson has implemented a plan based on your sugges-tion." He gestured across the Mississippi. "He has given orders to place our best sharpshooters in the trees and trenches. They are instructed to fire upon British commanders. I am to coordinate the same on the west side, while Morgan leads the defenses on the ground."

Drago scanned the tree-lined battleground. "I want Eva in a place she'll be hidden."

She was quick to argue. "I want to stay with you." Nowhere was safe unless it was by Drago's side.

He gave her his full attention. "I'll be nearby, but I want you up in the tops, hidden in the branches."

Nearby was better than alone.

Lafitte nodded. "Come then. It is time. The sun rises."

The deep charcoal of the night had indeed faded into the gray of morning. The fog remained denser near the water, but it was now easier to see beyond a few yards away.

Drago and Lafitte disappeared, then returned with armloads of Spanish moss. They tucked it into their belts, sleeves and collars, it covered their heads, and hung from their boots. Lafitte led them to a copse of trees adjacent to the battery and the river. Bernard and Harvey shimmied up a massive oak. Draped in the Spanish moss, they became nearly invisible. Drago directed her up another equally huge tree. When she climbed as high as she dared, he settled her in an upper crotch and checked that her rifle was primed and ready to fire. Then he checked it again. His expression flooded with concern. In the shadowed light of the dawn, his gaze was like a tornado, swirling with determination, confidence, courage and worry.

"Stay still and quiet, Eva. Keep your weapon ready, but don't fire unless it's to defend yourself, understand?" He cupped her jaw and rubbed his thumb over her chin, just grazing her lower lip. The sensation lingered like a hard-rung bell. "Stay in the tree until the battle is over. If something happens to me, go to the river. Lafitte has canoes and longboats hidden in the brush. Raul is waiting there; find him. He'll get you back to the convent. Watch after the twins."

She nodded, tears filled her eyes and fear gripped her throat, but she swallowed it. She would be strong and brave. "Where will you be?"

He nodded at a lower branch of the same tree, almost as thick as his waist. "Right below you." His eyes flickered with something both soft and flinty. "Stay safe." The sharply clipped words allowed for no argument. A captain's order, as if commanding it would make it so.

Her heart slammed into her chest. "You, too," she whispered.

He leaned in and kissed her, strong, tender lips moving with a desperate plea. She gripped his coat collar, then traced his face with her fingertips, memorizing every curve. He rested his forehead against hers.

"Eva." Emotion low and husky, rasped through his voice. "I love you."

His tortured tone said everything his words did not.

Stay safe.

Don't die.

His eyes locked with hers. She looked at him with every fiber of strength she could pull from her soul. Willing him to survive the battle. Her heart twisted almost painfully, and she responded the only way she could, the only way he'd understand. "I love you, too." Terror and love battled each other in her chest. She watched, frozen in a cold panic as he lowered himself to a thick crook and rested his rifle along the branch, sighting along the barrel toward the southern end of the field.

Somewhere nearby, Harvey, Bernard, Lafitte, and a dozen of his men loaded and sighted their weapons. Her pulse beat an erratic rhythm through her body, pounding through her veins in such a rush she almost couldn't hear. The battle would soon begin, and it was likely they wouldn't survive.

Together, they waited.

Chapter Forty-Eight

THE BRITISH ATTACK

Bright red rockets burst through the silent morning mist on the east side of the Mississippi and exploded, drawing everyone's terrified gaze.

Pakenham's signal for attack.

British drums began beating in an ominous tone. From behind Line Jackson, another drum beat a different cadence, either to send a message to American troops or to confuse the enemy. The perch gave her a nearly unobstructed view of Chalmette plantation's fields across the river. Tiny red dots lined up in squares and columns moved toward the Rodriguez canal, which the Americans had deepened. They used the mud to build a tall, thick wall, behind which Jackson's army gathered. The fog lifted, but the haze of gunfire replaced it. A smoke-tinted mass of thousands of redcoats marched toward the thin line of American resistance.

Eva swung her attention to the area in front of their battery and caught Lafitte checking his pocket watch. Had Drago's detour delayed them long enough to insert a wrinkle in Pakenham's plan of attack? No enemy soldiers emerged from the trees.

Yet.

Eva began to pray.

The roar of a cannon sprayed a British contingent with grapeshot. It ripped through a red-dotted square like a wind gust over a field of grass, felling them where they stood. A cloud of black smoke shot from another of Lafitte's big guns further down the line, and an immense boom rolled across the water. Hundreds more red specks dropped. Eva's stomach dipped in sickening horror. The ordered lines of soldiers continued to stumble over fallen comrades. A commander charged to the front on a white horse and was shot from his mount.

The snipers implemented their plan with grisly success.

The Chalmette battlefield erupted with gunfire and was soon thickly clouded with smoke. American gunmen calmly sent a hail-storm of bullets from behind the parapets. More British fell with each wave. She gasped at the lethal accuracy of the riflemen behind Jackson's line, wreaking havoc upon the enemy troops. She prayed for Corporal Blackwood's safety, thankful he was unfit to fight. The fall of every commander, some mounted, some on foot created confusion and stalled the British lines as troops waited for orders that didn't come.

The plan to cut off the head of the snake was working.

Eva felt the crushing weight of helplessness pressing on every bone. She swallowed a sharp sob. Chalmette's fields were now a red sea of fallen soldiers. Even with the ground vibrating from the cannon explosions and rifle cracks the screams of the wounded and dying reached her ears. Many of the British crawled toward the breastwork on their hands and knees. How many were young boys like Edward?

The ominous beat of drums continued, except now coming from a new direction. She glanced back to Morgan's line, and horror clawed at her chest.

Brighton and his troops had finally arrived. Redcoats filtered through the trees surrounding the field.

Hundreds of them.

Drago remained still, scanning the regiments flowing into the open. The slaves ceased their digging and ran. Followed by the militia.

Eva could hardly blame them. With no weapons, how would they engage the enemy? Stand there and shake their fists?

Lafitte cursed and dropped from his tree and began yelling in French. "Stand your ground and fight you, cowards!"

The few armed militia paused to fire their guns, but with no one to step up while they reloaded, they became easy prey for the British. Hugo was one of the first to drop his rifle and run for the trees.

Eva snorted in derision, surprised he'd stayed as long as he did.

Drago had his weapon trained on the far end of the muddy field. Brighton emerged, sword in hand, yelling for his troops to press forward to the battery. Fear swept over her like a harsh, icy wind. If they captured it, they would turn the guns on Line Jackson and decimate it.

The American militia continued to retreat; they tried to make a stand, but even she saw it was a lost cause. Brighton climbed the rampart in front of the armament and shouted, "Huzzah, boys! The battery is ours!"

Drago calmly released a long breath and squeezed the trigger. Brighton fell and didn't move. Drago reached for his powder and shot, then reloaded his gun. A few minutes later, another commander fell. Still, the army poured into the field and up the armaments.

"General Morgan has called for a retreat! The battery's been taken. Retreat!"

The command spurred Lafitte's men into motion. They dropped from the trees and crept toward the river.

"Eva!" Drago gestured toward Harvey and Bernard, who had descended from their perches. "Go with them! Find Raul!"

Her knuckles whitened on her rifle. "Not without you!"

His expression darkened. "I want you safe! Go!" Movement below caught his attention.

She gasped and followed his gaze to the battlefield. Brighton was still down and unmoving. But Lafitte was in trouble. He hid behind a pile of bulrushes, firing off a shot when he could. Behind him, a small group of redcoats quickly cut off his escape route.

Drago cursed under his breath. He couldn't get Jean's attention without alerting the enemy. He glanced up at her, a thousand words in his silver eyes. He said only four.

"Stay invisible, don't move."

He dropped and circled around behind the soldiers. Slowly, he eased the hammer back and aimed at the man closest to Lafitte. The click alerted the redcoats, but Drago's target fell before he could turn. His dagger sank into the chest of another, leaving his sword for hand-to-hand combat. With an enraged bellow, he attacked. Lafitte did the same and dispensed with two more, but not before the last one fired a panicked shot at Drago.

Eva bit back a scream as he stumbled and fell. The burn of anguish exploded with an intensity that charred her insides. Lafitte ran his saber through the soldier, then knelt and wiped at the blood streaming from Drago's head.

She grasped the branches with shaking fingers as she shimmied down the tree, heart ramming a hole in her chest. Ignoring the dull throb of logic, she prayed.

Please be alive!

The field had become blanketed in pandemonium. American militia turned and fled into the wood or toward the river. Others streamed out of the battery, shouting and firing off enough wild shots to slow the British enough to escape. Enemy troops stormed past the copse of trees where Eva hid. The British focused solely on taking the battery. Nothing else seemed to be worth their concern.

Drago hadn't moved.

God, please save him! Please, please, please!

A tight lump swelled in her throat, choking her. She swung her rifle over her shoulder and had just taken a step toward them when a rough hand grasped her arm and spun her around, bringing her face to face with Hugo.

Terror ripped the breath from her lungs, not so much because he grabbed her, but that he prevented her from helping the man she loved.

"This time, you come with *me*." The rancid stench of whiskey hovered in the air between them.

"No!" She twisted his fingers from her shoulder, but he only buried them in her hair and gave it a cruel yank.

He hauled her to the water's edge, flung her into a skiff, then pushed off the bank, allowing the current to take them downriver.

No! *Drago*! She had to get back to him.

Eva scrambled to her knees, ready to jump overboard if necessary. Gripping the side of the boat, she tried to get her feet under her but had no time to react to the swing of Hugo's meaty fist before it connected with her jaw.

Chapter Forty-Nine
HUGO'S REVENGE

E va awoke to the sound of a paddle dipping in and out of the water.

Drago.

The image of his crumpled body, blood streaming from his head, thundered through her mind, scattering painful doubts and fears everywhere. Her heart chilled into a horrible icy rock.

She didn't even have a chance to help him.

The battle had either ended, or she was well out of earshot. Her vision blurred, but after a few blinks, she could finally focus on the trees overhead, laden with Spanish moss. They were in the bayou. Sunlight flickered through the branches, and by its position, it was not yet midday.

The paddle strokes ceased, and the skiff bumped against something solid. Hugo's face loomed over hers.

"Good, you're awake." He pulled out a bottle and drank deeply. The sickening odor of whiskey assaulted her nose. "Come, Eva. We've much to discuss."

Grief and dread sucked at her limbs. She didn't care what he wanted. Without Drago, her world was gray and shadowed. She choked out her words. "Why have you done this?" Could he really still be angry with her after nine years? She lost a single missive, and his fury had exploded. Why did he still linger on past mistakes?

He finished the bottle and tossed it back in the boat, then looped a rope around a piling, securing the craft. "You stole something I need," he grunted, yanking her to her feet.

She whirled to face him, snarling and bitter. "I have nothing of yours, you spineless coward." He had a rifle and still, he ran.

"That's no way to talk to your benefactor."

Her mouth fell open. "Benefactor? You can't be that delusional."

Hugo grabbed her hands and tied them together in front of her body. At least it wasn't impossible to climb to the small deck encircling the shabby hut.

A loud splash startled her, and she knew without looking an alligator lurked nearby. At least six of the glowering beasts floated along the muddy bayou bank. Who knew how many more skulked in the shadows?

A tiny single room shack hunched before them. Hugo's hiding place. He'd brought her and other runners here when they had to stay out of sight for a while. He kicked open the rickety door and shoved her inside.

The place hadn't changed. A table, a small brick hearth with an iron kettle hanging next to it, and hammocks draped along the other three walls.

He lumbered over to a cupboard and removed a bottle. He shook it and nodded in satisfaction at the amount of liquid sloshing inside. His heartless stare sent sick whirls of dread through her stomach. "For over six years I fed you, clothed you, taught you the skills you needed to survive." He used his teeth to remove the cork, drained the bottle and slammed it on the table. "What did you do with it?"

He talked nonsense. "Do with *what*?"

Bleary, bloodshot eyes glared at her. "The map. The parchment you lifted from Renault's coat pocket. It showed the location of one of Lafitte's treasure troves. I saw him remove his coat and drape it over a chair. You picked it as instructed, but then you fled." His last words echoed in the tiny hut; spittle dripped from his lips. "Where did you hide it?"

"I—I told you that night. I lost it." She'd returned later to search, hoping to find her coat tossed in the alley, but it was so dark. She never recovered it.

Fear and fury churned in her belly at the memory of returning empty-handed, Hugo's rage and the red glow of the hot knife.

"No!" Hugo's small brown eyes darkened against the bloodshot whites in a demonic glare. "You lie!" Holding the bottle by the neck, he smashed it, then waved the wicked shard at her. "You wanted the treasure for yourself. You stole it from me and ran away. Now you've returned to the city for it, just like I expected."

She retreated until her back pressed against the rough wooden wall, heartbeat jerking in rapid jolts. "I ran because you split my face open with a hot knife," she snarled.

His expression twisted into an unrecognizable mask of livid madness. "Lies," he spat, lurching toward her.

Chapter Fifty

THE SURRENDER

When Drago regained consciousness, blood obscured his vision. The warm rush streamed down his face. Lafitte crouched beside him in a thicket of bulrushes near the river. Jean raised a finger to his lips. Harvey and Bernard were nearby, creeping closer to the water.

They shrunk into the reeds as hundreds of British soldiers advanced toward the abandoned battalion.

Lafitte's smooth whisper reached his ears. "Let's hope our men destroyed zee guns and powder before they retreated." He jerked his head toward the Mississippi. "Best to live to fight another day."

Drago groaned at the sharp pain lancing through his skull. He rolled to his knees and, with Lafitte's help, staggered to his feet.

"Where's Eva?" he rasped. She should be in one of the boats.

"Easy, Cap'n. Let's git you into the skiff." Harvey shrugged his bony frame under Drago's shoulder, and the extra support helped move him into the last tethered longboat. Someone pressed a handkerchief into his hand and he wiped the blood from his eyes.

Just as they shoved off, Bernard turned to study the east side of the river. "I'll be—" he murmured in shock.

Harvey's voice came out in an awed whisper. "They *surrendered*."

Drago's gut twisted in both regret and despair. He knew it was an impossible goal, but deep in his soul, he had hoped the American's wild spirit and fierce determination would somehow save the city. He sucked in a bitter breath and lifted his head to follow Harvey's gaze.

His heart gave a shocked jump in his chest, and he stared with disbelieving eyes. A British commander was slowly approaching Line Jackson under the white flag of surrender.

The Americans had *won*.

Chapter Fifty-One

LOYALTY AND LOVE

When Bernard related how he'd witnessed Hugo Dupré shove Eva into a dingy, a hard knot formed under Drago's ribs.

Lafitte ground his teeth and picked up an oar. "I know where the dog hides. Let's go." They piled into a skiff and shoved off, drifting downriver with the current.

As time passed, the knot tightened. What if the man harmed her? God had no reason to give him any consideration, but surely Eva deserved protection. Drago wasn't a praying man. Strong men took charge of their own destiny, actions, and decisions. Reliance on another revealed vulnerabilities best left veiled. After all, some of the soundest strategies involved exploiting and twisting the frailties of your enemy.

He'd always held that a helpless man was a weak man. Everyone knew that between the two, strength was always the victor.

The weak begged and bartered. Then they resorted to prayer and attempted to bargain with God, making outlandish promises in exchange for mercy, strength, guidance, or victory, because they were incapable of attaining what they wanted or needed on their own.

Why would God even bother when that someone possessed nothing to exchange for His effort?

They only prayed when they were helpless.

Weak.

Drago mashed his lips together. Who would want to help someone who asked for consideration *only* when they had nowhere else to turn? This situation had him feeling uncomfortably... helpless and weak. Eva was beyond his physical reach and he had no way to protect her. The only thing he could do at the moment was pray.

The irony wasn't lost on him. For the first time in his life, he had nothing to offer, promise or trade. God had no cause to listen to the likes of him.

What could he possibly barter for God's aid?

Eva's voice invaded his mind. *"No one is unredeemable, Capitaíne."*

He'd demanded loyalty from his men in exchange for a share in earned bounty and his protection. A conflagration of realization burned through him, both shocking and terrifying in its magnitude.

Loyalty.

Love.

Two things that could never forcibly be taken, only freely given. Such an offering must be wrapped in a solid oath, or it was worthless.

An oath... his word. His vow was the one thing he could offer to God. His vow was his bond. And he would vow loyalty and love.

Imagine combining God's power with those convictions! If he added to them every ounce of strength and will he could wring from his battered body until he collapsed from exhaustion... if he struggled to take one more step forward, then another and another. If he refused defeat... *imagine!*

Flames licked the walls of his chest, and energy pulsed through his veins. Drago Viteri Gamponetti dropped to his knees.

And prayed.

Chapter Fifty-Two
NOWHERE TO RUN

Eva had nowhere to run. With her hands tied, the best she could do was swing them at Hugo. Then what? Even if she disabled him, how would she handle the skiff?

Her gaze followed the broken bottle Hugo waved in front of her face, and fear, like the fingers of fog still gripping the bayou, coated her skin. She shivered. He would use it to cut her again, as he had that night years ago. Under the surface his rage roiled, toying with the edge of madness. He had wobbled on that insane edge then, just as he did now.

Hugo lunged, grabbed her by the wrists, and dragged her outside. The alligators eyed them warily, some on the bank, others submerged but for their wary and hungry eyes.

The sting shouldn't have surprised her, but it did. She hissed, gaping in horror at the blood dripping from her palm into the bayou. Hugo kicked a chunk of wood into the water, drawing the attention of the bayou's deadliest predators.

Alligators.

Watching.

Waiting.

Hugo gripped Eva's wrist and shook the blood oozing from

her hand into the water. "Tell me where you hid the map, Eva." He managed a thin, hard smile. "Tell me or I'll feed you to the gators one hand at a time." He shoved her precariously close to the edge of the dock.

She forced an even tone, despite her heart pounding in her ears loud enough to be deafening and fear dripping down her spine like melting snow. "It's gone, Hugo. I lost it." He was mad. And she was alone.

The image of Drago bleeding on the muddy ground left a horrifyingly empty hole in her chest. She choked back a harsh sob because she feared the worst.

He shook her again, the motion sending him off balance. He swayed back, then forward until his whiskey-soaked breath was hot on her face. "You looked at it, din' you? You looked at it. What did you see? Where's the treasure?" He waved the sharp glass in front of her eyes.

The lurking reptiles now floated only a few feet from the dock, their toothy grins expectant and pink. It was hard to think, to focus. She needed a believable story, something that might calm him. Perhaps a search for the map back in the city?

He swayed drunkenly and took an unsteady sideways step, and she saw an opening.

Survival instincts kicked in, Eva swung her fists up with all her might and connected solidly with his jaw. She cried out in pain as her hands met the pointed chin. Hugo's head snapped back, but to her horror, he didn't fall. He staggered, shook his head, then lurched for her, raising the broken bottle, ready to make good on his threat. The fingers of his free hand stretched for her throat. Eva screamed and twisted to the side, flinging herself behind him onto the rough-hewn wooden deck. She landed hard enough to knock the breath from her lungs.

Hugo jerked around at her sudden change of direction, his face contorted in a snarl. The quick movement altered his balance enough to cause him to stagger back. Willing her body to move and take advantage of his inebriated state, she hissed in a painful gasp and kicked him, adding to his backward momentum. She rolled to her side and pushed herself up to her hands and knees. To fight, she must be on her feet.

Hugo's startled shriek cut through the misty air.

Thrashing water quickly drowned out his gurgled cry.

She looked over her shoulder and gasped for breath, her heart still quaking against her ribs with violent aftershocks. Bubbles and blood drifted on the bayou surface, now murky with churned mud.

Hugo was gone.

And so were the alligators.

Chapter Fifty-Three

WHICH VOICE WILL HIM FOLLOW

D rago whipped his head around to glare at Lafitte. "I know a thirteen-year-old petticoat who can paddle faster than you. Put your back into it, man!" Drago's head pounded like a bloody hammer to an anvil, and pain sliced through his battered ribs, but he pulled his oar through the water like a giant beast with a single focus.

Jean merely raised a brow before taking another stroke. "Harvey, Monsieur Sauvage, I am not zee only one with a paddle, yet his wrath has unjustly fallen only on my strong, broad shoulders. As men of honor, you should share zee burden."

Bernard grunted in response. Harvey grumbled under his breath, lifted his oar from the water and placed it on his lap, drawing a groan from Bernard. "I told ye earlier, me shoulder's near broken from the kick of that blasted musket. Cursed thing were older than me. 'Tis a miracle I felled a moving target." He nudged Bernard. "Did ye see my shot though? Took 'im down before he could order his men to charge."

Bernard rolled his eyes. "I've already complimented your marksmanship, you bloated, strutting peacock. Now, will you please take a stroke? Unless you're too weak from singing your own praises..."

Harvey harrumphed and put his oar to use again. "I were hoping the blighter was Brighton." He mashed his lips together. "Wanted to avenge Manuel, that big ox. I shot at anyone yelling orders."

"I know, Harvey." Drago choked out the words. "Thank you." He scanned the bayou for a glimpse of Hugo's hut.

Harvey preened and picked up his tempo. "Don't need to thank me, Cap'n. I did it b'cuz it needed done." He paused to wipe the corner of his eye on his sleeve. He gave Drago a respectful dip of the head. "Saw ye shoot one commander betwixt the eyes."

So his shot was true. "That commander was Brighton," Drago ground out, almost surprised at the fluid anger that still flowed through his veins.

Harvey's face was solemn, but his eyes gleamed in undisguised glee. "Got his justice. Bloody white-livered cod fish."

"There!" Bernard pointed to the right. "I see a shanty."

Lafitte's expression was stoic, although his gaze sharpened. "Dupré's hide-out."

A small dingy floating lazily near the decking barely tugged on the dock line. It was the only sign the place was occupied. Acidic tension boiled in Drago's stomach and scorched a path up his throat. If Dupré had hurt Eva, he'd rip him into pound pieces.

They secured the boat to the piling. Jean took in the quiet structure and the half-open door, then studied the line of demarcation between the brown-gray bayou water and the thicker churned muck closer to the building and frowned, the edges of his mouth lined and hard. Drago's heart catapulted into his ribs. He slipped the knife from its sheath and drew his sword. Harvey hefted his musket.

They could creep up and use surprise to freeze the occupants, or simply charge inside. Not one to ponder long on such dilemmas, Drago went with his gut, leaped forward and flung his shoulder through the door of the tiny one-room shack.

Eva bleated in shock. She whirled next to a table splattered with dark blotches and shattered glass. Blood and frayed rope streamed down her wrist, an angry bruise colored her cheek, a cut split her lip. She crouched, wielding a wicked shard in her bleeding hand. He locked onto her sapphire eyes that first flashed in fear, then shock, and finally shimmered with relief.

A strangled sound lurched from Drago's throat. His weapons clattered to the floor, and he stumbled toward her. Eva met him halfway, and they collided bone to bone. She threw her arms around him, and he crushed her to his chest. His groan was ragged, not from pain or desire but from his insides crumbling. A wave of relief crashed through him so violently he was unable to stand. He sank to his knees, taking her with him. It took all his strength to keep himself from splintering.

Chapter Fifty-Four

FOXES AND HOUNDS

Eva couldn't believe her eyes. His face pale and bloody, head bandaged in a strip of torn cloth, Drago's massive shoulders filled the doorway. He was alive! Air left her lungs on a choked sob only to be jerked back in again. The urgent need to touch skin and breath and lips drove her into his arms. He curled her into his embrace with an anguished groan, buried his face in her neck and inhaled until his ribs stopped him before dropping to his knees with her.

"I was so afraid I'd lost you," he choked, clinging to her as if he was the only thing keeping her from floating away.

Eva blinked back the tears welling in her eyes. The sheer frigid burn of fear and loss had ripped through them both. Drago, so stoic and strong and commanding, was on his knees to keep himself from *breaking*. She heard it in his voice and felt it tremble through his body because the same sensations ripped through hers. They were raw and scraped, torn inside and out.

She placed her palms on his face and kissed him almost frantically. She tasted blood, the sting of the cut reopening, but didn't care. Skin, breath, lips.

Drago.

When she could breathe, she touched the bloodstained bandage on his head. "I feared you were dead." A tremor rumbled through her body. "You didn't move... all that blood—"

"Shhh." His voice, low and calm, still shook with emotion. He placed a gentle finger on her bruised cheek and frowned. "Did I not tell you I never engage in a fight I cannot win?"

She knew better than to smile, but she did anyway and endured the protest from her split lip. "Yet, you did this time."

He looked somewhat offended, although his eyes crinkled in amusement. "I certainly did not."

From the doorway, Lafitte's voice held a trace of both humor and pride. "By my records, it took thirty-seven minutes."

She was still confused. "Thirty-seven minutes?"

He offered his hand, and she took it, allowing the suave pirate to help her up. Drago winced, sucking in a sharp breath as Bernard and Harvey hauled him to his feet. He immediately reached for her, still needing the solid warmth of her body as reassurance. She gladly stepped into his embrace, needing the same from him. She hugged him, loosening her hold slightly at his soft grunt of pain.

Harvey crossed his arms and inhaled, expanding his bony chest to its full capacity. "That's the amount of time it took us to set those British curs running with their tails twixt their legs."

Her jaw dropped. "We won?" A flash of shock rippled through her body. "We *won*?"

Lafitte laughed as he turned toward the longboat. "In my experience, where there are battles between cunning and might, cunning always wins. It's like pitting a fox against a pack of hounds, eh *mon petite renaud?*"

Chapter Fifty-Five

NO MORE VEILS

March 18, 1815

I t was a beautiful day for a wedding.

St. Louis Cathedral was brimming with well-wishers of every kind. The *Dragon's* crew shuffled and shifted in a vain attempt to remain still, unlike Mother Marie Francois, Beatrice and the rest of the Ursuline nuns who stood stoically in the first few rows, calmly awaiting the start of the ceremony.

In his new shirt and jacket, Harvey strutted into the church like a rooster. Bernard waved him into the Sauvage pew with the rest of the family. Edward sat between the twins, apparently mediating some sort of debate between the two. Drago tried not to laugh out loud when Tristan reached behind Jacqueline's shoulders, then curved his hand around her head and over her mouth.

General Jackson and his officers dressed in their finest, with polished boots and starched shirts. Jackson had presented him a medal of valor and a copy of two letters. One the general had sent to President Madison lauding Drago's heroics, the other was a full presidential pardon for any illicit actions Captain Gampo may have taken while a Baratarian pirate, just in case the issue ever came up.

Jean Lafitte had agreed to serve as a witness and would give the bride to be wed. Pierre had gifted Eva with a beautiful silk gown, turning her into an angel. Drago would soon be her husband.

Husband.

For once, he had no twinges of guilt or hesitation that his past made him unsuitable or unacceptable.

Or unredeemable.

He would always have regrets.

Regret that he didn't demand another sweep of that pirate ship before giving the order to sink her. Regret that they didn't notice the child. Regret they didn't try harder to decipher what that frantic woman was saying. Perhaps that's why he flung his body between Julian and a swinging saber years ago, in hopes to offset such an egregious error in some small way.

Julian gave him a cheeky grin and a spry salute. Drago answered his new cabin boy with a tilt of his head and a wink. Indeed, it was time to let go of the past and embrace a future with Eva. With her, he was a whole man. An honorable man.

Jean escorted Eva to the alter, then bent over her hand, and with a glimmer in his eye and a wink, kissed her fingers before folding them in Drago's.

Eva smiled, and her radiance rendered Drago speechless. His mother's sapphire necklace glittered and ignited the azure fire in her eyes and matched the ring he slid on her finger as they completed their vows. Those who pillaged his cabin didn't think to look more closely behind the drawers of his desk. Foxes and hounds.

His wife. The Healer.

His bright, beautiful, raven-haired wife, who accepted his bloodied hands and black past, stole his heart and healed his soul.

DRAGO LIFTED HER VEIL, removed it and let it drop to the floor in an unwanted heap. Eva arched a quizzical brow.

"No more veils," he said, with a stern look and a tender smile. "Without you, I see only shadow. You are my light in the dark, Eva," he breathed. "I'll not allow you to be shaded from me." He rubbed his thumbs over her cheekbones and placed a kiss on the edge of her scar. "I don't deserve you, but I'm too selfish to do the honorable thing and leave you to shine for another more worthy."

Her heart swelled. Never had she felt so *cherished*. Thinking back to that dark night in Jamaica, when he stormed into the abbey and demanded she heal the little girl in his arms, she couldn't disagree more with his self-appraisal. But she only grinned. "Well, you are a pirate, after all."

He opened his mouth and hesitated. Instead of correcting her, his lips tipped up in the most disarming smile she'd ever seen. "And you're a thief. You stole my heart, *il mio amore*." He kissed her, and her heart hummed. She loved this man, heart and soul with every inch of her being.

Chapter Fifty-Six

VISIT FROM FONTAINE

No one seemed surprised when they missed breakfast. And lunch.

After a long hot bath together, they belatedly surfaced for the evening meal.

Exhausted, but happier than she'd ever been in her life, Eva smiled at her husband and sank into the chair he offered. Jacqueline skipped out of the kitchen and set a plate of charred bread on the table. Thankfully, a servant followed with plates of edible food —biscuits slathered in melted jam, smoked ham, and grits with shrimp. Everything smelled heavenly.

"Hello Captain Gampo, Mrs. Gampo," Jacqueline said, her eyes twinkling. "We put a new feather tick on your bed. Was it warm and soft? Did you sleep well?"

Drago tossed her a half-hearted glare as he took a seat. "Too many questions for such a young skirt."

Jacqueline laughed and hugged his neck, missing the satisfied warmth crinkling the corners of his eyes. "Julian is dying to know when we shall depart. He's most eager to begin his new duties." She hopped to a chair, sat and reached for her napkin.

"We?" Drago raised an inky brow.

Jacqueline's head snapped up. "Well, you certainly don't expect him to leave without *me*?" Her eyes widened, and she cocked her head, glaring like a statue.

Drago paused, a spoonful of grits hovering over his plate. "It's not his decision," he scowled.

Jacqueline opened her mouth to respond, but Tristan entered and interrupted her. "They have emerged from their den." He winked at his sister and smiled at Eva, then kissed her hand. "Good morning, Mrs. Gamponetti."

"Please call me Eva," she said, unable to contain a smile. "You all are the closest thing I have to a family. I should like us all to become familiar friends."

Jacqueline clasped her hands together. "It will be like having another sister!" Her bright grin faded. "I miss Stevie."

Tristan laughed as he took his chair. "I miss her, too, especially her cooking. You have big shoes to fill, Biscuit."

The young girl scowled. "I'm not a cook. I'm a healer." She reddened and cast a sideways glance at Eva. "Well...I wish to be. Eva has been allowing me to assist her."

"I see." Her older brother sighed and nodded at the plate she served. "That explains the burned toast."

Jacqueline winced.

Uncle Bernard entered, removing his gloves. "Good evening, everyone." His sons Victor and Adrian followed. Julian strutted in, smugly pocketing a coin while Harvey groused in his wake about being fleeced by a greenie still wet behind the ears. A chuckling Edward followed. They all sat except for Adrian, who stood by the door, casually checking his pistol.

Bernard propped his elbows on the table, laced his fingers. "Captain, a man is here to see you. He's waiting in the gaming hall."

"Oh?" Drago paused with his fork halfway to his mouth. "Did he give a name?"

While her husband's posture wasn't guarded, he wasn't as relaxed as a moment ago.

"He did," Tristan answered. "Monsieur Fontaine."

The *assassin*? Eva's mouth went dry. Had something gone wrong with the relics? She cast a horrified glance at Drago, who went from tense to absolutely rigid. He gave her hand a gentle squeeze.

"I'll go find him and have a word."

Not alone. Eva stood. "I shall come, too."

"No need." A dark-haired man framed the doorway, not as tall as Drago or Tristan, but just as muscular. "*Bonjour, Capitainé.*" Dark eyes shifted around the room, taking in every detail, assessing.

Eva's knees weakened, and she sank back to her seat. The man reached into his coat pocket and her heart gave a terrified jerk. Drago wasn't armed. She shot a panicked look to Adrian, who still held his pistol and towered over everyone else in the room. He warily followed the assassin with his eyes. Harvey drew his pistol and placed it next to his plate. At least they had some protection.

"*Bonjour*, Fontaine." Drago gestured to an empty chair. "Won't you join us?"

The man gave them a quick, gracious nod and sat across from Drago, an envelope in his hand, which he slid across the table, his attention never leaving Drago's face.

"King Louis sends his regards."

Drago reclined back in his seat. "I resigned my position as his agent."

Fontaine jerked his chin at the missive. "I have a distinct feeling you'll want to reconsider."

They stared at each other a moment. Drago finally reached for the parchment and broke the seal. As he began to read, he straightened, eyes slicing to Fontaine, his focus sharp and piercing.

"What is it?" Eva asked, both relieved the assassin didn't

attempt to kill them and terrified the instructions in the letter would lead to the same end. She could almost feel the burn of tension radiating from her husband's shoulders. Not as palpable as fear. More like the rolling thunder of fury.

A muscle rippled in Drago's jaw. "A member of the Spanish aristocracy was kidnapped while under the protection of the French king." The slight flare of his nostrils the only other indication of the gathering storm in his silver-gray eyes.

Victor's brows puckered. "The king sent a missive all this way for you? Does he not employ people in Paris who can address this?"

Eva clenched her jaw. Exactly. Except Victor was unaware how this king used his agents, or Fontaine's role. Her husband *couldn't* refuse.

Drago nodded absently, his gaze shifting to her face. In his eyes, she saw all the things he wouldn't say because it would break her heart. "He's giving me an opportunity to handle it."

"Good heavens," Uncle Bernard said. "Can you not decline and let one of his generals or agents take the mission?"

Drago locked stares with Fontaine. "I can, but I won't."

Eva's teeth began to ache, so she made an attempt to relax her jaw, already deciding to sneak aboard. Jacqueline wouldn't hesitate, but it's doubtful now she'd receive permission to accompany them either. She bit her lips together to squelch a confident smile. Julian couldn't deny both of them.

"Why can't you refuse?" Tristan asked, straightening.

Indeed, why not? Eva wanted to know the answer as well. It could be Drago was afraid to say no to the assassin, for fear of their lives. Or he was being blackmailed or threatened. If he took the assignment, would he demand she stay behind? There couldn't be a more horrible way to spend the first year of her married life.

That settled it. She was going whether he permitted it or not.

Meanwhile, Drago was grinding his teeth into dust. He jammed the letter into his coat pocket and rose to his feet. Eva stood with him. Whatever burden he was given, she would share it. He leveled a blank stare toward Tristan. "I won't decline because the aristocrat kidnapped was my cousin, daughter of the Marquess of Isla de Arousa." A storm raged in his eyes. "There's a ransom, but it is requested that I deliver it."

Shocked, Eva inhaled sharply and caught Drago's gaze, a thousand different thoughts, questions and fears flying through her head. He *had* to go. All other options dissipated.

Harvey stood. "I'll gather the men to ready the ship."

Fontaine stood and bowed. "I shall leave you to your preparations." He left the room, which had suddenly gone silent.

Adrian shoved his giant body away from the wall. Drago was huge, but Adrian was massive. "I'll go with you," Adrian said. At Drago's surprised expression, he shrugged. "You saved Julian's life four years ago, and Jacqueline's when she fell ill. You also—" He waved his hand in a circle that encompassed the entire city, then gave Drago a pointed stare. "A member of your family is in danger. I will do everything in my power to help." He addressed Tristan. "Father needs you here to run the gaming house." He shoved the pistol into his belt and crossed his arms over his wide chest. "We should leave a message in Baracoa for Stevie and Conal and the rest of the fleet. They'll come to our aide."

In Adrian's stoic stare, Eva saw everything he was not saying. Friendship, loyalty, brotherhood. *Family*.

Drago finally gave Adrian a curt, stoic nod. He took Eva's hands. She stared at their fingers and waited for him to tell her goodbye and inform her that he had to leave her behind so she would be safe.

Warm fingers stroked her cheek, then touched her jaw, tilting her face up. She raised her gaze to bright stormy eyes glinting with barely contained energy. "How would you like to become the first American female ship's surgeon?" he asked, a slow smile lifting the corners of his mouth.

They would journey together! "I'd be delighted," she said, with a grin of undisguised glee.

"Then I shall be her assistant," Jacqueline proclaimed.

The table went silent.

All eyes were on Eva. "It is not for me to say," she said to Jacqueline, who wilted the tiniest amount. "However, if your brother and uncle do not object, neither will I."

Jacqueline's eyes lit up with renewed energy.

Bernard pursed his lips together in thought, bushy gray brows shuttering his eyes from view.

Jacqueline persisted. "Julian and Adrian will both be there to protect me, should I need it." She said it as though it was a ridiculous possibility.

Harvey snorted. "A ship ain't no place fer a skirt—"

At Drago's scowl, the old salt raised his hands. "Unless they're family, o' course."

Family.

Drago clasped Eva's hand and kissed it. "And family they are." He shook Bernard's hand, then Tristan's, then Adrian's. "I thank you all." He slipped his arm around her waist. "We set sail as soon as we load the provisions we need."

Tristan squeezed Jacqueline's shoulders. "You had better behave, Biscuit, keep a keen eye open for trouble, and stay clear of it."

The young girl gave her brother a peck on the cheek. "Well, I try so hard to be good and avoid it when I can, Tristan, you know I do."

Edward choked, attempting to hide his laughter behind his napkin, which drew an irritated glare from this girl.

"One thing is certain," Drago said dryly, looking around the room at the group. "We shall not be bored."

Chapter Fifty-Seven
CHANGE IN DE WIND

The Louisiana shoreline faded into the horizon. Eva leaned on the rail near the helm of the newly christened schooner *Freedom*, a gift from the Lafitte brothers. Drago could now start a new life as a merchant mariner.

Should he so choose.

That decision would wait until they returned from Europe.

Drago Viteri Gamponetti, strong, dark and stoic, stood at her side, once again the commander, the leader of men. The grateful people of New Orleans had filled his hold with sugarcane, orange marmalade, and cotton bales. Its value would easily fund their mission to France. He wrapped his arms around her and kissed the scar on her temple, a gesture she accepted now, no longer shrinking away.

A small smile tugged at her mouth. Kalia's voice echoed in her head. Words from months ago…

"CHANGE IN DE WIND, Drago. Light calls to you, but de dark always a seductress. 'Tis you who must choose.

"Which voice will him follow? Him heart or him head?"

※

"You have a faraway look in those beautiful blue eyes," Drago murmured, as she stared at the mouth of the mighty Mississippi, its muddy fingers fanning out into the gulf water in the distance.

Warmth radiated around her spine and settled in sensitive places low in her belly. She turned toward him and stepped into his embrace. His arms always gave her strength and shelter. She felt bolder, braver next to him. She tilted her head and stared into those charcoal-rimmed, silver eyes and his handsome face. Her heart gave a familiar stutter.

She loved this man with every beat.

"I was thinking about what Kalia said to you in the moonlight, the night we took Jacqueline to the caves," she whispered.

He pulled her closer. She could almost feel their hearts thump against each other in a solid rhythm.

Drago lowered his head. "Him heart," he whispered against her lips, imitating Kalia's thick Jamaican tongue. "He will always follow his heart."

※

To receive an email alert for the next release: http://chloeflowers.com/contact/

※

Download the first Hearts of Adventure book FREE!Tap or type: https://dl.bookfunnel.com/r9u24vknuk

Also by Chloe Flowers

The Heart of a Tempest

A lady plotting her way out of an arranged marriage,

A smuggler with a cryptic invitation to a clandestine meeting,

A group of pirates out for revenge.

It's the perfect storm.

The Heart of a Siren

A deathbed confession.

A dark plot of revenge.

A band of ticked off pirates.

What else could possibly go wrong?

The Heart of a Bride

Remember me...

An accident rips sway the last five years of his life,

And turns his new bride into a stranger.

Her fight for his love soon turns into a fight for his life.

Other Pirates & Petticoats novels:

The Heart of a Pirate

Her twin siblings have been kidnapped.

The ransom is a ship called The Seeker.

She's not a real pirate.

But their lives depend on her playing the part.

The Heart of a Spy

He steals for the French crown.

She heals for the Catholic church.

He will heal her heart.

She will steal his.

☙❧

Coming soon: A new sweet contemporary small town romance series sure to capture your heart and tickle your funny bone.

Bridal Veil Falls

The town of Happily Ever Afters

Chloe's Website: www.chloeflowers.com

Letter to You

DEAR READER,

Thank you for reading my book! Please swipe to the end and consider leaving a review. Or tap here. Your opinion means a lot to me, and I'd appreciate any feedback you'd like to share.

Follow this link to sign up for new release alerts: http://chloe flowers.com/contact/

It usually contains book recommendations, some of the recipes the characters in my books cook up, as well as a fun contest or giveaway. You'll also hear about my bee hives! I'll send you a FREE ebook download to read or give to a friend.

Fondly,

Chloe

P.S. Are you an organ donor? I am.

For more information, go to: https://www.organdonor.gov/ register.html

⁂

You can reach Chloe via snail mail (and if you'd like your print

book signed, send it here, along with your return address). She
does her best to personally reply to every letter.

Flowers & Fullerton Publishing
303 North Court St.
Box 37
Medina, Ohio 44258

Website: http://chloeflowers.com
Publisher: www.FlowersandFullerton.com

About Chloe

CHLOE SUPPORTS THE NATIONAL BREAST CANCER FOUNDATION.

Chloe Flowers is an award-winning author and the recipient of the University of Akron, Wayne College *2018 Writer of the Year* Award. She writes small town contemporary women's fiction, and historical women's action and adventure romance novels about scoundrels, pirates, and spunky, independent heroines.

Chloe keeps bees, and identifies her hives by the different flowers she paints on them. Her pets have always been named after her favorite characters or action heroes: Indiana, Luke, Gimli, Thelma, Rocket, Al Giordino, Severus, Mushu, Mérida, Jack...Dead Pool (he's a goldfish).

Chloe's biggest fault is the apparent inability to say "no" whether it's in response to a call for aid or a double-dog-dare to hike home through 30 acres of a snow-covered forest at midnight...during a full moon. It was early morning during said adventure when she came upon a group of sheriff's deputies searching for a lost girl. So, of course she offered to help (turns out, they were searching for her).

She is a member of the Great Lakes Fiction Writers, Contemporary Romance Writers, Regency Fiction Writers and The Author's Guild.

She has given workshops and presentations on creating a critique group, how to provide effective critiques, story structure, marketing and self-publishing lessons to writers groups, library patrons and school children.

Chloe has a weakness for good red wine, Calvin & Hobbes comics, pie, dark chocolate and brown-eyed guys with beards, which is probably why she digs pirates, men in uniform and treasure hunters and writes about action and adventure and of course romance, which is the greatest adventure of all.

❧

facebook.com/chloe.flowersauthor

x.com/flowers_chloe

instagram.com/chloeflowerswrites

bookbub.com/authors/chloe-flowers

pinterest.com/chloeflowers

NEW ORLEANS CREOLE JAMBALAYA RECIPE

Unless they're from the NOLA region, most people don't realize there are two kinds of Jambalaya: Creole and Cajun.

The Creole version uses tomatoes and is also referred to as "red" jambalaya. There are other subtle differences between the two in preparation.

If you have the spices to make your own Creole seasoning, do it. I grow thyme and oregano in my garden, because they are hardy and perennial. I root basil in jars on my kitchen window, and then transfer them to a pot or the garden in the spring. I dry and store them in airtight containers, and use them all year long. I'll share my method below.

This recipe serves 8 (I always make extra to freeze).

INGREDIENTS
    5 Tbsp. unsalted butter
    2 lbs. Chicken breast (cut into bite-sized chunks)
    1 lb. Andouille sausage (cut into 1/4 inch slices)
    5-6 cloves of garlic (minced)
    3 stalks of celery (diced)

2 cups of chopped onion (I use 1 yellow onion and 1 Vidalia onion)

1 green pepper (diced)

1 yellow or red pepper (diced)

(Or you can use 2 green peppers, but I'm all about color)

3-4 Tbsp. Creole seasoning (or make your own-recipe follows)

2 cans (14.5 oz.) diced tomatoes

3 tsp. hot sauce

2 tsp. Worcestershire sauce

4 cups chicken broth

3 bay leaves

1 tsp salt (add more to taste later)

1 lb. raw medium shrimp

2 cups uncooked rice (Carolina long grain is yummy)

2-3 green onions thinly sliced

Creole Seasoning

Put all this into a coffee grinder or blender:

Double it if you want to make extra.

2 tsp. paprika powder (sweet-not spicy Hungarian)

2 tsp. garlic powder (you can also use dried minced)

2 tsp. onion powder

2 tsp. dried thyme

1 tsp. dried oregano

1 tsp. dried basil

1 tsp. cayenne pepper

1 tsp. salt

1/2 tsp ground black pepper (freshly ground is best)

Instructions

1. Coat chicken with **2** tablespoons of Creole seasoning (you'll use the other later). Let it marinate.

2. Meanwhile, melt the butter in a large skillet or Dutch oven, then add the chicken and brown it.

3. Toss in the sliced andouille sausage, and cook until the sausage browns a little.

4. Add the Holy Trinity. (onion, celery and bell pepper) and garlic and sauté for 5 minutes.

5. Add tomatoes, hot sauce, uncooked rice, Worcestershire sauce, chicken broth, bay leaves and salt.

6. Add 1-2 tablespoons Creole seasoning. Start with 1, you can add more to taste.

7. Bring to a boil then reduce the heat to medium, cover and simmer for 25-30 minutes, stirring occasionally (every 5 minutes) until the rice is tender.

8. Add the shrimp and cover. The shrimp should steam cook in 2-3 minutes. They are done when they're pink. You can also add the shrimp midway through the simmer stage. I'm not a fan of overlooked shrimp that's chewy, but as long as it is cooked through and pink, you're good.

9. Sprinkle with a pinch of sliced green onions and enjoy with cornbread or warm crusty French bread.